Grace Will Lead You Home

A NOVEL

by
TAMARA TILLEY

Grace Will Lead You Home

By Tamara Tilley

Library of Congress Cataloging-in-Publication Data is on file at the Library of Congress, Washington, DC.

ISBN 13: 978-0578517858

Quoted Scripture: King James Version

Cover design: Design 7 Studio
Cover images: Shutterstock
Photo credit: Rachel Lauer

ARCHER
PRESS

Dedicated to

Walter
The love of my life.
Here is to another forty years!

ACKNOWLEDGEMENTS

I am so thankful for those of you who encourage me to continue in my writing journey.

I am thankful for my family and friends for their love and support.

Thank you- Mom, Michele, and Charlene for taking hours out of your days to help with the editing process.

Thank you, Rachel, for our quick photo shoot, and thank you, Madi, for your unwavering enthusiasm.

Thank you, Scott Saunders for bringing my visions to life with spectacular book covers.

And last, but never least, thank you, Jesus, for giving me stories that point people to You

ONE

Cassie looked at her Maurice Lacroix watch as she pushed open the gym door. The anticipation building inside her was like nothing she had ever felt before.

"I can't believe you'll be gone an entire month," Jill said as she tossed her gym bag over her shoulder. "No wonder you've been putting in extra hours at the gym."

"Yeah, right!" Andrea said belligerently. "Cassie has been a perfect size three for the five years I've known her."

Cassie tensed at Andrea's backhanded compliment. Even though her friend was right, no one knew the real reason Cassie worked so hard to maintain her *perfect* figure.

No. Don't go there. Things are better now.

"Tell me again where you'll be going?" Jill asked as they crossed the parking lot.

"Ireland, London, Spain, Italy, and Switzerland," Cassie listed, excited just thinking about it. "Then we're taking a ten-day cruise down the Rhine through France and Germany. After that, we go to Amsterdam where we'll be staying in a penthouse suite overlooking the Amstel River."

"I've seen brochures for those river cruises," Jill said. "They're not like those massive cruise ships with tennis courts, water parks, and screaming kids running everywhere. They're sophisticated and romantic. They attract a completely different clientele."

"And Mark insisted we book the most expensive suite on the ship. It has its own wraparound balcony, a spacious sitting area, and gorgeous furnishings. It's going to be incredible."

"But why go now? It's going to be cold this time of year."

Textbook Andrea. If there was a negative, she was sure to find it. "Because this was the best time for Mark's schedule. Besides, we will be indoors a lot of the time, touring museums

7

and art galleries, exploring restaurants and cafés. And when we're on the ship, we will be snuggling together on the balcony of our amazing suite watching the scenery pass by. It will be quiet and intimate. Just what we need."

"I could never talk Dan into something like that," Andrea whined as she passed her foot under the back bumper of her Mercedes. "Last year, his idea of a grand vacation was a trip to the Bahamas with a business meeting sandwiched in the middle." She dropped her gym bag in the trunk, then passed her foot again. "I already told him I'm going to Italy this year without him. And, the money I save by leaving his workaholic butt at home is going to buy me a whole new wardrobe."

"You're not actually going by yourself, are you?" Jill asked.

"No, I'm taking my sister. I need someone to count my drinks and keep me in line, so I don't do something reckless."

Jill and Andrea continued to debate the finer points of the perfect vacation while Cassie's thoughts turned inward. She was both nervous and excited about their upcoming trip. Not only was it a dream vacation, but it would give Mark and her a fresh start—a chance she never would have imagined possible just a year ago.

"Cassie!"

She flinched, not realizing she had tuned out her friends kibitzing. "Sorry, Andrea, my brain is all over the place today. What did you say?"

"I asked—for the third time—when do you leave?"

"Ahh . . . tonight. I have some last-minute errands to run this morning, then I'm going to surprise Mark at work with lunch."

"What's he doing at work on a Saturday? Especially the Saturday before vacation?" Andrea asked.

"He's been putting in extra hours these last few weeks, tying up loose ends and making sure his VIP clients are evenly divided among his associates. I'm hoping by the time I get there; I can persuade him to leave early."

Jill squealed with excitement. "How exciting! You're going to have such an amazing time. Take lots of pictures."

"Of landmarks," Andrea clarified with a dry laugh. "I don't want to see a *complete* pictorial of what you did while you were gone. There is only so much you should share with your friends."

Jill laughed while Cassie blushed at Andrea's outrageous comment. Exchanging hugs all around, Cassie hurried to her car feeling giddy and excited, and all the things she hadn't felt for so long.

Okay, Cassie said to herself as she pulled out from Fitness Sphere's parking lot and into the stream of traffic. *First the nail salon, then the cleaners, then lunch with Mark. Please, please, please, let him be willing to leave early.* She knew she was taking a risk; Mark did not like it when she showed up at the office unexpectedly. He'd ranted on more than one occasion how unprofessional it looked when wives showed up unannounced and distracted their husbands when they should be working. But since it was a Saturday, and none of the partners should be there, Cassie figured it wouldn't be that big a deal.

I'll play it by ear. If he's too busy, I'll just drop off lunch and go. Besides, I'll have him all to myself for a whole month without work monopolizing his time. What's one more afternoon?

Cassie waited for the traffic signal to turn green, her fingers drumming on the steering wheel.

What if he's engrossed in a deal? Or meeting with one of his partners? I don't want to upset him by interrupting. Maybe I should call?

"Call Mark's phone," she said to her voice control, but before it connected, she canceled it. "Where's the fun or spontaneity in that?" *No. I just won't ask him to leave. I'll bring lunch, no strings attached.*

In the ten minutes it took Cassie to drive to the nail salon, she changed her mind half a dozen times regarding lunch.

Why am I acting like this? Things are different now. Mark has changed.

Cassie shuddered, an emotional trigger whenever her thoughts traveled to darker times. Mark's work had been a major obstacle in their marriage, but it was not the most hazardous.

Shake it off. Dwell on the good, not the bad.

It had been her mantra for the last year.

Only the good.

Cassie thought back to the first time she'd seen Mark. She'd been in New York three years and had just started working the late shift at an all-night café. It was only her second night on the job when Mark strolled in looking like a fashion model straight from a photo shoot. His deep complexion, coffee-colored eyes, and charismatic smile mesmerized her, and the designer silk suit he wore had suave sophistication written all over it. But Rachel—one of the other waitresses—gave her the quick 411 on him. Business office around the corner. Routinely stopped in on his way home. A major workaholic. Always ordered a Black Tie to go. Never had time to sit down.

But that night, Mark's routine changed. He went out of his way to introduce himself to her, then sat at the table she was clearing and struck up a conversation. It was the first of many.

Night after night, Mark showed up at the café, sat in Cassie's station, and swapped stories with her. His stories were all about business; hers were about art school and crazy customers. Cassie found him charming, and his commanding presence filled the room, but never once did she consider Mark might be interested in her. He was so far out of her league it wasn't even funny. She just figured they were sharing polite conversation, anecdotes about their day, nothing more.

But soon enough, Mark invited her out. The first time he did, it caught her completely off guard. She deflected his invitation to a business function, using her hectic schedule as an excuse. She explained that juggling school, work, and her studies allowed no time for a social life. Mark accepted her refusal with a gracious smile but insisted he would ask her out again. Cassie wrote it off as harmless flirting. He was a gorgeous businessman, wealthy, and probably had supermodels on speed-dial. She, on the other hand, was just a third-year art student, barely making ends meet. She knew the novelty of their relationship would eventually wear off, and when it did, he would go back to spending time with his high-end friends, and she would go on being a barista until the art community discovered her talent.

Then he asked her out again.

When she refused a second time, he asked if their age difference bothered her. She assured him age was just a number. Even so, when she found out he was nine years her senior, she was shocked. Never would she had guessed he was that much older than her. Clearly, he wore his age as easily as his Tommy Hilfiger ties.

Two months into their nightly repartee, Cassie finally conceded. Mark showed up later than usual and proceeded to tell her about his latest venture. She sat down at the end of her shift and completely lost track of time. When she realized they had talked the night away, and there was no way she could make it to class on time, Mark convinced her to play hooky. Laughingly, he claimed it was a sign they were meant to spend the day together. His smile was so engaging, so charming; she agreed to go.

From that day on, they spent every spare moment together. At first, their dates were simple. But soon, movie dates turned into Broadway openings. Hot dog cart dinners in the park evolved into fancy dinners at five-star restaurants. And when Cassie embarrassingly explained she didn't have the wardrobe for some of his favorite haunts, packages from swanky boutiques showed up at her apartment.

Cassie soon realized Mark wasn't only wealthy, but influential. No matter the restaurant or the time, not a dinner went by without someone walking over to their table to shake Mark's hand or give him a pat on the back. Even women would interrupt their candle-lit dinners to make time with Mark. Cassie found these intrusions awkward and intimidating. It was obvious these women were flirting with Mark, and at times, he seemed a little too accommodating, kindling insecurities in Cassie. But Mark assured her it took different kinds of *grease* to keep the wheels of business turning, and she had nothing to worry about.

But Cassie did worry. She knew Mark wanted to take their relationship to the next level. After all, he was a thirty-year-old man, not a college junior. And as much as Cassie liked to think of herself as a rebel—leaving home at an early age, striking out on her own, turning her back on the do's and don'ts of her childhood—she couldn't shake the conversations she'd had with her mother regarding abstinence and intimacy. Her mother had challenged Cassie not to sacrifice her virginity for anything short of amazing, passionate, lasting love, and never to confuse love with sex. And even though Cassie hated her mother for leaving her, she was afraid if she disregarded her advice altogether, the memories of her mother would evaporate, and she would have nothing left.

Until Mark, abstinence had been a non-issue. She was in New York for one reason, and one reason only: her art career. That was her main focus. That and a job to pay for the expenses not covered by her scholarship. She'd been driven and had stayed on course, and Mark respected the boundaries she had laid down.

Until the night he took her home.

They had been dating for two months before Mark took her to his Fifth Avenue apartment. That was when she realized the extent of his wealth. Mark's apartment wasn't *on* the twenty-fifth floor. It *was* the twenty-fifth floor.

The penthouse.

When the elevator doors opened, she stepped directly into the entryway of Mark's lavish, magazine perfect apartment. The view, the architecture, the decor, everything fit together flawlessly.

Immediately, Cassie felt out of place in the opulent surroundings. She didn't feel she had what it took to fit into Mark's world. She was a nobody from a no-nothing town. She didn't come from a prestigious family, have a career, or even a degree. In fact, she had missed so many classes in the last two months—because of time spent with Mark—she had dropped out of art school before they could kick her out. She gave the associate dean an elaborate story about complications with an ongoing health issue. And since she had a stellar record with a promising future—according to one of her professors—she was given the semester off to take care of her health without jeopardizing her scholarship.

But standing in Mark's elaborate penthouse, knowing the elite circles he traveled in, Cassie wondered if she would ever be able to measure up.

"What do you think?" Mark moved closer, staring at her with his warm brown eyes.

"It's beautiful."

"Not nearly as beautiful as you," he said as he gently caressed her cheek with the back of his hand.

She wanted to believe him, wanted to belong in his world.

"Here, I'll show you around." Mark reached for her hand and gave her a tour. From the terrace balcony, to his richly paneled study, to the gourmet kitchen, everything in Mark's apartment was done on a grand scale. Then they walked the marble hall that led to the master suite. Mark opened the double doors, and Cassie nervously looked around, knowing she shouldn't be there.

Mark stepped closer. "I want to share my life with you, Cassie. I want to give you all of this." Then, dipping his head to the nape of her neck, he uttered his ultimate desire. "I want all of you."

Cassie's inhibitions slid to the floor along with the silk dress Mark slipped from her shoulders. That night she had made a decision. She would never go back to the town of Liberty, her efficiency apartment, or the world of Cassidy Martin. She would only move forward into the world of Mark Grayson.

As she lay awake that first night, Mark pressed against her back, she struggled with what she'd done. Her mother's words taunted her. The self-deprecating barbs from her conscience condemned her. She muffled her cries, turmoil and resentment churning inside her, giving way to anger.

If you cared, Mom, you wouldn't have left me. You and your god abandoned me a long time ago. It's my life, and I am going to live it how I want to. You can't tell me what to do anymore. I'm a grown woman. I will make my own choices. And I choose Mark.

Cassie moved in with him the very next day.

TWO

"Okay, Cassie, you're all set," the manicurist said with a smile.

Cassie looked up, realizing she'd been daydreaming. Withdrawing her newly polished fingertips from the drying contraption, she stood, carefully laying her purse strap over her shoulder. "Thanks, Amy. I'll see you next month."

"Yes, you will, and I'm going to want to hear all about your trip."

"Deal." Cassie smiled, then headed to the new BMW Mark had surprised her with the previous month. She slid into the supple leather interior already planning her next stop.

The dry cleaner, then Mark's office for lunch.

As she drove, she couldn't help but smile as she fantasized about all the fun things they would be doing in the weeks to come. A romantic walk along the Thames, a gondola ride at sunset, coffee and dessert at a French café.

It's going to be perfect.

Rushing from the dry cleaner, Cassie carefully laid Mark's cleaning on the back seat and made sure it was secured so it would not move around. She flinched involuntarily, remembering the time Mark shoved her to the bathroom floor and berated her because his suits got wrinkled. *Stupid! That's what you are, Cassie! The most important meeting of my career—of my life—and you expect me to wear this?* He threw the crumpled suit on the tile floor, then pushed her face in it like a dog being punished.

Stop it! She scolded herself.

It's different now. He's changed.

She tried to shake off the negative memory, angry her conscience trampled her excitement and replaced it with doubt. But she couldn't help it; the memory was strong.

It was the first time Mark had been violent with her.

The first time she saw the crack in his armor.

They'd been married less than a year when she realized there were two sides to Mark. The charmer—the man who won her heart, and the tyrant—the man who was controlling and abusive. She had learned fast what she needed to do to avoid the back-handed side of Mark's temper. Unfortunately, she wasn't always successful. However, over the last year, his dark moods had become a thing of the past. That's why the second honeymoon— a chance at a fresh start.

Everything is going to be fine, she reassured herself as she drove to Mark's favorite deli and picked up lunch.

Cassie entered the prestigious office building where Mark's company leased a floor of suites. With her new Gucci sandals clacking on the marble tile, she crossed to the elevator banks, noticing the atrium and lobby weren't nearly as crowded as they would be on any given weekday. Balancing the to-go box from the sandwich shop in one hand, she pressed the button for the twentieth floor with one of her newly polished fingers. The door immediately opened, and she stepped in. When the elevator doors reopened, Cassie rushed down the hallway, feeling like a kid on Christmas morning. Barely containing her excitement, she swung open the large glass door with the name *Gray and Sons* etched on it. She always smiled at the play on words but hoped one day soon they would have a son who would follow in Mark's footsteps. Hurrying to his office, she burst through the door and cheered, "Surprise!"

Mark quickly scrambled to his feet, leaving the woman he was entangled with on the couch. Cassie watched as he attempted to tuck in his shirt, then she turned and saw Amanda— his assistant—buttoning her blouse and straightening her hair.

Cassie stood, unbelieving, her hands shaking. Dropping the carton of food in the doorway, she stumbled backward out of Mark's office and hurried toward the large glass double doors. Pushing through those, she bolted toward the elevator at the end of the hall. She heard Mark yelling at her to stop, but she didn't. She couldn't. Once inside the elevator, she repeatedly pressed the Close button.

Close already. Come on, close.

Looking up, she saw Mark turn the corner and rush toward her. He was within inches of the elevator when the doors finally closed. She heard him shout a string of profanities, and bang against the closed door before the elevator started its descent.

Pressing herself against the back wall, she tried to slow her breathing, but her heart raced so fast she felt like she was going to pass out. She bent over, fighting the pinpoints of light, but nausea crept up her throat threatening to explode onto her new sandals.

How could you, Mark? How could you do this to me?

The atrium. The lobby. The parking structure. They were all a blur as she hurried to get away. Her hands were shaking so bad, she fumbled with her key fob, dropping it on the cold cement. With quaking fingers, she picked it up and pressed the button. The taillights flashed, and the alarm chirped. Quickly, she pulled the door open and slid in. Just as she pushed the ignition button, her cell phone chimed. *Mark.* She wanted to answer it, scream at him all the questions running through her head, but she couldn't do it. She did not want to hear his excuses. She did not want to give him a chance to explain. As far as she was concerned, there was no explanation. There was no excuse. Mark had played her for a fool, and she had been naïve enough to believe him.

Racing home, she nervously paced around their apartment like a caged animal. Crying hysterically, she felt like she was losing control of her body. Of her life. Of everything. When the phone rang, she ignored it. Knowing she had to get out of there before Mark came home, she hurried to their bedroom. There, at the foot of the bed, sat her already packed suitcases. Grabbing the collapsible handle of the largest one, she stacked the smaller suitcase on top, and threw the overnight bag over her shoulder. As she headed for the door, she heard Mark's voice fill the living room.

"Cassie . . . Cassie, baby, let me talk to you. Come on, Cassie, pick up! Cassie!" he shouted. "Pick up the phone! Let me talk to you!" She stood like a zombie staring at the phone, terrified to move, terrified to defy Mark. But if she stayed, and allowed him the chance to explain, he would manipulate her like he had done so many times before. But how much worse would it be if she ran? He *would* find her. Then what? Cassie leaned against the elevator door, knowing she couldn't stay, but afraid to leave.

Where can I go? I have nothing without Mark.

The courage she felt just seconds ago was gone. Dropping her overnight bag onto the floor, she backed away from the elevator. Then, from out of nowhere, she heard a whispered voice telling her to run. Startled, she swung around, expecting to find someone standing behind her. She scanned the living room and hall, but no one was there.

I imagined it.

Her mind was playing tricks on her. Stepping away from her luggage, she turned toward the bedroom.

Run, Cassidy. Go home!

There it was again. It had to be the voice inside her head. Her gut. Instinct. Whatever it was people called it. Or she was going crazy. Nevertheless, the urgency she felt that very second was empowering. Looking over her shoulder at the phone, she listened as Mark cursed and swore. "Don't you dare defy me, Cassie! I'm warning you!"

Flinging her purse and carry-on over her shoulder, she pressed the elevator button. The doors opened immediately, and she quickly dragged her suitcases inside. She had nothing to say to Mark; nothing worth staying for. She had tried to make it work, tried to believe him, but his actions pretty much said it all.

She was done trying.

Driving proved difficult through the blur of tears. Cassie kept reliving, dissecting the last several months, questioning everything. She thought the change in Mark's behavior was proof he cared. A rekindling of his love for her. A renewed dedication to their marriage. Now she realized the changes started about the same time Amanda was hired as his new assistant.

Cassie replayed the phone conversations she'd had with Amanda. They exchanged pleasantries and compliments like friends would. From time-to-time, Amanda encouraged Cassie to come by the office and steal Mark for lunch or even the rest of the day. She helped by clearing Mark's calendar and freeing up his time. Cassie thought Amanda's support and encouragement had been instrumental in the revitalization of their marriage. Now she realized nothing could be further from the truth. *She wasn't helping me; she was just making sure I didn't stumble upon their escapades. How could I have been so stupid?*

———— • ————

An hour later, Cassie found herself standing in the middle of JFK Airport, clueless what to do next. She had used a travel agent to book their trip, and before that, Mark had always taken care of their travel arrangements. The most she'd ever done is book a one-way flight to New York. Now she had to figure out how to take a first-class ticket to Ireland and exchange it for a destination stateside.

By the time Cassie had her ticket, made it through security, and found her gate, she was numb. She had walked from one end of the concourse to the other, fought with three different ticket agents, two supervisors, and a manager, insisting she didn't care how much money she lost by transferring her ticket; she just needed it changed. And if that wasn't enough, her phone vibrated in her purse every few minutes sending chills down her spine. And when it didn't vibrate, she was terrified she would turn around and find Mark standing behind her. Now, with her phone in her hand, she ignored the list of calls from Mark and dialed a number she had pushed to the recesses of her mind. She waited, listening as the phone rang. When the familiar voice on the other end of the line said, "Hello," she took a deep breath.

"Dad, it's me . . . Cassidy."

THREE

"I'd like to come for a visit. If it's all right with you?" The pause was so long, Cassie thought she lost the connection. "Dad?"

"It's your home, Sunshine. Of course it's all right."

Not a *that sounds great, honey* or *I can't wait to see you, sweetheart.* Cassie wanted to yell, "Forget it!" and hang up, but she had nowhere else to go.

"I'm not sure when I'll be landing. I'll call you before I get on my connecting flight."

"Okay. I'll wait for your call."

It had been more than five years since Cassie had last spoken to her dad.

The conversation had not been a pleasant one.

There was a lot of yelling and shouting on her part, and a healthy dose of her father's self-righteous incriminations. He voiced his disappointment at her New York lifestyle, and preached that she needed to get her life right with God. He also said—in not so many words—Mark was not welcome in his home if they weren't married.

So, that was that.

She hadn't spoke to her father since, not even to invite him to her wedding.

And now he's going to get his chance to say, 'I told you so' to my face.

Cassie sat in the terminal waiting for her flight, hating herself for running back home. She had promised herself a hundred times she would never return to Liberty, with its small-town ways and small-minded people, but here she was slinking back with her tail between her legs.

Resting her head back against the chair, she closed her eyes, remembering the day she left. It seemed like a lifetime ago when she boarded a plane to New York with a scholarship in hand and determination coursing through her veins. But she was no longer that wide-eyed girl juggling two jobs, cramming for finals, and painting with a heart full of passion. In fact, she didn't even go by the same name. It was Mark who started calling her Cassie. He teased that Cassidy sounded like a white-trash hick from a backwoods town, not the name of a sophisticated up-and-coming artist. Cassidy agreed with him, though inwardly she had been crushed. It was the first of many changes Mark made as he groomed her to fit into his world.

A world she had just left behind.

———— • ————

Cassidy jolted awake as the plane touched down, reality hitting her like a slap in the face. She wasn't in Europe about to enjoy a second honeymoon. She was on her way home to face her father.

To explain the mess she had made of her life.

But it's better than facing Mark.

At least her father wouldn't hit her.

She exited the small plane and walked across the tarmac into the airport. If you could call it that. The entire building consisted of a single gate, a minuscule lobby, and a security checkpoint with a stainless-steel conveyor belt and a walk-through metal detector. It was worlds apart from the airports she had grown accustomed to.

Immediately, she saw her father waiting by the ticket counter. Taking a deep breath, she walked over to where he was standing and gave him a timid hug and a sheepish smile.

"Hi, Dad."

He took her shoulder bag from her hand and smiled back at her. "You look tired, Sunshine."

She ignored the nickname. "Yeah, you could say that."

"Do you have more bags?" he asked.

"Two."

Silently, they walked to the lobby's side door and waited for someone to wheel over the cart with luggage on it. Cassidy pointed out the two pieces of luggage that matched her overnight bag and watched as her dad dutifully grabbed them from the shelf.

Again, without speaking, they walked to the parking lot where Cassidy recognized the old, faded blue pickup from her childhood. Without fanfare, her father tossed her expensive designer luggage into the hay-littered bed of the truck, right on top of a rusted bale of wire. Cassidy climbed onto the old bench seat and stared out the passenger window, feeling numb.

She caught her dad glancing her way a few times and decided to break the silence. "I left Mark."

"I kind of figured it was something like that." His words were slow and soft.

"I really don't feel like talking about it, but I thought you at least had the right to know."

He nodded like he understood the stipulations she was making. "I won't pry, Sunshine, but I can be praying."

Her shoulders stiffened, and her teeth clenched. Her dad had not changed in the least. He still felt a prayer tossed to a vindictive god could solve the world's problems. But she hadn't changed over the years either. So, she did what she had done a million times before.

She closed her eyes and tuned him out.

———— • ————

When Cassidy felt the truck turn off the highway and onto the long dirt road, she opened her eyes and saw her childhood home. Coming to a stop next to the front porch, she looked up, feeling like she had stepped back in time. Something she swore she would never do.

Her father lifted her suitcases from the truck bed, while she grabbed her overnight bag from where it sat on the seat next to her. She walked up the broad steps of the wrap-around porch and entered the living room with a sigh. Looking around, she couldn't believe it. Nothing had changed. It looked just like it did the day she left after graduation.

Silently, she headed upstairs to the bedroom that had been hers as a little girl. Everything was exactly as she had left it. The same white canopy with the pink bedspread. The matching desk and standing mirror. The shelf over the dresser displaying her many awards.

Her father walked in behind her and set her suitcases on the floor of the almost empty closet—her old flannel shirts the only things she'd left behind. He waited for her to say something; she could feel it. "I don't feel like talking," she finally said, interrupting the uncomfortable silence.

"I understand," he said as he walked away. "Good night, Cassidy."

When she heard the door click behind her, Cassidy felt a twinge of guilt at the way she had treated him. After all, she was the one who had asked to come home. It wasn't his fault she was running from Mark and hating her life. But tonight was not the time to hash all that out. She could apologize in the morning.

The overwhelming fatigue Cassidy felt was both physical and emotional. Her mind kept playing flashbacks from the scene she had walked in on. Mark and Amanda, their bodies twisted together. How many people knew of his infidelity and had kept it from her? Was Mark and Amanda's affair limited to the office, or did it explain some of the extended business trips he had been on in the last few months?

Exhausted, Cassidy looked through her luggage for something suitable to sleep in. Rifling through an array of seductive lingerie and alluring evening wear brought fresh tears to her eyes. She had packed with a second honeymoon in mind, not a night spent in her childhood bed.

You're such a fool!

Unable to stomach the idea of wearing the sexy lingerie, she decided a cotton sundress would have to double as a nightgown. Changing in the adjoining bathroom, she slipped the gauzy dress over her head. Pulling back the covers from her bed, she caught the fresh laundered scent. *Did Dad wash the sheets after I called? Why? Why would he bother? It's not like he wants me here.*

Not having the energy to debate her father's intentions, she crawled between the sheets, hoping to sleep away the nightmare that was her life.

FOUR

What is that thumping?

Cassidy could not identify the annoying noise, and her eyes were not willing to acknowledge if it was morning. But when the thumping continued, she squinted and remembered she was no longer in New York.

The nightmare was real.

Mark was having an affair.

She was home . . . in Wyoming.

"Cassidy, you need to get ready for church." Her father's voice was tender yet firm.

Church? Are you kidding me? She groaned. "I need some sleep, Dad. Go without me."

"Cassidy, I understand you're going through a tough spell, but the house rules haven't changed. If you're staying in my house, you will go to church. I'll wait for you out front."

She heard his footfalls on the stairs and yelled, "I'm not a child anymore! You can't tell me what to do!"

It's not like I'm moving back home. I just need somewhere to clear my head.

Cassidy argued with herself, even as she did what she was told. She got up and rummaged through her suitcase, tossing things around. Then she smiled. "You want me in church. Fine. I'll go to church."

She found the few pieces she'd packed in case of warm weather and held them up in front of her. *Perfect.* She slipped on the short floral skirt and rolled the waistband to make it even shorter, then pulled on the sheer red blouse—without the camisole that went with it—leaving her black lace bra completely visible. Gliding her feet into her Louboutin pumps, she turned to scrutinize herself in the full-length mirror. *I look like I belong in a gentleman's club.* "Oh well," she whispered, "if he's going to force me to attend church, he'll just have to put up with my wardrobe choices."

Cassidy walked out onto the front porch with her chin in the air, and paused, waiting for a lecture on modesty. Except her father was already in the truck, so she had no choice but to get in. He glanced at her exposed legs, and then to her eyes, but said nothing as he pulled away from the house.

Her plan failed. She was going to church—like it or not.

Cassidy felt self-conscious as she walked across the church parking lot. She quickly tugged down her skirt to its appropriate length but could do nothing about her see-through blouse. The outfit meant to shame her father was only proving to make her stick out like a sore thumb, the chill in the air making matters even worst.

The looks she received from the congregation stemmed from gracious embarrassment to disapproving disgust. Men looked at her then quickly looked away. Women all but gasped, and the few teenagers in the crowd gawked like she was a Playboy centerfold. All Cassidy wanted to do was sit down and disappear into the woodwork, but her father insisted on introducing her to everyone they passed on their way into the sanctuary.

"Cassidy, you remember the Fosters," her father said politely.

"Cassidy . . . heavens . . . it's been awhile, hasn't it?" Mrs. Foster's eyes darted from her see-through blouse to her exposed legs and back to her blouse again. She forced a smile, obviously uncomfortable.

"Yes, ma'am. Seven years."

"Well," she gave Cassidy another thorough look, "at least you still have your manners."

The couple walked away, whispering as they did.

"Come on, Dad, let's just go sit down."

The service seemed to drag on forever, but when the pastor finally said the closing prayer, Cassidy quickly slipped out of the sanctuary and waited in the truck. She just couldn't handle watching one more person look at her father with a sense of pity. On the drive home, her father tried to discuss the morning sermon with her, just like he used to do when she was younger.

"What did you think of the message?"

She starred out the passenger window and shrugged.

"People today don't want to acknowledge Satan is alive and well."

She sensed he was waiting for her to say something.

"Cassidy?"

"I wasn't listening, okay? I told you I needed to sleep, but you insisted I go! Well, you got your way. I went to church. But that doesn't mean I listened."

He turned away from her, glanced out his side window, then back at the road ahead of him.

Another awkward drive in silence.

The minute her father put the truck in park, Cassidy hurried into the house. Immediately, the aroma of pot roast filled her senses with memories of Sundays past. Her mother always had a wonderful lunch ready for them after services. But instead of the smell stirring her hunger, it stabbed at her heart. Rather than joining her father for lunch or for supper, Cassidy stayed in her room the rest of the day, tossing and turning, one painful memory after another.

FIVE

When Cassidy awoke the next morning, some of the numbness she had felt the previous day began to subside. Getting out of bed, she hovered over her suitcase, trying to decide what to wear. She chose a pair of J Brand skinny jeans and a white halter top. "Not exactly ranch wear, but it will have to do."

Putting on a cardigan, she went downstairs and walked out onto the front porch. She could see her father working by the open barn door, but knew she wasn't ready for another bout of guilt and recrimination. Slipping around the corner and down the steps, she started walking with no real destination in mind.

Nothing had changed.

Everything looked the same.

It was as if time had stood still.

She wandered around the property, enjoying the unseasonably warm day. But as it neared noon, she made her way back to the house. Realizing she needed to be civil toward her dad, she thought making lunch for the two of them might help smooth out some of the tension.

In the kitchen, she dropped her sweater across the back of a chair and quickly fixed sandwiches. She was just finishing up when her dad walked in.

"I'm sorry about church yesterday," she said in a rush as her father looked at the lunch she had prepared. "I know it means a lot to you. I just don't see the need for God in my life," she chuckled sarcastically, "not that I'm doing such a great job on my own."

Her father didn't correct her or debate with her, he simply smiled and said grace before eating.

"Mark had an affair," Cassidy blurted out in between bites of her sandwich. "We were all set to go on a second honeymoon for our fifth anniversary when I caught him with his assistant."

"Mark isn't a believer, is he?"

26

Cassidy stared at her dad in disbelief. "What does that have to do with anything? I'm his wife! Shouldn't that mean something?"

"Unfortunately, the world no longer recognizes the sanctity of marriage. Relationships are disposable. Everything is based on happiness. If you're not happy, find someone who makes you happy. That's what the world says."

Shocked, Cassidy sat back in her chair. "But he said he loved me. He was in my bed, making me promises. We were going away on a second honeymoon."

"But Cassidy, your marriage was not built on a solid foundation. How is it you thought he would be faith—"

"I can't believe you're defending him!" Cassidy shot up from her chair and crossed the kitchen. "I knew you were disappointed with me, but I never thought you would turn against me. What happened to all that God stuff about forgiveness? What about—" Cassidy fought the emotion in her voice. "Forget it! I knew it was a mistake coming here. I'll leave in the morning." She turned and hurried from the kitchen and out the front door.

Pushing away tears, Cassidy walked through the pasture, feeling completely alone.

Why did I even come here? What did I expect? She walked without purpose or direction. *But where else can I go?*

Looking at the expansive land—rolling hills on every side—it mocked her, reminding her how insignificant she was.

Once again, she was a nobody.

With no future.

With nowhere to go.

A gust of wind blew across her face, sweeping stray hairs across her lashes. Closing her eyes, Cassidy turned into the breeze, allowing it to dry her tears so she didn't have to admit they were there. Though it was warmer than usual for November, the breeze chilled her exposed shoulders. But she didn't care. It helped numb her pain. And in a strange way, the press of the breeze full on her face made her feel not so alone.

Taking a couple of deep cleansing breaths, she scolded herself for being so weak, then continued her walk. However, when she looked ahead of her, she was met with an unsettling memory.

Standing off, in the distance, was the original homestead her grandfather had built. A place that held both good and bad

27

memories. To her father, it was an old dilapidated building used for storage, but her mother had turned a small corner of it into a magical place for just the two of them. They would go there and have tea parties, girl time, and overnight adventures. But the last time she had been there was anything *but* magical.

Even though Cassidy knew she should return to the house, she walked toward the old building, as if it was a nemesis needing to be conquered.

She crossed her arms across her chest, warding off the chill in the air, but could do nothing for the chill in her bones.

When she climbed the back steps, she noticed the planks creaked but no longer sagged. Looking down, she saw new boards had replaced the dried and splintered ones.

Why would Dad do that? He only uses the place for storage. Then she opened the door.

"What in the world . . ."

She couldn't believe what she was seeing. Gone were the bales of hay and piles of fencing wire usually stored there. Instead, there were new pine floors—shined and varnished—and a modern kitchen. Crossing in front of the small kitchen nook, she pushed the swinging door opened and was shocked to see a fully restored living room.

What's going on here?

The fireplace that had nearly crumbled years ago was repaired and sported a massive wood mantel. A huge picture window filled the west wall, and another window on the south wall was framed out with a sitting area complete with padded window bench. Cassidy's eyes leapt from one corner of the room to the other. More pine wood floors. An over-stuffed couch. Coffee table. The old homestead was now a beautiful cottage.

This is incredible.

Remembering the last time she was here, she looked up, her eyes immediately drawn to the open-beam ceiling. The massive center beam taunted her, as if to say, 'we meet again.' Her heart raced, and her skin turned clammy at the memory of what she almost did that night. She dropped her head and closed her eyes.

Why God? Why bring me here? So you could remind me of that night? That I didn't have the guts to go through with it? Make me hate this place all over again?

"You don't belong here."

Cassidy froze. She was hearing voices again. Had God just told her she didn't belong? It was true. She didn't. But she and God weren't exactly on speaking terms.

Looking up, she turned around and saw a loft behind her, the shadow of a person standing next to the rail. However, the harsh rays of light filtering through the large picture window made it difficult for her to see. Squinting, she put a hand to her brow. When she blinked, the figure was gone.

Great! Now I'm imagining things too.

Dumbfounded, she closed her eyes and shook her head, trying to rationalize what just happened. When she heard footsteps on the stairs hugging the north wall, she saw a shadow descending the steps and moving toward her. She wanted to run, but her feet refused to move.

"This is my house; you're trespassing."

Cassidy was too scared to say anything. She just stood there staring . . . staring into eyes that were strangely familiar.

"I said, 'This is my house.' So, I'm asking you nicely to leave." His words were pleasant but firm.

"I'm sorry, I . . . I didn't mean to intrude," she said, nervously. "This is my father's property. I haven't been home for some time and didn't realize he sold this building." She smiled, trying to regain her composure.

"My name is Cassidy."

———— • ————

Wil had never seen Cassidy Martin at such a loss for words. When she was in high school, everything about her was smooth as silk: the way she spoke, the way she dressed, her beautiful blond hair. She was perfect. Everything that is, except for her attitude.

After her mother died, she became self-centered and self-righteous. She was too good for their little town, and she let everyone know it. She left the minute she graduated.

He hadn't seen her since.

Not until that morning in church.

This is going to be interesting.

SIX

"I know you, don't I?" Cassidy asked, quizzically. She felt like she should recognize the man in front of her but couldn't pull his name from her past. He was very tall, with broad shoulders, a sturdy jaw, and chestnut brown hair. His looks and physique were quite appealing. Surely someone this good-looking would not have escaped her memory.

He cleared his throat, looking uncomfortable under her scrutiny. "I realize you didn't intrude on purpose, but if you don't mind, I have some errands I need to get done."

Embarrassed, Cassidy shook off her soul-searching. "Of course. Yes. I'm sorry." Walking toward the door, she turned around, chancing one more look at the man. When his gaze locked on hers, his rich brown eyes held the hint she needed.

"Wilbur? Wilbur Marsh?"

Cassidy's mind tried to make the connection between the handsome man standing in front of her and the awkward teen she had known in school. Wilbur Marsh had been the quintessential nerd when he walked the halls of Central Valley High School. Ultra-conservative family. Black-rimmed glasses. Homemade flannel shirts. Baggy pants held up by suspenders over scrawny scarecrow-like shoulders. He looked like a character from the cover of a Saturday Evening Post magazine.

He was the ultimate target in school and the butt of everyone's jokes. Someone was always pulling a prank on Wilbur. She never involved herself in any of the stunts, even when she felt the other students were being cruel. She felt sorry for Wilbur, but not enough to put her popularity on the line. Through it all, his demeanor never changed. He never lashed out or named the people involved. He just took it. It was as if persecution was a badge of honor for him.

Talk about a late bloomer.

When Cassidy realized she was staring again, she quickly

apologized. "I'm sorry I didn't recognize you sooner. It's just that I've been away from Liberty for a while, and names seem to have escaped me." She tried to sound sincere as she gave him another satisfying glance.

"Or it could be you never gave me the time of day when you did live in Liberty," Wilbur said matter-of-factly.

Cassidy felt her face flush when Wilbur gave her a scrutinizing glance, and from the look on his face, she was coming up short.

"Look, I have some things to get done this afternoon, so if you don't mind . . ." Wilbur walked to the front door and opened it, clearly asking her to leave.

I can't believe it! Cassidy thought as she walked out the front door and onto the porch. *Wilbur, the nerd, is giving me the brush off?* She didn't know how many more hits her ego could take. First Mark. Now Wilbur. She wasn't sure if it was pride or spite that kicked in, but she was not going to let this opportunity go.

Mark hurt her.

Cheated on her.

Made her feel like she was less than nothing.

Well, turnabout is fair play, sweetheart. You burn me; I'll burn you.

Fabricating her most alluring smile, she looked up into Wilbur's riveting brown eyes. "Maybe we could get together later and talk over old times. I'd love to hear what you are up to these days." Cassidy leaned against the railing of the small porch, tossing a sultry look over her shoulder. She knew he would agree. After all, he was the school geek, and she was the most popular girl in their graduating class. When he stepped closer, she grinned while gliding her fingers down the length of his arm.

See, I still have it.

However, Wilbur quickly snatched her hand, stopped her stroking. "The only 'old times' I remember are of me being used for everyone's entertainment, and you being too stuck-up to care."

His stare cut through Cassidy like she was made of putty, causing her quick temper to flare. "That's not fair!" She stood, pulling her hand away. "I never did anything to you or to provoke those pranks."

"You're right. You did absolutely nothing. You were too

busy thinking only of yourself."

His words were so cold, so measured. He didn't even have to raise his voice for Cassidy to feel the weight of his insults. Her anger simmered below the surface. Men usually fell all over themselves to get her attention. They were charming and suave. They always had a ready compliment, not an insult. "Listen, Wilbur—"

"No. You listen. I think it's time for you to go back to New York. I'm sure you're more comfortable there with your upscale apartment, pretentious friends, and wealthy husband. Besides, you shouldn't be gone for too long, especially if he's anything like you." He glared at her, condemnation in his stare. "You know what they say, 'When the cat's away the mice will play.' I would hate for his eye to wander in your absence. That would never do for the Central Valley High Homecoming Queen."

Cassidy's reflexes were quick and sharp. Before Wilbur could react, she slapped him hard across the face. Covering her mouth in shock, she stood stock-still, waiting for him to react—but he didn't. He just rubbed his jaw while staring at his feet.

With tears pooling her eyes, Cassidy bolted from the porch, running with no destination in mind, because no matter how far she ran, she could not get away from the person she'd become.

Wilbur's words penetrated deep inside, the accuracy of his statement painful and harsh. She did not like the picture he drew of who she was, or what she had become.

He has no right to judge me! He knows nothing about me! Sprinting turned into a jog even as her legs grew weak due to the rugged terrain. *How dare he act as if he—*

Her foot caught on an exposed root from a sturdy oak tree, pitching her forward. Throwing her hands out in front of her, Cassidy tried to brace herself, but momentum worked against her. Crying as she tumbled head over heels down a steep knoll, she came to an abrupt stop, pain slamming into her forehead.

When she opened her eyes, points of light danced in front of her, making her feel like she was going to puke. Trying to sit up, she gasped at the pain and closed her eyes against the dizziness. "Thanks, God!" she cried out. "I can always count on you to kick me when I'm down!" She wasn't sure how long she sat there cursing God, but she did know she was emotionally spent. When she decided to take a few minutes to rest before heading back to the house, her body was quick to agree.

SEVEN

Joseph looked at the clock on the living room wall for the last time before hurrying down the front steps, getting into his truck, and heading toward Wil's place.

He was worried about Cassidy and didn't know what to do.

She had stormed out of the house hours ago, mad as a hornet, and it was all his fault. He didn't mean for his words to be so combative or to push her away. He simply pointed out what seemed to be so obvious to him.

Unfortunately, being at odds with his daughter was nothing new. It had become the sum of their relationship after her mother's death. While he had chosen to draw strength from God, Cassidy had turned her back on God, blaming Him for her mother's accident.

He spent years trying to reach his daughter and help her through the tragedy that had darkened both their lives, but he had never been able to break through. He could not penetrate the barrier she had built. Her on one side, God and him on the other. Cassidy became an angry, defiant, self-absorbed person. They spent her entire senior year arguing about one thing or another, and when they weren't arguing, Cassidy was ranting about their little hole-in-the-wall town and how she couldn't wait to get out. The same town his family had called home for over a hundred years.

Pulling up in front of Wil's place, Joseph hurried up the porch steps and knocked. He was grasping at straws but didn't know where else to look. He flinched when Wil opened the door so abruptly.

"Oh . . . hey, Joseph."

"Sorry to bother you, Wil, but you haven't seen Cassidy, have you? She's home visiting and—"

"I know. I saw her at church." He leaned against the door

jamb and crossed his arms against his chest. "Why didn't you mention she was coming home for a visit?"

"It was unexpected," he said, removing his hat and swiping his forearm against the sweat of his brow. "So, I guess you haven't seen her in the last few hours?"

"Actually," he rubbed his jaw, "she did stop by here expecting to find the old storage shed. I guess you never told her about our arrangement."

Shoving his hat back on his head, Joseph sighed. "No. I never did."

———— • ————

Wil could see Joseph was visibly upset, which angered him even more. Cassidy had wandered off, thinking only about herself, not considering that her father would worry.

"I'm sure she's fine, Joseph. She probably just lost track of time."

"But when she left the house she was upset. Extremely upset. She's hurting, and I said some things that made her . . . I didn't mean to . . . I . . . she . . . I'm just afraid . . . afraid she might do something . . . foolish."

Wil looked into the elderly man's eyes and saw not only the love he had for his wayward daughter, but genuine fear. "What do you mean, 'she's hurting?' "

"She didn't come home for a visit, Wil." Joseph twisted his hands together. "Cassidy left her husband."

"What?" Wil was stunned. "Why?"

"She found out he was being unfaithful. I don't know much more than that, but I do know she's very upset. She's not her normal . . . you know, not her normal . . ."

Joseph was at a loss of words, but Wil knew exactly what he was having a hard time saying. Cassidy had become a very cold, calloused person after her mother's death. She was emotionally distant and shut people out, her way of protecting herself from getting hurt.

Wil thought about his interaction with her earlier. *She didn't look hurt when she was making a pass at me. At least not until I turned her down.*

"Listen, Joseph, I don't think you need to worry. Cassidy was just . . ." Wil looked at the concern in the man's eyes and didn't want to hurt him further. It would crush Joseph if he found out

34

about his daughter's behavior. "Look, you probably passed her on your way out here. Or maybe she went into the house through the back door, and you didn't see her. Why don't you go home and see if she's there? If not, call me, and we'll figure out where to go from there."

"Maybe you're right. She's probably just cooling off somewhere." Joseph sighed. "Sorry for bothering you, Wil." He turned, shoulders slumped as he headed back to his truck.

After watching Joseph drive away, Wil turned in the direction Cassidy had stormed off to earlier. *I can't believe I said those things about her husband. Even though I was apparently right.*

Scanning the horizon, Wil continued to scold himself for being so cold and uncaring, precisely what he accused her of when they were in school. The only difference . . . he wasn't a kid. He knew better and should have been the bigger man.

Grabbing a bottle of water out of the refrigerator, he took a swig just as his phone started to ring. Pulling it from his pocket, he saw it was Joseph.

"Wil, she's not here. I'm really concerned. It's been a long time since Cassidy has been on the ranch. She could have easily gotten turned around, that, and she left so fast, she didn't take a jacket with her or anything."

"Okay, well . . . she couldn't have gone far on foot. If Cassidy is as upset as you think she is, she probably just found a quiet place to think. I'll take a look around here. Why don't you look by the creek?"

When Joseph hung up, Wil pocketed his phone and headed out the front door. Climbing into his F-150, he drove to a couple places he thought Cassidy might be. And sure enough, in less than fifteen minutes, he spotted her in the distance, sitting under an oak tree.

Shifting into neutral, Wil descended the knoll faster than he should have, angry Cassidy was pouting like a ten-year-old while her dad was worrying himself sick.

Kicking up a trail of dust, Wil knew Cassidy had to see him coming, but she just sat there, not even bothering to get up. Slamming the truck into park, he hopped out and marched over to where she was hunched against the tree. "I hope you're happy, Cassidy! Your dad has been looking everywhere for you and is beside himself with worry. And here you are feeling sorry for yourself."

She slowly turned toward him. When she did, Wil saw her hair was matted with blood, and she looked dazed.

"I tried . . . I tried . . ." Her words were slurred and jumbled. "really, I did. I thought I . . . I felt dizzy and decided to rest. Just for a minute . . . I was waiting . . . to feel better. I didn't mean to worry Dad . . . really I didn't."

She looked at him with a helplessness he'd never seen in her before.

"I must have . . . fallen asleep."

Wil knelt next to her, concerned by her mumbling. He reached for her, gently turned her toward him, but she gasped at his touch.

"Cassidy, what happened?"

She looked at him but couldn't seem to focus. The gash over her right eye was serious.

"We need to get you back to the house. Are you hurt anywhere else?"

She didn't answer, but she was shivering, and Wil could tell she was cradling her right arm.

"Come on, let's get you home."

He gently helped Cassidy to her feet, careful not to apply pressure to her arm. She staggered and lost all color in her complexion. He held her close for support, but she quickly pushed away from him, stumbled to her knees, and retched. Wil stood by helplessly as her body continued to flinch involuntarily. When she stopped heaving, Wil knelt next to her.

"Let's try again, Cassidy," he said, softly, "but slower this time."

Carefully, Wil helped her stand and waited as she gained her balance and steadied her stomach. She continued to shake as he guided her to the passenger side of his truck and lifted her onto the seat. Wanting to get her home as quick as possible, he took off up the hill, the vehicle jostling over every rut and rock, Cassidy gasping and moaning with every bump and dip. They had barely traveled fifty yards when she opened the door. Afraid she was going to tumble out, Wil grabbed her arm to study her as she heaved outside the truck. He cringed at the pain he heard as she coughed and sputtered. Knowing she could go no further, he pulled up close to his front porch and gently lifted her out of the vehicle and carried her inside.

"What are you doing?" she grimaced with her eyes squeezed shut.

"You need to lie down. Somewhere stationary." He lowered her to the couch in front of the fireplace, pulled a blanket up over her, then hurried to the kitchen for a bowl and his penlight.

Sitting alongside her, Wil tucked the bowl in next to her other side. "This is in case you feel like you're going to puke."

She cringed. "You don't need to yell. And I'm not going to be sick. I just need a minute to rest."

"I didn't—"

She cringed again.

Wil whispered, "I wasn't yelling."

"Then stop talking and just let me lay down here for a minute."

Wil bit back a retort, then stood, his phone in hand. Walking away from where Cassidy lay, he spoke quietly, "Joseph, I found her. No, she's at my house. I think you'd better come here."

EIGHT

Wil hung up the phone and walked back over to where Cassidy lay. When he sat down alongside her, the cushion of the couch dipped slightly, eliciting a soft moan from her.

"Cassidy, I need to look at the gash on your head."

Though she didn't answer, Wil carefully pulled her hair back from the open wound.

Definitely needs stitches.

He pressed his hand to her cheek, glad to feel some warmth returning.

At least she's not going into shock.

"Cassidy, I need to check out your arm. Let me know where it hurts, okay?"

She groaned.

When Wil brushed her hair back over her right shoulder, he realized the blood matted in her hair wasn't solely from the gash on her head. She had a serious chunk of skin missing from her shoulder.

Okay. I'll come back to that.

Wil gently took her arm in his hand. She whimpered slightly as he worked his way down the bone from the elbow, slowly squeezing, waiting for a reaction. When he applied pressure to her wrist, she cried out.

"I'm sorry. I know it hurts, but I need to look a little closer. I'll be as gentle as I can."

He carefully turned her arm over and pressed in a few more locations. Even though she cried out at his prodding, he was pretty sure it wasn't broken, just badly sprained.

"Cassidy . . . Cassidy listen to me. I need you to open your eyes."

Her lashes fluttered, but she had a hard time keeping her eyes open. Wil pressed his finger to her right eyelid, then shined his penlight in her eye. She flinched at the assault but didn't pull away. He did the same to her other eye and watched as she followed his directions. Look right. Look left. Look at me. Follow my finger. She also answered his litany of questions. Her name. The day. Her age. And if she knew where she was.

Wil heard a commotion outside just before Joseph catapulted himself into the room, almost stumbling over his own feet. "How is she? What happened? Is she going to be okay?"

"Slow down, Joseph," Wil said quietly as he moved away from Cassidy's side. Joseph lowered himself beside his daughter to see for himself that she was okay.

"She's going to be fine, Joseph. Cassidy has a slight concussion, some cuts and scratches, and a badly sprained wrist. The gash on her head will need a couple of stitches, but she's going to be fine."

Joseph's eyes darted from her head to her wrist, to her shoulder. "Are you sure? Shouldn't we get her to the hospital?"

"She'll be fine. Besides, she's not going to want to travel right now. The concussion is making her nauseous. That's why I brought her here instead of home. The drive was wreaking havoc on her stomach."

"She's so still. What if she's unconscious, or slips into a coma? Injuries like this can escalate really fast."

"Look, if it will make you feel better, we can take her to the hospital, but I'm telling you, it will cause her more discomfort than she is experiencing right now."

Joseph looked between him and Cassidy, clearly unsure what he should do. "She looks so pale and frail."

"I'm not frail, Dad," Cassidy groaned, though her eyes were still closed. "And I don't want to go to the hospital. I don't want to move at all. Just let me rest here for a little while. I'll be fine."

Joseph waited a second, then looked at Wil. He signaled for Joseph to follow him into the kitchen.

"Look, Joseph," he whispered, "let me take care of Cassidy here. She'll need to be watched throughout the night, and she's going to need a few stitches to close the gash on her forehead. I'll bring her home in the morning, and if you're still not convinced about her well-being, you can take her to the hospital. That is, if she'll let you."

Joseph paced a few steps and furrowed his brow while rubbing the whiskers on his cheek.

"Trust me, Joseph. I promise I'll take good care of her."

"Of course I trust you, but this is my daughter we're talking about, not a steer or a stallion."

Wil crossed his arms across his chest, waiting for Joseph to decide what he was going to do.

"Okay. She can stay here but only if you think it's best."

"I do. Now, why don't you go home and get some rest? If you're going to have to play nursemaid tomorrow, you'll need all the sleep you can get tonight."

After saying goodbye to Cassidy, and only receiving a moan in return, Joseph walked to his truck alongside Wil. With a hand on Joseph's shoulder, Wil tried to encourage him. "Come on, she's going to be fine."

Joseph turned to Wil, looking sadder than sad. "She wasn't always this way, you know. Cassidy was the sweetest, most loving little girl before she lost her mother. I would give anything to turn back the hands of time, but I can't." He massaged his brow, looking older than his years. "I love her so much, but I feel powerless to save her. When she left here nine years ago, she was angry and bitter and blamed God for her pain. Day after day, I've prayed for her heart to soften, to find her way back home. But not like this. Brokenhearted, and now physically hurt. She'll blame God. Push Him further away. And there is nothing I can do but pray."

"But Joseph, that's the best—"

"I know." He raised his hand, cutting him off. "I don't discount the power of prayer. But I know my daughter. I'm not sure she can take much more."

NINE

She felt his presence and opened her eyes. Wilbur sat on the coffee table alongside her, a black medical bag next to him. He leaned in close, visually examining the wound on her head.

A doctor. Score one for the nerd.

"I'm going to need to stitch this up."

She panicked and tried pushing herself to an upright position, but her head felt like it was going to explode, and her stomach lurched once again with disapproval.

"Cassidy, you need to take it easy." He pressed his hand to her good arm, encouraging her to lay back down. "I know what I'm doing. You just need to lay still and not move around."

She watched as he pulled instruments from his bag and laid them on the coffee table next to him, then he shifted to sit next to her on the couch.

"This is going to be a little cold, but it will help numb the area."

She clenched her teeth as he swabbed the area over her right eye. When he was done, she let out a soft breath.

"See, that wasn't so bad." He smiled.

Cassidy didn't answer. She just stared at him hoping he knew what he was doing. When she saw him pick up a disposable razor, she put out her hand. "What are you going to do with that?"

"I need to shave around the laceration. Just a little bit so I can clean it out and see what I'm doing while I'm stitching it."

She stared at him for a second, wondering if he was vindictive enough to do something stupid, then closed her eyes, not having the energy to care. She felt the grate of the razor against her scalp, and the tickle as a small clump of hair tumbled down her cheek. He was careful, his touch gentle, then he pressed a cloth to her brow.

"I'm going to lay this here while I irrigate the wound, so nothing gets into your eye."

She hissed, squeezing her eyes closed as the cold liquid tingled and stung. "Sorry," he whispered, his thumb wiping away the liquid dribbling down her cheek.

Cassidy could feel pressure and a pulling sensation about her temple, but she didn't experience actual pain. Wilbur worked slowly and carefully, but it wasn't too long before he removed the cloth.

"All done," he said as he started to clean his instruments with an antiseptic sponge.

Cassidy raised her hand to inspect the area, but before she could touch her forehead, he pulled her hand back down to her lap.

"You need to leave it alone. I would put a bandage on it, but I think that would be more uncomfortable. It would just pull at your hair."

She watched as he tore open a medicated wipe, and asked, "What is that for?"

"Your shoulder. You have a nasty gash on it too."

She looked at her shoulder and saw a pretty good size piece of flesh scraped away. The second Wilbur touched the wipe to it, she flinched, jerking her shoulder aside. "That hurt!"

"I'm sorry!" he snapped, then softened his tone. "I'll try to be more careful, but it's pretty deep and I need to make sure it's clean."

She could tell he was trying to be gentle, but it still hurt.

A lot.

Even though her shoulder felt like it was on fire, Cassidy grit her teeth, laid still, and held her breath.

When he sat back and began to collect the gauze wrappers and bloody swabs, she exhaled and closed her eyes, feeling emotionally and physically exhausted.

"Don't go to sleep on me now, I still need to take care of your wrist."

She opened her eyes. "It's fine. Just a little sore."

"It's not fine. It's badly sprained and needs to be wrapped."

She sighed with frustration, wanting nothing more than to be left alone so she could cry in private.

"Come on, Cassidy, suck it up. This is your own fault. If you hadn't flown out of here half crazed, you wouldn't be in this pain, or given your father a heart attack when he couldn't find you. He's an old man and shouldn't have to deal with your self-destructive behavior. So, stop thinking only about yourself."

Why did his words hurt so much? He wasn't being fair. This wasn't her fault. It was Mark's. He's the one to blame. He's the reason she's home and angry and . . .

Then why did she allow Wilbur's words to hurt so much?

Because they were true.

Closing her eyes, she turned toward the couch, determined to be the model patient. She didn't flinch or protest when he lifted her hand up and down as he circled the bandage around her wrist, pulling it snug. She bit her lip to keep from crying. Swallowing her pain, she refused to give him the satisfaction of seeing her cry.

"All done," he said as he rested her arm across her stomach.

She didn't acknowledge him, she just kept her face pressed against the couch cushion.

"Cassidy?"

"Fine. You're done," she mumbled into the cushion.

"Cassidy, look at me."

When she refused, he framed her chin with his strong fingers and forced her to look his way, allowing him to see the tears running down her face.

"Why didn't you tell me I was hurting you? I would have gone slower."

"What would it have mattered? It was going to hurt anyways. Besides, someone as self-centered as myself deserves the same amount of pain she's dished out over the years, right?"

———— • ————

Wil felt terrible. As much as he *didn't* appreciate Cassidy or the way she treated her father, he certainly did not take pleasure in seeing her in pain or hearing his harsh words thrown back in his face.

"Look, I'd give you something for the pain, but I can't. At least not for the first twenty-four hours. We need to keep you alert and coherent."

Cassidy brushed at the tears trailing back to her ears. "I'll be fine."

Stoic. No, stubborn. It was obvious she was going to make a point of hiding her pain.

Frustrated with himself more than with her, Wil went to the kitchen to get a washcloth and basin. Running cold water into the bowl, he then soaked the cloth and rung it out with more force than was necessary. Walking back to where Cassidy lay, he sat down beside her. Though she was silent, her eyes asked him why.

"You've got dirt all over you."

She reached for the cloth. "Then I'll do it."

"You can't see your own face. Just let me do it."

He brushed the cloth across her forehead and cheeks, then gently washed the dirt on her arms and shoulders. When he pressed the cloth to her neck, he noticed the plunging neckline of her halter top was revealing more than she probably wanted. When their eyes met, and Cassidy's face flushed red, he was sure of it. Reaching for another blanket draped over the back of the couch, he covered her with it and slid it up to her shoulders.

"There. Now I have some things I need to get done, but I'll check on you periodically."

After making a few calls, and finishing a few chores, Wil spent the remainder of the evening sitting in the over-stuffed chair across from Cassidy. Waking her every hour, he checked her eyes and asked her questions to make sure she was coherent. She responded without irritation and then closed her eyes and turned toward the couch cushion, shutting him out. He didn't think she fell back asleep that easily, but it was obvious she didn't want to talk to him either. Even so, Wil didn't sleep; he couldn't. Guilt gnawed at him. Guilt because he knew he was to blame for the condition she was in. If his words had not been so cruel, so spiteful, so accurate, she wouldn't have run off and gotten herself hurt. Caring for her, even if she didn't want to speak to him, was the least he could do.

TEN

Cassidy woke to the smell of bacon. She inhaled the scent, grateful it didn't turn her stomach. Slowly, she opened her eyes. The room didn't spin like it had the night before, so she decided to take her chances. Standing, she waited to see if she felt dizzy or sick.

Standing . . . check. Now to see if I can walk without falling flat on my face.

Hearing noises coming from the kitchen, she decided that would be her goal. With each measured step, she felt shaky, but not dizzy. When she pushed opened the swinging door, she saw Wilbur standing at the stove. He looked good, even from behind. Fitted jeans. Cowboy boots. Waffle-weave thermal shirt stretched across sculpted shoulders.

Don't even go there. You already embarrassed yourself once.

She cleared her throat. "May I use your bathroom?"

Startled, Wilbur spun around. "Cassidy, what are you doing up?" He put down the spatula and stepped to her side, his hand immediately going to her waist for support. "You should be lying down."

"But I need to use the bathroom," she whispered.

"It's upstairs. I'll help you."

"No," she turned back around. "I can do it on my own."

"I don't know, Cassidy, it's a lot of steps, and they're kind of steep. Are you sure?"

"I'm sure. You know me, I only think about myself," she said as the door swung shut behind her.

Cassidy hated herself for throwing Wilbur's words back in his face. He didn't deserve to be treated that way. After all, he was only trying to help. Shrugging off her self-incrimination, she stood at the foot of the stairs and looked up. Encouraged that she didn't feel like she was going to puke, she held onto the banister.

Taking one step at a time, she stopped midway to catch her breath. When she did, she couldn't help but glance at that stupid beam again.

How can an inanimate object taunt me?

When she reached the landing, she sighed with relief then looked around.

Amazing!

Bookshelves covered one entire wall, and a writing desk sat nestled in the alcove overlooking the living room below. The king-size bed was elevated on a distressed wood platform, the same wood that was used for the bookshelves, headboard, and matching nightstands. Though the bed took up most of the floor space, it fit the room perfectly. Obviously custom built. She continued admiring the finely crafted details and masculine accents as she crossed to the pocket door on the far side of the room. Stepping inside the bathroom, her appreciation grew for the design and architecture. Light cascaded through the multi-paned window. And even though the room was small, the attention to detail was still there. The fusion of sleek lines and antique fixtures gave it an eclectic feel that was warm yet modern.

Whoever designed this bathroom knew what they were doing.

Looking around, she caught her reflection in the vanity mirror, and gasped. Small black stitches stuck out from her blood matted hair. Her right eye was discolored and swollen, and she had a good size bandage on her shoulder. She looked horrible, which did nothing for her demeanor.

You deserve it. Now, you look as damaged as you are.

When Cassidy left the bathroom, she was struck again by the rightness of Wilbur's loft. Sharp lines. Warm tones. Bold edges. Rugged beauty.

It suits him.

Then she saw the black leather Bible laying on the night stand. It drew her in. Sitting on the edge of the bed, she reached for the well-worn book and stared at it like it was a relic deserving respect. She felt tears well in her eyes, and a pain squeeze her chest. Her mother often read to her from a Bible much like this one. Cassidy's heart ached for her mother like she had not felt for some time. Pressing the book to her chest, she curled up on the side of the bed.

"Cassidy?"

She opened her eyes and saw Wilbur crouched alongside her. But where was she?

"I got worried when you didn't come back downstairs for breakfast."

She blinked, then saw the Bible clutched to her chest. Closing her eyes, she tried to make sense of everything.

Wilbur's loft. His bed. His Bible.

"I'm sorry." Cassidy swung her feet to the floor, wincing at the movement. Feeling beyond humiliated, she set the Bible back on the nightstand. "I wasn't being nosy. I just saw it . . . and, well . . . it brought back some good memories . . . and your bed was . . . I just sat down for a moment. It was comfortable." She looked anywhere but at him. "I guess I fell asleep."

"It's okay. I should have taken you to bed last night . . . I meant offered you my bed . . . to sleep in . . . alone."

They exchanged awkward looks, and Cassidy couldn't help but grin as Wilbur blushed. "Did you say something about breakfast?" she asked, moving the conversation to a safer subject.

"Yes!" He stood, clapping his hands together nervously. "I have breakfast waiting for us downstairs."

"Sounds good." She stood slowly.

Clutching the handrail with her good hand, Wilbur held on to her right elbow, setting the pace—a slower than slow pace. She wanted to pull away. Do it herself. Prove she did not need his help, but when she stumbled, she was glad for his steady hand.

Pushing through the kitchen door, the same sunshine that lit the upstairs bathroom greeted them, softening her disposition. She took a seat in the corner nook, her back to the window, drinking in the warmth offered by the sun. When Wilbur placed a plate filled to capacity in front of her, she laughed. Staring at the stack of bacon, an omelet oozing with cheese and finely diced vegetables, and two small biscuits already split and buttered, she shook her head. "This all looks wonderful but there's no way I'll be able to finish even half of it."

"That's okay. You don't have to eat it all. I just wasn't sure what would sound good. Eat what you want and leave the rest."

Before Cassidy could lift the fork to her mouth, Wilbur took the seat across from her, their knees bumping slightly, then he bowed his head to pray. "Lord, thank You for sparing Cassidy last night and for giving her a fresh start this morning. I pray she finds what she's looking for. Amen."

Cassidy felt a wave of belligerence. *Who said I was looking for something?* And even if she was, she certainly did not need God's help to find it. As much as she wanted to argue with Wilbur and put him in his place, she decided to let it go. After all, he had helped her out. If anything, he'd at least saved her a trip to the hospital.

Taking small bites of the feast in front of her, she paced herself, not wanting to do anything that would make the queasiness return. But Wilbur . . . he ate his food with voracity.

No wonder he filled out after high school.

When he caught her staring, she quickly looked away.

"What?"

"I didn't say anything." Cassidy quickly put a forkful of eggs in her mouth.

"What were you staring at?" Wilbur pressed.

She took her time, swallowing before she spoke. "I guess I was just surprised by the size of your appetite."

"Well, as you might recall, my evening was interrupted last night, so I missed dinner."

"Excuse me," she fired back. "I didn't mean to *interrupt* your evening. It wasn't exactly what I had planned either. Sorry to be such an inconvenience."

"Hey," he sat up straighter. "I was only kidding. Don't be so defensive."

"I'm not being defensive," she said, while repeatedly stabbing her omelet.

"Well, the eggs on your plate are already dead, so you can stop taking your anger out on them."

"I'm not angry!" Cassidy insisted.

They sat in silence, neither continuing their side of the argument.

Cassidy sat with her elbow on the table, her head propped in her hand. No longer feeling hungry, she pushed the remainder of her breakfast around on her plate.

"You barely touched your food."

"I'm not really that hungry."

"Then why don't you go ahead and lie down for a while. You're looking a little green."

Without saying another word, she scooted from the breakfast nook, and braced herself on the table as she stood. Wanting to look stronger than she felt, she straightened up and pushed open the kitchen's swinging door but had to grab onto the door jamb when she felt her legs buckle.

"Cassidy!"

She felt Wilbur's arm slip around her waist.

"I'm okay." She looked over her shoulder as she spoke, and he was right there. Looking at her. Nearly nose to nose. "Ahh . . . my legs . . . I lost my balance."

"Sunshine, are you okay?"

She spun around to see her dad rushing toward her, the front door hanging open.

"Dad!"

"Sunshine . . . what are you doing up? Here let me help you." He reached for her elbow and looped his arm around her.

She knew the minute Wilbur let go of her, his warmth gone.

"I'll be in the kitchen if you need me," he said as he took a step back.

Her dad led her to the couch, where she pulled her feet up under her and allowed her head to rest on the overstuffed pillows of the couch.

"How are you feeling, Sunshine?"

"Would you stop calling me that!" she bristled. "I'm not a little girl anymore!" Her bitter tone brought sadness to his eyes. "I'm sorry, Dad. I didn't mean to snap at you. It's just I would prefer you didn't call me that anymore."

"Okay, Cassidy, whatever you want."

She closed her eyes, her outburst zapping her of what little energy she had. Feeling herself drift, she didn't fight it.

"Sun— . . . sweetheart, Mark called."

Her eyes shot open, and she sat up so quick she made herself dizzy. Grabbing her forehead, she groaned, "What do you mean 'Mark called?' How? He doesn't even have your number."

"Well . . . actually, he called your phone. When I was passing by your room, I heard it go off and thought I should answer it. In case it was important."

"Dad! That's what voicemail is for." Cassidy threw her head back, causing both her eyes and her stomach to swim. "I didn't want him knowing where I was." Staring at the ceiling, she asked, "What did he say?"

"Well . . . he was nice. Polite. And when he found out you'd had an accident, he sounded very concerned."

"Oh, Dad, please tell me you didn't?" She clenched her fist, anger coursing through her veins.

"He's your husband, Sun—" He cleared his throat. "I thought

he had a right to know."

"A right to know? Really? As far as I'm concerned, he gave up his 'right to know' the minute he started sleeping with his assistant."

Cassidy had not heard Wilbur walk into the room, but she saw him now, and caught the look of sympathy on his face.

A look that morphed into pity.

"That's right!" she glared at him, her anger turning to rage. "The most popular girl in school can't satisfy her own husband. He'd rather have sex with his assistant than with me. And I didn't even suspect. Late meetings. Out of town conferences. I bought it all. Every last lie. Until I walked in on them together. I guess I was so desperate to make my marriage work, I ignored the truth. Desperate people do desperate things. Obviously, or I wouldn't have come back to this no-nothing town and thrown myself at a hired ranch hand."

"Cassidy!" her father snapped, but she continued.

"Sorry to bruise your ego, Wilbur. Don't flatter yourself by thinking it was your good looks that attracted me. I just wanted to get even with Mark. I wanted to inflict on him as much pain as he caused me, and I thought you'd be an easy target. I figured you would jump at the chance to sleep with the homecoming queen. However, I forgot you were such a goody-two-shoes, just like my dad."

"Okay young lady, that's enough!" Her father barked, his voice firm, his jaw set. "You might be hurting, but that's no reason to hurt those who want to help you. We have done nothing to deserve your stinging words."

Cassidy lowered her eyes, embarrassed she was being scolded like a child, but more embarrassed about the things she had said. It was true. Wilbur didn't deserve her venom. It was Mark she was angry with. She was about to apologize, but her dad was not finished.

"If you want to be mad at someone, you can be mad at me. Because, not only does Mark know where you are, he's on his way here."

Anger was quickly replaced with terror. *What am I going to do? He's not going to come all this way and expect to leave without me. But what will he do if I refuse to go? He wouldn't dare hurt me in front of my father. No. He's too smooth for that.*

"I'm sorry, honey, when he asked for directions, I thought it was a good thing. He was coming for you."

"It's not your fault, Dad," she whispered, trying to press down her fear, to keep it from her voice. "I'm a big girl now. I shouldn't expect you to run interference for me."

Her thoughts raced, grasping for a solution. *Maybe I can get a flight out of here before he shows up?* She thought about it, then fingered the stitches on her head. *I can't even walk straight. How am I going to get on a plane feeling like this? She thought again. I'll just refuse to speak to him. He can't come here and put demands on me.* Then a chill shook her. *But would he hurt Dad?*

She flinched when she felt a hand close around hers, then looked at Wilbur sitting on the coffee table in front of her, his eyes filled with concern.

"Cassidy, what's wrong?"

She pulled her hand away. "Nothing."

"Don't lie. You're white as a sheet, and you completely checked out. We were talking to you, but it was like you weren't even here. And then when I touched your hand, you flinched."

"You startled me."

"And you whimpered."

She looked at her father. "I'm fine."

He looked at Wilbur. "Could you give Cassidy and me a few minutes?"

Wilbur stood, and she listened as he walked across the room and closed the front door behind him, but she refused to look at her father.

"You're afraid of him, aren't you?"

She chuckled sarcastically. "Wilbur Marsh? Hardly."

"Mark."

She clenched her jaw.

"He hurt you, didn't he?"

She looked at him, exasperated. "Of course he did. Haven't you heard a word I've said? He slept with another woman."

"That's not what I meant."

She looked away, but not before her father saw tears flood her eyes.

———————— ● ————————

Joseph walked out and joined Wil on the porch.

"Can I ask another favor, Wil?"

"Sure, Joseph, anything."

"Cassidy doesn't want to see Mark right now. Can she stay

here until he leaves? Normally, I would encourage her to face her troubles, but I don't think she can handle it right now. She's too fragile, too upset, and . . . and I think there might be extenuating circumstances. I'll meet with Mark and explain to him that he is welcome to come back when Cassidy's feeling better. If that's okay with you?"

Wil didn't answer right away.

Joseph couldn't blame him. Cassidy did nothing to hide her true colors, not exactly endearing herself to Wil. He had his answer, so he turned to walk back into the cottage.

"She can stay."

"Are you sure?"

"Yeah, I'm sure. But listen, she's going to find me all up in her face if she doesn't watch that mouth of hers."

Joseph nodded before walking back inside the house. He stayed only a few minutes, then announced he would be leaving.

"I'll call once Mark is gone." He leaned over and gave Cassidy a kiss on the top of her head. She remained silent.

When Wil walked him outside, Joseph extended his hand. "Thank you. You've already done so much for Cassidy."

"No. What I've done, I've done for you. Cassidy doesn't want my help."

———— • ————

Wil lingered on the porch after Joseph left, not looking forward to going back inside. There had been a time when he had been infatuated with Cassidy—even harbored a school-boy crush—but after her mother died, she changed. First, she became withdrawn. Then, her internal sadness turned to steely-eyed anger. Finally, her self-centeredness overshadowed her beauty. Her looks could not help her at that point. As far as Wil was concerned, she had an ugly spirit and a blackened heart. She needed God's help now more than ever. However, in her current situation, he didn't see her reaching out to anyone, much less God.

Wil knew what he was talking about. Cassidy didn't know it, but he had suffered his own losses, faced his own demons. The only difference was he had acknowledged he was powerless to survive those trials without help from God. He hoped—for Cassidy's sake—she learned the same thing before it was too late. It was obvious she was on a self-destructive path, requiring God's intervention.

However, convincing her of that was a whole different story. Sighing, he pushed off from the porch rail and went back inside.

ELEVEN

Cassidy heard Wilbur walk back into the living room but kept her eyes closed. She didn't feel like talking to him, small talk or otherwise.

She could feel him staring, lingering in the room, so she pretended to be asleep. Eventually, his muffled footsteps headed toward the kitchen, then she heard the sound of running water.

Good. He's probably doing the breakfast dishes. That will give me at least a few minutes to myself.

She opened her eyes as she thought about Mark, wondering how furious he would be when he found out she wasn't home.

If Dad had just left my phone alone.

But the more she thought about it, the more she realized, Mark probably knew where she was all along. The GPS tracker on her phone would have told him exactly where she was. She cursed herself for not thinking about that sooner.

But why come after me? You want Amanda, fine, you can have Amanda. I just made it easier on you. But knowing Mark's possessive personality, he probably wanted it all. The wife and the mistress. *Yeah, well, I might be ignorant and naïve, but I'm not stupid enough to stick around for that.*

When she heard the water stop in the kitchen, she quickly closed her eyes. She felt the slight wisp of air from the kitchen door swinging open, then heard creaking from the stairs. Next, she heard Wilbur's muffled words as he spoke on the phone.

"Hi. I know I said I would swing by, but something has come up. Of course I will. You promised me a home-cooked meal. I'm not going to turn that down. Can I get a rain check? Okay, thanks, Jessica. I'll be by soon."

Jessica? Who's Jessica?

"Hi, it's me. I'm not going to be able to make it today, but I can come by tomorrow." He chuckled. "I know, I know. You can assure

Madi I'll be there when she needs me." He laughed some more before hanging up.

Madi?

"Hi, Sadie. I'm not going to . . ."

Jessica, Madi, Sadie?

"Can you give Heather a message for me? Just tell her . . ."

What in the world? He sure isn't the shy, reserved guy I remember from high school.

Four dates.

Four different women.

And he canceled them all because of me.

She felt a little offended. She had just assumed he had turned down her advances because he was still the nice little church boy she remembered growing up with.

Obviously, she was mistaken.

How dare he be so judgmental toward me when he's living the life of a playboy.

She wasn't sorry he turned her down. It would have been a colossal mistake. Even though she might not be holier-than-thou, the still-small-voice that taunted her from time to time was telling her turnabout was *not* fair play.

When Wilbur came downstairs, he glanced her way before disappearing into the kitchen. He returned just seconds later, his medical bag in hand.

Plopping down on the coffee table, he said, "I need to change the bandage on your shoulder and check your stitches."

Cassidy didn't respond, she just stared at the ceiling.

"Are there cobwebs up there?"

She looked at him, "What?"

"You keep staring at the ceiling. I'm wondering what you see up there."

A fifteen-year-old girl, with a rope in her hand, wanting to escape the pain, but not having the courage to do it. She gave the beam a final glance then turned to him. "Nothing."

He shrugged his shoulders "Fine. Then how are you feeling? Any dizziness?"

"A little."

"How about your head? Does it still ache?"

"Yes."

"I'll give you something for that."

Wil examined her stitches, changed the bandage, then wiped a few of her cuts and abrasions with an antiseptic swab. When he finished, he wadded up the trash and went to the kitchen. He returned with a glass of water and a mild painkiller.

Cassidy took the meds, swallowed them with a swig of water, handed the glass back, then just stared at him.

"What?" he asked.

"I didn't say anything."

"No, but you look like you want to." He could see the indecision in her eyes, and it irritated him. "What? It's obvious you have something to say. So, just say it."

"Fine. I don't want to cramp your style because you feel like you need to babysit me. I would hate to come between you and your social life."

"What?" he said, utterly confused.

"Oh please. I heard you canceling your dates. Not exactly a one-woman man, are you?"

Wil thought a moment, then realized how Cassidy could have gotten the wrong idea. He was ready to correct her but decided to have a little fun instead. "I hope that doesn't offend you, especially since I turned you down. But I already have my hands full and I don't think I can juggle just one more female. It's hard enough keeping everyone's temperament and personalities straight."

Cassidy was so shocked, she was speechless.

Wil hurried to take her water glass back to the kitchen because he was having a hard time keeping a straight face. The expression on Cassidy's face was priceless. It felt good giving her some of her own medicine for a change, even if he was being less than honest. He didn't lie. It was just the phrasing he chose that gave Cassidy's imagination a chance to run wild.

He replayed their banter in his head, then stifled a laugh.

TWELVE

Cassidy opened her eyes, but it took a minute to sort out her surroundings. A phone was ringing. It must have been what woke her. Not knowing what time it was, she looked around more intently, but there was no clock to be found. Closing her eyes, she quickly reviewed the last things she remembered.

Breakfast with Wilbur.

Her dad coming over.

She gasped. *Mark is on his way here.*

Remembering how she found him tangled in Amanda's arms sickened her. She wasn't sure what hurt most, the betrayal, the humiliation, her stupidity for putting up with Mark's manipulation and intimidation or being so naïve to have believed his lies.

Wilbur walked past her and disappeared into the kitchen. When she heard him wrestling with pots and pans, she assumed it must be around lunchtime. She stretched her legs off the couch and pushed her aching body up to a standing position. The tumble she took had done more than give her a gash on the head and a concussion. It seemed like every muscle in her body was twisted into tiny little knots.

Walking slowing to the kitchen, she stood in the doorway and watched Wilbur for a few minutes, then asked, "You know, I still don't know why you're here?"

He turned sharply toward her, then went back to what he was doing. "What do you mean by 'here?' " he asked curtly.

"Here. On the ranch. Did Dad sell you this plot of land? Do you work for him? What's the deal?"

"Sort of."

"What do you mean, 'sort of?' Either you work for him, or you don't. It's not that hard of a question."

"I help your dad with the herd and the other animals in

exchange for housing."

"Why? Shouldn't you be living in town closer to the hospital?"

He turned around, a smirk on his face. "I'm not a doctor, Cassidy, I'm a vet."

"What? Wait a minute, you're telling me my dad let a vet work on me instead of taking me to the ER?"

"Actually, if memory serves me, you didn't want to go to the hospital."

"But that's because you looked like you knew what you were doing."

"I did know what I was doing."

"But I'm not a steer!"

"It doesn't matter. I stitched you up, bandaged your wounds, and saved you the cost of an ER visit. You're welcome."

Before she could say anything more, Wilbur turned his attention back to lunch.

She wanted to argue, threaten him with a lawsuit, anything to wipe that smug look off his face, but she just didn't have the energy. And what would it accomplish? After all, he had taken care of her and saved her from a grueling drive to the hospital. No, she decided to concede this one, and move on to another subject.

"Well if you ask me, you're getting the better end of the deal. This place would go for big bucks on the Airbnb market. Dad could easily advertise this as a romantic getaway or honeymoon retreat. A dude ranch for two, for people who want to experience western living without all the commercialism." She looked around the cottage-style kitchen. "But I never would have thought this old building had such potential, or that my dad would take the time and money to renovate it. And so well too. Who knew Dad had such a flair for style?"

"He didn't. I did, but thanks for the compliment." Wilbur carried two plates to the kitchen table, then glanced her way. "What? Does it surprise you that the high school geek has style?"

Cassidy tried to formulate something witty or sarcastic to say, but with Wilbur staring at her, she drew a blank.

"Come on, let's eat." He took a seat at the table and waited for her to do the same.

Cassidy was poised to say something when he bowed his head and started to pray out loud.

"Thank you, God, for this day and this meal, and that Cassidy's injuries weren't more serious. Be with us throughout the day and in all we do and say. Amen."

She mumbled an 'amen,' then cleared her throat. "Wilbur, I do appreciate what you did, and I'm glad I didn't have to go to the hospital last night. So, thank you for running interference with Dad."

"Well, first of all, can we drop the Wilbur? I haven't been called that since high school, and I would prefer not to go back to it. Call me Wil. And second, you're welcome. I was glad I could help since I feel partly responsible for your accident."

"Why would you feel responsible for me being a klutz?"

"Because if I had handled our earlier conversation better, maybe you wouldn't have run off like that."

When Cassidy thought about how she had acted and what she had said, her face heated up and her throat tightened. "Yeah. About that . . . I ahh . . ."

"Hey, forget it. That's behind us. Why don't we try a fresh beginning?" Wil held out his hand to Cassidy as if he was introducing himself for the first time. "Hi. I'm Wil Marsh, and you are?"

Cassidy smiled, then grasped his extended hand. "Cassidy Grayson."

They ate in a companionable silence. Obviously, the excitement of late had fueled Wil's appetite because he had no problem putting away a huge turkey sandwich and was already working on a rather large helping of potato salad.

Cassidy, on the other hand, pushed her salad around on her plate, still feeling a bit queasy. She wasn't sure if it was from the conk on the head or the thought of Mark coming to see her. Either way, her appetite was non-existent. After taking a few more bites, she decided to fill the silence, anything to get her mind off Mark.

"So, tell me, why did you become a vet? I would have thought you'd be a rocket scientist or brain surgeon or something ridiculously intellectual."

"I was going to be a doctor, but I hit a few bumps in the road when I was in medical school. When I recovered from that, I realized I didn't want to be cooped up in a hospital in a huge city or give up small-town living and the great outdoors. I decided I got along with animals better than people. So, I changed my major and became a veterinarian."

"Were your parents disappointed? I mean, that's quite a drop in salary and prestige. Not that they were ever social climbers themselves."

Wil was silent, his mood shifting.

Oops. Definitely a sore spot.

"Let me guess. They laid hands on you and prayed for you to repent of your foolish ways. But in the end, they loved you anyway because that's what parents do with their wayward kids."

He took a swig of his soda, then stood. "My parents are dead, and I would prefer not to talk about it." Putting his dishes in the sink, Wil headed for the back door. "I have some chores I have to do. Help yourself to whatever you need. I'll be back in a couple of hours. Keep the cordless phone with you so if you run into any trouble you can call your dad. I'll see you a little later." Wil pulled his Ariat ball cap on and walked out the swinging screen door.

Cassidy was stunned. Shocked even.

Wil's parents were his world. All through school they were at every assembly and every open house. If Wil was involved in it, they were there. Cassidy knew it was their love and support, and conservative upbringing that allowed Wil to tolerate the joking and ridicule he got from the other kids. He might have been a geek in school, but at home he was ten feet tall.

After cleaning up the lunch dishes, Cassidy sat on the couch, tired from what little energy she'd exerted and angry at herself for what she'd said about Wil's parents. Though she drifted in and out of sleep, she wasn't really getting any rest. If she wasn't stressing about Mark—nervous about what he might do—she was thinking about Wil, intrigued with the man he'd become. Remembering a picture of Wil with his parents on the desk upstairs, she decided to poke around a little, see if she could find something that might explain what happened to them.

After catching her breath from climbing the stairs, Cassidy studied the large expansive loft. But when she realized she was once again staring at the massive center beam, she scolded herself. *Forget it! That was nine years ago.*

But it reminded her what a mess she had been before leaving Liberty. *Of course, I didn't come back in much better shape, did I?*

Shaking off the memory, she made her way to the desk and picked up the sterling frame. The picture had to have been taken a couple years after graduation. Wil looked polished, his physique stronger and his features attractive, nothing like the scrawny boy in high school. Cassidy saw more pictures of his folks on the bookshelves that lined the other wall.

So what happened to them? Were they ill? Both of them?

She picked up what looked like the most recent picture. They looked healthy. Cassidy remembered how she felt when she lost her mom and couldn't imagine how Wil must have felt. *How on earth did he cope with losing both parents in less than nine years?* She was mulling this over when she heard the front door open and close.

Glancing over the short wall of the loft, she saw her father standing by the front door. He looked anxious, rolling his hands around, one over the other. Carefully, Cassidy descended the stairs. But when her father turned toward her, it wasn't anxiousness she saw in his eyes; it was something else, something she couldn't quite put her finger on.

"What is it, Dad? Is Mark here?" She crossed the room to the couch. "If Mark sent you to come get me, he can forget it. I don't want to hear his apologies or his excuses. He's insane if he thinks I'm going to go back to him after what he—" Cassidy stopped her ranting when her father's expression changed once again. To pity.

"What is it, Dad? What did he say?"

He swallowed, clearing his throat, but didn't answer her question.

"Dad . . ."

"He left papers for you to sign. Divorce papers."

Cassidy reached for the sofa table to balance herself, and her dad reached out to her. "I'm sorry, Sunshine."

Cassidy didn't hear what her father was saying, the word *divorce* stuck in her head. Making her way around the sofa, she sunk into the cushions.

Divorce papers.

Mark didn't want her.

He didn't want to apologize or plead with her.

She wasn't even worth fighting for.

She was an unnecessary piece in the puzzle of her own life. Everything she'd come to know, become accustomed to, was no longer.

What did this mean?

She should be relieved. She should be thankful Mark would never hurt her again, but the unknown seemed more ominous.

Where do I go from here? If I'm not Mrs. Mark Grayson, who

am I? How can I go back to New York and face my friends?
The circles she traveled in were afforded to her because of her social status. But now she was a nobody.

"Cassidy . . . Cassidy, honey, it's going to be okay."

Her dad laid a caring hand on her knee. She wasn't even aware he had sat down next to her because of the cyclone of questions monopolizing her thoughts. She began to feel claustrophobic, like everything was closing in on top of her.

Getting to her feet, she hurried to the front door, threw it open, and rushed out onto the porch. She leaned on the rail and took in a few deep breaths.

———————— • ————————

Wil was pulling up in front of the house when he saw Cassidy spring out the door. He jumped out of his vehicle and took the front steps two at a time.

"What is it, Cassidy? What's wrong?"

She continued to take long dragging breaths. She could barely breathe let alone answer his questions. When Joseph came to the door, Wil looked at him for answers. Joseph just nodded for Wil to follow him inside.

He was torn.

Cassidy looked like a simple wind could knock her over, but when Joseph retreated inside, Wil had no choice but to follow.

"What happened?" he whispered. "Cassidy looks like she's going to crumble into a million pieces. Is it her husband? Was he here?"

"He was here all right." Joseph said rather flustered. "But he didn't come to get Cassidy. He came to serve her with papers."

"What?" Wil was shocked.

"You heard him." Both men turned and saw Cassidy standing in the doorway. "He doesn't want me. My own husband doesn't want me." Tears streaked her face. "Dad," she turned to her father, "I need to go home now."

Wil watched as she walked down the stairs and climbed into Joseph's truck.

God help her.

Because she was going to need it.

———————— • ————————

Cassidy walked into the house and saw the stack of papers lying on the coffee table, and the small white envelope on top of them. She didn't need to read any of it to know what it spelled out.

She felt like a complete and utter failure.

A personal note from Mark, written on the stationary she helped him pick out, lay on top of the stack. She picked up the envelope, feeling the near weightlessness of it, then tossed it back down.

A single piece of paper sums up what I was to you? She shook her head and brushed at the tears on her cheek. *He had no intentions of talking to me. Begging for my forgiveness. Pleading with me to come back. I wasn't even worth the effort.*

What a fool. The things she'd endured to make her marriage work. The years she had spent tied up in knots, afraid of the man she should love above all else. And what was she to him? She was nothing more than an acquisition, one he had grown tired of. A contractual agreement that had reached its expiration date.

THIRTEEN

Joseph was beyond worried.

After Cassidy's accident and the bombshell Mark had dropped on her, she took refuge in her childhood bedroom. At first, he understood she needed time to herself to absorb all that had happened and figure out her next step. But after a week had passed, he grew anxious, especially since she wasn't eating. He kept trying to coax her from her room, but nothing worked. On days when his worry turned to panic, he knocked on her door until she begged him to go away. At least then he knew she was coherent enough to answer.

He cried out to God to intervene where he had failed. He knew it was because of God's grace she was home and not self-destructing somewhere else. But what would he do if he couldn't reach her, if he couldn't help her before it was too late?

Never could he imagine something more awful than losing his precious Catherine. But watching his only child slowly killing herself was beyond all he had ever suffered.

Wil checked in with Joseph daily, hoping to hear Cassidy had turned a corner. And every time he did, his compassion for her lessened. He knew a divorce had to be devastating—he wasn't minimizing that—and he had a feeling there was more to her hurt and pain then she was letting on. But he was afraid her behavior was life-threatening, not only for her but for Joseph as well.

Wil saw it in the old man's eyes. He was dying a little each day. All because Cassidy was choosing to give up on life.

Without being too obvious, Wil spent his mornings in the barn. It was his way of keeping an eye on Joseph. He fed Gent, worked on little projects, tinkered mostly. But it gave him a chance to observe

Joseph, to make sure he hadn't reached his breaking point.

He was working on one of the stalls, replacing a few rotted boards, when a large delivery truck pulled into the yard. He watched Joseph descend the front porch stairs as the driver got out of the cab, walked to the back bumper, and pushed up the large rolling door.

"I have ten boxes for a Cassie Grayson," the driver said, as he handed a clipboard to Joseph, then jumped up on the tailgate.

Joseph looked at the clipboard then at Wil. "They're from New York. Mark must have sent Cassidy's things." Joseph scribbled his name on the sheet of paper then dropped the clipboard on the tailgate. "I don't want her to see these—not yet anyway."

"Don't worry, Joseph, we'll put them up in the hay loft. They can stay there until you're ready to tell her about them."

For a fifty-dollar tip, the truck driver agreed to carry the boxes to the barn and lift them to where Wil was perched halfway up the ladder. Wil hefted them up into the loft, then took the time to stack them in the back corner out of sight. When he was done, he hopped down from the ladder, and brushed himself off. "Okay, now that—" Wil stopped when he saw Joseph's eyes, red and glassed over. Walking over to where he stood, Wil put a hand on his shoulder and gave it a hearty squeeze. "Come on, Joseph, she's going to be fine. Eventually."

"I don't know what to do, Wil. I can't reach her. When her mother died, she closed herself off from me and God, but she never gave up altogether. She was too stubborn for that. I find myself praying for those days. At least then I knew she was a fighter and her basic instinct was to survive, even if it meant leaving town. Now, I think she wants nothing more than to give in to the depression that is slowly killing her."

Joseph's face was haggard and drawn, causing Wil's anger to simmer just below the surface. "Look, Joseph, why don't you let me talk to her?"

"That's just it, Wil," he threw up his hands in defeat, "she's not talking."

"I know, I know, but let's see what happens." Wil thought about what he was going to say to Cassidy. It wasn't going to be pretty, and he preferred Joseph wasn't around to witness it. "Look, you were headed to the south pasture, right?"

"Yeah."

"Well, go ahead and do what you were doing. I'll let myself into the house and see if I can talk some sense into Cassidy."

"I don't know, Wil."

"Come on, Joseph. Trust me."

Joseph glanced at the house and sighed. "Okay, but please be careful. I don't think she can take much more." With shoulders sagging and his head down, Joseph walked to his pickup and drove away.

Wil took a deep breath, trying to press down the animosity he felt toward Cassidy. As he climbed the front stairs, he prayed he could make her see what her behavior was doing to her father. If she wanted to ruin her life and be self-destructive, she needed to do it somewhere else, not where Joseph would shoulder the responsibility and guilt if she decided to do something drastic.

Climbing the stairs, Wil took another cleansing breath, stopped in front of Cassidy's door and knocked.

No answer.

"Cassidy, it's Wil. I want to talk to you." He made sure his voice was calm, hiding the anger he felt.

No answer.

"Come on, Cassidy. I can be just as stubborn as you. Open the door."

Nothing.

"Look, you can either open the door, or I'll force it open. Your choice."

Wil waited, but when there was no response, he put his shoulder into the door. Splintering the doorframe, the door flung open, slamming against the wall, causing the entire room to shudder. Cassidy flinched where she lay curled up in a ball beneath her bed covers but didn't say a word.

Stepping into the room, Wil's nostrils were immediately assaulted by the stench that comes from an unbathed body. He was convinced she hadn't bathed or showered since locking herself in her room.

"Gees, Cassidy, it reeks in here." Wil crossed to the window and pushed it open. It smelled worse than any locker room or gas station bathroom he could remember being in.

Still, Cassidy did nothing to acknowledge his presence. She remained curled up facing the wall.

"I can't talk to you in this stench; I can barely breathe."

She was probably counting on that, but it didn't deter him in the least.

"I'm warning you, Cassidy, you better have something on under those filthy covers, because if you don't get up right now and get in the shower, I'm going to drag you in there myself."

He waited for her to move, but she remained motionless. "Okay, have it your way." Wil stepped forward and yanked the blanket and sheet from her grasp. Horrified, he couldn't believe what he saw. Her lingerie was soiled and stained, her skin a sickly shade of gray, her hair matted like straw.

Shocked, Cassidy snatched the sheet back, pulling it up to her chin. "Who do you think you are?!" she yelled. "Get out! You have no right coming in here. Just get out!" She curled into a fetal position and faced the wall.

"You have exactly five seconds to get from that bed to that shower," he pointed, even though she wasn't paying attention, "before I drag you in there myself."

She turned venomous eyes on him. "You wouldn't dare!"

"Bet me!" Wil fired back.

He waited. But when it was obvious Cassidy had no intentions of moving, he grabbed at the sheet clenched in her hands and ripped it from the bed. Wading it and the blanket up in a ball, he shoved them through the open window, screen and all.

"What do you think you're doing?!" Cassidy yelled, looking at him with contempt.

"They stink and need to be washed. So do you." He stood staring at her, arms crossed against his chest. Waiting.

Cassidy told him—in no uncertain terms—exactly where he could go.

"Fine! Have it your way!"

He grabbed her arm and yanked her from the bed. Cassidy kicked and slugged, trying to break free, screaming as Wil wrestled to control her swinging arms and flailing legs. The language she used shocked even him, her words crude and obscene. *I'm glad Joseph isn't hearing this*, he thought as he backed into the bathroom.

Stepping over the side of the tub, he planted his feet, so he didn't lose his balance. Turning the water on, he engaged the shower head, then held Cassidy's face under the icy stream.

Screaming, she took in a mouthful of water and started choking. She hollered for Wil to stop, but he continued to hold her face under the shower spray, even though she coughed and sputtered. Cassidy began to cry and begged him to stop. Once he heard defeat in her tone, he let go of her.

She sank to the porcelain, drew her legs up to her chest, and sobbed. Turning off the water, he stepped from the tub, drenched and exhausted. He looked at Cassidy as her body convulsed with emotion, then covered her with a towel, embarrassed by her exposure.

Looking down at his soaked clothes and boots, he sighed. *Good job, dummy. You really thought that one through.* Walking out of the bathroom, he stared out the bedroom window, not knowing if his ill-conceived stunt did anything to snap Cassidy out of her funk.

When he heard the rings of the shower curtain slide across the rod, and the water turned back on, he pulled the bathroom door closed, but didn't let it latch. He didn't want to have to break down just one more door if Cassidy decided she wanted to go another round.

Wil finished stripping the bed of the remaining sheets, tossing them out the door, then went to the linen closet in the hallway and grabbed another set. Flipping the mattress, he finished making up the bed just as the shower water stopped. When the bathroom door opened, steam bellowed out, along with Cassidy in a little white sundress.

She didn't bother looking at him, she just walked to the other side of the room and scrunched up in the rocking chair. She crossed her arms against her chest, her long blond hair dripping over her shoulders. Leaning her head back against the chair, she finally made eye contact with him. "Can I get some privacy?" Her tone was cold, void of any emotion.

"Sure. Just close your eyes," Wil retorted.

"You need to go now."

"Cassidy . . ."

"Look, Wil," her voice was barely more than a whisper, "I'm not going to do anything stupid if that's what you're afraid of."

"Fine, you're not going to do anything stupid, but you still need to eat."

"I'll eat when it's time for dinner."

"Is that an invitation? Why thank you. I don't mind if I do. In fact, I'll even cook."

"No thank you. I can cook for myself."

"Okay, you're cooking, but I'm still staying to make sure you follow through."

"Look, Wil, I'm tired, and upset, and hurt, and . . . why won't everyone just leave me alone?" She closed her eyes, emotion in every word. "I just want to be left alone."

Wil waited a moment before he spoke. "If you had wanted to be alone, Cassidy, you wouldn't have come home. If you're willing to admit it or not, you're afraid to be alone."

Cassidy had a retort ready, but Wil raised his hands in concession. "I'll go, but if you're even a minute late to dinner, I'll be back to get you. Understand? Because I'm not playing games."

Cassidy just turned her head to the window, offering no reply.

Wil gathered up the foul-smelling sheets lying in the hallway, then went downstairs and circled the outside of the house to retrieve the bedding he had flung through the window. He also picked up the torn and bent screen, then put everything in the back of his truck.

Joseph was on his way back to the house as Wil drove up alongside of him.

"I couldn't concentrate on what I was doing. I had to come back. Did you talk to her?" Joseph looked hopeful.

"Yes. She's none too happy with me, but I don't care."

"What did you say to her?"

"Let's just say I tried to help her cool off and gave her a douse of reality." Wil thought about how cold the water was. It would have been funny if not for the pain he saw in Cassidy's eyes. His behavior had been rough, but he didn't regret his actions. "I told her if she was even a minute late to dinner, I'd come back to remind her of our deal."

"If you were able to talk any sense into her at all, I appreciate it, really I do."

"Just call me if she's AWOL."

"I will . . . and thanks again."

Luckily, Joseph didn't notice Wil's clothes were dripping wet. He was glad he didn't have to explain his actions, because he doubted Joseph would have agreed with his tactics.

Wil, wet and soggy, stepped from his pickup, grabbed the pile of sheets, and headed to the back porch. Stripping to his boxers, he put his clothes, along with the bedding in the washing machine. He pulled at the back of his neck, massaging his tight muscles, trying to release the tension that had settled across his shoulders. Slowly, he climbed the stairs and headed for his own shower, a shower that proved a little more soothing then the one he had just had.

Twenty minutes later, Wil scrubbed a towel through his hair and relaxed on his bed. Reaching for his Bible, he read in Ecclesiastes that there was a season for everything under heaven, even hate. No doubt, Cassidy was in that season, but Wil knew it would pass. Scripture said so. Glancing at his bedside clock, he waited for the phone to ring, but five o' clock came and went without a call from Joseph.

Wil kept busy the rest of the evening, straightening the living room, cleaning the kitchen, reading. He was pulling Cassidy's sheets from the dryer when the phone rang.

"Hey, Joseph, is everything all right?"

"Yes, I think so. Cassidy came down for dinner. She didn't eat much and said even less, but that's okay. I think she's turned a corner."

"I'm glad to hear it. Call if you need anything."

"Sure thing . . . and Wil . . . keep praying. She doesn't have an easy road ahead of her."

"No road is easy, Joseph. Some are just bumpier than others."

FOURTEEN

It had been a week since Wil pulled Cassidy from her bed and forced her into the shower. And with each day that passed, he checked in with Joseph regarding her condition. For the most part, the updates were positive. Cassidy wasn't talking much, but at least she wasn't spending all her time in her room. And she was eating a little more each day. Whenever Wil drove by the house, he glanced toward her bedroom window, praying she would find the strength she was looking for.

Wil made his way toward the barn, this time checking on Joseph. Yesterday he said something about replacing some shingles on the roof and some loose boards on the backside of the barn, and knowing Joseph, he was stubborn enough to do it himself instead of asking for help.

Sure enough, Joseph had just loaded up his tool belt with nails when Wil rounded the barn. It took some talking, but Wil was finally able to convince Joseph he shouldn't be on the roof at his age. Joseph blustered and grumbled but allowed Wil to do the work while he fixed a section of fence running parallel to the road into town.

A couple of hours and a few choice words later, Wil lowered himself from the roof of the barn, convinced that the next time it needed work, he would hire someone else to do it. He had never been afraid of heights and was secured to the roof with a gizmo he'd come up with. Even so, jockeying for position while moving the stack of shingles and keeping his balance was a little more than he had bargained for. But he was done. All that was left was cleaning up the old shingles and remnants he'd tossed off the roof.

"I guess I should thank you."

Wil turned around and saw Cassidy standing against the rail of the fence. She looked good. She was still way too thin—the bulky sweater she was wearing nearly swallowing her up—but she definitely looked better than the last time he saw her.

"For what?"

"Shock treatment," she said with just a hint of a smile.

"Well, before you thank me, I think you should know I didn't do it for you. I did it for your dad. He was dying a little each day, and I couldn't stand by and watch it any longer."

Cassidy's shoulders slumped, clearly wounded by his response. She hung her head, turned around, and walked away.

You just couldn't say you're welcome, could you? Wil chastised himself. *Instead of being polite and accept what was clearly an apology, you took the cheap shot and threw it back in her face.*

It had taken a lot of courage for Cassidy to come talk to him; the least he could have done was be a little kinder.

Fine, he moaned to himself. *I'll go apologize.*

After he put the last of the tools away, he took a deep breath and headed toward the house.

Cassidy was sitting on the window seat alongside the fireplace when he walked in. She cast a look in his direction, then turned back to the window.

"I'm sorry I was short with you." Wil crossed the room as he spoke.

"You don't need to apologize. I deserve whatever I get."

"That's not true, Cassidy."

"Whatever." She continued to stare out the window.

"How's your head feeling?"

"Itchy."

"Stitches will do that to you. How about your wrist and shoulder?"

"My shoulder still hurts. I must have hit it harder than I thought."

"I can take a look at it, if you'd like?"

"I'm okay."

Feeling stupid just standing there, Wil slowly made his way to the door.

"Wil, can I ask a favor?"

"Depends on what it is?"

"I need to go to town tomorrow. I was wondering if I could borrow your truck?"

"No, but I can take you. You shouldn't be driving with your hand and shoulder banged up anyway."

"I'm fine, really."

72

"Like I said, I'd be glad to drive you."

"Forget it."

"Cassidy, I'm not putting you off. I have three stops of my own to make. If you don't mind running errands with me, I'll take you were you need to go."

She sighed, still looking out the window. "Fine. What time should I be ready?"

"How about eight o'clock?"

Cassidy nodded, but that was all, so Wil left. When he stepped out onto the front porch, he smacked his hat against his leg.

Why is she being so obstinate? One minute she's apologizing, the next she's treating me like an inconvenience.

Wil shoved his hat back on his head, got in his vehicle and drove home. When he got there, his message machine was blinking. He pushed the button, then went to the kitchen for a bottle of water.

"Hi, Wil. Madi needs your help. I hope you get this message soon."

The machine buzzed off as Wil grabbed his medical bag and ran out the front door.

———— • ————

Cassidy noticed Wil racing down the driveway and wondered where he was going and why he was in such a breakneck hurry.

What do I care? As long as he's not hovering over me.

FIFTEEN

Cassidy was ticked.

She had gotten up early and made sure she was ready *before* eight o'clock, so she wouldn't slow Wil down, but now he was a no-show. Frustrated, she stormed to the barn looking for her dad.

"Dad, do you know where Wil is?"

"No, Sunshine. I haven't seen him yet this morning. Why?"

Cassidy cringed. "Dad, please stop calling me that!"

"Sorry," he acknowledged his blunder, then asked, "Why are you looking for Wil?"

"He's supposed to drive me into town today. He said he would pick me up at eight o'clock, but it's already eight-thirty."

"If you needed to go into town, why didn't you ask me? I'll be going on Thursday."

"Because I need my divorce papers notarized and sent today, and I figured you wouldn't want to be a party to my ultimate demise."

"Sunsh—, ahh, Cassidy, I know it's not all your fault. I could tell by Mark's attitude, he wasn't going to change his mind. When I asked him to reconsider and not act so rashly, he—"

"You what?" Cassidy gasped. "You had no business even talking to him. What were you thinking? He cheated on me, Dad. And that's not all he did." Cassidy stopped, realizing it was futile to argue over something she could not change. And she certainly didn't want her dad to know all the sordid details of her marriage. Taking a deep breath, she waited a few seconds before speaking again. "Let's just drop it, okay? But I still need to get to town. Can I use the pickup?"

"Are you sure you feel good enough to drive?"

"I'll be fine, Dad. I might be belligerent, but I'm not incapable."

Cassidy went back inside the house to grab her jacket, purse, and paperwork, then snatched the truck key off the hook by the door and left. After letting the engine warm up, she turned the wheel towards the long driveway, but at the last minute decided to go to Wil's place and give him a piece of her mind.

Pulling up in front of the cottage, she was surprised to see his truck wasn't there. *Maybe he broke down,* she grumbled. *The way he was driving last night, maybe he crashed it.*

Deciding to see for herself, she knocked on the door several times with no answer. Trying the doorknob, she found it unlocked, so she let herself in. Looking around it was obvious Wil wasn't home.

Did he stay out all night?

The answering machine, with its blinking light caught her attention. She thought about it for a second, knowing it was wrong, but she walked over to the table and pressed the Play button anyway.

Listening to the last message, she was shocked. "So that's why he was in such a sure-fire hurry last night. He was off with some woman named Madi."

"What are you doing?"

Cassidy spun around and saw Wil standing in the open doorway. Immediately, she knew she had overstepped her bounds. Stammering, she tried to come up with a good explanation as to why she was in his house, listening to his answering machine, but it was no use. "I'm sorry, Wil. I shouldn't have . . . I mean, I didn't . . . I was just angry that you—"

"Fine. You're sorry," Wil cut her off. "But that still doesn't answer my question. What do you think you're doing?"

Still stammering, Cassidy tried to explain. "You stood me up. You were supposed to pick me up at eight o'clock. I came to wake you." Cassidy looked at the answering machine before continuing. "I guess it isn't oversleeping that has you running behind schedule."

Wil grinned. "Nope, sleep was the furthest thing from my mind last night. In fact, it got so hot, I don't think I could have slept even if I wanted to. Madi was almost more than I could handle. She—"

"I don't need to listen to this." Cassidy interrupted before marching out of the house and down the stairs. She threw the truck into gear, but before going to town, she was going to clue her father in on exactly what kind of guy Wil was.

Okay, Dad, let's see what you think of your God-fearing Boy

Scout when you find out he's been lying to you.

Cassidy couldn't wait to knock Wil off the pedestal her father had put him on.

Roaring across the pasture, she slammed on the brakes in front of the barn and cut the engine. "Dad . . . Dad . . ." Cassidy yelled as she marched across the yard.

"What is it Cassidy? What's wrong?" Joseph emerged from a stall as Cassidy entered the barn.

"It's Wil."

"What's wrong? What happened?"

"I just thought you should know your devout little follower is no better than any other hot-blooded American male."

"Sunshine, what are you talking about? I thought you went to town?"

"I was. I mean I am. I just decided to check on Wil first, you know, make sure he was okay. And you know what? He wasn't even home. In fact, he hasn't been home all night. He was out shacking up with some woman."

The look of confusion on her dad's face angered Cassidy. He had no problem thinking the worst about her, but when confronted with the truth about Wil, he seemed unwilling to believe it.

"I think you might be confused, Cassidy. Wil would never behave that way."

"I can't believe you! Why are you defending him? You scolded me and disciplined me when I went to New York and moved in with Mark. You told me my behavior was sinful and how disappointed you were with my choices. You went on and on about the evils of sex before marriage. When I wanted to bring Mark home to meet you, you wouldn't even allow it since we were already 'living in sin.' You made it very clear; we were not welcome here unless we were married.

"But now . . . now when you're faced with the fact that Wil is sleeping around, and probably doing it on your own property, you want to defend him?"

"Wil, is what Cassidy said true?"

Cassidy spun around, not realizing Wil had followed her to the barn. But she was glad. Now her dad would find out for himself.

"Go ahead, Wil. Tell Dad what you were doing last night. Tell him all about Madi and how hot she made you." Cassidy could feel victory. Finally, someone other than herself was going to get the lecture.

"You were with Madi?" Her Dad looked at Wil, concerned.

"Yes, Joseph, I was with Madi." Wil looked stoic.

Ha! Caught! Let's see you wiggle out of this one choir-boy.

Cassidy waited for her dad to drop his eyes in disappointment. She waited for him to launch into a lecture like he had done to her so many times before. But to her surprise, her dad burst out laughing, joined by Wil.

"What's so funny?" she demanded. "Why are you two laughing?" They ignored her, making her even madder. "Dad, answer me!"

He looked at her. "And how did you know Wil was with Madi?"

"She was in my house, listening to my answering machine," Wil offered.

Her dad turned disapproving eyes on her. "Cassidy, is that true?"

She felt like she was having a bad dream. Her dad wasn't even asking Wil about his escapades, but it was obvious he was upset with her for trespassing. "No way! No way am I going to stand here, and have you lecture me about what I did, while you completely ignore the fact that Wil is a hypocritical jerk."

She turned to leave, but Wil stepped in front of her, standing dangerously close. "Get out of my way, Wil."

"Not until you listen to what I have to say."

Crossing her arms across her chest, she glared at him.

"You see, Cassidy, I did spend the night with Madi. And though she was nervous, I did everything in my power to make her comfortable and keep her relaxed."

Cassidy could not believe her dad was letting Wil carry on like this. She tried to leave again, but Wil grabbed her arm and spun her around.

"Leave me alone." She jerked her arm, trying to break free.

"Not until I'm done telling you what happened last night."

"I don't care about your conquests."

"Well, you're going to listen anyway."

"Dad . . ."

"Listen to what he has to say, Cassidy."

She felt like she was in an episode of The Twilight Zone. Not only was her father demanding she listen to Wil, he was actually going to stand by and listen too.

Yanking on her arm, Wil waited for their eyes to lock. "Madi

77

is a pregnant mare. She went into labor last night, and I was there to help her deliver."

When Wil let go of her arm, she took a step back, mortified. She could feel the color draining from her face as the two men once again started laughing. She couldn't believe the fool she had made of herself. Feeling defeated and humiliated, she hurried toward the barn's double doors.

"Hey, you still want that ride into town?" Wil asked, laughing.

"Forget it."

Cassidy stormed out of the barn, got into her father's truck, and floored it.

By the time she reached the city limits, Cassidy had control of her anger. Taking a deep breath, she looked around the downtown area and quietly laughed to herself. Nothing had changed. The town square still looked exactly the same, with its city hall, courthouse, and manicured park. It could easily be the setting for an old-time movie.

Pulling into the city parking lot, she killed the engine. Wrapping her jacket tight around her, she hurried across the street and down the sidewalk. With papers in hand, she climbed the front steps of the courthouse, a crushing pain squeezing her chest. She had to stop to catch her breath, the reality of the situation overwhelming her. She still couldn't believe her marriage was over, that Mark had so easily dismissed her, breaking every promise he had made to her.

Why do I care? I should be happy to be out from under his manipulative, controlling ways. To not have to hold my breath every time he comes home from work, wondering if he is going to love me or hit me. I should be thankful I got out with my life.

But she realized it wasn't her heart as much as it was her ego that was wounded. She had tried so hard to be everything Mark wanted her to be. He wanted thin—she exercised seven days a week. He wanted the perfect hostess for the dinner parties he liked to throw— she took cooking lessons and spent hours pouring over recipes so she could impress his upscale friends and coworkers. He always insisted their penthouse be a show place at all times, leaving her to feel like a guest in her own home. But she had done it. She had spent the last five years doing everything she could to fit into Mark's world.

But it still wasn't enough.

Was I ever enough? Maybe he had mistresses all along, and I was just too stupid to realize it.

"Can I help you?"

Startled, Cassidy looked at the clerk at the information desk, remembering why she was there. "I need to get something notarized."

"Down the hall, third door on the right."

Cassidy walked down the marble hallway, admiring the beautiful architecture. The last time she'd been in such an ornate building is when they filed their marriage license.

She chuckled at the irony.

Opening the door with the simple inscription 'Notary', she walked up to the small counter. "I need to get something notarized and filed."

"One moment, please."

SIXTEEN

And just like that, Cassidy's marriage was over. Granted, it would take weeks to finalize it, but that was just a formality. Climbing into the pickup, she wasn't sure what to do next. She didn't want to go home, at least not yet. She had made such a fool of herself in front of Dad and Wil, and she wasn't ready to face either one of them.

So she drove.

And the more she drove, the more she realized she was wrong about Liberty. It *had* changed.

A lot.

Driving past the high school, Cassidy counted the new neighborhoods and subdivisions filling the gap between town and the old mill. She was stunned. After all, who would actually *choose* to move to Liberty?

She pulled off at the rutted road that led to the pond, the truck bucking and jostling over every pothole and divot. *I can't believe no one has bothered to pave this road.* It was the only road to the pond, and everyone and their brother used it, especially during summer.

Parking as close to the shore as possible, she turned off the motor and sighed. Closing her eyes, she remembered the good times before her mother had died and allowed herself to get lost in the memories.

When a hawk screeched, Cassidy opened her eyes, feeling a little disoriented. *Did I fall asleep?*

Sitting up straight, she realized she must have dozed off. With nothing left to do, she started the truck and headed back down the uneven road.

Once she reached the highway, her conscious and subconscious battled within her because there was still one place she had not visited. Driving in a direction she did not want to go, her heart led her to a place her mind had tried so hard to forget.

Slowing down, she pulled onto the shoulder of the highway, the old truck sputtering as it came to a stop. She walked around the side of the pickup and down the weeded embankment. She saw the cross from where she was—even with the wind whipping her hair in front of her eyes—but she moved closer still. Bending down, Cassidy allowed her fingers to touch the forged metal memorial her father had erected in her mother's honor.

"Mom, I'm lost without you," she whispered, tears flowing down her cheeks. "I don't know what to do. You would be so ashamed of the choices I've made. I've tried hating you for leaving me, but I only miss you more. I want to start over, but I don't know how." Cassidy swallowed back the emotion welling up in her throat. "I'm scared, Mom. I feel so alone. Dad doesn't understand me, and I don't understand how he can still serve a god who took you away from us. It makes no sense. Nothing makes sense anymore."

Cassidy stared at the cross and the plaque that stood as a reminder her mother was no longer there for her. She didn't feel horror like she did the night she was summoned to the hospital and told her mother had died of internal injuries. She didn't feel rage like she did when she was told it was the drunk driver's second offense. No, what she felt now, was hopelessness. She was at a complete loss with no future in sight.

She sat down in the tall grass, pulling the collar of her jacket up, not caring if she got dirty. Staring at the small monument, she thought about her life in New York.

If I had never met Mark. If I had just finished school—stuck to my art—everything would be so different. But she *had* met Mark. *I should have left the first time he hit me.*

But she didn't.

Instead, she made excuses for him. Blamed herself. Accepted his apologies, and the gifts he gave her when he felt guilty. And then the abuse got even worse, more dangerous, more painful, and was coupled with threats. *If you embarrass me in front of my clients, you'll be sorry. If you tell those hags you run around with anything about our personal life, I'll knock your teeth out. If you go to the police, I'll know.*

And then it got better.

Or so she thought.

Feeling a chill, she looked up and saw the sun had begun its descent. She had no idea how long she had been sitting there, but she knew it was time to go home and face the music.

Walking up the hillside, she climbed into the truck, then glanced one more time at the cross barely visible from the road. Taking a deep breath, she turned the key in the ignition.

But nothing happened.

"No. No! No!!"

Cassidy tried and tried to get the engine to turn over, but it was no use. Slamming her hands against the steering wheel, she winced and grabbed her wrist. That's when she noticed the gas gauge was resting neatly on the E. Driving around town, she hadn't realized she was running out of gas.

Frustrated, she threw her head back, hitting it against the rear window causing a sharp pain to shoot down her neck. *My life is one stupid, painful decision after another.*

Sitting in the truck, in her self-induced pity party, she watched as the sky grayed into twilight. She knew she needed to call for help but didn't know who. It would be painful for her father to find her here, but it would be too embarrassing to call Wil for help. Besides, she didn't even know how to reach him.

"I don't understand You, God!" she yelled. "Here I am pouring out my heart, trying to figure out life, and You just can't help but stick it to me when I'm down. Can't You give me a break here? For once, couldn't You just help me instead of making my life miserable?"

Gasping, Cassidy jumped when her purse vibrated next to her. Reaching for her cell phone, she answered the call, even though she didn't recognize the number. "What?" she snapped.

"Gees, how'd you know it was me?" Wil teased. "Or do you always answer your phone with such a cheerful attitude?"

"What do you want, Wil?" Cassidy bristled.

"I was worried about you. You were pretty mad when you took off this morning, and it's getting late. I just got the feeling something wasn't right. But obviously you're fine, so I'll leave you alone."

"No! Wait!" Cassidy yelled before Wil could hang up.

She heard his frustrated sigh. "What?"

"I ran out of gas, and I don't want to call Dad. Would you mind coming to get me?" Cassidy hated having to ask for his help, but she had no choice. She couldn't bear to see her dad here, in this place.

"Where are you?"

"By Mr. Wicker's old place."

"What are you doing out there?"

She cleared her throat to answer, but nothing came out.

"I'll be right there."

The old highway didn't see many travelers, but the ones who did pass by, were kind and friendly, stopping to offer their assistance. Cassidy politely waved them on knowing Wil was on his way.

Unfortunately, sitting on the side of the road gave her too much time to think. She had just blamed God for not helping her, when Wil called out of the blue. She tried convincing herself it was a coincidence, but somehow, she could not put it out of her mind.

Twenty minutes later, Cassidy watched as Wil pulled off the highway, kicking up dirt as he came to a stop. Grabbing a gas can from the bed of his truck, he rounded the back bumper then glanced over toward the cross in the brush.

Cassidy got out of the truck and followed him. "I'm sorry to bother you like this," she said as he removed the gas cap.

"No bother." Wil was polite, but not overly friendly.

Cassidy stuck her hands in the pockets of her jacket, knowing she needed to apologize for more than just the inconvenience of him having to bail her out.

"Look, I'm sorry I went into your house and listened to your answering machine. I was completely out of line. I had no right."

"Nope," was all he said as he tilted the gas can and filled the tank.

Cassidy waited for him to say something more, but he was silent. She could feel her temper rising the longer Wil ignored her.

"I said I was sorry. What more do you want, a written apology?"

He said nothing.

"Well, if the silent treatment is all I'm going to get, two can play at that game."

"I doubt it," Wil mumbled under his breath.

"Excuse me . . . what did you say?" Cassidy followed Wil as he walked toward his truck. "The polite thing to do is talk to a person when they speak to you, not ignore them."

Wil swung around so fast Cassidy had to jump back to keep from running into him.

"Polite? What do you know about polite? You're an arrogant, spoiled brat who thinks life owes you some big favor. You huffed out of here nine years ago a selfish, self-centered person. You turned your back on God and your dad. But, now that your little fairytale marriage has fallen apart and your life as a pampered socialite is over, you come running back here expecting everyone to tiptoe around you and dance to your tune. Well, you know what? You're wrong."

"How dare you?" Cassidy almost shook with rage. "How dare you stand there and judge me! You have no idea what I've been through. You're right though, I did give up worshiping some higher power who would take the life of a little girl and destroy it with one pass of his hand. I did lose respect for a father who only talked about the sovereignty of God and made me feel as if I had no right to mourn or be angry. I realized then, I was the only one looking out for Cassidy, so I did what I had to do. I made my choices and I'm living with the consequences, but it's my life, and you have no idea what it's been like. You with your farm boy mentality, always doing the right thing, thinking everything will be fine. It's obvious you've arrived Wilbur Marsh, but once you experience a little disappointment in life, you'll see what I'm talking about. Until then, you can keep your lectures and your self-righteous attitude to yourself."

Cassidy turned on her heels and walked toward the driver's side door, but with one swift jerk of her arm, she was pulled back around to face Wil. His hold on her arm was so tight it was painful. His eyes fiercer than she'd ever seen them.

"Do you think you're the only one in the world who has dealt with tragedy?"

"Being picked on in school hardly qualifies as tragedy, Wil."

He clenched her arm a little tighter.

"Okay, well how about watching your house go up in flames. The only place you ever felt loved and accepted. Or having the firemen tell you there's nothing they can do as they physically restrained you from trying to rescue your parents. Or how about watching as they remove the charred bodies of your mom and dad from the ashes of the only life you'd ever known.

"See, Cassidy, tragedy is everywhere and happens to everyone, but you wouldn't know that because your thoughts have never traveled farther than yourself." Wil released his hold on her. "Maybe that's why your husband left you for another woman.

Maybe he realized there wasn't enough room in your life for anyone but yourself."

Wil didn't give her a chance to respond, he just got into his truck and skidded onto the highway.

Cassidy was stunned. Horrified. She slowly climbed inside the truck and softly shut the door. She sat there for several minutes, resting her head on the steering wheel, allowing Wil's words to sink in.

Why didn't dad tell me what happened to Wil's parents?

Then again, why didn't I bother to ask?

Wil was right. She had thought only about herself since coming home. She couldn't imagine the pain and anguish Wil must have felt losing both parents at the same time, standing by, helpless to do anything. At least when she lost her mother, she hadn't witnessed the accident that took her life. When she was allowed to see her in the hospital, she looked peaceful and beautiful. Wil never got the opportunity to say goodbye. Now it made a little more sense why Wil lived on her father's property.

Cassidy sat in the truck once again dreading going home. No matter what she did, she found herself hating life.

Hating *her* life.

When she finally got home, she found her dad sitting in front of the fireplace, elbows on his knees, head in his hands. She quietly crossed the living room, trying not to disturb him, but only got as far as the landing of the stairs.

"You okay, Cassidy?"

"Yeah, Dad." She started up the stairs.

"Is your mom's cross still in good shape?"

She turned to him, surprised. "How did you know?"

"Wil told me where you ran out of gas."

She swallowed back her emotion. "Yeah. Looks good."

Cassidy's heart ached for her dad. He and her mother had been so in love, even after twenty years of marriage. But after the accident, he said, 'It was God's will. It wasn't for him to understand, but to trust.' Cassidy disagreed. She was angry with her dad because he continued to serve a god who thought nothing of destroying their family. But now, hearing the brokenness in her father's voice told her he missed her mother still.

Closing her bedroom door, Cassidy crawled onto her bed. She pulled her pillow tight against her chest and thought about her dad. He had aged. Walked slower. Tired easier. Yet here he was still taking care of the ranch. The herd. The horses. Obviously, Wil helped out, but was it enough? *I should be the one taking care of him. I should be the one making sure he's okay.*

But no, she had been so wrapped up in her metropolitan lifestyle, so stubborn, so defiant, she had never looked back and considered what she had left behind.

After soaking in a bath, Cassidy lay on her bed, staring at the ceiling. She was still in a melancholy mood, looking for answers that seemed unattainable.

Unattainable because she refused to look in the right places.

———— • ————

Joseph watched his daughter slip upstairs and disappear into her room.

He had brought Cassidy before the Lord every day since she was born, praying she would grow up with a love for the Savior. But he saw her gentle spirit crushed by the death of her mother and could tell she was still searching for the happiness that continued to elude her.

First, it was her art. She was going to go to college. Study her craft. Make a name for herself. It was the vehicle she used to leave her childhood behind and start over. But she didn't *go* to New York; she *ran* from a life she didn't want.

Then it was Mark. An older man. Experienced in life. An unbeliever. He showed her a whole new world, afforded her opportunities she never would have had otherwise. But all he did was lead her further away from God. Wounding her in the process.

Now she was back home. More battered and broken than when she left.

Joseph went to bed weary, pleading with the Lord not to let Cassidy self-destruct before she realized peace would not come to her apart from God. Those were the last words on his lips before he drifted off to sleep.

SEVENTEEN

Waking early the next morning, Cassidy stared at her unpacked suitcase still sitting on the floor. She pulled out a pair of designer jeans and a mohair-blend sweater she had bought at Barney's, then headed for the barn. She heard her father on the far side of the stables, so she walked over and watched as he worked.

"Good morning," she said as she hitched her foot up on the lowest rung of the stall.

Startled, he gave her a half-smile. "You're up early."

"My daddy always told me 'the best part of the day happens when most people are still asleep.'"

His smile grew.

Watching in quiet, she followed him to another stall. "Dad, where's Honey?"

He sighed, his shoulders drooping slightly. "I had to put her down last year. She came up lame, had an infection. She was old."

"Oh Dad, I'm so sorry. I know she was your baby."

"That she was. We lost her mama when she was born, but I was determined not to lose her too."

"I remember that night. We all took turns feeding her until she got stronger."

He smiled again, and Cassidy could tell he was lost in a memory.

Following him to the next stall, she asked, "So, who do you ride now?"

"Rooster here." He patted the tall stallion and stroked his withers. "He looks menacing, but he's just a big baby."

Moving from one pen to another, Cassidy helped her dad measure the oats and split the bales. They worked in relative silence, an unspoken ease between them. Doing morning chores together seemed like old times. Surprisingly, Cassidy felt a sense of contentment working alongside her dad after all these years.

Noticing the hay stock was running low, she moved to the hay loft ladder. "Dad, I'm going to pull down some more hay."

"Uh . . . no . . . that's okay, Sunshine." He hurried toward her. "You don't need to do that, I can do it later."

She started to climb. "It's no big deal. Besides, you shouldn't be climbing up here, especially when . . . hey, when did you start using this for storage?" She pulled herself up into the loft and squatted next to one of the boxes. "Wait a minute, this has my name on—" It took a few seconds before she realized where they had come from. She looked down at her dad in disbelief.

"I'm sorry, Sunshine, I was going to tell you, I just wanted to give you some time."

Ripping the tape off the box, she pulled the flaps open.

"Come on, Cassidy. Come down from there."

After rifling through a box of clothing, she opened another one. It was filled with photo frames and albums, everything depicting her life with Mark. She held a picture of them together, a week after they were married. She studied Mark's eyes, searching for the man she had fallen in love with; all she saw was a man who had both lavished and terrified her for the last five years, a man who had grown tired of her and packed her away in a bunch of boxes.

Angry, she ripped open another box and gasped. All her art supplies were dumped inside. Carelessly dumped. Brushes and tubes of paint laid haphazardly among her sketch pads. Her pouch of chalks—the felt pouch her mother had made her—laid opened, pieces of chalk everywhere. But even worse, her old paint palette of colors was upside down, stuck to the last canvas she had worked on. Her eyes stung and her heart ached, not so much because the picture was ruined, but because Mark had thought so little of her work.

"You okay, Sunsh . . . Cassidy?" Her dad peaked over the ledge of the loft.

"Not really, but I will be." She swiped at the tears wetting her cheeks. "Now get off the ladder so I can lower some hay." She turned to the winch and quickly lowered bales to the barn floor. Her dad worked on stacking them, doing his best to keep up. After lowering her box of paint supplies, Cassidy climbed down from the loft with an armful of clothes and a pair of expensive Balenciaga sneakers tied together and tossed over her shoulder.

When she met her father's eyes, she looked away, hating to see pity. The—*my daughter is a screw-up and I feel so sorry for her*—look. "I'm okay, Dad. I'm just going to take this stuff to my room."

Cassidy slammed her bedroom door, dropped the box of art supplies on the floor, and tossed the pile of clothes and pair of shoes onto her bed. She paced, angry and frustrated. Mark had packed her up and moved her out, just like he did the living room decor he'd tired of.

I was nothing more than a disposable accessory to him.

Pulling off the mohair sweater and expensive jeans she had put on earlier, she exchanged them instead for an older pair of Calvin Klein's and a Ralph Lauren button down. Even still, she never would have imagined when she bought her designer threads, she'd end up wearing them in the dust and grime of the great outdoors.

She looked at herself in the mirror, turning front to back, surprised her jeans hung lose. For the last month, she had tried to lose five pesky pounds because the skimpy lingerie she'd bought for their trip left very little to the imagination. She had wanted to look perfect for Mark.

The irony made her laugh.

Not only had she lost the weight, but she had lost the man as well.

Needing a distraction before she fell apart, she went to the kitchen and started making breakfast. By the time her dad was finished with his morning routine, she had eggs, hash browns, bacon, and toast ready to go. When he entered the kitchen, she greeted him with a smile and a strong cup of coffee.

"Cassidy, this looks wonderful."

"Well, my cooking skills might have changed over the years, but I can still make a mean breakfast."

Her father gave her a quick hug, sat down, and prayed.

Cassidy watched, but didn't join in.

After a few bites, her dad chuckled.

"What?"

"Do you remember the time you decided to make your mom and I breakfast in bed for our anniversary? You figured if chocolate chips tasted good in pancakes, they would taste even better in omelets."

Cassidy laughed. "It took Mom forever to scrape burnt chocolate out of her cast-iron skillet, and when I carried the trays upstairs, I sloshed orange juice all over your food. And you ate every chocolatey orange flavored bite. How did you stomach it?"

He grinned. "I knew I'd rather have a killer case of heartburn than chance hurting your feelings."

Cassidy didn't know how to respond. She'd been emotionally distant from her dad for so long, she'd chosen to block out the good memories from her childhood. When her mother died, she'd been angry with him because he chose to cling to God instead of blaming Him. Up until that day, her dad had been her hero, her rock. But after the accident, all she saw was a weak shell of a man. She realized now, even though she still felt God was her enemy—her dad was not. It was time she treated him with the respect he deserved, even if she didn't believe in his god.

"This was great, Cassidy," her father said as he got up from the table.

"Good. I'm glad you enjoyed it," she said as she wiped circles on the kitchen counter, then turned to him before he could leave. "Look, Dad, I don't have much of a game plan right now. This all kind of took me by surprise, and it might take me some time to figure out where to go from here. But if it's all right with you, I'd like to stay here for a little while, at least until I decide what to do next." Cassidy paused for a moment, waiting for her dad to say something, but he was silent. "I'm more than willing to do my fair share around the ranch," she rambled on. "I know it's been a while, but how hard can it be to shovel manure and feed chickens." Fidgeting with the dishcloth in her hand she finally blurted out what she was trying to say. "I want to come home, Dad, if that's all right with you?"

Cassidy's heart sank when her father still didn't say anything. *I can't believe it. He really doesn't want me here.*

She watched as he carried his dishes to the sink. She couldn't blame him for not wanting her to stay—not really. She had rebelled, behaved horribly, said mean and hateful things to him and disrespected his god for so many years. Now she was reaping the penalty for her actions.

But when her dad finally turned to face her, she saw his eyes were red and watering. "Cassidy, sweetheart, I've prayed for this day for nine long years." He choked back emotion as he opened his arms wide. "Welcome home, Sunshine."

Cassidy walked into her father's open embrace and allowed her tears to fall freely against the front of his shirt. She didn't know what her future held, but right now she didn't care. She just wanted to be held by her father, to feel his strong protective arms around her once again. Just like when she was a little girl.

He held her tight until her tears stopped. Taking a step back, she dried her face with the tail of her shirt, then straightened her shoulders. "Enough of this. We still have chores to do."

"No sweetheart, you go ahead and take care of your stuff. Wash your things if you need to. I'm going to town for some supplies. That is, unless you want to come with me?"

Cassidy politely declined the invitation. One trip to town in a week was plenty.

After watching her father pull away, she found herself back in her room, rummaging through her box of art supplies. She pulled out the canvas that had been carelessly dumped in the box and scrutinized her work. It was good, but it wasn't great. She didn't understand that about her work. She put her heart and soul into it, but somehow it didn't come across in the finished work.

Cassidy came to the realization, she wasn't as good as she gave herself credit for. Yes, she had sold a few pieces at local galleries in New York, but she was never going to become the breakout artist she once hoped to be. She shrugged her shoulders. "Oh well, that doesn't mean I still can't enjoy the process."

Gathering the chalks that weren't crushed or broken, she put them back into the felt pouch, picked up one of her sketch pads, and headed outside. She really didn't have a specific destination in mind, but she knew she would know it when she got there.

Ending up next to the creek, she walked over to where the water trickled over jagged rocks and a low-slung tree branch stretched across the water. Sitting down, she leaned against the tree trunk, unrolled her chalk pouch next to her and did something she had not done for the last three years.

At first, she felt stiff. Her sore wrist and tender shoulder impeded her movements and interfered with her strokes. But after a few minutes, with her chalks streaking across the textured paper, she found her rhythm, losing herself in a world she had missed more than she realized.

When she was done, she held out the rough sketch at arm's length and critiqued it. It wasn't very good, but she didn't care. She knew she could get it back. She was rusty, but nothing a little practice and a little more recovery time wouldn't take care of.

Looking up at the changing sky, Cassidy realized she'd lost track of time and probably needed to head home. Slowly, she walked through the pasture, enjoying the gentle breeze. Rotating her shoulder a few times, she was surprised that after two weeks, it still bothered her. But then she remembered how she flung the bales of hay around. *Serves me right.*

Cassidy approached the house, then stopped when she saw Wil standing on the porch. Immediately, her stomach knotted. After their last *conversation*, Cassidy wasn't sure she was ready for another one of Wil's chats. Climbing the porch steps, she walked slowly toward the front door.

"I don't know what you said to Joseph this morning, but he looks ten years younger."

Cassidy stopped. "I didn't really say much, other than I wanted to stick around for a while."

"I'm sure that was it. He's missed you, you know."

"I'm beginning to realize that."

They were quiet.

Wil leaned against the upright of the porch and looked out over the land. Cassidy stood clutching her sketch pad to her chest, not knowing what to say.

"I'm so sorry about your parents," she finally blurted out. "I can't imagine how difficult that must have been for you."

"Thank you."

Again, silence filled the air.

"I'm sorry things didn't work out for you in New York, but I see you haven't given up your art."

Cassidy looked down at her sketch pad. "Oh, I was just fooling around. It's not very good with my hand and shoulder bothering me, but it did feel good to pick it up again."

"I thought you were pursuing your art in New York."

"I was, but then I met Mark and it . . . well, it kind of took a back seat."

"That's a shame. You were good."

"Good for Liberty's standards, not so good for New York's."

Quiet again, Cassidy wasn't sure what else to say. Small talk seemed rather silly after the knock-down drag out fights they'd had. Taking a deep breath, she shuddered slightly as a breeze swept across the porch. "It's turned chilly out here. I'm going in. Would you like something to drink?"

Wil shrugged a shoulder. "Sure."

She went directly to the kitchen and opened the refrigerator; Wil followed behind. "Looks like we have orange juice, iced tea, and water. Dad still doesn't believe in having soda in the house."

"Water is fine." Wil reached for two glasses and set them on the counter.

After filling the glasses, she turned to say something to Wil and glanced at the clock hanging on the wall. "Oh shoot! It's almost lunch time. I had no idea I was outside so long." Opening the refrigerator again, she grabbed everything needed for sandwiches and laid it all on the counter. When she reached up to get plates from the cupboard, she winced slightly, rotating her shoulder, trying to work free the stiffness.

"Your shoulder is still bothering you that bad?"

"Yeah, but it will be fine. I just think I went down on it harder than I thought. It also didn't help that I moved bales of hay around this morning."

While Cassidy assembled sandwiches, she couldn't help but notice Wil scrutinizing her every move. It creeped her out. Spinning around, a mayonnaise-laden knife in her hand, she pointed at him. "Look, Wil, I'll make you a deal. You stop watching my every move, and I'll make you a sandwich for lunch."

He arched a brow. "Deal."

It took only a few minutes for her to make Wil's sandwich. When she was putting everything back in the refrigerator, he reached around her and poured himself a glass of iced tea.

"Why didn't you tell me you wanted tea instead of water?"

"I don't. But I've eaten enough meals with Joseph, to know this is his drink of choice."

Cassidy bristled, feeling jealous of Wil's relationship with her father. She had no right to be. It was her own fault. Even so, it still hurt thinking her father's bond with Wil was stronger than their own.

"Hey, what's all this?"

Cassidy turned to see her dad standing in the doorway. "Sorry, Dad, it's not much, but I kind of lost track of time."

"Are you kidding? This is wonderful. Breakfast *and* lunch, you're going to spoil me."

"Well, it's nothing fancy."

"Any meal I don't have to make is a feast in my book."

"But Dad, I thought you liked cooking? You used to work

side-by-side with Mom all the time."

"That I did, but not because I liked to cook. I just liked being close to your mother."

Dumbfounded, Cassidy took a seat. *I can't believe I didn't know that. He did all the cooking after mom died. I just assumed he . . . I never even offered to help.*

Wil and her dad bowed their heads for prayer, so Cassidy followed suit—out of respect.

As they enjoyed their meal, her dad spoke to Wil. "You never told me how Madi's delivery went."

Cassidy choked on her swig of water. Just hearing the name reminded her what a fool she'd made of herself. Wiping her face with a napkin, she chanced a look at Wil, and saw the smirk on his face.

"It went as well as could be expected," he said, amusement in his tone. "With it being her first foal and all, she did pretty well. She has a chocolate-colored filly with a blaze on her muzzle. A real beauty."

Wil and her father continued to talk about horses, feed, repairs, and Wil's growing practice. The more they talked, the more irritated Cassidy got. The conversation between the two of them was easy and natural, while she sat there feeling like an outsider with nothing to say. With her frustration building, she could hardly wait for lunch to be over. When her father swallowed his last bite of sandwich, she jumped to her feet to clear the dishes.

"That's the best lunch I've had in a long time," he said as he stood. "Thank you, Sun . . . ah, Cassidy."

"You're welcome, Dad."

"Yeah, Cassidy, it really hit the spot," Wil added.

She ignored him as she reached across the table for the dishes. Wincing, she snatched her arm back, and tried again with her left arm. Setting the dishes on the drain board, she turned and saw Wil watching her. He glanced at her shoulder, then met her eyes. He didn't need to say anything. She knew exactly what he was thinking.

"It's fine," she mouthed, not wanting her dad to know.

"Uh-huh." He didn't look convinced, but he let it go as he followed her dad into the living room.

She rolled her eyes while reaching for the refrigerator door. *Why does he have to be so irritating?*

"Joseph, I'm scheduled to attend a conference in Cheyenne this weekend, but I don't have to go if you need me here."

"Why would he need you here?" Cassidy asked, handing her father a thermos of tea.

"I was talking to your dad."

"But you were talking about me, right?" she challenged.

"No. I was just making sure—with all that's going on—Joseph would be okay without me here."

"Well, let me assure you, I can give Dad all the help he needs. We will get along just fine without you."

"Excuse me, but I'd rather hear that from your dad, since I've been the one helping out around here for the last three years."

It was like a punch in the gut. A direct hit. She wanted to say something, defend herself, but Wil was right. He'd been the one helping her dad when it should have been her. Not having a snappy retort or quick comeback, Cassidy turned and walked away.

———— • ————

Wil drove home, kicking himself. He should be making it easier on Cassidy, not harder. She was home. An answer to Joseph's prayers. And it looked like she intended to stay, at least for a little while. He should be happy for Joseph's sake.

Then why wasn't he?

He thought a moment . . .

Because he was waiting for the other shoe to drop, keeping his defenses in place for the time when Cassidy got bored and took off again. Her reasons for leaving Liberty had not changed.

The town was still small.

Her mother was still gone.

She still blamed God and was at odds with her father because he didn't.

Unless Cassidy realized she was the problem, nothing would change, and she would just end up leaving again.

Then it would be up to him to pick up the pieces. And quite frankly, he wasn't sure Joseph would be able to handle it. He was older now. Not as healthy as he had been when she left nine years ago.

But your antagonistic attitude and barbed comments could be the very thing that pushes her away. His conscience scolded him. *Then you would be the one responsible for Joseph's broken heart.*

Sighing, he shifted into park, and rested his arms and

forehead against the steering wheel.

God . . . you're right. It's not my place to judge, or to dish out punishment. I need to encourage Cassidy, not tear her down. I need to nurture her relationship with her father, not come between it.

Sitting up, he nodded, decision made. He would do his best to get along with Cassidy, put his pettiness aside. Be her friend, not her adversary.

At least he would try.

EIGHTEEN

Though Cassidy groaned every morning when she got up before the sun, it was worth it to see her father not work so hard. His initial response to her proposition had been bullheadedness, balking when she reminded him that he was getting older. But in the end, he had finally agreed. She would oversee the morning feeding routine, and he would shorten his workday by one hour. It had only been a few days, but it was working. Even though he groused when she called him in for the night, her dad was sticking to his end of the bargain, so she continued with hers.

Cassidy's mornings were grueling, but the rest of her day was enjoyable and productive. Before lunch, she would go outside to sketch. Each day she looked for a different vantage point in which to capture the best light or traipsed off to another section of the property in search of unique subjects or distinctive compositions. She enjoyed being outside, and even though the air at times was chilly, it was invigorating and made her feel alive.

Every day, after lunch, she gave herself a new task. So far, she had cleaned every inch of the kitchen, from the top shelf in the pantry to behind the refrigerator. She had tossed dry goods long past the expiration date and repapered every drawer and cabinet. She had deep cleaned the living room, from ceiling cobwebs to dusty baseboards, and had even cleaned both the front and back porches, dusting off screens and wiping down siding. But, the most rewarding thing she did by far, was make dinner for her dad. She had prepared a couple of the fancy recipes she had perfected while in New York, but her dad was a meat-and-potatoes kind of guy. Comfort food is what he preferred, and Cassidy had to admit, she missed the simplicity of a good steak and a starchy fat-filled side dish.

Unfortunately, the shoulder she had hurt weeks ago continued to aggravate her. Though her wrist and forehead had healed just fine, her shoulder was getting worse. She changed the bandage daily, and used warm compresses at night, but the wound refused to scab over for any length of time. Of course, it didn't help that she kept catching the bandage on her clothing when she got dressed or bumped into it while doing her chores.

Up until now, she'd considered it a nuisance more than a problem. But today when she woke up, it felt warm to the touch and was beginning to seep. Knowing it was stupid to suffer needlessly when a doctor could give her something for it, she debated whether she should mention it to Wil.

Why . . . he'll just scold me for not taking care of it right.

She deliberated, listing the pros and cons, but in the end had decided if it wasn't feeling better by Monday, she would go to the clinic in town.

As for today, she had a very important task to do. It was time she put New York, and her life with Mark behind her.

After lunch, she climbed into the hay loft and sifted through the boxes Mark had sent her. It was cathartic to go through each item, remembering when she got it and what the occasion was. She had cried a lot and cursed even more, but three emotion-filled hours later, she had everything divided into four stacks: throw away, give away, store for spring and summer, and a box of warm clothes she could use right now.

"Okay," she took a cleansing breath and dried her face, "now to get these boxes from here to there." She glanced over the edge of the loft to the barn floor below.

The winch helped her lower the boxes to the ground floor, but she still had to climb down the ladder, unfasten the boxes, and arrange them in stacks. Back and forth, up and down, she didn't stop until all the boxes were down. Out of breath and sweating, she looked at the two stacks that needed to go to her room. One stack she would store in her closet for later; the other stack had stuff she could use right now. Mustering what little energy she had left, she muscled a box into her arms, walked across the yard, climbed the stairs, and deposited it in her room.

"That's one," she counted off, then repeated her steps until every box was moved.

After dropping the last box on her bedroom floor, Cassidy collapsed across her bed. "I thought spin class was hard," she panted, waiting for her breathing to return to normal. Once she knew she wasn't going to pass out from overexertion, she sorted through her clothes, hanging up some, and folding others before putting them in her childhood dresser. After breaking down the empty boxes and taking them to the mud room, Cassidy returned to her room. Seeing her purse and carry-on bag stacked in the corner, she decided to continue her purge therapy.

Sitting on the floor with her back against the bed, she pulled her phone from her purse. She had ignored every incoming call, every text, every voicemail. It was her way of cutting herself off from her former life. She had nothing left to say to Mark and had not wanted to listen to the numerous questions her friends were sure to ask.

But she was feeling stronger now. And wanted to put the past behind her.

Immediately, she erased every message from Mark, refusing to give him the satisfaction, since nothing he had to say mattered anymore. Then, she listened to a few messages from her travel agent, each call more insistent than the one before. "I get it. No communication, no refund," Cassidy yelled at her phone, before deleting the rest of the agents calls, along with wrong numbers and telemarketers. But when she saw Andrea's name on the screen, she pressed Play.

"Hey, Cass. I'm here if you need me. You did the right thing. I wish I had the guts to leave Dan, but I'm not as strong as you. He might be a cheat, but he appeases his guilt by giving me a very generous allowance. He thinks I don't know about his escapades, or that every time he goes on a *business trip*, he takes his whore with him. But I don't care. A mistress is a small price to pay for the lifestyle he affords me. But I'm glad you finally know the truth. And if it's any consolation, you were too good for Mark. He's a grade-A jerk. He deserves the likes of Amanda. She's playing him, and he doesn't even know it. He'll get his. Just wait and see. Well, call me if you need to talk or get drunk." Cassidy heard Andrea's signature laugh right before she disconnected the call.

I can't believe she knew and never told me.

Cassidy considered Andrea her best friend, even confided in her at one time that her marriage was on shaky ground. She didn't dare tell her Mark was abusive, but Andrea knew they had their troubles, and never once hinted that their problem might be infidelity.

I guess since Dan is Mark's right-hand man, she was afraid to do anything to upset her own gravy train.

Slumping back against the bed, Cassidy scanned through the remaining calls, shocked to see none of her other friends had bothered to call her. Not Chloe, not Kira, not even Jill. Then again, maybe they weren't her friends after all, considering everyone in her life was there because of Mark. Wives of Mark's co-workers. Women Mark encouraged her to spend time with. She'd lost touch with her friends from art school and the coffee shop, mostly because Mark didn't approve of anyone he didn't know.

When did I stop being me, and become only what Mark wanted me to be?

Staring at the ceiling, she quickly replayed the last few years in her mind, remembering every negative comment he made about her figure, how he never missed a chance to insinuate she was fat.

He insisted on picking out her wardrobe when they went to high-end functions and teased her when she put on a pound or two at the holidays. The only time he praised her is when she was far below what she thought looked healthy.

And then there were the plastic surgery brochures he would casually lay on her nightstand. He suggested—more than once—that she consider augmentations to accentuate her lesser features. And even though the thought terrified her, she had actually considered it, thinking it would make him happy.

I was just another one of his acquisitions, something he could prance around in front of his friends and business associates.

And I let him do it.

But after five years, he'd grown tired of her, just like he had his custom Ferrari and platinum Rolex. She'd been replaced by a newer model with younger features and a more enhanced appearance.

Getting to her feet, Cassidy walked over to the window, needing the fresh air to combat the churning in her stomach. She closed her eyes but refused to cry. Taking a couple of deep breaths, she opened her eyes and stood up straighter.

Okay, pity party over.

Turning to her desk, she tidied up the area where she dumped her sketches and chalks at the end of each day. Sticking out from underneath the pile, she noticed the letter Mark had left with her dad. The one she refused to read until she was ready.

Well . . . today is the day.

Needing to put it all behind her, she ripped open the light blue, parchment envelope, remembering the day she helped pick out his personalized stationery.

I wonder if he knew then that he would be using it to write me a Dear Jane letter?

Unfolding the single sheet of paper, she read his familiar script.

Cassie,

I'm sorry you found out about Amanda this way, but I'm glad it is finally out in the open. I never intentionally meant to hurt you. I'm just not cut out for monogamy. It's not in my DNA. Hasn't been for a while.

So . . . Amanda wasn't the first.

Cassidy swore, clenching the letter in her hand, balling it up in her fist. She was poised to throw it in the trash, but stopped, knowing she needed to read the rest and get it over with. Smoothing out the wrinkled paper, she continued.

But if it's any consolation, you were special enough I wanted to give it a try. You were so beautiful, so different from any woman I had ever met. I thought if I molded you into the perfect woman, the perfect wife, I would be happy. But I realize that wasn't what I was looking for. If I had to put it into business terms, I guess 'the art of the deal' turned out to be more fulfilling than the acquisition. So, you see, it's not your fault. It's just who I am.

Perfect wife? Who is he kidding? Did he really think abusing me, terrorizing and belittling me would bring out my better qualities? She thought a moment. *Then again, that's who he is in the business world. He bullies and obliterates his competition on a daily basis. He's right . . . it is who he is.*

Even though you signed a pre-nup, and a non-disclosure agreement before we were married, I still want you to be compensated for your time. So, I've had my lawyers draw up papers and have instructed them to give you a very generous settlement.

Finally . . . the whole reason for writing me in the first place. To remind me to keep my mouth shut.

Take care of yourself, Cassie. You've come so far in the last few years. Any man would be happy to have you. Unfortunately, I'm just not that man.

Mark

Feeling rejected and angry, and needing some time to process, Cassidy went downstairs and quickly wrote her dad a note, explaining that she was so tired from moving all the boxes, she was going to call it an early night. She then made him a sandwich and propped the note up against it and left it in the refrigerator.

A little after five o'clock, her dad tapped on her bedroom door. "Cassidy, honey, are you okay?"

"Yeah, Dad, just tired," she said in a fake cheerful voice.

"Okay then, I'll see you in the morning."

She pressed her face to her pillow to muffle her cries.

NINETEEN

Sunday morning, Cassidy woke up stiff, tired, and emotionally exhausted. She could barely raise her arms in front of her because of all the straining she'd done moving the boxes from the hay loft. And thanks to Mark's letter, she'd spent the rest of the evening in a self-induced pity party, beating herself up for allowing Mark to manipulate and intimidate her for most their marriage.

Needing a hot shower to soothe her aching muscles and wash away her negative disposition, she stepped into the stream of water, only to wince and step back.

Her shoulder was on fire.

Great! Just one more thing to contend with.

Discouraged, and slightly weepy, she washed her hair—as best as she could with one hand—then finished showering. Gathering her dripping hair, she pulled it over her left shoulder and turned her right shoulder toward the vanity mirror. She twisted and turned, scrutinizing her wound, trying to see what was preventing it from healing.

"Cassidy . . ."

She heard a slight knock on her bedroom door.

"Are you awake?"

"Yes, Dad. I'll be down as soon as I'm ready."

Doing her best to juggle both her blow dryer and hair brush, Cassidy dried her hair, applied a little make-up, then stood in front of her bedroom closet. Now that she had a larger wardrobe to choose from, she looked for something that would be comfortable on her tender shoulder. A pink angora sweater set, with tank-top shell and long-sleeve cardigan, was the lightest thing she could wear without exposing the ugly bandage. Pairing it with a floral maxi skirt, she looked in the mirror, pleased with the end result. After the fashion disaster she wore the first time

103

she went to church, she purposely chose outfits with her dad in mind. Not to embarrass him, but to please him.

Arriving at church, Cassidy smiled and shook hands with a few people, but quickly found her seat. She went to church out of respect for her dad, but still felt hypocritical being there. When he joined her in the pew after indulging in some small-town chatter, he turned to her and smiled.

"Did I tell you how beautiful you look, Sunshine? You're the spitting image of your mother."

Her throat knotted. "Thanks, Dad," she whispered while fighting back tears. He took her hand in his and gave it a squeeze before turning his attention to the pastor as he called the congregation to prayer.

It took several minutes for Cassidy to regain her composure, her father's words catching her completely off guard. But even though her thoughts were elsewhere, she still heard the words of the pastor as he spoke about her least favorite Bible character—Job.

"Imagine it, people. Put yourself in Job's shoes. Actually, that would be sandals."

The congregation chuckled.

"Job experienced excruciating pain and incredible loss, but his trust in God never wavered. That's what true faith is.

"Think about it . . . how great would God be if His people's faith was tempered by the trials of this world? If our loyalties ebbed and flowed like the waves of the sea? We've all experienced loss, some of us more than others. And I'm *not* saying that the staggering grief many of you have endured due to the loss of a loved one and the anger that accompanied that grief, separates you from God. But *I am* saying those events do not nullify who God is. He is our Creator. Our Redeemer. He loves you with an unshakable love. He has tough skin and can handle a spiritual chest-pounding filled with: Why me? Why now? Why did You let this happen?

"But . . . at the end of that conversation . . . you have to let Him in. You must allow God to be the *only* God—big G—in your life. Through good and bad, highs and low, pain and suffering. God remains and will always be God."

When the pastor paused and scanned the audience, their eyes locked. It was only for a split-second, but it was as if he was asking, "Are you listening?"

Cassidy was sure it was her imagination, but it made her feel awkward, like everyone knew what a mess she'd made of her life. It was hard enough sitting still with the pain radiating from her shoulder, but public scrutiny made her even more uncomfortable. As soon as the pastor finished, she hurried out of the sanctuary and across the parking lot to wait for her dad in the truck. She watched him slowly make his way out of the vestibule and down the steps, talking to everyone in his path. *For being such a quiet man, he sure turns into a social butterfly on Sundays.*

When he got into the truck, he pulled from the lot while talking about the 'powerful message' the pastor had given. He kept glancing her way, waiting for her to engage him, but Cassidy was quiet. Even though she had listened, she was frustrated with what the pastor had said. And since she didn't want to get in an argument or a debate with her dad, she kept her opinion to herself. Closing her eyes, she leaned her head against the passenger window. Her dad got the hint and drove the rest of the way home in silence.

After swapping her skirt for a pair of jeans, Cassidy pulled off her cardigan and gently peeled back the bandage on her shoulder. She didn't like what she saw.

When did Wil say he would be home? Was it today or tomorrow?

She was beginning to think one of Wil's lectures would be a small price to pay in exchange for something to help alleviate the pain.

Pulling her sweater back on, she made her way to the kitchen. When she looked out the back window, she saw her dad stoking the coals on the grill, so she gathered the ingredients needed to make macaroni salad. Working in the kitchen was fast becoming one of her favorite parts of the day. Her dad was so appreciative of every little thing, even the simplest dishes.

Unlike Mark.

Cooking for him was a stressful ordeal. No matter how hard she tried, he always had something critical to say. It had gotten so bad that most of their meals were eaten out or brought in by a delivery service. 'You just don't know what you're doing in the kitchen, Cassidy,' he told her on more than one occasion. 'I'd rather pay than be disappointed.'

Shaking off the negative memories, Cassidy put a few pots of water on to boil and foiled some corn for the grill. When her dad came into the kitchen to get the steaks, she handed the corn cobs to him, wincing when she stretched out her hands.

"It's still bothering you, isn't it?" He nodded toward her shoulder.

"Yeah. Stupid thing just won't go away," she said, trying to sound casual. "I was thinking I might go to town tomorrow, see if the doctor at the clinic can give me something for it. I just didn't want to worry you."

"Has Wil looked at it?"

"No."

"He'll be home this evening. I think you should give him a call."

"I'll see."

"Cassidy, Wil could—"

"I'll take care of it, Dad," she said, trying to hide her irritation. "Don't worry about it."

He was poised to say something more, but she raised a brow, challenging him. He threw up his hands in defeat. "I won't say another word." He turned around and let the kitchen door shut behind him.

Cassidy continued what she was doing in the kitchen, boiling noodles and eggs for the salad and deviled eggs for her dad. It was his favorite side dish, and it made her happy to see him smile.

Lunch was just the two of them. No frills. Simple. And it was perfect. It amazed Cassidy that she could feel such peace just by sharing a meal with her dad.

After he shoved a fourth deviled egg into his mouth and swallowed, he took a sip of his tea and said, "So . . . tell me about your sketches. I've seen you all over the property. I bet the trees have grown a lot since the last time you drew them."

"They have."

"So, what would you sketch in New York? High rises? Taxis?" He chuckled. "Oh, I guess there's always Central Park."

She swallowed deep, embarrassed. "I haven't sketched in years. I . . . ah . . . kind of lost interest." *No. Mark told you, you were wasting your time.* "I'm pretty rusty, but I'm really enjoying myself," she said, casually, even though she knew it was so much more. She felt like she was coming back to life.

After lunch, her father dozed in his favorite chair, a book in his lap, his glasses perched on the end of his nose. Cassidy went on her daily walk, enjoying the sun and loving the landscape she had once thought ugly. Trees with branches tangled together, bark scared and weathered. A twisting stream that spilled over rocks, causing ripples in the crystal-clear surface. Small rock formations that rose out of nowhere, as if they'd been placed there by an unseen force. For so long, she had convinced herself Liberty was boring and vacant. But now, the calm and quiet seemed to be exactly what she needed.

Resting at the base of a tree, she took in the panoramic view around her and without warning, she started to cry. Out of nowhere, she just broke down, heavy sobs racking her body. With acres between her and her father, Cassidy let it all out. Unlike last night, she didn't need to muffle her anguish or choke back her sobs. She didn't need to pretend to be strong or in control. She was sure it was the pain in her shoulder that weakened her resolve, but she didn't care. She let her body rid itself of the emotional hurt and anger she'd been suppressing for years.

Losing track of time—something that happened quite often these days—she looked toward the hilltops and saw dusk settling in hues of amber and gold.

Time to get home.

Standing up, she brushed off her backside, and turned toward the house, surprised she had walked so far. She would need to hurry, or her father would worry.

She walked as quickly as possible but had to be careful to navigate the ruts and holes. When the warmth from the sun was replaced by a chilly breeze, she pulled her sweater snug around her, but it did little to ward off the cooler temperature.

As she crested a small knoll, she caught her breath, her insides fluttering. Backlit by the setting sun, she saw Wil, crossing the field, walking toward her with his head down. She felt nervous and surprisingly, a little excited to see him.

Why? All we do is bicker. He's a royal pain in my—

When he looked up, she stopped contemplating her feelings. He stood with his arms crossed against his chest, waiting as she approached.

"When did you get back?" she asked, when she was close enough to be heard.

"Just a little while ago. I came to see Joseph, and he sent me out to look for you."

"I went a little farther than I thought," she explained as she walked with her arms wrapped around her. When she reached Wil, he turned and fell in step beside her.

"It's chilly out. You must be cold in that little sweater."

"Just a little bit. I was enjoying the sunshine but forgot how quickly the temperature can change." She shivered slightly as she walked with her head down. When she felt something drop across her shoulders, she shrieked, letting it fall to the ground.

"What's wrong with you?" Wil shouted. "I was just trying to be nice." He stooped to pick up his jacket, but when he stood, their eyes met.

Cassidy quickly looked away, hoping to hide her tears, but it was too late.

"Hey, what's wrong?"

"It's nothing. Really." She smiled, trying to look stronger than she felt. "My shoulder is still bothering me a little. I was going to go to the clinic tomor—"

"Why didn't you tell me?" he interrupted. "I would've looked at it."

Cassidy started walking again, Wil in step beside her. "I didn't think it was that big of a deal, not until Saturday. I must have done something to aggravate it because now it hurts more than before."

"I'll look at it when we get to the house."

"It's not that big of—"

"I said, 'I'll look at it,' " he snapped, walking in determined strides, making it hard for her to keep up.

Out of breath by the time they reached the house, Cassidy climbed the front steps and followed Wil into the living room. He pointed to the couch.

"Sit down and take off your sweater."

She smiled. "You're going to have to buy me dinner, at the very least, before asking me to take off my clothes."

"Very funny," he said, not even slightly amused.

She carefully took off her sweater, then watched as Wil gently removed the yellow-stained gauze. "Dang it! Cassidy," he shouted, causing her to flinch. "Why didn't you tell me it had gotten this bad?"

"Because it wasn't *that* bad," she shouted back. "I told you, I must have aggravated it when—" Emotion swallowed her words, the pain too great to continue arguing. Wil must have realized how badly she hurt because he apologized and softened his tone.

"I'm going to go get my bag, okay? I'll be right back."

Cassidy nodded.

"What's going on in here?"

She looked up to see her dad leaning against the upstairs railing.

"Cassidy's got a bad infection," Wil answered. "I'm going to get my bag. I'll be right back."

Wil rushed out the front door while her fathered hurried downstairs. "You okay, Sunshine?" He sat next to her on the couch.

"I don't know what's worse, Dad, the pain or the humiliation. It wasn't this bad on Friday, or I would have had Wil look at it." Cassidy craned her neck as her father inspected her shoulder for himself.

Only seconds passed before Wil was back, medical bag in hand. He looked around the room, frustrated.

She watched him, then finally asked, "What's wrong?"

"I'm trying to figure out the best way to go about this."

"Go about what?"

"I need to irrigate the wound and flush out the infection. Something must be embedded in it for it to be so inflamed."

Cassidy didn't like the sound of that. "What exactly do you need to do?"

Wil sat beside Cassidy and looked her straight in the eye. "I'm not going to pull any punches, Cassidy. This is going to be painful. I can give you something for it, but even that is going to hurt. I know this is going to sound weird, but I think the kitchen table is the best place for me to work. You can lay down, and I'll have better light to see what I'm doing. And I won't have to worry about staining the couch or making a mess on the carpet."

She was going to be sick.

Remembering how much it hurt the first time he cleaned it made her stomach roll. And she knew this time was going to be ten times worse. She closed her eyes, taking deep even breaths.

"I can take you to the hospital, if you'd rather. You can be seen by a real doctor there instead of letting me do it."

She looked at Wil and saw the rejection in his eyes, thinking she didn't trust him.

"Will a doctor do it differently?" she asked.

"No. The only difference is the hospital table would be sterile, covered in white paper, while ours is oak covered in a gingham tablecloth." He smiled nervously.

Getting up, Cassidy saw Wil's shoulders sag in defeat, but when she turned toward the kitchen, he jumped to his feet.

"Joseph, can you get a pillow and a blanket?"

Her father hurried upstairs, while she walked into the kitchen, followed by Wil. She leaned against the table, feeling sick to her stomach. Her legs were like rubber, and her skin was clammy. She felt cold but was sweating at the same time.

"Hey," Wil leaned down so he could look her in the eye. "I know you're afraid, but I promise I'll be as gentle as I can." He stroked a tear off her cheek. "And if at any time you need me to stop, I will. Okay?"

Her head was swimming, the room spinning. And if that wasn't enough, Wil's gentle words and soft tone made her want to cry even more.

"Maybe we'd better just go to the hospital." Wil took a step back.

"No!" She reached out and touched his forearm. "I trust you, Wil, really I do."

"Are you sure?"

"I'm sure." She chanced a smile.

He placed a light kiss on her forehead and gave her good arm a reassuring squeeze before turning to the kitchen counter and opening his medical bag.

What was that for?

Cassidy was stunned by Wil's show of affection.

He just kissed me . . . like he'd been doing it for years.

She stared at him even though he was turned around.

Don't make a big thing out of it. He's only trying to put me at ease, that's all.

But she still found it very unsettling.

Joseph cleared the table of the salt & pepper shakers, napkin holder, and the small bouquet of wildflowers Cassidy had gotten in the habit of picking. Then, he vigorously wiped down the gingham tablecloth before placing a pillow at one end. Wil looked at Cassidy as she stood beside the table.

"I feel ridiculous climbing up on the table. The last time I did that, I was reaching for a cookie and got swatted."

"Well, I promise I won't give you a swat, but if you're a good patient, I'll give you a cookie."

Wil's levity was lost on Cassidy. She knew he was only teasing, but it wasn't helping.

She sat on the edge of the table, swung her legs around and lay back. The tablecloth bunched under her, so she wiggled and squirmed until it laid just so. With her head on the pillow, she turned to her dad. "I'm going to try really hard not to swear, but I can't make any promises."

He nodded, then pulled the blanket over her shaking body.

Wil scrubbed his hands over the sink, dried them, then pulled on blue latex gloves. When he leaned over her, he looked extremely serious and way too handsome.

"Okay, I'm going to give you a few shots to numb the area. I'm not going to kid you, it's going to hurt, and it won't completely deaden the area, but it will help."

"Okay."

Cassidy quickly turned her head and reached out for her father's hand. When she felt the first shot pierce the swollen area of her shoulder, she clenched her father's hand and squeezed her eyes shut. The second shot was less painful, and the third shot had only a pressure sensation. Cassidy felt a cool liquid flow over her shoulder, making her shudder. Opening her eyes, she looked at her dad. His head was bowed, his lips moving in silent prayer. She couldn't bring herself to watch what Wil was doing, so she closed her eyes once again and tried to take deep breaths as a stinging sensation was felt deep within her shoulder.

———— • ————

"Joseph, I'm going to need some washcloths or dish towels, something to absorb the liquid I use to flush out the infection."

He opened a drawer and handed Wil a stack of kitchen towels.

Wil folded a towel and tucked it up under Cassidy's shoulder, then smiled at her. "Okay, here we go."

He ripped open a small package containing a sterile scrub, and as gently as possible, cleaned the surface of the wound, removing the thin layer of crusted puss that covered it. When he poured antiseptic fluid to flush the wound, Cassidy flinched, sucking in a breath, and curling her lips together.

"Sorry. Do you need me to stop?" he asked.

She just shook her head and closed her eyes.

He repeated the process several times, tossing towel after saturated towel into the sink, until the wound was bright red, and he was sure he'd gotten all the infection.

But he still needed to find the cause of it.

Using his pen light, Wil shined it on the fleshy wound. He used fine tipped tweezers to root around, hating each time Cassidy winced or flinched with pain. Moving a little closer, he saw something foreign. Pressing the tweezers together, he pulled back, only to come up empty.

"Okay, Cassidy, I see what I'm looking for. Hang in there. I'm almost done."

Wil dug a little deeper, feeling Cassidy's body tense even more. He pinched the tweezers together but lost his hold on the deeply embedded splinter. He took a deep breath and tried again.

Cassidy groaned. "I don't know how much more I can take."

"Breathe, Cassidy. I've almost got it. I don't want to lose my position now. It . . . is . . . right . . . there."

She started to shake.

"Hang on, Sunshine. He's almost done."

Wil knew Cassidy was at her breaking point, but he was so close. Pressing deeper, he surrounded the splinter and squeezed the tweezers together, then pulled them out. Staring at the bloody little tongs with the sliver of wood grasped between them, he sighed with relief, "Got it!"

Cassidy turned, took one look, and passed out cold.

TWENTY

"Cassidy . . . Cassidy, wake up." Wil spoke softly as he mopped her brow with a cool washcloth. "Come on, Cassidy, open your eyes."

She opened her eyes but was having a hard time focusing. "Are you done?"

"Yep. It's all bandaged and ready to go. You'll need to take it easy for a few days, and I'll change your bandage at night, but we should see improvement as early as tomorrow."

She rolled to one side and tried pushing herself up to a sitting position.

"Here, let me help." Wil stood alongside the table and assisted her to a sitting position.

"Did I swear?"

He laughed. "No. You were a good girl."

"When will the dizziness go away?" Cassidy asked, before closing her eyes and planting her head in the center of his chest.

Joseph looked on with concern. "Is this normal, Wil?"

He chuckled, "Not exactly normal, but she'll be fine. She's just exhibiting a hypersensitivity to the medication I used. She should feel it wearing off within the hour." He turned back to Cassidy. "Come on, let me help you to bed."

Her head rolled back. "No. I'm okay."

Wil laughed. "You're not okay. You would fall flat on your face if I wasn't standing in front of you. Come on. I'll help you."

"No, just help me to the couch. I'm fine really. I just feel a little wobbly."

With his arm securely around her waist, Wil helped a shaky Cassidy to the living room. He lowered her to the couch and brought her feet up to rest on the cushions. He pulled off her shoes, then watched as she closed her eyes. Soon her breathing was slow and steady.

113

Staring at Cassidy, Wil felt his heart racing and an ache travel through his body. The feelings he felt for her were wrong. Dead wrong. She was vulnerable and still legally married. She was in no condition to start a new relationship. And as for him, it would be spiritually crippling to pursue a relationship with Cassidy, knowing she had no desire to open her heart to God. No . . . the most he could do for her is pray and be her friend. Maybe in time she would stop running from God.

Wil went to the kitchen and cleaned up the paper wrappers on the floor and the instruments on the table. He was sterilizing his equipment when Joseph joined him in the kitchen and reached for a mug from the cupboard.

"How about a cup of coffee, Wil?"

"Sure."

When Wil finished what he was doing, Joseph set a cup of coffee on the counter in front of him. They stood and drank in silence, Wil's thoughts and emotions spinning out of control.

"You don't need to feel guilty, Wil."

He looked at Joseph. *Can he really tell what I'm thinking? Are my feelings for Cassidy that obvious?*

"She'll understand," Joseph continued. "You had to do what you had to do. She'll recover."

Wil realized Joseph thought his guilt came from the pain he had caused Cassidy, not the fact that he was looking at her in a whole new light. He didn't answer Joseph. He was too busy chastising himself for not keeping his feelings in check.

His entire adult life he prided himself on not being swayed by the physical. He had received a lot of female attention in college once he out grew his awkward stage, and his roommate was always encouraging him to experiment with what life had to offer, but Wil stood firm. He wanted to be an example to his friends in college. He wanted his commitment to God to be what people remembered about him.

But now . . . now Wil found himself drawn to Cassidy, like a moth to a flame. She exuded a sensuality that captivated him and a vulnerability that made him want to wrap her in his arms and protect her from the pain and disappointment of this world.

It's physical. That's all it is. We have no common ground. Not where it matters most.

"Wil!"

He looked up, realizing Joseph was talking to him.

"I'm sorry, what did you say?"

"The conference . . . how'd it go?"

"It was interesting, a lot of great information."

Wil had also done a lot of thinking about his career and his future at the conference. In fact, that was the reason he had come to see Joseph in the first place, before getting sidetracked with Cassidy's injury.

"Joseph, I wanted to talk to you about a few ideas I had regarding my future."

"You're leaving, aren't you?" Joseph sighed. "I knew this arrangement was only temporary when you moved here, but after a few years, I thought you had settled in and decided to stay."

"It's been great, Joseph, really. I've enjoyed our time together immensely, but if I'm ever going to expand my practice, I need a real office; some place where people can come to me. I don't mind doing house calls for horses and cattle, but I'm driving clear across town to check out a cat's infected eye or a pup with a burr in its paw. I could get more done and be more available if people brought their smaller pets to me."

Wil paused and waited for a reaction from Joseph. He finally lifted his head and asked, "You gonna move to town too?"

"I'm thinking so. The old hardware store is up for sale. It's right in the middle of town, a great location, a lot of floor space, and it has an apartment upstairs."

"That place doesn't suit you, Wil. It's sandwiched between two other buildings. You always said you needed your space, that you belonged in the outdoors. You can't move to the middle of town and hold up in that old building. It's not right."

"That's what you said when I asked to use the old homestead. You said it wasn't good enough for a barn owl and look what I've done with it. I can do the same thing with the hardware store. It will just take a little more time. Besides, Cassidy's going to need a place to stay. She likes what I've done with the place, and it will keep her close to home."

"Is that what this is all about? You want to give up your place, so Cassidy has somewhere to live? Well, it's not necessary. She's doing just fine with me."

"Come on, Joseph, you can't expect her to live in her childhood bedroom the rest of her life. She's not a little girl anymore. She's going to get antsy and want her own space."

"She hasn't complained about it yet, and Lord knows she

speaks her mind when things aren't to her liking."

"You're just being stubborn, Joseph, and you know it. Cassidy might not be complaining about the living arrangements right now, but that's only because she's hurting and doesn't want to be alone. But sooner or later, she's going to feel stronger and want her independence. When that happens, you can bet she—"

"I can hear you, you know," Cassidy shouted from the other room. "If you're going to talk about me, I'd appreciate it if you did it in front of me where I can defend myself. That is, if you haven't already decided my future for me."

Wil and Joseph looked at each other, knowing they'd been caught speaking out of turn. Walking into the living room, they each sat in the wing chairs by the fireplace. Cassidy lay on the couch, looking pale, but the flash in her eyes proved she was very much awake.

"So, what's the big pow-wow about?"

"I'm thinking about moving to town," Wil volunteered.

"Why move to town when you fixed up your place so nice?"

"Because I need an office, and I found a place in town that's perfect. It even has an upstairs apartment. It's exactly what I need. It wouldn't be ready for a while, but when it's done, you could have my place."

"I don't get it. You're already so busy with house calls and patients, why set up shop where even more people can bother you? Don't you realize, the minute they know you live upstairs, they'll be calling you in the middle of the night and all hours of the day? You'll never have time off or time to yourself. Sounds like you're setting yourself up for more than you can handle. I wouldn't do it if I were you."

Cassidy's condescending attitude angered Wil. She acted as if she had a say in what he did with his life.

"Well, you know what, Cassidy, I wasn't asking for your advice or your opinion." He got up and crossed the room, setting his coffee cup on the kitchen counter. Picking up his bag, he walked toward the front door.

"You know what's wrong with you, Cassidy? You know nothing about being part of a community. Sure, you had your circle of friends in New York, but where are they now? Nowhere to be found because they weren't real friends to begin with. They were people who fed off you. What you could give them. Your status. Your position. And you're guilty of doing the same thing. You see people as a waste of time, unless they have something to offer you.

"I, on the other hand, love being part of a community. I appreciate the company and the friendship it brings. I enjoy providing a service to people and helping them when they're in need. I don't expect riches in return, sometimes just a firm handshake from a farmer or the smile in a child's eyes is enough. But I'm sure you can't understand that. It's nothing you can measure on the NASDAQ or attach a dollar sign to."

Wil turned to Joseph. "I'll be headed into town tomorrow to make an offer on the property. I'll let you know how things go."

———— • ————

Cassidy jolted when Wil slammed the door. When she turned to her father, she saw a disappointing look on his face.

"I'm sorry. I was just speaking the obvious." Cassidy rested her head back on the pillow. "He's just too big-hearted for his own good. He has no idea that people are taking advantage of him. Wait until he gets bothered in the middle of dinner, or the middle of the night, or when he tries to take some time off. He'll see. He'll see I was right, and he was wrong. When will he learn—"

"No Cassidy!" Her father barked. "When will you learn?"

She was shocked. Her father never used to raise his voice to her, and now it seemed to happen all too often. He jumped up from where he was sitting, his face crimson.

"Cassidy, the whole world is not as you see it. The crowd you ran with in New York does not represent the people of Liberty. Wil is not the naïve farm boy from your youth. He's a man who has suffered a great deal and is stronger because of it. He knows what he's doing and will make sound judgments for his future. I knew it was only temporary when he moved onto the ranch. I knew he would have his own office one day. I also knew I would dread seeing him go."

He stopped a moment, as if reflecting on the last few years.

"Wil has been like a son to me. He took care of me last year when I had pneumonia and three years ago when I broke my leg."

He turned to her, the fire back in his eyes.

"I will not have you disrespecting him like that, especially when he's looking out for your best interest too. If he leaves, you'll have a place of your own. He thinks you need your space and shouldn't have to live with me. It took him three years to fix up the homestead, and now he's willing to walk away from it so you can have your own place."

"I didn't ask him to do that." Cassidy lashed back.

"You're right, Cassidy. You didn't. But that's the difference between you and Wil. He's willing to sacrifice for others while you only think of yourself, and you know what? I blame myself. After your mother died, you changed. I told myself it was just a phase, that you were hurt and angry. I thought if I showed you love and patience, used kind words and a gentle attitude you would come back around. But I was wrong. I allowed you to become ill-tempered and self-centered. And look what it's done to you.

"Your mother would be heartbroken."

———— • ————

Cassidy couldn't sleep.

She tossed and turned all night, trying to shake off her father's wounding words, but they lingered in her mind, prodding her like a hot branding iron.

Her dad had never spoken to her with such anger. Discipline maybe, but never anger. And the worst part was, he had chosen to defend Wil over her. Wil held a higher position than she did in her father's life. She was the daughter he always had to pray for, the screw-up, the wayward child. But Wil . . . Wil was the golden boy, the good child, the son he never had.

I didn't even know he had broken his leg or suffered from pneumonia. What else don't I know about?

She had missed so much by being away, by cutting off communication between them. It was her own fault she felt like an outsider. She had walked out on her dad, leaving the door wide open for someone else to walk in. Wil had picked up where she had left off and treated her father better than she did.

Wil shouldn't have to leave because of me. He deserves to be here.

Cassidy debated long into the night, finally admitting to herself, she was an outcast who desperately wanted back in. She wanted things to change. She wanted to be there for her father, repair their relationship, be someone he could count on. She needed to put her resentment toward Wil behind her and earn her father's respect.

However, her sharp tongue and quick temper was not the way to go about it.

First thing in the morning, she would apologize to her dad, then do everything in her power to restore their relationship. One she had long ignored.

TWENTY-ONE

The next morning, Cassidy got up early, dressed, and headed to the stables. She was done with most of the feeding before her dad appeared. When he did, she couldn't hold back the tears. She walked over to where he stood and without saying a word, fell into his arms. She sobbed as he stroked her back, held her tight, and hushed her cries.

"What's this all about, Sunshine?"

"I'm sorry, Dad. I'm so sorry for everything. I know I'm not the person you want me to be, but I want to change that. I want to make you proud of me. I don't ever want to give you a reason to yell at me again."

She stepped back and brushed at her tears.

"Please don't give up on me, yet. I love you so much. I know I haven't said it often enough, or shown it lately, but I really do love you."

She fell into his arms again.

"I don't know what I would do without you."

Joseph strained to make out Cassidy's muffled words. She spoke into his chest, but it went straight through to his heart. He rocked her like he did when she was a little girl and held her tight as his own tears fell into hair. "I love you too, Cassidy. More than you'll ever know."

Holding up her head, she looked into his eyes and smiled. Joseph kissed the tip of her nose and gave her another tender squeeze.

"I'm finished out here," Cassidy said in a scratchy voice, wiping tears from her face. "How does breakfast sound?"

"Wonderful." Joseph grinned wide as he wrapped his arm around his daughter and walked back to the house. Internally, he praised

God and prayed for Cassidy. She still had a long road ahead of her. But he knew, if she reached out to the Lord, she would find in Him a firm foundation.

One that would grow over time.

———— • ————

Wil walked toward the old hardware store, excitement fueling his steps. This felt right. Something he'd wanted to do for years. Having Cassidy back, someone on the ranch to look after Joseph, was just the push he needed.

As he approached the old downtown building, he saw a woman get out of her car and step up onto the curb. She was attractive. Tall. Long legs. Red hair. Fitted blazer, trim skirt.

And a smile that triggered warning bells.

"Hi, I'm Ella," she said as she extended her hand. "We spoke on the phone."

"Wil Marsh. Thank you for meeting me here."

She smiled. "My pleasure. I was glad to do it, especially for a bona-fide hero."

"Excuse me?"

"My niece has been singing your praises for weeks. Her kitty, Polka Dot, was nipped by a horse, and you came and 'rescued her.' Sarah's words. She ranks you somewhere between Doc McStuffins and Paw Patrol."

Wil chuckled. "I remember. White cat with black spots. It wasn't that serious. Probably more traumatic for Sarah than her kitty. But I know how important it is for a little girl to have something to cuddle at night."

"Big girls need something too," Ella said seductively. "I guess I'll have to get me a kitten."

Wil chose not to respond. He knew a come-on when he heard one and didn't want to encourage her further.

Ella unlocked the door, and they both stepped inside the old hardware store. Once his eyes adjusted to the dark interior, Wil scanned from one side of the building to the other.

A blank canvas. Perfect!

"It's a lot bigger than I expected."

She smiled. "Three thousand square feet."

Immediately, he started visualizing how he would section off the open space. A reception area. Four maybe six exam rooms. A supply closet. Surgery room. An office for him. Maybe even—

"Wil . . . would you like to see the upstairs?" Ella asked.

He'd obviously checked out, his mind reeling with ideas.

"Sure. Lead the way."

Slowly, Ella eased up the stairs, her hips swaying a little more than necessary. Wil made sure there was a healthy distance between them before climbing the stairs. When he reached the top, one expansive room stood before him. The living area was spacious with three narrow rectangular windows overlooking Main Street. The kitchen was open to the rest of the room and definitely in need of repairs, and there was a large dining area where an old table and three rickety chairs still stood. He loved the openness of the area, but soon realized there was no place for a bedroom, or a bathroom for that matter.

"Isn't there a bathroom?"

"Yes, on the third floor," she said with a grin.

"Third floor?"

"Surprising, isn't it? The property is quite deceiving from the outside." She opened what looked to be a pantry cupboard, only to reveal an enclosed staircase. Once again, Wil waited before climbing the stair behind her.

When he reached the landing, he was amazed. The room was huge, even though a section was closed off for the bathroom. He walked across the hardwood floors, to the closed door and looked inside. Cracked mirror. Rusty fixtures. Moldy shower. "Okay, so this will be a gut job."

"Yes, the kitchen and bathroom are in rough shape and will need to be completely renovated, but you have to admit, the building offers more than you expected." Ella walked to the far side of the room and looked out the windows. "And the view is great."

"You're right." He joined her, glancing down at Main Street. "The rest of the building is in good shape. The floors just need to be sanded and stained. The beams look solid. But I think I would replace these windows, make them bigger. Bring in more light."

"Well, you don't want the windows to be too big. This is a bedroom after all." Ella moved closer to him. "You'll want to protect your privacy."

It was obvious Ella was letting him know she was available and interested, but her seductive overtones had the complete opposite effect on him. She was a beautiful woman, there was no denying that, but her forward personality was very unattractive. Besides, his mind was focused on business.

"I'm definitely interested."

Ella's eyebrow arch and her smile deepened.

Immediately, Wil realized his mistake. "In the property. I'm interested in the property and would like to make an offer."

Her smile faded slightly, but only for a moment. "Wonderful! Let's go to my office and write it up. Then we can celebrate over lunch."

"Actually, I have a noon appointment. Maybe some other time."

She stared at him. No, more like she stared *through* him. "Later then. I'll hold you to it."

Wil followed Ella to the second level, took another look around, then to the ground floor. He was brimming with ideas, plans, energy. He knew this was right. It would take some time to fix it up, but when he was through, it would be the perfect office space and a place he could call home.

Wil met Ella at her office and filled out the necessary paperwork. She continued her flirting, working their future date into the conversation whenever she could, but he politely steered clear, keeping their conversation on business.

Heading home, Wil could not wait to share his news with Joseph. It would be hard to leave the ranch and the man who was like a father to him. But it was the right thing to do. The timing was perfect. Cassidy was home. And even though she wasn't necessarily happy about it, she needed some space to get her life back on track and time to rebuild the bond between father and daughter.

TWENTY-TWO

Cassidy was seeing life through new eyes. She walked around the house, the barn, the yard, feeling different, looking toward the future. It was time to move on. She needed to put the hurt and pain from her past behind her.

The loss of her mother.

Mark's abuse and betrayal.

They had each carved out a piece of her heart. But she had to move forward. Remember the good, let go of the bad. It was time to get reacquainted with her dad and the life he had made for himself in her absence.

After morning chores, breakfast, and some sketching, she made lunch for her and her dad. He said grace, then asked about her sketches, like he used to do, wanting to know when he was going to get to see them. Cassidy wasn't ready to show anyone her work yet, knowing her technique was still pretty rough. So, she just shrugged and changed the subject.

When they were done with lunch, she gathered the dishes, put the leftovers back in the refrigerator, and ran some water in the sink.

"Okay, sweetheart, I think I'll head on out, see if I can get another section of fence repaired," her father said before swallowing the last of his iced tea.

"Hey, Dad, just curious . . . did Wil say what time he would be back?"

"Nope. Just that he was going to look at the old hardware store. Why?"

She twisted the dish towel in her hand. "Because I should probably apologize for what I said yesterday, about people taking advantage of him. I mean, it's true. People *are* going to take advantage of him. But that's up to him to deal with. It's none of my business. And I feel bad I wasn't more enthusiastic about his plans."

"Joseph!"

Cassidy jumped as Wil's voice boomed from across the living room.

"Lands sake, boy, what's gotten into you?" Joseph chuckled when Wil burst into the kitchen.

"It's perfect! The hardware store is absolutely perfect! I made an offer a little lower than the asking price, but Ella didn't think it would be a problem since the owner is very interested in getting the place sold. Ella said she would contact the seller right away with my offer. She was sure they would accept it."

Cassidy heard only one word. "Who is Ella?" she asked, trying not to sound too interested.

"She's the real estate agent I'm working with." Wil turned back to Joseph. "It's going to need a lot of fixing up, but it has good bones. Did you know it has a third floor?"

"I didn't, but that makes sense. The few times I was upstairs with Russ, I never saw more than a kitchen and a living room."

"Yeah, there's a third floor with a huge bedroom and bathroom. The bathroom is a complete gut job, so is the kitchen. And the downstairs is entirely open, so I'll be starting from scratch, but that's fine. I'll get to design it the way I want. I won't have to work around existing walls or floor plans."

It was the most animated Cassidy had ever seen Wil. He strutted across the kitchen, waving his hands around as he explained his ideas.

"Ella suggested a few contractors she thought would be good for the job. Of course . . ."

There's that name again. Cassidy tuned out Wil, wondering who this *Ella* person was, and why he was putting such stock into what she said.

"What's that look for?"

Cassidy looked up and realized Wil was talking to her.

"What? Nothing. I was just thinking it sounds like a lot of work." Cassidy tried to sound nonchalant.

I'm doing it again. Why should I care if it sounds like a lot of work? Like he said last night, he isn't asking my opinion or my permission. If it's what he wants to do, he should go for it.

"It is going to be a lot of work, but so worth it. I'll have my own place, designed the way I want it. But don't think you're going to get rid of me anytime soon. I'll be starting from scratch and still working. I plan on finishing the upstairs first, so I can move in. Then, work can start on the downstairs." Wil stopped what he was saying to answer his phone.

"Really? Already? That's great, Ella. Thanks for handling things so quickly." He looked at Cassidy then turned slightly, whispering into his phone, but she could still make out what he was saying. And if her instincts were correct, Ella was on the prowl, trying to secure a dinner date with Wil while he diplomatically declined.

Wil quickly pocketed his phone. "My offer was accepted. If everything goes smoothly, it will be mine in a couple weeks."

"How nice of her to get back to you so quickly," Cassidy poked. "It's a shame you can't take her up on her dinner invitation."

Wil looked at Cassidy, and she could feel a lecture coming on about being so nosy, but he took a beat, then turned to her dad.

"I have a couple of appointments this afternoon, and then I really need to start making some plans. I'll see you guys later." Wil went to leave but was only half way to the front door when he turned around and said, "I'll be back to change your bandage later this evening."

"Well, don't let me interrupt your plans. I can take care of myself."

"Oh, no you don't. You screwed up my handy work once already. This time I'm not taking any chances. I'll see you later tonight."

"I'm a grown woman," Cassidy grumbled as he closed the door. "I can take care of myself."

"He was only teasing with you, Cassidy." Her dad smiled as he headed for the door.

"He's just so smug all the time. I don't need him scolding me whenever we talk. I am an adult, you know."

"Oh, come on honey, that's just his way. Wil is not going to come right out and say it, but he cares about you." He placed his hat on his head and looked at Cassidy with a raised brow.

"Right. He cares for me like he would a thorn in his side."

"That's not true and you know it."

He closed the door behind him as Cassidy headed for the stairs, mumbling and carrying on a one-sided conversation. "It is to true. The only reason he's even nice to me is out of respect for you. I don't care. I mean I'm glad he's been here, but now that I'm home it's time for him to move on."

Cassidy knew she was speaking only to herself, but she said it anyway. Wil had obviously been a lot of help in her absence, and it was evident how much her dad enjoyed his company. Even so, Wil leaving the ranch would be a good thing. It would give her and her dad more time to bond without outside interference.

TWENTY-THREE

Wil drove home ecstatic with the news. He was finally going to have his own place *and* an amazing office space. Even so, when he walked in the front door of his place, he stopped and looked at all he was giving up.

He had taken the old rickety homestead and turned it into a very comfortable home. He gazed around in a melancholy kind of way and then shook it off. Yes, he would miss the rugged fireplace and the original log walls, but his new place could be everything this place was and more.

Taking the stairs two at a time, he sat at his desk, pulled out a notepad, and started making a list of the equipment he would need for each exam room and his office. Stopping, he switched gears and began writing down the materials and tools he would need to fix up the living area. Then he realized he needed to take yet another step back. He couldn't do anything without measurements.

Reaching in his back pocket for his phone, he scrolled his contacts, then dialed.

"Hi, Ella, it's Wil."

"Wil, what a nice surprise."

He heard the overly friendly tone in her voice and wondered if it was wise to ask her for a favor. She was a nice person, and very good-looking, but he didn't feel an attraction for her, and didn't want to give her the wrong idea.

"Is this business related? Or did you reconsider my dinner invitation?"

"Actually, I was wondering if you could meet me at the hardware store, so I can take some measurements? I'm anxious to get started with the design plans."

"Tell you what, I have one more appointment this afternoon at three o'clock. How about if I go home and change, then meet you at the store around four. I'll help you with the measurements."

"That's not necessary. I'm sure you have more important things to do."

"Not at all. Besides you'll need someone to hold the other end of the measuring tape if you're going to get accurate measurements."

Wil realized she was right. He would need a second pair of hands to do the job right. "Okay, I appreciate the offer. I'll meet you there at four o'clock."

"Actually, would it be too big of an imposition if you picked me up at my place? My car's making some odd sounds, and I can't get it into the shop until Thursday."

"Sure." He jotted down her address. "See you at four."

Wil hung up the phone, wondering if he made a mistake accepting Ella's help? Sure, he needed it, but he also knew any attention he showed her might be misconstrued as interest on his part.

Don't make a big deal out of it. She's probably helpful to all her clients. It's part of her job.

———— • ————

Wil made a few house calls on his way into town. When he pulled up in front of Ella's place, it was a little before four. Her car wasn't in the driveway, so he double-checked the address he'd plugged into his phone. Just as he did, Ella pulled up to her garage and quickly walked around the back of her car. Wil stepped out of his truck and walked to the curb.

"I'm so sorry; I'm running a little late. Come on in. I'll only be a moment."

Swinging her purse over her shoulder, and with her briefcase in her other hand, Ella dashed up the front steps of her quaint ranch-style home. She left the front door open for Wil, so he followed her in and stood in the living room.

"I'm just going to take a quick shower, then I'll be right out." She said as she kicked off her high heels and hurried down the hall.

Wil looked around the modest living room. From the high-gloss hardwood floors to the white beadboard trim, the room looked like a picture out of a design magazine. There were fresh flowers on the coffee table and another bouquet on the large dining room table. Built-in shelves in the living room held beautiful old books and what looked like personal mementos. Wil glanced at the framed pictures. Ella holding a sold sign. *Probably her first sell as an agent.* Poolside in a bikini. With a man at a bar, drinks in their hands. Standing with another man near a lake. But there were other photos of just a man. He glanced at them, then took a double take.

Is that Derrick Edwards?

He studied one of the pictures closer, realizing it was his nemesis from high school. Edwards had been a real jerk back in the day, but not just to him. Drinking, carousing, and partying with a different girl every week had earned him the nickname *One and Done Derrick.*

Just seeing his image brought back horrible memories for Wil. Derrick had taunted him on a weekly basis and made him the victim of most of his pranks and jokes. Derrick had been bad news, and his run-ins with the school advisors and local police had been a weekly occurrence.

No wondered he ended up how he did.

Wil looked at another picture of Derrick with his arm around an underclassman. One of the nerdy girls, who hung out in the back of the library. Definitely not Derrick's type. Then he put it together. It was a picture of a younger Ella. *Wow, has she changed!* Gone were the glasses, braces, and all-around awkward teenager. She was almost unrecognizable.

But what would a guy like Derrick want with a girl like Ella?

Wil sighed. *Maybe that explains her flirtatious personality. It's her way of getting attention.* If Wil had to wager a guess, Derrick probably used her for cheap entertainment, and Ella consented so she'd be accepted. He hated the thought of her—or any girl for that matter—being taken advantage of.

Wil heard the shower water stop as he continued to look at the pictures with both interest and irritation. Ella walked into the room wearing a pair of white denim cut-off shorts and a fuchsia tank top, the bright color complementing her bronzy skin.

She looked at the bookshelf and sighed, "So, now you know my secret."

"Secret?" Wil said, puzzled.

"You still don't recognize me, do you?"

He shrugged. "I figured it was you in the picture." He pointed to the one with Derrick.

"Yep. That was me. Chubby. Four-eyes. Acne. Luckily, I've

changed since then." She smiled as she smoothed her hands over her hips. "Even my name. I always hated it. Eleanor sounds like a crippled old lady."

"Eleanor! Yes! Now I remember," Wil said, finally putting the pieces together.

"Yep . . . that's me. Eleanor smellanor. Eleanor the elephant." She looped her arm around his and gave it a squeeze. "You see, Wil, we really do have a lot in common. We were both shy and awkward in high school but look at us now. We're successful, independent, and a lot more put together."

Wil slipped his arm from hers and pointed at a picture. "But what were you doing with Derrick Edwards?"

"That's right." She crossed her arms across her chest, looking a little irritated. "You *would* remember Derrick."

"Yes. But unfortunately, our relationship wasn't based on friendship."

"Yeah, I know. He did some pretty awful things to you. I never did understand how he could be so cruel. But none of us realized the demons he was dealing with in his head."

"Well, the demons won." Wil thought back a few years ago to a newspaper article explaining Derrick's suicide. "I guess he won't be harassing anyone anymore."

"Yeah. I guess not." Ella sighed, then walked down the hall.

When she returned to the living room, her hair brushed, sandals in her hands, Wil realized she was strangely quiet.

She slipped on her sandals and a thin little sweater, then grabbed her purse and smiled. "Ready?"

"Sure, but aren't you going to be cold? I know we've been having warmer weather than usual, but by the time we're done it's going to be chilly."

"I'll be fine. Until I see snow on the ground, I'm a shorts and sandals kind of girl."

"Okay. Whatever you say." Wil walked behind Ella as they headed to his truck. He couldn't help but notice how attractive she looked with her long, sculpted legs and her almost too short, shorts. But his mind was on the abrupt way she ended their conversation regarding Derrick. He could only imagine why.

After opening the truck door for her, he jogged around to the driver's side and got in. "I'm sorry if I said something to offend you. I mean, it's no secret Derrick was a bully in school, but I should have kept my comments to myself. It's obvious you had some kind of a relationship with him. I just never remember seeing you two with each other in school."

"That's because we *weren't* together in school. Heaven-for-bid the popular senior be seen with the fatty sophomore. That would have ruined his reputation. No, not many people knew we were brother and sister. It would have ruined his image."

"What? Derrick was your *brother*?" Wil was shocked.

"Well, step-brother. But he was all I had. And even though he was mean and rude and bullied others, he wasn't like that to me. When he was away from his friends, he wasn't at all the person people thought he was. He talked to me all the time about how disappointed he was with life. He felt he had ruined his at a young age. Addicted to drugs. Alcohol abuse. Adults didn't trust him. Cops hated him. But girls loved his bad-boy image. They became an addiction, just like the drugs.

"He used girls for his own pleasure but was disgusted with them at the same time. He felt if girls were willing to throw themselves at him, they got what they deserved." Ella looked at Wil, then looked away. "At times he would become violent. More than once, I walked in on him slapping around a girlfriend who wouldn't perform to his satisfaction. He was lucky none of the girls pressed charges. Of course, they knew it would be worse for them if their parents found out they were with the town delinquent."

"What about your parents? Did they know what was going on?"

"They were either too stoned or too drunk to care. Most times, they didn't know where Derrick was or what he was doing. The couple of times the cops dragged him home, my mom acted horrified, and his dad rattled off the punishments and restrictions they were going to put on him. But as soon as the cops left, they'd go back to their drinking or smoking. The next morning, they wouldn't remember a thing.

"My mom was too passive, and my stepdad was a chauvinist. Mom wouldn't interfere with his disciplinary measures, and Derrick unfortunately learned how to treat women from his father's example."

Ella looked at Wil with haunted eyes.

"Derrick hated his life but didn't have the strength to overcome it. When he found out he had AIDS, he shot himself. He left a note saying he was too big of a coward to go through the pain and torment of life as a leper."

A silent tear ran down Ella's cheek.

"My niece, Sarah, was a product of his lifestyle. Amy has turned out to be a pretty good single mom, and so far, Sarah and Amy haven't tested positive for the virus. It terrifies me to think what Sarah will do when she finds out the truth about her father."

Wil didn't know what to say. Unexpectedly, the flirty Ella had exposed the not-so-happy life she had grown up with. All he could do was apologize. "I'm sorry, Ella. I had no idea. I don't know what else to say."

"That's okay, you didn't know. Most people didn't. Besides, I'm the one who should be apologizing for putting such a damper on what should be an exciting day for you." She smiled, flipping a switch on the conversation. "So, tell me what you're planning for the place."

Wil took the hint and changed the subject. By the time they pulled up to the curb outside the hardware store, he'd given her the basic outline of his plans. While he unloaded the ladder from the back of his truck, and grabbed the other supplies he'd brought with him, Ella unlocked the front door and let them in.

"Now you're sure it's okay we're in here, right?" Wil asked as he put the supplies down on the floor.

"We're fine. I talked to the owner, and he said as long as you didn't start working on the place before escrow closes, he didn't care if you were in here. So, where do you want to start?"

"Let's get the dimensions of the full room. I know what the paperwork says, but I think I would like to measure it for myself. I don't want to have all my plans finalized, to find out the original measurements were off."

"Whatever you say. I'm at your disposal."

There was that smile again. Was Ella really just wanting to help, or was there something more to it? Wil tried to relax and take her help at face value, but a part of him knew he'd better stay on his toes.

After taking every conceivable measurement of the downstairs, Wil explained to Ella how he visualized the space.

"It sounds like you know exactly what you want, but it also sounds pretty expensive. You could always start with just two exam rooms and then add more as they're needed?"

"No, I want to do at least four to begin with. I always thought it was ridiculous to walk into a veterinary clinic with a small waiting room filled with every animal imaginable. Between the barking and hissing, and birds going crazy, pets are all strung out before the vet even gets a chance to see them. No, I want to have a small reception area and use the extra space for exam rooms— rooms where people with appointments can wait for their time slot. In fact, I'm leaving room to expand to six, in case I need more."

"You sound like you plan on being in Liberty for a while." Ella said as she stepped closer to him.

"I don't have any plans of leaving, if that's what you're asking. Of course, that's up to the Lord. If He leads me somewhere else, so be it, but for now this is home."

Wil scribbled some notes. Drew rough sketches. Double-checked measurements. He scanned the room, adding notations where needed. And each time he did, he caught Ella staring at him. Whenever their eyes met, she just smiled.

Upstairs, they repeated everything again, taking every possible measurement. Then he set his sights on the kitchen, envisioning his plans. "I'm thinking stainless steel appliances and black granite counter tops."

"Oooh, I love the industrial look," Ella said. "Sleek. Modern."

"Not too modern," he corrected. "I'll warm it up with cherry wood cabinetry or maybe reclaimed wood. Since I want an open concept between the kitchen and living room, it needs to feel warm and comfortable, not cold and medicinal."

"Oh, I agree. A kitchen should be warm and inviting, just like the living room," she said, sounding a little *too* agreeable.

When they moved to the third floor, he looked around with a heavy sigh. "This is where the real work will begin. I want to start here so I can move in as soon as possible."

"You plan on living here through the renovations?" Ella asked, sounding a little surprised. "Don't you think that will drive you crazy? All the noise, and dust, and . . . stuff everywhere?"

"Not really. Besides, I plan on doing a lot of the work myself. I just need a contractor for the bigger things, like wiring, and plumbing, and permits if necessary."

She shrugged like she didn't agree. "So, do you need me to list your old place?"

"No. It's actually not mine. I mean it is, but not really."

She laughed. "Well, that explains it."

He smiled, realizing he wasn't making any sense. "What I meant was, I live on Joseph Martin's property. I renovated the old homestead into a small cottage. After he saw the work I put into it, he said it was mine to keep, but I never had any intentions of holding onto it long term. And now with his daughter back in Liberty, it will be a nice place to pass on to her."

"Ah, yes, the talented Cassidy Martin. I guess her art career didn't take off like she had hoped."

Hearing a tinge of satisfaction in Ella's tone, Wil immediately came to Cassidy's defense. "She *is* talented. She just got sidetracked while living in New York."

"Oh, that's right. I heard she was in the middle of a messy divorce."

His jaw tightened. "Your rumor mill is a little off base, Ella. Cassidy's divorce isn't messy. Her husband cheated on her, so she left him and came home to be with her father. End of story."

Realizing he had snapped at Ella, Wil dropped the subject and turned his attention to the dilapidated bathroom. Looking at the rotted-out shower stall, a pedestal sink that had seen better days, and a toilet with a missing seat and tank lid, he envisioned what he could do with the place.

Ella wiggled through the doorway, brushing up against him. "So, what do you have planned for in here?"

"Well, first I'm going to blow out that wall and extend the place by about four feet. Then, I'll install a large whirlpool tub *and* stand-up shower. Over there," he pointed to the wall opposite them, "I'll replace the sink with a vanity that has plenty of countertop space. And over here," he stepped to where the toilet currently sat, "I'll enclose this area and make it a separate toilet room."

"Sounds amazing. Maybe you missed your calling and should be an interior designer instead of a vet."

"Nope." He shook his head. "I like what I'm doing. Working with animals suits me just fine."

After Wil finished explaining his vision for the bathroom, they got to work measuring the bedroom space. Side to side. Corner to corner. Ella gave her opinion on what she would do, and Wil politely listened. Standing in front of the small dormer-style windows, he studied the area, stepped back from the windows, then stood in front of them and turned to the rest of the room. "These really need to be bigger. I can add shutters for privacy if I need to, but I want to make sure there is plenty of natural light. If I'm going to be inside all day, I need to make sure my bedroom doesn't feel like a cave."

Wil set the ladder in place next to the windows, but before he could move, Ella began to climb the rungs. "Here, I'll hold the measuring tape for you." As she stretched toward the ceiling, Wil got an eyeful of legs, abs, and a little more when her short-shorts rode up. Convinced it was intentional, he turned away, irritated she would be so bold. Pulling on the measuring tape, he squatted down next to the wall, jotted the measurement he needed, then stood. As he did, Ella teetered on the ladder, losing her footing. Letting out a panicked squeal, she fell forward into Wil's arms, knocking him back against the wall.

Wil stood flat against the wall, not sure what to do next. His hands were still on Ella's waist, and she was still pressed up against his chest. He felt his complexion heat up and quickly dropped his hands. He waited for her to take a step back, but she didn't. With her hands on his shoulders, and her emerald eyes locked on his, she slowly leaned in.

"Ella, don't." Wil gently pushed her a few inches away. "I think we need to go."

She stepped back, looking embarrassed and hurt. Clearing her throat, she tugged on the hem of her snug-fitting shirt, then hurried toward the stairs.

You handled that like a pro. Wil scolded himself, hating that he'd hurt her feelings. But what else could he have said? He wasn't interested in her, at least not *that* way.

He caught up with her by the time they had reached the main level of the building. "Ella, wait . . . please." He reached out for her arm, stopping her.

She pulled her arm free, then turned around. "You sure are fickle, Mr. Marsh," she said with crimson red cheeks and a stiff chin. "What is it, go or stay?"

"I didn't tell *you* to go, Ella. I said *we* could go since I got what I came for."

"And, clearly, that isn't me," she mumbled under her breath.

He cringed. "Look, Ella, you're a beautiful woman, and I didn't mean to insult you, but I'm not looking for a relationship right now."

"And I don't have what it takes to make you think otherwise?" She stood defiantly with her hands planted on her hips.

"It's not that. I'm just not in the market for a girlfriend, or a wife, or anything else at the moment. Right now, I'm focusing on my career. It would not be fair to start a relationship when my time is going to be monopolized by all of this." He spread his arms out.

Ella crossed her arms against her chest and looked at him, her pouting lips morphing into a smile. "You know, you could have just told me you're gay. Then I wouldn't feel so bad."

He chuckled. "Would that have really made you feel better?"

"Probably not." She shrugged. "But at least my ego wouldn't feel so bruised."

He waited a second before asking, "So . . . can we still be friends? Because I do appreciate the help you've given me so far. But if this is going to be awkward for you, I'll understand."

"Yes, we can still be friends. It would be childish for me to say otherwise. Besides, maybe if you spend more time with me, I'll be able to wear you down."

He cocked his head, frustrated. "Look, Ella, I—"

"I'm kidding," she cut him off with a giggle. "Gees . . . can't a girl have a sense of humor?"

"Yes," he said with a smile. "As long as you can take as well as you can give."

Wil walked Ella to his truck. "Look, as long as you don't get the wrong impression, how about we grab a bit to eat? I didn't mean to keep you this long, so the least I can do is offer you dinner."

"Thanks, Wil. Actually, I would love a bite to eat. How about Mario's? We could share a pizza."

"Sounds good to me."

They left the hardware store and head around the corner to Mario's.

"Is pepperoni and olives okay with you?" Ella asked as they slid into opposite sides of a booth.

"Sure."

The waiter was there almost immediately with glasses of water.

"Are you ready to order?" he asked.

"Yes," Ella took the lead. "A large with pepperoni and olives and a pitcher of Coke. Put it on my account. Tucker."

"Yes, ma'am."

"Now I know why I didn't make the connection between you and Derrick," Wil said, after the waiter walked away. "You have different last names."

"True. We didn't have the same last name. I was three when

my mom married Derrick's dad. However, Tucker is my married name."

"You're married?!" *I'm taking a married woman out to dinner?*

"Relax, Wil, I'm divorced."

Thank goodness.

"Do you remember Matt Tucker, one of Derrick's friends?"

Wil thought back to a character who was almost as bad as Derrick. He also remembered hearing something about him being arrested on a statutory rape charge. "Wasn't he . . ."

"*That's* why we're divorced," Ella clarified, acknowledging she knew what Wil was thinking. "We had been married about a year when I found out what he was doing. Even though the girls he was with were consenting, they were still underage. When their parents found out, they banded together and had Matt arrested."

"He was still breaking the law," Wil said, sounding more defensive than he meant to. He could tell Ella was ready to fire back when the waiter interrupted by setting down their pizza and pitcher of soda. When the waiter walked away, Wil asked, "Do you mind if I pray?" cutting off her rebuttal again.

She huffed. "No. Go ahead."

Wil quickly thanked the Lord for the property deal, Ella's help, and asked Him to bless their food. When he looked up, Ella was just staring at him.

"I'm not excusing his behavior, Wil," she said, launching into her defense. "Imagine how I felt, the stupid housewife, sitting at home, believing the pack of lies my over-sexed husband told me day in and day out. Matt always made me feel like a second-class citizen. I was sexually abused by my stepfather and ignored by my mother. I witnessed the horrible things my brother and his friends did but clung to the attention Matt showed me. I was overweight, and very unsure of myself back then. His attention, even though sometimes negative, made me at least feel like I was a somebody."

She took a swig of soda, then continued. "Matt tried to blame his behavior on me, said if I had been a more satisfying wife, he wouldn't have had to look for fulfillment elsewhere. I was embarrassed and humiliated. After the trial, I left town with no intentions of coming back."

"Why did you come back?" Wil asked as he ate the now tasteless pizza they had ordered.

"My parents had gotten involved with some cult. They were convinced money and possessions bred negative energy. So, they left the house, their cars, their belongings, everything to me. I had my real estate license by then and came back to town with the intentions of selling everything. The house was in bad condition, so I had to put a lot work into it to get it ready to sell. Somewhere along the way, I fell in love with the place and decided to stay."

"Doesn't the house and the town hold bad memories for you?" Wil asked as he poured himself another glass of Coke.

"It did at first, but I have to admit, if it wasn't for hitting rock bottom and deciding to do something with my life, I wouldn't be where I am today. I got in shape, refined my people skills, and became the number one salesperson in my region. I make no apologies for who I am and what I've accomplished. I'm very happy with the life I've created for myself, and I have the satisfaction of knowing I did it all on my own."

Wil wanted to point out to Ella that God had obviously protected her through some very harrowing times, but he didn't think she would appreciate his insight. She felt she was a self-made woman and had no one but herself to thank for her success. Maybe he would be able to bridge that conversation with her at a later time, but for now, he felt it was best to change the subject.

So, they chatted over pizza, Wil doing his best to keep the subject matter light and general, steering Ella away from anything regarding their personal lives and previous relationships.

When Wil drove Ella home, he followed her up the front walk to her door. She unlocked the house, but he entered first and turned on a nearby lamp, then took a cursory look around before she walked in.

"Such a gentleman," she said with a sexy smile. "Why don't you stick around. We can have some dessert."

With Ella's flirty attitude back, Wil knew he needed to make a quick exit. "I don't think so, but thanks again for your help this evening. I really do appreciate it. I hope tonight's conversation didn't drudge up too many unhappy memories for you."

She stepped closer, looking at him through fluttering eyelashes. "If it does, can I call you for company?"

Boy, she doesn't give up easy.

"If it's a friend you need, Ella, I would be more than willing to help—but only as a friend."

"Then how about spending Thanksgiving with me, as a

friend?" she asked, a huge smile on her face. "It's the day after tomorrow, and I haven't made any plans. Well, I usually spend it with Sarah and Amy, but cooking for you would be so much more fun."

Persistent. I'll give her that.

"Actually, I have standing plans with Joseph," he said as he backed toward the front door.

"But his daughter is home this year. I'm sure Cassidy would love to have him all to herself."

Wil hadn't even thought about it. He just assumed he would spend it with Joseph, like usual. But even if he didn't, he knew giving Ella any kind of encouragement would not be a good idea. "I appreciate the invite, Ella, but I'm going to have to pass."

He trotted down Ella's front steps and got in his truck, wondering if he was going to celebrate Thanksgiving with all the fixings, or spend it alone with a microwave dinner.

TWENTY-FOUR

Pulling off her sandals on the way to her bedroom, Ella thought about her day with Wil.

He really is intriguing.

There was something challenging about going after the unattainable—the elusive. She knew Wil's background. He'd been raised with conservative values, lost his parents, and lived the quiet life of a loner.

But if he moves to the city, maybe I can change that. It was obvious he was affected by my stories of woe.

Yes, her personal life stunk. But she was resilient and had put it all behind her.

But I might have to bring it out from time to time, to play on his sympathies.

And then there was the prayer.

I guess the rumors are true. He really is a 'God' person.

She plopped down on her bed and lay back. Staring at the ceiling, she laughed to herself.

He would probably be shocked to find out he was locker room fodder at the local gym.

Older women called him sweet and thoughtful. A good Christian boy. But the younger women were more descriptive, even suggestive. They talked about his personality, appreciating his charm and compassion; but they were even more specific when talking about his well-honed physique.

After returning from college, women took notice at the transformation in Wil. He'd gone from junk to hunk. Awkward to amazing. He was considered quite the catch in town but was completely oblivious to the attention and stares he received, which made him even more attractive. Ella thought about how she could get closer to him.

Maybe I need to start setting time aside for church on

Sundays. She sighed. *What a major snooze. Or . . . I could just casually stop by the hardware store once he starts working on it. Offer my help.*

Ella rolled her eyes when she thought of their earlier conversation. *Oooh, I love the industrial look. Sleek. Modern.* "I sounded like an idiot," she groaned. "Next time, I'll wait for Wil to make his point, *then* I'll agree with him."

And then there's Cassidy.

Ella realized she had hit a nerve when she talked about Cassidy's divorce.

Maybe that's why Wil isn't taking me up on my offer. He said he wasn't interested in a relationship, but maybe he's already in one.

She would be more careful with her comments in the future. Demeaning another woman's character was not the way to a man's heart. Making him forget about her completely was much more profitable.

Ella knew she had the means to make him forget, but what would she have to do to make him take notice? She thought of a couple of angles she might try. After all, she saw the way Wil blushed when she was pressed up against him.

At least he isn't completely immune to the shape of an attractive woman.

Of course, that was right before he basically told her he wasn't interested. But she just smiled to herself.

He's resistant but not immune. Underneath that Superman exterior is still a warm-blooded male.

Ella got up from her bed and moved to the bathroom vanity. Looking in the mirror, she smiled.

"He can't resist my advances forever."

———— • ————

Wil still wondered about Thanksgiving, but distracted himself with thoughts of his new building, and all the ways it would change his life.

He'd be able to attend animals in a fully stocked exam room instead of on kitchen counters or back porch steps. Have a kitchen he could both cook and entertain in. Walk upstairs to a jetted tub at the end of a strenuous day.

It was going to be a lot of work, but it was going to be amazing in the end.

Even his time with Ella wasn't so bad. Though the conversation had gotten pretty personal, Wil could tell she just needed someone to talk to. She needed a friend, even though it was obvious she wanted something more. Maybe he would see if he could get her and Cassidy together. They had a few things in common, and Wil felt Ella's conversation would probably be better shared with another woman.

Talking with Ella made Wil think about Cassidy and the difficulties she was dealing with. Mark's affair had to have taken a toll on her ego. She was a beautiful, talented young woman, yet Mark had made her feel expendable.

The more Wil thought about Cassidy's problems, the more he tried to figure out ways he could help. For whatever reason, he seemed to bring out the worst in her. They could only talk and carry on a conversation for so long before they ended up bickering. Even so, there was something he felt when he was near her. Maybe that was why he didn't look at Ella with interest.

Wil struggled with his thoughts all the way home.

It was pretty late when he pulled into the drive. He slowed in front of the house and saw the living room light was still on. Grabbing his medical bag from the floorboard, he walked up the steps of the porch and gently tapped on the door, knowing Joseph was probably already in bed.

"Who is it?" Cassidy whispered from the other side.

"It's Wil, who else were you expecting?" he asked sarcastically

Cassidy opened the door and looked at him with contempt. "Well, I certainly wasn't expecting you to be rude enough to come at this time of night."

"Oh get off it, Cassidy. It's only ten o'clock. I'm sure this is considered early in New York."

Walking past her, he sat down on the coffee table and started pulling out supplies from his bag, but Cassidy hadn't budged from the front door.

"Come on Cassidy, I don't have all night. I need to check your shoulder." Wil finally looked up from where he was sitting, and realized Cassidy was dressed for bed. She wore oversized flannel pants and a little camisole top that barely covered her midriff. He glanced down and fumbled with his supplies, waiting for her to take a seat on the couch.

She took her sweet time, but finally walked across the living room and stood right in front of him. "I was dressed for bed, you know."

He looked up at her. "I can see that." He waited for her to take a seat on the couch, then positioned his bandage scissors against her shoulder and started cutting. He could feel Cassidy staring at him, and knew she was doing her best to make him feel uncomfortable. However, he got the last laugh when he quickly pulled the last piece of tape from her shoulder.

"Ouch!" She slapped his arm, then looked at hers. "You did that on purpose just to irritate me."

When Cassidy reached for the wound, Wil slapped her hand away. "Don't touch. Your hands aren't clean."

Cassidy sat with her fists clenched on either side of her, and Wil was sure he could hear her teeth grinding together. But she didn't say another word while he changed her bandages.

When he was finished taping the new gauze in place, he cleaned up the discarded wrappers and closed his bag. "It looks good, Cassidy."

She didn't answer, so he got up to leave.

He was halfway across the living room before she said anything. "You were out pretty late."

Wil smiled, knowing Cassidy's curiosity would get the better of her. He turned back around. "Ella and I were doing some measuring at the hardware store. It took a little longer than expected, so we went out to dinner. Sort of a celebration."

Okay, maybe that was stretching it a little bit.

Wil waited for Cassidy's verbal volley, but she didn't say a thing. She just got up from where she was sitting, turned off the side table lamp, and started climbing the stairs, leaving Wil in the shadows from the front entry's night light. She stopped on the landing, but only for a second. "I'm sure you can see your way out, Wil. Have a good night."

When Wil got home, he poured himself a cup of coffee, and sat in the quiet of his own living room, dissecting the banter between Cassidy and him.

And the lack thereof.

He had dangled Ella's name in front of her on purpose, curious what she would say. But she didn't say a word. Even her 'good night' lacked its normal amount of sass.

Had he hurt her feelings?

He had mentioned Ella's name on purpose to get a reaction out of her, to see what she would say. It was stupid on his part—immature really. But he wanted to see if Cassidy had feelings for him, like he was feeling for her. Nevertheless, in his juvenile attempt to flush out her feelings, he forgot she was going through a very traumatic time. She had just left her husband. Not because her feelings for him had run its course, but because she caught him in the act with another woman. Her husband cheated on her. Sent her divorce papers. Pretty much said you're not good enough.

And what did I do? Try to stir her up.

He'd even been so flustered by her non-sparring attitude, he had forgotten to ask about Thanksgiving.

Heading to bed, Wil realized he had to give Cassidy her space. As much as he would like to help her forget about Mark and the difficulties she was having, he realized bickering with her was not the way to go about it.

It would serve him right if he didn't get invited to Thanksgiving dinner.

And I have no one to blame but myself.

———— • ————

Cassidy lay awake in bed agitated with Wil . . . or was she agitated with herself? She liked toying with him because she knew he was safe. He would never forfeit his convictions for a little female companionship.

But Ella seems to have gotten his attention easy enough.

She had convinced herself it was Wil's purity that kept him at arms-length, preventing him from making a move on her. Then Ella came into the picture.

Cassidy sulked, staring at the ceiling of her bedroom. *Face it, you don't have what it takes to keep a man's attention.*

She thought about Mark. As much as she hated to admit it, she missed him. She realized it wasn't love she missed, because it was obvious that wasn't what they had shared, but she missed being with someone.

Admit it. You're needy and shallow.

As much as she liked to come across as an independent, free-spirit, she felt worthless without the attention of a man.

Had that been part of Mark's plan?

She pondered her life with him. They'd had an exciting, adventurous, and sometimes wild lifestyle. Traveling to exotic locations. Partying with influential people. But Mark's dark side was always there. Ominous. Prevailing. Instilling just enough fear to keep her in line.

To please him, she had participated in things that were sordid and sometimes unsettling. On occasion, she had experimented with recreational drugs to melt away her inhibitions and had developed a drinking habit in the process. Even so, it still wasn't enough.

Mark enjoyed sensory stimulation like movies and magazines. Things that constantly reminded Cassidy she wasn't satisfying him, so she tried even harder to be what he wanted her to be. She ignored the times he was ugly, abusive, and the terror he stirred inside her. She kept trying to come up with different ways to please him, to keep his attention. But obviously, nothing she did had been enough.

Cassidy felt herself succumbing to the depression she had tried so hard to keep at bay.

What is it about me that isn't enough for a man?

She tossed and turned most of the night, searching for something just out of reach.

Self-worth was simply unattainable.

TWENTY-FIVE

Cassidy's alarm woke her the next morning.

She rolled over, pushed the Off button, and stared at the dark room that surrounded her. She groaned, not wanting to get up, but knew she needed to.

Crawling out of bed, she shivered, then moaned. The warm snap they'd been enjoying was gone. Replaced with the normal chill of November.

After pulling on a pair of tailored jeans, she fished around in her dresser drawer for a long-sleeved thermal, then put her favorite cable-knit sweater on over it. *A seven-hundred-dollar Prada sweater, and I'm mucking stalls.*

This was her new life.

The barn was dark at five o'clock in the morning, so Cassidy turned on the overhead light. An amber glow flooded the stables and beckoned the start of a new day.

Talking to the horses as she fed them, immediately changed her mood. She was surprised how good it felt. Life in New York City was nothing like this.

Maybe that's why I'm enjoying it so much.

She hummed as she completed the morning chores and was just finishing up in one of the stalls, when Wil walked in with his head down.

"Hey, Joseph, you're up a little ear—" His eyes widened in surprise when he saw her. "Cassidy, it's you." He walked to the side of the stable and hitched his leg up on the rail. "What are you doing up so early?"

"I've taken over the morning chores. To lighten Dad's load."

"But Joseph isn't usually out here until six o'clock. Why so early?"

Cassidy continued brushing Rooster. "I don't have the routine down as well as Dad, so it takes me a little longer. If I waited

147

until six o'clock, he would beat me to it. This way, he can't try to do the work without me."

He watched her for a little while. Cassidy wasn't sure if he was impressed or waiting for her to do something wrong. When he turned to walk away, she asked, "Was there a message you wanted me to relay to Dad?"

"No. Just checking in with him, that's all." He kept walking.

"Wil?"

He turned back around. "Yeah?"

"We will probably have Thanksgiving dinner around three o'clock, if you're interested. I mean . . . if you don't already have other plans." She tried to act casual, like she didn't care one way or another if he accepted her invitation.

He got a stupid grin on his face. "Cassidy, are you inviting me to dinner?"

She gave him a drop-dead stare. "Only because I know Dad would like you there."

"But you wouldn't?" He smiled.

Ooh, why does he always have to be so smug?

"Look, if you already have plans, I don't care," Cassidy said, feeling flustered. "At least I can tell Dad I asked."

Watching as he pushed the toe of his boot around in the dirt, she could tell he was smirking. He turned to leave but spoke over his shoulder. "See you tomorrow around three."

———— • ————

When Cassidy returned from the market, she quickly unloaded the bags, double-checking the list in her hand. Earlier, she'd gone through the old recipe box on the counter and pulled out all her dad's favorite side dishes. It was a feast in the making.

I hope I can pull this off.

She wanted it to be nice for her dad.

Special.

And there was a small part of her that hoped Wil would appreciate her efforts too.

After putting the groceries away, she headed outside to do some sketching. She tried a couple of different locations, but her mind just wasn't in it. Even though she wanted to blame it on the cold, she couldn't. It was tomorrow's meal that kept running through her mind. After another thirty minutes of scribbling, she gave up and went back into the house. Scrutinizing the living room, she decided it could use some tidying up before tomorrow.

TWENTY-SIX

Cassidy was up bright and early the next morning. However, instead of cursing the dark, she was excited to start the day.

After finishing with the animals and her chores, she turned her attention to Thanksgiving dinner.

By the time her father came downstairs, the turkey was stuffed and in the oven. Two of his favorite Jell-O salads had been whipped up and were in the refrigerator chilling, and she was busy making an apple pie from scratch.

"Everything smells wonderful, Cassidy," her dad said as he entered the kitchen with a healthy inhale.

"Yea, but dumb me, I forgot the turkey would be in the oven all day. I'm not going to be able to bake my pies until after dinner. Then, we'll have to wait even longer to eat them," Cassidy said, irritated she hadn't thought about it sooner.

"Don't worry about it, Sunshine. We'll need at least an hour or so for our dinner to digest. It will be perfect timing."

She knew her father was only trying to make her feel better, so she smiled and let it go. She wasn't going to let anything spoil the rest of the day.

———— • ————

Everything was almost ready. The turkey was cooked to perfection and cooling on the counter, and the side dishes were simmering on the stovetop. She put her pies in the oven, then glanced at the clock. A little after three. Then she heard the front door open and shut. She smiled. *Right on time.* Wil and her dad's conversation got louder as they approached the kitchen.

"Wow!" Wil said as he looked at all the serving dishes on the table and the pans still on the stovetop. "You've outdone yourself, Cassidy."

"Did you doubt I could do it?" she countered, crossing her arms

150

against her chest.

"No. That's called a compliment," he said, giving her one of his killer smiles. "Everything looks and smells amazing."

"Oh . . . I thought you were teasing me." She hated herself for overreacting. *Why does he always make me feel so off-balance?* She fumbled with the hot pads in her hands. *Move on. Keep going. Don't overthink everything he says.*

"Well, everything is almost ready. Dad, why don't you start carving the turkey while I dish up the rest of the food?"

"How about I let Wil carve? He's got the hands of a surgeon. I'll pour everyone some sparkling cider."

While Cassidy spooned the potatoes into a large bowl and drained the corn, she found herself watching Wil as he worked on the turkey. When he looked her way, he smiled. She pretended not to notice.

Finally, they took their seats at the table. Her dad sat in his usual place at the head of the table. Wil sat on his right and she sat on his left. Reaching out his hands to each of them, she placed her hand in her dad's. However, she wasn't prepared for the hand Wil extended across the table to her.

When she looked up at him, Wil smiled. She hesitantly rested her hand in his, then bowed her head while her father blessed the food with a prayer of genuine thanksgiving.

She listened to her dad and Wil discuss a myriad of subjects. Business. Inflation. Religion. Progress. They covered it all. She envied the way they talked with such ease and was happy just to listen. But occasionally, Wil or her dad would ask for her opinion. She would give it, then they would move on to another subject. She enjoyed listening to them debate different issues. In fact, she enjoyed everything about the meal. The food. The conversation. The company. And the way her hand still tingled from the squeeze Wil had given it as he said 'Amen.'

When it looked as if everyone was done, Cassidy stood up and started clearing the table.

"Cassidy, I must say, this has to be one of the best Thanksgiving meals I've ever had," Wil said as he pushed back from the table.

"Yeah, Sunshine, everything was terrific."

She felt her cheeks heat up at their compliments, so she mumbled a quick thank you, then moved to the oven to check on the pies. "These are going to take a few more minutes. Why don't you guys go sit in the living room while I clean up the rest of this mess?"

"Oh no," Wil stood, "you did all the cooking; we can do the cleaning." He picked up his plate and walked it over to the sink.

"No deal. You'll just get under foot. I'll have this cleaned up in no time."

"Are you sure, Sunshine?" Her father said as he got to his feet. "You've done so much already."

"No Dad," she looked at him, overwhelmed with emotion. "I haven't done nearly enough. I have a lot of years to make up for."

He pulled her into a hug and spoke in her ear. "Just having you home is all I need."

She returned his embrace, willing herself not to cry, then turned back to the sink. "Now go. Both of you. I'll let you know when the pies are done."

She didn't turn back around until she was sure they were gone. *Wow! Where did that come from?* Cassidy asked herself as she cleared more dishes from the table. *And what was with Wil squeezing my hand like that?* She wasn't sure if he meant anything by it. But that, along with her father's hug, had just about done her in emotionally. She needed time to think, to put some space between them. That's why she had refused their help. She needed some time to herself.

After folding the dish towel, and laying it on the counter, she looked around the kitchen at the clean surfaces and polished appliances. Once again, she was surprised how rewarding it felt to do something so domestic.

Without asking if they were ready for their dessert, Cassidy went ahead and dished up two bowls with generous slices of apple pie and double scoops of vanilla ice cream. When she walked into the living room carrying the dishes, her dad and Wil moaned, claiming they were still too full from dinner.

Then they proceeded to devour every last bite.

Before too long, the evening had come to an end. Wil walked his and her dad's dishes into the kitchen, and her dad disappeared upstairs after wishing them both a good night. Cassidy was tired from the work she had put into the meal, but it was a good tired.

An accomplished tired.

Slowly, she walked around the living room, turning off lights and straightening pillows.

"Dinner really was great," Wil said as he crossed the living room and stood by the front door.

"Thanks. I enjoyed making it." Cassidy watched as Wil fidgeted with the door handle, like he wasn't ready to leave.

"What is it?"

"I was wondering if you would be interested in seeing the hardware store?"

"Oh!" Cassidy was excited at the thought of it, but then calmed her tone. "No, that's okay. I'd probably just be in the way."

"How could you be in the way? The building is huge. Besides, I wouldn't mind bouncing a few ideas off you."

"I don't think I would have any useful suggestions. I haven't hung out in many veterinary offices." Cassidy moved to turn off another light.

"Well, maybe not with the downstairs, but you could give me a woman's opinion on the upstairs apartment."

Cassidy rolled her eyes. "I thought that was why your real estate *friend* was following you around, so she could give you *personal* help."

Wil chuckled. "So, that's what this is all about. You're jealous."

Cassidy swung around and saw the smirk on his face. "You're crazy! Why would I be jealous? I couldn't care less who's giving you advice or who you're spending your time with. I'm sorry to wound your ego, Wil, but you seem to have forgotten one little thing. I'm still married. And I would just as soon shoot myself in the foot than jump into another relationship."

His grin widened. "Well good. Now that I know you're not after me for my insanely good looks, dazzling charm, or hefty back account, would you consider giving me a hand?"

Cassidy laughed. She wouldn't exactly call it charm, but Wil's invitation was tempting. Interior design was a passion Mark had not allowed her to explore. She'd been expected to fit into his world, not change it. "Fine. When?"

"Tomorrow afternoon? I could meet you downtown."

"Fine," Cassidy said as she climbed the stairs.

"Great! I have a few follow-up appointments, but I'll call you when I'm done. And, Cassidy . . ."

She stopped and turned to him. "Yeah?"

"Thanks."

TWENTY-SEVEN

Cassidy had gone through a dozen outfits before she caught herself.

I'm being ridiculous. It's not like we're going on a date. We're going to be talking about windows, flooring, square footage.

Deciding on a pair of jeans—her favorite Burberry figure-hugging jeans—and her stiletto boots, she liked the overall effect. Tall. Thin. Leggy. Pairing them with her favorite blue silk blouse—because it matched her eyes perfectly—she stood in front of the full-length mirror and admired her image. Pulling on her Givenchy leather jacket, she decided she liked the way it made her outfit look a little more casual. *Three-thousand-dollars' worth of casual.*

But she felt comfortable.

Ready.

Ready in case Wil's real estate agent just happened to drop by. Even though Cassidy wasn't interested in Wil, she certainly wasn't going to allow Ella to get her hooks into him. If the woman showed up, Cassidy planned on running interference.

Just enough to bring out the lady's not so pretty side.

Because every woman on the prowl had one.

Cassidy cruised downtown, taking in all the sights and sounds. Instead of jockeying the old pickup into curb-side parking, she decided to use the public lot at the end of the street. Getting out of the truck, she slammed shut the rusty door, then straightened her jacket and smoothed her hands down the front of her jeans. As she walked toward the old hardware store, she studied the town with new eyes. It was quaint. Nostalgic. Not dilapidated like she remembered it.

Funny what perspective will do for you.

Strolling down Main Street, she walked by the shoe repair store with its funny little boot-shaped sign, then passed the fabric store with its patchwork valance draped across the large picture window.

Cassidy recalled many wonderful hours spent in that store with her mom, choosing just the right material for doll clothes and quilt squares. Cassidy closed her eyes at the memory, forcing herself to enjoy it instead of letting her anger overshadow it. Continuing down the street, she passed the old barber shop. When she heard cat-calls and whistles, she grinned.

Sounds like I chose the right outfit.

Cassidy stopped in front of the old hardware store and looked up. It was big. Bigger than she remembered. Cupping her hands against the large glass window, she peered inside to see if Wil was already there, but it was hollow, dark, and empty.

Once her eyes adjusted to the darkness, she strained to see, but there wasn't much to look at. Four walls and a couple of posts. Hearing the recognizable sound of high heels clicking on cement, Cassidy turned and saw a woman walking her way. She was beautiful. Tall. Red hair. Wearing a pencil skirt.

It had to be Ella.

Who else would dress to the nines in a town like this?

The woman's navy suit and cream-colored blouse looked smart. Business-like. Even so, Cassidy didn't miss the way the buttons of her blouse pulled and strained across her chest. She was obviously well-endowed and did nothing to hide it.

As soon as the woman saw Cassidy, her steps slowed, and her eyes scanned. The telltale signs of sizing up the competition. And Cassidy had no intentions of correcting her. She just smiled. *Let her think whatever she wants.*

"You must be Wil's agent?" Cassidy said as she extended her hand and offered a fake smile.

"I am," she said, arrogantly. "Wil must have told you all about me."

"Not really, but you're wearing a blazer with your company's logo on it. It was a pretty safe assumption," Cassidy said, coolness in her tone.

She didn't like her.

There was just something about the woman. Her tone. The way she sashayed down the sidewalk. The sound of Wil's name on her lips. *Whoa . . . wait a minute. Maybe I am jealous.* Cassidy questioned herself, but quickly disregarded the thought. *I am not interested in Wil. I just don't want to see him get hurt. And this woman has trouble written all over her.*

"I see you two have gotten acquainted." Wil jogged up,

crashing into Cassidy's thoughts.

"You could say that." Ella smiled at Wil, completely ignoring Cassidy.

"I asked Cassidy to come down and give me some pointers on decorating."

"Oh?" Ella turned to her. "Did you work in a vet's office in New York? I thought you left Liberty to pursue your art career."

Cassidy felt her jaw clench, and her muscles tighten. "I did. But I also enjoy interior design. Wil asked me to stop by and listen to his ideas for his living space. You know, to get a woman's point of view," Cassidy said, watching Ella's smile tighten.

That's right, sweetheart, Wil wants my opinion.

Ella wrapped her hand around Wil's forearm and gave it a squeeze, a sign of being territorial if Cassidy ever saw one.

"Well, Wil certainly doesn't need any help where design is concern. He walked me through his ideas the other night, and I thought they were simply fabulous. He definitely has a romantic side. His bedroom is going to be spectacular, and I can't wait to see it when it's done."

Ella's message came through loud and clear. She thought she was going to have the inside track into the private life of Wil Marsh. Cassidy glared at her, but Ella just smiled in return.

"Uh . . . okay . . . so . . ." Wil stuttered, obviously picking up the underlying tension. "I appreciate you coming down and letting us in, Ella. We'll make sure the place is locked up when we're through. I don't want to take up too much of your time."

"Nonsense. You're not taking up my time. I enjoy this part of my job." She unlocked her door and waited as the two of them walked in.

"I bet!" Cassidy mumbled under her breath as she walked through the threshold into the musty interior.

Just as Ella closed the door behind them, her phone chimed. She answered it with a smile that soon faded. "Oh, come on, Carol, can't you take care of Mr. Brewer? You know he's just going to take me on another wild goose chase. He's not interested in a house. He's just lonely." Ella sighed and tossed a fake smile in Cassidy's direction. "Oh, all right. I'll be there in a few minutes." She disconnected the call and dropped her phone into her purse.

"I'm sorry, Wil. I have to meet with another client. I'll leave you to explain your great ideas to Cassidy. I'm sure she'll agree with me and see them as wonderfully unique."

"I'm sure I will," Cassidy said barely containing the smile that threatened to give her away. Ella's little plan to follow them around had backfired. Now Cassidy would be able to hear about Wil's plans without having to listen to Ella's every comment. Wil thanked Ella again before shutting the door behind her, then turned to Cassidy. "Well?" He spread his arms wide. "What do you think?"

Cassidy glanced at the concrete floor and bare walls. *It sure is a blank canvas.* She tried to visualize a receptionist window and a lobby full of animals. When she turned full circle, her stare collided with Wil's. He quickly looked away, pretending to be engrossed with a section of wall—a very *blank* section of wall.

She smiled, then asked, "So, are you going to explain to me your grand plans?"

"Sure." Wil regained his composure. "Let's go upstairs."

When they reached the upstairs landing, Wil crossed to the other side of the room. "This is the living room and kitchen area."

"So, what do you plan to do with it?" Cassidy asked as she walked into the dilapidated kitchen space.

"I'd like to put a bar area here." Wil said as he waved his arms around an open space between the kitchen and living room. Cassidy raised a brow, encouraging him to go on. "I'm thinking black granite countertops and cherry wood cabinetry. I'd like a clean look, but I don't want it to feel too sterile."

She shrugged.

"What?"

"Nothing. It sounds nice."

"But . . ."

"But what?" Cassidy avoided Wil's stare.

"Come on, Cassidy. I can tell you're thinking something. What is it?"

"I told you, it sounds nice."

"But you would do it differently, right?" Wil asked.

"It doesn't matter. It's your place, not mine."

"Yes, but I asked you here so you could give me some ideas."

Cassidy debated if she should say anything. It was Wil's place, and it sounded like he already had a plan. Who was she to interfere? She glanced around one more time, then asked, "Why do you want to put a bar here? I thought you wanted to keep the room open?"

"Well, I do. I just thought it would be a nice place for entertaining."

"Oh that's right," Cassidy rolled her eyes, "I forgot about all those extravagant social functions you've been throwing lately."

Wil was about to correct her, then laughed. "So, how would you do it?"

"Well, if it was *my* kitchen, I would put an island here with maybe a smaller bar area at the end of it. Putting the bar on the side will help to keep the room open instead of sectioning it off." Cassidy moved to the area she was talking about. "I would also install a cooktop with an indoor grill right here."

"Go on," he said, crossing his arms against his chest.

She hesitated. "Come on, Wil, I came here to hear your ideas."

"Yes, and I brought you here so I could hear yours."

His look encouraged her to continue.

"Well, I would put a double stacked oven here on the right and the refrigerator over there. I think with the large appliances anchoring the counter space it will make it more efficient. For task lighting, I would use some under-cabinet lighting. Over the island, I would use something a little more substantial and warm, so it looks more like an accessory instead of a necessity."

"And the sink?"

She eyed the counter area. "Well, I would do one of two things. Either, put in two sinks, one in either corner, or put a large farmhouse style sink in the middle of the counter."

"What would be the advantage of both?" Wil asked, sounding interested.

"The two smaller sinks would be versatile. One could have a built-in strainer for washing fruit and a cutting board for preparing vegetables. The other one could have a long-necked faucet for filling large pots with water. If you had a farm-style sink, it could still have the same accessories, you just wouldn't be able to do more than one task at a time."

"What about windows?" he asked, standing next to the small window in what would be the dining area. "Since natural light can only come from the ends of the room, I would like to replace this window with something larger. But who knows what kind of framework I'm going to find once I open the walls."

"Just incorporate whatever you find into the design," she said, not the least bit perplexed.

"What do you mean?"

"Say you have three studs that can't be removed," she mimicked where and how they would run the length of the wall. "You could add vertical windows as long as you like, then add crossbeams to frame them out. Make it look intentional. You could always add a cherry veneer to the studs, so they appear decorative instead of structural."

"So, you're saying tear down the wood wall completely and have a glass wall instead?"

"Except for the beams."

Wil walked through the kitchen. She could tell he was trying to visualize it. "Could you sketch it for me, so I have something to show a contractor?"

"Sure, but it is just an idea, Wil. You don't have to do it. It's your kitchen. You need to do what's right for you."

"Are you kidding? You just took all the guesswork out of it for me. Except for deciding what kind of sink and how the final window design will look, I'll actually have something on paper, instead of in my head." Wil seemed genuinely excited. "Okay now . . ." With a slight hand to her waist and a gentle push, he propelled her into the middle of what would be the living room. "How would you set up the living room? Keep in mind I need space for a dining room table."

Cassidy rattled off a few ideas, loving that someone was interested in her opinion.

Wil shook his head in amazement. "You really have a flair for this, Cassidy. You obviously don't need a canvas to be artistic."

"Thank you." His compliment meant more than he would ever know. Just to have someone acknowledge she had talent. The few times she had tried to do something different at home, Mark had said her designs were amateurish. Unsophisticated.

"Cassidy . . . are you okay?"

She looked up at Wil. "Yeah. Sure. Uh . . . what about your study? Is it going to be in your bedroom or in the living room?"

"Neither. Well, at least not to the extent it is now. Most of the books I have in my bedroom will go in my office downstairs. I'll just have personal books up here, but nothing like what I have now."

"But you'll still need a nice bookcase in here?"

"Or in my bedroom."

"Do you really want to infringe on your bedroom space with

a bookshelf?"

"Well, let me show you how much space we're talking about."

Cassidy followed Wil upstairs to the third level, surprised by the size of the room. "You're right. Even with the slanted walls, it's still quite large, but there is no closet. You'll have to take up floor space in order to gain the storage you need." Cassidy peaked into the bathroom. "Wow."

"Yeah. I know. Total gut job. Plus, I thought I would bump it out another four feet."

"Oh, nice. It will give you some good space to work with." She walked to the far side of the room, to the windows overlooking downtown.

"I want to replace those, to add more light." Wil said as she fingered the sills.

"With what?" Cassidy wondered.

"I'm not sure yet. If I make any changes to the outside of the building, it must be approved by the Historical Society. They want to make sure the downtown area retains its original charm. Have any ideas?" Wil asked with a defeatist attitude.

"Yes!" Cassidy said with excitement. "I have the perfect idea. If you put a single French door here, at the peak, with an arched transom window at the top for detail, you can put a smaller arched window on each side, and then a smaller one yet. You would have five floor-to-ceiling windows offering plenty of light and lots of style. You could even add a small step out balcony. The Historical Society shouldn't have a problem with that. It would still have an old-time charm to it." Cassidy looked to Wil for approval. He was smiling from ear to ear.

"So, what about the closet issue? How am I going to pull that off? I mean, I'm fine with just having a dresser, but I guess I should look to the future."

"What do you mean?" Cassidy blurted out before she could stop herself.

"Eventually, I hope to settle down. Though this place wouldn't be suitable for a family, it would be a fine starter place for when I meet that certain someone."

Cassidy giggled and spoke with a regal accent. "Oh, but of course, sir, and have you found that certain someone?" Cassidy joked.

"Maybe I have." Wil's tone turned serious. He looked away from Cassidy and in an instant, she realized what she had done. She had just designed the perfect house for Wil to share with Ella. It had to be her. Who else would he be talking about? Ella was beautiful, smart, intelligent, and above all, obviously had her sights set on Wil.

In an instant, Cassidy felt the wind sucked from her sails. The fun and the excitement she'd been sharing with Wil just lost its appeal. She was confused by her own feelings. She was sure she wasn't interested in Wil *that* way. He'd been a friend these last few weeks—that's all. Obstinate, pigheaded, and arrogant, but a friend just the same.

But if that was the case, why was she so upset at the idea of him ending up with someone like Ella? Maybe because she'd seen her fair share of '*Ellas*' while in New York. Women who latched onto eligible bachelors, then rode their coattails until they got bored, or drained their bank accounts, whichever came first.

Cassidy studied Wil. *Surely he sees through Ella's coy demeanor and knows what kind of woman she really is?*

And Ella . . . though Wil was very attractive and had prospects of being successful in business, was she really going to get much out of him financially? An up-and-coming veterinarian would hardly be held responsible for huge alimony payments. Cassidy was deep in thought when Wil nudged her.

"Earth to Cassidy," he said with a smile.

She quickly smiled back at him.

"Sorry, I guess I got a little distracted." She walked toward the stairs, Wil following her. "Look, Wil, though my ideas might sound well and good, they're going to be very expensive. I think you should look at more practical ways of renovating this place." Cassidy talked over her shoulder as she headed for the next flight of stairs, her words cold and brittle. Wil grabbed her arm and stopped her before she descended to the main floor. She reluctantly turned around and saw Wil's rich brown eyes filled with frustration.

"What's with you, Cassidy? You've taken my simple ideas and made them inventive and spectacular. Why are you suddenly being so negative?"

"Because they're not realistic," she said matter-of-factly. "If you told me your budget had no limit, then they would be good ideas. But right now—"

"My budget has no limit," he interrupted with a mischievous

161

grin.

Cassidy just stared at him. "What are you saying?" she huffed. "That money is no object?"

He smiled like a kid on Christmas day. "I'm saying money is no object."

"I don't understand. How do you have that kind of money? Your practice has barely taken off."

"It was from my parents."

"Your parents!" Cassidy said with a little too much shock in her voice. "Your parents were farmers and very—"

"Conservative." Wil cut her off. "Look, just because we wore handmade clothes and drove an old truck, doesn't mean my parents were dumb and uneducated."

"I never said they were dumb, Wil." Cassidy did not miss the hurt in his eyes.

"But that's what you were thinking, right? You figured they were dumb hicks who could barely afford to rub two nickels together. Well, let me tell you about my father. He was quite the businessman. The land he owned here in Liberty was not the extent of his holdings or his investments. This is just where he chose to raise his family—to raise me. He wanted to give me a different kind of up-bringing than most kids got in our day. He wanted me to appreciate a simple life and hard work. He wanted me to be proud of my accomplishments, not because they were given to me, but because I had earned them."

Wil took a second to clear the emotion from his throat.

"And my mother . . . my mother was amazing. She grounded me in God's Word and helped me understand that all we have is a gift and should be treated as such. So, you see, I might have been raised in a simple way, but not by simple people."

Wil's mini-sermon left Cassidy speechless. She was awed by the devotion and the respect he had for his mother and father. He didn't tell her of his wealth as a means to impress here. He did it as a tribute to the man who had raised him.

Cassidy felt humbled and humiliated. Had she ever spoken about her mother and father with such admiration or respect? No, she had cursed her mother for dying and hated God for taking her. She was embarrassed to tell people where she was from and what her father did for a living.

No, Cassidy's perspective and outlook on life was cynical and jaded. Every man for himself was the motto of big business. In her eagerness to be a somebody, she'd become a nobody in the shadow of her rich and powerful husband.

Cassidy felt Wil's warm hands on her upper arms. She looked up expecting to see hurt in his eyes, but instead saw compassion. "Look, Cassidy, I know the sweet girl you were before your mother's death is still deep inside you somewhere. We just have to wash off enough of that big city cynicism to find her."

"I don't know, Wil. I'm not sure I can have the Pollyanna attitude you have. I'm too obstinate for that or maybe too afraid to let my guard down. The last time I had hoped for the best, I found my husband with another woman. I'm not sure I can ever be that hopeful again."

"I know you feel like the world did a number on you, Cassidy. But you have a choice. You can either fight back or be swallowed up by it."

She thought a moment, but before she could form a rebuttal, Wil draped his arm around her shoulders and led her down the stairs. "So, when can you have those drawings done?"

"You're serious? You really want me to draw up plans for your apartment?"

"Actually, I'd like for you to do the whole thing. We could come back here after you have the plans for the upstairs done. Then I could explain what I need for an office, examination rooms, and reception area."

"But, Wil, I have no experience working with a builder. I see what I'm talking about in my head, but I don't know if I can translate that to paper."

"Then you'll learn as you go. If I'm not mistaken, you looked like you were enjoying yourself up there. I'm sure it wasn't the company, so it must have been the work." He gave her a wink, then closed the front door behind them. After jiggling the handle to make sure it was locked, they walked toward the parking lot. "I do have one more favor to ask you."

"What?" Cassidy groaned, sure he was going to ask her dating advice. And if he did, she would have to be honest about her impression of Ella.

"I want you to do the artwork for the reception area."

"You do? But I don't do animals. I do structures, landscapes, stuff like that."

"You used to draw horses."

Cassidy quickly remembered one of her drawings winning an

art contest at school. "You remember that?"

"Of course I do. I voted for you."

Cassidy smiled at the memory. Winning that contest was the defining moment that set her course toward an art career. Unfortunately, she had ended up back in Liberty no more famous than when she left. Oh well. New York was behind her now.

A distant memory.

It was time to map out a new future.

She looked up at Wil, his excitement contagious. "So, what did you have in mind?"

TWENTY-EIGHT

Cassidy went straight to her room and started sketching ideas for Wil's apartment. After several starts and stops, and a bedroom floor littered with crumpled papers, she finally hit her stride.

She was excited.

Energized.

Alive.

She was doing something tangible, and it felt great.

Wil's kitchen materialized right before her eyes. She didn't stop at the farmhouse sink and black granite countertops. She sketched an island, barstools, pendant lighting, and copper accents throughout. She even added copper flecks to the countertops, to give them warmth so they didn't look too sterile.

Then she moved on to the windows in the living room and dining room, allowing her imagination to run wild. She sketched several options, each a different look depending on what structural challenges they would have to work around. Long windows. Picture windows. Glass blocks and the French door concept she'd already pitched to Wil.

When she was done with the bedroom sketches, she reviewed everything again, admiring her work. *It's going to be beautiful. No matter what Wil decides.*

Glancing at the clock, Cassidy jumped off her bed. *Oh my gosh, how'd it get to be so late?*

Ignoring the mess on her bedroom floor, she hurried downstairs to start dinner. She opened the refrigerator just as her father walked in the back door.

"Hey, Dad, I'm running a little late. Why don't you go ahead and take your shower? I should have these leftovers warmed up by then."

He nodded. "I'll do just that."

Cassidy pulled out containers with Thanksgiving leftovers in them and set them on the counter. When she turned back for more, she was startled to see Wil standing in the kitchen doorway. Squelching a curse, she hurled a nearby hot pad at him. "You scared me half-to-death! Don't you ever knock?"

Wil laughed. "I could, but this was so much more entertaining. I thought you were going to jump onto the countertop."

Cassidy ignored his chuckling. Instead, she swung the refrigerator door open far enough to knock him off balance, then grabbed the remaining leftovers. Setting them on the counter, she reached for the upper cabinet. Wil put his hand on hers.

"Here, I'll get them." He smiled his dazzling—*you can't stay mad at me*—smile as he reached for three dinner plates.

As much as Cassidy wanted to be irritated with him, she wasn't. Wil's sincerity and charm always seemed to be his saving grace.

"So, have you thought much more about the designs for my apartment?" he asked while she pulled lids off the plastic storage containers.

Not wanting to admit she thought of nothing else since getting home, she tried to keep her remarks casual. "I've put a few ideas together, but I still think you need to hire a professional," she said as she divvied up leftover onto two of the three plates.

"All I want is a picture, something to show a contractor," Wil said as he worked on his own plate. "Remember, I've had a little experience remodeling. I'll probably do a lot of the work myself, but I need something on paper, in case I have to pull permits. I just need to make sure what I want is structurally doable."

"But how do you know I know what you want?" she asked as she put one of the plates in the microwave and pressed the reheat button. "I could design something horrible or use a lot of pinks and frills." Cassidy laughed at the thought of Wil cooking in a kitchen colored in pink and decorated with flowers.

"I think you know exactly what I want." Wil didn't look at Cassidy when he spoke, but she felt he was talking about more than just decorating. He glanced her way just as her dad entered the kitchen.

"What's with the mess in your room, Cassidy? You've got papers tossed everywhere. Are you working on a new project? Because that's what your room always looked like when you were working on a project."

"Ahh . . . actually, I was cleaning out my portfolio. It's no big deal." Already feeling flustered, she chanced a look at Wil. From the smile on his face, she knew she'd been caught. Ignoring his penetrating stare, she busied herself putting the Jell-O salads on the table.

Luckily, Wil started talking to her dad about his place, leaving her to finish what she was doing.

Her dad poured himself a glass of iced tea from the pitcher on the counter, then took a seat at the table, apparently oblivious to the interaction between her and Wil. Cassidy grabbed a can of soda from the refrigerator and offered one to Wil.

"Soda? What's the occasion?" he teased, pinning her with his stare.

"The occasion is called; Cassidy did the shopping." She handed him a can, but quickly looked away. With everything reheated, she sat down across from Wil, and bowed her head as her father said grace.

She heard her dad praying but wasn't really listening, her thoughts completely jumbled. Did Wil realize the confusing feelings he stirred inside her? He was getting comfortable around her.

Too comfortable.

You're overreacting. Thinking too much. Wil has every right to feel at home here. He's been around for the last three years. Unlike you. Her conscience taunted

"Cassidy, are you okay, sweetheart?"

Cassidy popped her head up, realizing her dad had finished praying. "Yeah, I'm fine. I was just thinking about something." Cassidy quickly shoved a forkful of potatoes in her mouth. If her mouth was full, she wouldn't have to answer any questions.

She listened as Wil went on and on about his new office space and apartment. To hear him talk, it was like he had already moved in and seeing patients.

"I was excited to buy the place, but after listening to Cassidy's ideas for the upstairs apartment, I can't wait to get started."

Cassidy felt a twinge of pride. It had been a long time since anyone had acknowledged her talents.

It felt good.

When the three of them were done eating, Cassidy cleared the table and refused Wil's help with the dishes. She shooed both men outside onto the porch where they continued talking.

After finishing with the dishes, she looked out the kitchen window and saw Wil and her dad still talking, but the expressions on their faces were more serious than she expected. She found herself leaning closer, as if by moving a few inches, she would be able to hear what they were saying. When she caught herself, she backed up.

It's none of your business. Just leave it alone.

Wil was probably still talking about his building, but maybe her dad was giving him a dose of reality to go along with his pie-in-the-sky ideas. She finished wiping down the counters, then went upstairs to straighten her room.

After throwing away the balled-up pieces of paper scattered around her room, Cassidy sat in the middle of the floor and laid out the sketches around her. With a critical eye, she scrutinized her favorite designs. They were good. Real good. She picked up the sketch of the master bedroom and smiled. It was intimate, romantic, in rich shades of golds and reds. It had a fireplace, a sleigh bed, and a cozy sitting nook. All the things she had ever envisioned for the perfect bedroom.

Her bedroom.

She gasped at the realization. *I can't give this to Wil. It's too personal. This isn't his bedroom—it's mine.*

"Are those sketches for me?"

Cassidy jumped. Sitting with her back to the door, she didn't see or hear Wil walk in.

"No." She quickly gathered them together and stood. Taking a deep breath, she pressed them to her chest and turned around. "I'm still working on them."

"Can I at least see what you have so far?" Wil reached for the papers, but Cassidy took a step back.

"No. They're not that good."

"Why don't you let me be the judge of that?" He lunged forward and snatched them from her hands. She tried to grab them back, but Wil kept them at arm's reach. "Hold your horses. I want to see what you've come up with so far."

Cassidy reached for them one more time, but Wil easily kept them from her. "Knock it off," he laughed. "Or I'm going to lock you in the closet."

"Right! How mature." She crossed her arms against her chest and glared at him.

He looked through the papers slowly and quietly, not saying a word.

"I told you they weren't that good. I was just messing around."

"Cassidy . . ." He glanced at her then back at the sketches. "These are incredible. The details, the colors, they're perfect."

"Really?"

He moved to the edge of her bed and sat down, consumed with her drawings. "Yes, they're great, but I'm confused." He glanced back and forth between two different sketches. "Is this an alternate view of the same room or an optional design?"

Cassidy sat down next to him. "It's two different designs." She leaned over to point out the differences in the two sketches. "Here, I put up a wall to separate the bed from the rest of the room in case you want more privacy. That makes for a sort of dressing area over here and gives you a wall to build a closet. In this drawing," she leaned closer still, "I kept the room more open and expanded the bathroom to include a walk-in closet."

Wil scrutinized both designs. "Which one do you like best?"

Cassidy thought about it. She liked both designs because they served two different purposes, but she did have a favorite. She was about to point to that design, then stopped. "It doesn't matter what I think, it's your bedroom." Cassidy turned, realizing how close they sat. Their eyes caught and for a moment neither of them broke the connection. Then, just as quick, Cassidy pictured Wil and Ella together. She got up from the bed and crossed the room, trying to shake off the feelings she was having. "It's your house. You're going to have to choose for yourself."

He stared at her, like she was a puzzle to be solved, but she quickly turned away.

"Look, Wil, I have some things I need to do. Take the drawings with you and look them over. Decide for yourself which ones you like best."

He continued to stare, then snapped out of it. "Sure . . . I'll do that. But let me look at your shoulder before I leave."

"It's fine. I checked it before dinner."

"Are you sure? It will only take a min—"

"It's fine. Really."

Wil slowly moved to the door. "Okay, then I guess I'll see you tomorrow. Thanks for dinner, Cassidy, and the work you did on these sketches. I really appreciate it."

After she heard the front door close, she exhaled the breath she'd been holding and collapsed on top of her bed.

What was that all about? Why was he looking at me like that?
She pondered their interaction. *Don't blow things out of portion.
He's appreciative. Thankful. That's all. You're grasping at straws if
you think a guy like Wil would be interested in a woman like you.*

She jumped up from her bed and walked into the bathroom.
Plugging the tub, she turned the water on high. When she reached
behind the door for her towel, she caught her reflection in the
mirror. Standing there, staring at her likeness, she saw the self-
centered, belligerent girl who had shut out her dad when he needed
her most. She saw the woman who ignored her conscience and all
she'd been taught as a child, so she could fit into Mark's
manipulative, controlling world. She saw the hardened woman
she'd become because the life she thought she wanted had betrayed
her and made her out to be a fool. She watched as a tear slipped
down her cheek as she thought about all she had sacrificed.

It was sobering.

Illuminating.

She swiped at her tears, wishing she could whisk away her
feelings as easily, then sighed. "He deserves so much more."

———— • ————

Wil went home and plopped down on the couch. Staring at the
ceiling—still wondering what Cassidy saw when she looked up—he
struggled with his feelings. It was obvious she was keeping him at
arm's length. Maybe he was pushing too much.

*I'm just trying to make her feel needed . . . show her she still has
a lot to offer.*

Even so, she was dealing with all the baggage that comes with a
divorce, and he needed to allow her time to handle things her own
way.

I need to give Cassidy her space.

Just then the phone rang. Caller ID showed who it was. At first,
he was going to let the machine answer it, but common courtesy
won out.

"Hi, Ella, what's up? Actually, I do have some drawings of what
I am looking for. Have you seen any of his work? Okay . . . tell him
to meet me at the hardware store tomorrow? I know, I know. I'll
stop calling it that as soon as it's mine. All right, I'll see you then."

170

TWENTY-NINE

Wil, Ella, and her cousin Blake stood in the middle of the ground floor space of the hardware store. They'd already walked the building and now Blake held Cassidy's sketches in his hands.

"Wow! Who is your designer?" he asked.

"Actually, Cassidy isn't a designer; she's an artist."

"Well, these are pretty innovative, considering what you have to work with." He shuffled through them again. "So, do you want me for the job?"

"Possibly. Ella tells me you're a great contractor, that you're a *details* guy, and you appreciate true craftsmanship. After looking at the building, do you think these designs are doable?"

"Anything is doable. I mean, it's only money, right?" he laughed smugly.

Wil was having second thoughts about this Blake guy. He was arrogant and cocky. The way he carried himself. Comments he had made as they walked around. But if he was as talented as Ella said, he could be the perfect guy for the job.

"I know this is a big job, but I have some construction experience and plan on doing a lot of the finish work myself. I could probably do the whole job, given enough time, but it's time I'm in short supply of. That's why I need a contractor. Someone who can meet deadlines, file the necessary permits, and knows the ins and outs of zoning issues and requirements."

Blake shook his head and laughed while scrutinizing Cassidy's sketches. "I charge extra for people who think they can do their own renovations. If I'm going to be expected to go back over your work and fix your mistakes, it's gonna cost you more."

"You know what, Blake," Wil snatched the sketches from his hands, "maybe you're not the man for the job."

"Wait a minute, Wil." Ella said as she pressed her hand to his chest. "Blake doesn't understand how talented you are." Ella turned to her cousin. "Wil explained to me how he completely remodeled a storage shed into a cottage. You'll have nothing to worry about with his work."

"If you say so," Blake smirked, but Ella glared in return.

Wil watched as an unspoken conversation transpired between Blake and Ella, before Blake turned to him and smiled.

"I'm sorry, Wil. I didn't mean to insult you. But if you could see some of the disasters I've had to clean up because homeowners thought they knew what they were doing, I think you'd understand my hesitance." He smiled, but when Wil didn't join him, Blake cleared his throat, and his demeanor turned serious. "I really would like to be in on this project and meet your artist. There's a lot of talent in these sketches, and I would love to pick her brain on some other projects I'm working on."

Wil was glad Blake recognized Cassidy's talent. It would do her good to have someone besides her dad and him compliment her work. "I'll see what I can do about setting up an introduction, but right now, I have an appointment out on Green Valley Road. Ella, I'll leave you to lock up."

Wil headed toward the front door.

"Wait a minute. Did I get the job or not?" Blake asked.

With his hand on the doorknob, Wil turned around. "Write up a detailed proposal and get back to me as soon as you can. If it looks fair, the job is yours."

Ella watched Wil pull away, then turned to Blake. "You almost blew it, you idiot. Sometimes you are so full of yourself, you don't even realize how rude you sound."

"Sorry." Blake shrugged, clearly not caring. "So, when do I get to meet the other woman?"

Ella sighed with frustration. "She's *not* the other woman. I just want to make sure it stays that way."

Ella's reason for enlisting Blake's help was two-fold. Not only was he a very talented contractor, but he was also extremely attractive, and at the moment, unattached.

"I'm not sure when Cassidy will come around next, but I have no doubt she'll stop by once the work in underway. That's where you come in. I want you to . . . let's say . . . be a distraction. Talk plans with her. Take her to a few of your other job sites. Shower her with compliments and attention. If she's the Cassidy Martin I remember from high school, her ego will eat it up. Then maybe I'll get enough time with Wil for him to see I'm not just a real estate agent. I have more to offer him than Cassidy does. A lot more."

THIRTY

Cassidy did not see much of Wil the last couple of weeks, which was a good thing. She really needed time to figure out her life, and when Wil was around, she just could not seem to think straight. So, to fill her days, she took long walks, spent lots of time sketching, and helped out as much as she could around the ranch.

She had just stepped from the shower after a day spent in the pasture, when her cell phone rang. She didn't even realize she still had it plugged in. It was sad to think her phone had been working all this time, but none of her friends from New York had even bothered to call her.

"Hello."

"Cassie?"

She took a deep breath before answering. "Hello, Mark."

"How are you doing, Cass?"

"Fine." But was she? Just hearing Mark's voice sent her reeling. It was like he had some kind of twisted hold on her. Even though she was furious with him and wanted to lash out at him for the way he'd manipulated her over the years, and the pain he'd caused her, the other part of her wanted to apologize for running, see if they could try again, and pretend everything was all right. Knowing she'd never be good enough for a man like her father or Wil, she figured living with Mark—even with his unfaithfulness—was all she deserved.

"You never sent back the papers I sent you. I wasn't sure what to make of it."

"What papers?"

"The papers . . . with my letter. I left them with your dad. I know you must have seen them because you sent back the divorce papers."

Cassidy was trying to think. Did she read any other papers? She remembered reading his letter of apology and signing the divorce papers next to all the little arrow markers, but she didn't remember seeing any other papers.

"Mark, I'm not sure what you're talking about. I thought the divorce papers where the only thing in the envelope. I signed at all the arrows, had it notarized, and mailed them back. Do you mean you haven't filed for divorce yet?" Cassidy's mind spun at the thought of maybe having one more chance.

Stop it! Stop it right now! You might not deserve a man as decent as Wil, but you sure as heck deserve someone better than Mark.

"No, honey, I filed." His tone was patronizing, killing her like a slow blade across her throat. "I got all those papers back. It was the settlement I was referring to."

"What settlement?" Cassidy tried to sound civil but with each new question she wanted to scream. She wanted to tell Mark how wrong he was and how he was going to live to regret letting her go. She didn't want a settlement, she wanted a husband. One who would promise to love, honor, and respect her. None of which he had done.

"Cassidy, I included a settlement in that package. I asked for you to sign it and send it back to me."

"What's to settle? You're a manipulative jerk, and I'm an idiot for believing you loved me." *That's it! Fight for yourself!*

"Cassie, please. I didn't call to upset you. I just wanted to make sure you were okay . . . in the future. Look, I set up an account in your name and have been depositing money in it. I will continue to deposit money in it for the next five years."

"Why?" Cassidy wiped at her uncontrolled but silent tears. "I signed your prenup when we got married. You don't owe me a thing."

"But I want to make sure you're okay, that you're taken care of."

"Then take care of me, Mark. Come and get me. Tell me you're sorry and that we can start over." Desperate Cassidy was back and sounding more pitiful than ever.

After a long pause, Mark finally spoke. "I'm sorry, Cassie, really I am. Things just didn't work out for us."

"You're right. Because I was all wrong for you. I tried to love you and make things work. I put up with your abuse and your demeaning behavior." Cassidy paced across the room and threw open the window, needing air. "I'm sure Amanda will be perfect for you because you two are cut from the same cloth. You're both cheats. The only question is, who will cheat on whom first? Goodbye, Mark. Have a nice life because that's what I intend to do."

Cassidy threw her phone down on the bed and stood before the window. Her feelings ranged from furious to fearful. From love to hate.

He doesn't care about me. He is only thinking about himself.

Mark must have thought, since she didn't return the settlement papers, she had something else in mind. Maybe he was afraid she was going to press charges for the things he had done to her. Or publicly humiliate him in front of his colleagues and clients. He wasn't trying to take care of her, he was trying to buy her silence.

Suddenly, she felt claustrophobic.

I've got to get out of here.

She quickly got dressed, grabbed her coat, and hurried outside.

The light in the barn was dim and the air was cold. Fall was quickly turning into winter. Cassidy saw her breath as she moved in closer to the stalls.

Rooster, Sassy, and Whiskers all looked over at her, their ears perked up. They had become familiar with Cassidy and probably thought they were getting an evening snack. Even Gent, Wil's horse, looked at Cassidy with curiosity.

She grabbed Whiskers' harness and quickly looped it around the three-year-old's ears. Leading him out of the stall, Cassidy latched him to the hook by the tack room door, then retrieved his blanket and saddle from inside. Cassidy's shoulder ached under the weight of the saddle, but she didn't care. However, when she swung the tack up on the gelding's back, the pain was enough to take her breath away. Leaning against Whiskers until the pain subsided, Cassidy took a couple of deep breaths, then cinched the saddle in place with her good arm. Whiskers bobbed his head and pawed the ground, full of spirit and eager to go for an evening ride. "Okay, boy. Just give me a minute." Muscling herself up into the saddle, Cassidy led Whiskers out of the barn.

Dusk was lying across the mountains, and an auburn ribbon split the evening sky. It would be dark soon, but no darker than Cassidy's emotions.

When she heeled Whiskers, he responded with a leap. He took off down the dirt road and over a knoll before Cassidy could give him further directions. It didn't matter since she had no specific destination in mind. She was just running.

You're pathetic. You pleaded with your abuser to take you back.

How is it Mark could make her feel so empty and worthless? The power he had over her reminded her how weak and needy she was.

This is not who I want to be. I'm stronger than this. I'm talented. You'll see. I'll make something of myself without your help or your connections.

She would prove to Mark it was he who had made the mistake.

Cassidy realized Whiskers was grunting with every stride, sweat on his withers, even in the cool night air. "Sorry, boy." She pulled on the reigns and slowed his stride. "I didn't mean to push you so hard." Turning him around, they headed home at a much easier pace.

Cassidy saw lights on at Wil's place and decided to stop by and see how things were going at the hardware store. As she approached the cottage, she heard voices from the porch.

It was Wil and Ella.

She stopped where she was, not wanting to be seen. Their voices were muffled so Cassidy couldn't make out what they were saying, but she didn't miss the kiss Ella gave him. After Wil walked back inside, Ella headed to her car, and Cassidy turned to go.

"Cassidy . . . is that you?" Ella called out.

She cringed. It was obvious Ella had seen her. There was nothing she could do but acknowledge her. Dismounting Whiskers, Cassidy walked over to where Ella stood by her car.

"Hi, Ella. I was just out for a ride when I heard you and Wil. I didn't want to disturb you, so I decided to hang back until you were gone. Sorry if I startled you."

Ella was fiddling with the buttons on her blouse, acting nervous. "Oh no, you didn't startle me. I saw you. I'm just a little embarrassed is all. I mean . . . I didn't intend for anything to happen. I just wanted to congratulate Wil on the closing of his new office space . . . and . . .well, you know how it is?"

"Yes . . . I guess I do." Cassidy looked at the two buttons still unfastened. "Well, good night, Ella." Cassidy started to lead Whiskers away.

"Hey, Cassidy, before you leave, can I ask a favor?"

Cassidy turned back around.

"My cousin, Blake, he's the contractor who will be working on Wil's place. He absolutely loved the sketches you did for Wil and was wondering if he could get an introduction."

Cassidy was puzzled. "Wil never said anything to me about it."

"Well, I'm sure that was his way of protecting you. You know, being as sensitive as you are right now. I'm sure he didn't want to pressure you into anything that might send you spiraling again."

Cassidy clenched her jaw, infuriated Wil had been talking to Ella about her. It was enough to make her want to march into his house and set him straight. It was one thing if he wanted to carry on with Ella. He was an adult and that was his business, but he had no right talking about her personal life with others.

"Well, I don't know what you're talking about, Ella. I'm a big girl. I don't need people to protect me. I can take care of myself."

"Oh honey, don't take me wrong. I think it's kind of sweet, you know, the way a big brother takes care of his little sister. It's just . . . well . . . Blake is quite charming and very good looking. I think Wil was probably being a little over protective, that's all."

Cassidy seethed inside. How dare Wil screen who she talks to. "So, Ella, tell me when I can meet this Blake. I'm flattered he likes my sketches and would love to hear what he has to say about them."

"Great! How about I have him give you a call tomorrow? In fact, he should be at Wil's most of the day. Since the place is officially his, I know he won't want to waste any time getting started."

———— • ————

Cassidy slammed the door of the tack room and marched toward the house. She was ready to slam the front door, when she noticed her dad reading in the living room. She didn't want to disturb him or have to field any questions, so she closed the door quietly and headed for the stairs.

"You okay, Cassidy?"

The concern in her father's voice stopped her. She turned to see him looking at her over the rim of his reading glasses.

"I'm fine, Dad, why?" Cassidy edged up the corners of her lips into what she hoped was a convincing smile.

"I heard you talking to Mark. I wasn't ease-dropping, mind you; I was just walking by."

She waited for the inevitable question.

"Do you really still love him, Cassidy, after everything he's done?"

Cassidy crossed the room and sat down opposite him. She took a deep breath as she tried to gather her thoughts. "No Dad, I don't love him. In fact, I'm not sure I ever did."

"Why do you say that? It's obvious you're still hurting."

Cassidy took a minute to answer. Speaking her feelings out loud would make them more real, expose the person she'd become.

"Dad, I think what hurts the most is that I failed. I failed as an artist. As a wife. At life. And I have no one to blame but myself. I don't know if I was ever in love with Mark, or if I was only in love with the idea of Mark."

Cassidy walked over to the fireplace trying to rid herself of the chill coursing inside her.

"I wanted to prove I was better than anyone in this stupid little town. I wanted to prove Cassidy Martin was too good and too talented to waste her time in Smallville, U.S.A. The only thing I proved is that I was a stupid little farm girl taken in by the trappings of the big city. I realize I didn't have friends in New York; I had acquaintances. People liked me because of the money and the social class Mark represented. My whole life there was a lie."

She swallowed hard, trying to control her emotions, but the truth of it all hurt.

"Mark didn't love me. He was taking marriage for a spin and decided to trade me in for his freedom. It was like I had a lease on life in New York. The lease ran out and here I am. A nobody again." Cassidy looked at her dad, her hurt twisting into anger. "Your daughter's a failure, Mr. Martin, clear and simple."

She walked from the fireplace to the stairs. "There's leftovers in the frig, Dad. Go ahead and eat without me."

————— • —————

Cassidy left before Joseph could utter a single word of disagreement. And what he'd just witness did not bode well. A callousness had risen in her demeanor as she spoke. He was afraid another wave of self-destruction was on its way.

Resting his head in his hands, he whispered, "God, please don't let her plummet too far before she looks up."

THIRTY-ONE

The next day, Cassidy awoke with a sense of determination. If Liberty was where she was destined to live, then she might as well start living.

If this Blake guy is as interested in my plans as Ella says, maybe he can help me find some work.

Cassidy parked in front of Wil's new building. She pulled at the hem of her hip-length tweed jacket as she got out of the truck and took a quick glance at her reflection in the side mirror. She wanted to look her best when introduced to Blake. Ella had already told her he was good looking, so she wanted to make an equally as good impression on him. Business-like but not stuffy. The red silk blouse she'd chosen shimmered in the rays of the sun, and her fitted black slacks accentuated her every curve.

She sauntered into the office space, her stiletto heels clicking against the old wood floor. Hearing voices upstairs, she scaled the steps to the third floor. Wil looked surprised to see her, but Ella just smiled. Out of the corner of her eye, Cassidy saw someone standing on the other side of the room.

A tall man with sandy-blond hair, wearing well-worn jeans and a tight-fitting black T-shirt, gave her the once over. She couldn't help but do the same.

Manual labor definitely agrees with him.

"Am I interrupting?" Cassidy asked as she walked toward Wil and Ella.

"No, not at all," Wil answered. "We were just going over your sketches. Blake," Wil turned to tall, tan, and gorgeous, "this is Cassidy Martin, the artist I told you about. Cassidy, this is Blake Simpson. He'll be the contractor working on the renovations."

Blake stepped forward and extended his hand to Cassidy. "It's nice to meet you, Ms. Martin. Your designs are quite creative. In fact, I have a few projects that need a little polishing. Maybe you could take a look at them?"

Blake let go of her hand, but not her eyes. His riveting stare made it hard for Cassidy to think. "Thank you, Mr. Simpson. I'm not a professional by any means, but I would love the opportunity to do more designing. It's a creative outlet for me."

"Good." He smiled. "Then maybe when I'm done here, we can go to a site I'm working on in Green Valley. It's going to be a huge undertaking. Ten thousand square feet. Three levels. And a prima donna for a housewife."

"Wow, sounds exciting."

She looked at Wil, hoping to see some encouragement, but only saw a rigid expression. When his phone rang, he turned away to answer it.

Cassidy walked over to where Blake was reviewing her sketches.

"What you designed here," he pointed at the floor to ceiling headboard she'd drawn, "how it separates the room, creating a closet area, it's really unique."

"Or practical. Have you ever known a woman to survive without a closet?"

He laughed. "So . . . not only is your design innovative and functional, but you're also looking out for Wil's future. You know, the old adage, 'Happy wife. Happy life.'"

She casually glanced at Wil. "Yeah. Something like that," she whispered.

"Duty calls," Wil said as he stuffed his phone back in his pocket. "I have to go to the Randall's."

"The Randall's out on Highway 29?" Ella perked up.

"Yeah, on Meadows Road."

"Do you think you can give me a lift home? I rode in with Blake, but if you're headed in that direction, you could drop me off so Blake wouldn't have to backtrack."

Wil looked from Blake, to Cassidy, and then back to Ella. "Sure. No problem."

"Great." Blake interjected, rubbing his hands together like a mad professor. "That will give me time to pick Ms. Martin's brain for ideas." He turned to her. "How about we get a quick bite to eat, then I can show you the layout of the Gentry place?"

Cassidy saw a flicker of irritation in Wil's eyes but ignored it. If he was going to spend time with Ella, he had no business interfering with who she spent time with, especially when it could mean a job offer.

"That sounds fine, Mr. Simpson."

"Blake, please. Mr. Simpson is my father."

"Okay, as long as you drop the Ms. Martin. It's actually Mrs. Grayson, but Cassidy will do just fine."

Ella smiled alongside Blake but when Cassidy looked at Wil, she could tell he wasn't thrilled with the arrangement.

"Okay, well, we'd better get going if you have an appointment," Ella said to Wil, then clutched onto his elbow and smiled. "These stairs are a little rickety. You don't mind, do you?"

Cassidy watched as they crossed the room, but before they were completely out of view, Ella looked back over her shoulder and smiled. Cassidy recognized the look. It was a smile of challenge.

Challenge accepted.

———— • ————

"So, Ella, tell me about Blake," Wil said as he pulled away from the curb.

"Well, he's a graduate from Texas A & M where he got a degree in engineering. He's worked all over the world. New York. Amsterdam. Tokyo. Australia. And most recently, he turned down a very lucrative job offer in Chicago, because he didn't want to live in a suit and tie world anymore."

"And . . ."

"And what?"

"Is he married, single, divorced . . ."

"What does that have to do with his qualifications?" Ella asked, even though Wil knew she understood why he was asking.

"I saw the way he looked at Cassidy. It's not just her sketches he's interested in."

"Is that a problem, Wil? I mean, maybe a little male distraction would be a good thing for Cassidy right now."

"No. She's not ready for that."

"I beg to differ," Ella giggled. "I saw the way she looked at Blake."

"No. She was just flattered he appreciated her talent. She's not ready for another relationship. Her divorce isn't even settled yet."

Ella moved closer to Wil as he pulled into her driveway. "That's just a formality." She ran her hand down his arm and in a gentle voice said, "Wil, I don't want to hurt your feelings or anything, but just because Cassidy isn't interested in *you*, doesn't mean she's not interested in men."

Wil was ready to fire back, but again, Ella patted his arm and allowed her hand to slip to his thigh. "Look, Wil, Cassidy as much as told me she appreciates the brotherly attention you've shown her. That's how she sees you, as a big brother. Please don't let her interfere with what we might have together."

"But, Ella—"

"I know you said you just want to be friends, but be honest, the only reason you said that was because you were trying to leave room in your life for Cassidy. But as you can see, she's moving on. She's bouncing back just fine. Cassidy's a very intelligent woman. I think she knows what she wants."

Wil allowed the truck to idle while he digested what Ella said. Maybe she was right. Cassidy and he were always rubbing each other the wrong way. Maybe their individual personalities were just too different for them to blend. He only wanted the best for Cassidy. He wanted to see her happy. He just wasn't convinced Blake Simpson would be the one to respect her as she should be or treat her like she deserved.

Ella placed a light kiss on Wil's cheek. "Call me?"

Wil looked at her and saw the affection she was so willing to give him. He smiled. "Sure, how about lunch tomorrow?"

Ella beamed. "That sounds great. In fact, we can have lunch here. I have a great Spicy Mongolian Beef recipe. Can you handle hot?"

He didn't miss the double entendre, but he chose to ignore it. "I'll call you tomorrow."

THIRTY-TWO

Cassidy walked with Blake to the little sandwich shop around the corner. They each ordered, but Blake insisted on paying for everything.

After they took their seats at a corner table, and Blake unwrapped his pastrami on rye, he asked, "So tell me, what other projects have you worked on?"

"None." She laughed. "I'm sure Wil told you I'm an artist not a designer." Cassidy opened her ham and cheese and began to pull the unwanted shreds of lettuce from the mayonnaise-laden bread.

"You're kidding me, right?"

"No, really. I mean I've always enjoyed designing, and I doodled plans on how I wanted to change my apartment in New York, but I've never done anything for someone else."

"That's incredible, because your sketches are as good, if not better, then anything I've seen of late. And I've worked with some pretty prominent designers over the years."

Cassidy covertly studied Blake's features while he talked. He was quite handsome, and in excellent shape. But she was pretty sure he was several years older than her, especially after using a phrase like 'over the years.' He was not new to the construction business, but he hid his real age well behind a toned physique and captivating eyes.

"So," Blake said after taking a swig of his soda. "Did you ever incorporate your designs into your New York apartment, because if you did, I would love to see any pictures you might have."

"No, I never did. My hus—" Cassidy stopped abruptly, not sure what to say.

"It's okay," Blake said with a compassionate tone. "Ella told me you're going through a divorce. I understand how that is, I've been there myself."

Relief swept over Cassidy. Finally, someone who might

understand how she's feeling. "What happened? I mean with your marriage?" When Blake looked away, Cassidy realized what an idiot she was. "I'm sorry. That was completely out of line. I had no business asking such a personal question. Please accept my apology."

"No, it's all right. It was a while ago." Blake took another bite of his sandwich and swallowed. "Kim decided monogamy wasn't her thing. We were living in Chicago at the time, and I was consumed with my career, trying to make a name for myself. I gave her too many lonely nights, and enough time to allow her mind and her eye to wander. I knew Kim was feeling neglected, so I tried to come home earlier and show her a little more attention. I thought things were getting better."

Blake paused as if reliving a moment in time. "She no longer acted depressed when I got home late at night, and she stopped calling me hour after hour asking me when I was coming home. I should have seen the signs. Things weren't better. She just found attention somewhere else.

"I was trying so hard to give her the life I thought she deserved. The long hours, the big deals, I thought I was doing it for us. Then one day, I decided to surprise her with a romantic weekend getaway." Blake took another sip of his soda before continuing. "I was the one who was surprised. She'd been having an affair for several months without me knowing. Shows how perceptive I was. I came home to pack for the weekend. Kim didn't realize I was in the house when she came home with her lover. They were panting all over each other when I walked into the room."

When Blake stopped again, Cassidy wanted to assure him he didn't need to continue, but she didn't. She wanted to know she wasn't the only one who had been so naïve, so blind, she didn't see the signs around her.

"Kim looked at me that day with indifference. She wasn't sorry she'd been caught; she was relieved. She no longer had to live a lie. She asked me for a divorce on the spot. So, I packed my bags and left while she and her boyfriend sat together in my living room."

Cassidy sat in silence. She didn't know what to say. Her appetite had disappeared, and her heart felt overwhelmed with sympathy for Blake. Their situations were almost identical, the outcome strangely the same.

"That's when I moved here. I never did like big-city life. I was a square peg trying to fit into a round hole. I was doing what was expected of me, but not what I wanted. Everyone was telling me how far I could go and how talented I was, but I wasn't happy. Sure, I wanted to be a contractor. I love working with my hands and seeing visions come to life. But multi-level high rises and state-of-the-art structures were not what I wanted to build."

Cassidy hung on his every word, knowing Blake could truly identify with what she was going through.

"So, I moved here and started working on homes, started working with real people again." Blake finished his sandwich then turned the tables on her. "So, what's your story?" He leaned back in his chair as he shook the last crumbs from his chip bag into his mouth.

Cassidy nearly choked on her soda. She watched as Blake lobbed his chip bag into the trash, then turned his attention back on her.

"Well . . . I . . . I mean . . . Mark . . . not me . . . I wasn't . . ." Cassidy stuttered, sounding like an idiot who couldn't string three words together.

Blake reached across the table and laid his hand over hers. "It's okay, Cassidy. You don't have to talk about it if you don't want to."

She carefully slid her hand from under his and reached for the napkin across her lap. "It's not that, it's just . . ."

"I know it must be hard on you," Blake interrupted. "I've had a few years to deal with it, but this is all new territory for you. So, for what it's worth, if you ever need to talk, I'm here. I'm not the judgmental type either. My philosophy is live and let live." He wiped his mouth on a napkin before tossing it into the trash can, then turned to her and smiled. "Ready to see a monster of a house?"

Cassidy was relieved by the change of subject. "Sounds good to me."

———— • ————

Wil pulled up in front of his building right behind the truck Cassidy drove to town. He looked at his watch. *I was gone for over two hours.*

And Cassidy was still out with Blake.

He walked inside, stared at the four walls, and thought about what Ella had said earlier.

Does Cassidy really see me as just a big brother? She must know my feelings are deeper than that?

But then again, maybe not.

Wil had been careful to give her space, thinking she needed time to think, to deal with her situation. Maybe he should have been more forward, showed her he really cares.

"No," he said, then started to pace. "I did the right thing. Cassidy needs time to regain her equilibrium. She's hurt and angry and has a tendency to be self-destructive. And a rebound relationship with a guy she's just met is only going to make matters worse."

Wil took a moment to examine his feelings for Cassidy, surprised how easily he was willing to ignore the fact that she was still legally married and at odds with God.

But her marriage had been an act of rebellion, Joseph said so. And it was over for Biblical reasons. Mark broke their marriage covenant long before divorce papers were filed. Maybe she never loved Mark to begin with.

Even with her anger issues, and her fractured relationship with God, Wil could not help but think there was still hope for Cassidy. She just needed time to think.

Hopefully Blake wouldn't prove to be too big of a distraction.

THIRTY-THREE

Even though there was only a shell of a building to walk through when they arrived at the Green Valley home, Cassidy had no problem visualizing it in her head. Blake described each room in detail, and then went on to explain some of the design issues they were dealing with.

When they were done walking the enormous home, Blake rolled out the blueprints for the house on the tailgate of his truck. "So, what do you think?"

"Well . . ." she crossed her arms against her chest, trying to ward off the chill in the air. "you said Mrs. Gentry wants an intimate feel in the living spaces, but enough room for lavish parties. So, why don't you put in retractable glass doors between the great room and the patio instead of French doors? She can achieve the cozy, warm, feeling she's looking for with decor choices, but when she has a party, the retractable doors can disappear into the walls, allowing the party to flow out onto the covered patio, giving her double the space. As long as her parties aren't in the winter," Cassidy laughed.

Blake stared at her with a look of revelation. "That's it! I can't believe I didn't think of it sooner. With Helen leaning towards a French country style, I immediately defaulted to French doors. But I could easily frame out the panes of glass to *look* like French doors. Cassidy, you're a genius!"

Blake had his arms around Cassidy before she could react. It was just quick side hug, meant only as a thank you. Even so, it caught her way off guard. Luckily, Blake didn't seem to notice her awkwardness.

"Got any other ideas?" he asked, excitedly.

"Well, this area right here," she pointed on the blueprints, "you said it's where a large built-in is going to be."

"Right?"

"Why when you have a media room and a game room?"

"Because Mr. Gentry insisted he wasn't going to be shooed off into another room whenever he wanted to watch a ball game. He insists the house be functional. Not just a show piece for his wife."

"But having the entertainment center against this wall," she pointed, "and the sofas here," she pointed again, "you're sectioning off the room. People will be sitting with their backs to the rest of the house and most of the view."

"I know, but it can't be helped. Hal insists on having a TV in the main room."

Cassidy chewed on her lip while she studied the plans. "Okay. How about this, since Mrs. Gentry wants an open feel, how about a credenza here, in the middle of the room and either a large couch or sectional against the wall or twin couches flanking the credenza."

"How does that help anything? Now the TV is the main focal point. Helen will have a fit."

"You didn't let me finish," Cassidy said with a Cheshire Cat grin. "When the TV isn't in use, it disappears *inside* the credenza. With a flip of a switch, the TV lowers inside, and what you have left is a beautiful custom furnishing. Surround sound can be put in the ceiling, and everything would run off a phone app."

"Okay, that's it," Blake said with a wave of his hands. "I'm giving you copies of all these plans, and then I'm going to arrange a meeting with you and Helen Gentry."

"Oh, but I couldn't."

"Believe me, Cassidy, you can, and you should. And . . . you'll be more than compensated for your time. Helen has already gone through two interior designers, and she was beginning to look at me like I was next on the chopping block. Maybe if I bring you in on this project, I'll work my way back into her good graces."

Blake rolled up the plans to the house while Cassidy pondered the idea. She was excited but terrified. She always thought she had a talent when it came to design, but Mark never encouraged it, so she let it go. Blake, on the other hand, dealt with designers all the time. He knew what was good and what was just okay.

But he truly seems impressed.

When Blake squeezed her hand, she jumped and quickly

withdrew.

"I'm sorry. I didn't mean to startle you. You just seemed to zone out on me," Blake said as he raised the tailgate of his truck and gave it a quick shove.

"I'm sorry. I guess I was just thinking about what you said. Do you really think my ideas are good?"

"No." He shook his head, then smiled. "They're exceptional."

"Really?"

"Listen, Cassidy," he leaned against the bed of his truck, his demeanor all business. "This project is one of my biggest since going out on my own. And the Gentry's are very well connected. I would not jeopardize this or future deals just to make you feel good. Your talent is real. The way you looked at those plans, listened regarding the vision of the client, and came up with a solution, that's natural. Instinctive."

Cassidy's pulse raced with excitement even as negative memories volleyed around in her head. *Leave it alone, Cassie. Leave it to the professionals, Cassie. Don't be ridiculous, Cassie.* The many times she tried to redecorate or reinvent their penthouse, Mark always shot her down. Unless he was paying hundreds of thousands of dollars to a top-notch designer, he wasn't happy.

She walked around the side of the truck, glancing at Blake across the bed. *But Blake seems genuinely impressed. Like he said, why would he jeopardize such a lucrative deal just to compliment me?* He smiled back at her, a rather sexy smile. *Because he might be interested in something more than just my design ideas?* Climbing into the cab, she considered the possibility of his interest extending past professional reasons.

So, what if it is more than professional? The thought had no more crossed her mind when her conscience bantered back. *But what about Wil?*

Inwardly, she groaned, hating her analytical mind. *What about Wil?* She was sure he had something going on with Ella. *Besides, I'm beneath his standards. He wouldn't want to date me; he'd want to save me. A relationship with him would be filled with so many dos and don'ts, it would be like dating my dad.*

Blake started the truck and slowly drove down the rutted driveway. "You know what, Cassidy, I like you. You're easy to talk to." He glanced her way and wink.

She almost laughed out loud. *I guess I don't have to wonder.* Blake was clearly interested, and it made her feel good. In just a few short hours, he had buoyed her self-confidence and made her feel like she was a person with something to contribute. And the way he looked at her made her feel desirable again.

"What would you say to dinner and a movie tonight?"

Wow, he certainly doesn't believe in wasting any time. But now that the questioned was posed to her, she wasn't sure if she was ready. Silently she weighed her feelings.

"Don't tell me you're hung up on Wil?" Blake asked as he sped toward town.

"No," she snapped, sounding a little too defensive. "It has nothing to do with Wil," she softened her tone. "I'm just not sure I'm ready to go out yet; that's all."

"Well good. Then at least I know I have a chance," he smiled back. "Besides, Wil seems like a real stuffed shirt. Quite frankly, I don't know what Ella sees in him. He might be good-looking, but so what? He seems like such a bore. Wil obviously doesn't know a good thing when he sees it." Blake chuckled. "Kind of like Ella. She's beautiful, out-going, sexy, but Wil has barely given her the time of day. And if he's not careful, he's going to miss his chance."

Cassidy sat thinking about Wil and Ella. She agreed with Blake's description of Ella. She was all that and more, but Blake had it all wrong if he didn't think Wil was interested. Cassidy saw Ella leaving Wil's house. At night. Long after respectable business hours. Why wouldn't Wil be interested?

She felt a twinge of hope. *Maybe he does have feelings for me?*

Cassidy carried on a casual conversation with Blake while mentally tallying Ella's pros and cons. *The pros are obvious. Beautiful. Successful. Single.* But what were the cons? *She's a bit aggressive.* Maybe Wil didn't like the way she hovered so close or hung onto him. Cassidy could see how that would be a turn-off for someone as conservative as Wil. *Maybe she drinks too much or has an addiction, or a bad reputation around town? Nah, Wil doesn't buy in to gossip. He wouldn't make a judgment call without talking to Ella directly.* And from Ella's behavior, Wil hadn't come right out and told her no. *Then what?*

Blake continued to talk about his projects, old and new. Cassidy commented when necessary to keep up her end of the conversation, but in her mind, she was still playing score keeper with Ella's pros and cons.

"I guess I would have to say my most bizarre project was putting a Jacuzzi tub in a church's baptistery. It was one interesting church. The pastor looked like . . ."

Church.

That's it!

Cassidy had gone to church with her dad every week since she'd been home but never saw Ella there. Not once. *That must be it. She doesn't share Wil's faith.*

Pleased with her internal sleuthing, Cassidy tuned back to Blake's story about the Jacuzzi, but then it dawned on her. She didn't share Wil's faith either.

Then how could he possibly be interested in me?

"Cassidy!"

Blake's abrupt tone got her attention. "I'm sorry, Blake. What did you say?"

"You weren't listening, were you?"

"No. I was. Jacuzzi. Baptistery. Strange looking pastor."

"I asked you about dinner and a movie. You never gave me an answer."

Staring down at the floorboards, she knew there was no way she felt like going out now. Not when she'd come to the realization Wil and she would never work out. "I'm sorry, Blake. I just don't think I'm ready to date yet. Besides, my divorce isn't final, so it would be in poor taste to be seen around town with another man. I have already given the gossip mill more than my fair share of fodder."

"Then I'll make you dinner at my place, and we'll discuss the Gentry house. It will be a business meeting, and an opportunity to get to know each other better." Blake's grin was mischievous to say the least. He definitely had more than business on his mind. "Come on, Cassidy, loosen up. Maybe Wil's ho-hum lifestyle is rubbing off on you."

Blake pulled in behind Cassidy's truck in front of the hardware store and killed the engine. "So, what do you say?"

Cassidy didn't answer. She was too surprised to see Wil leaning against the side of her vehicle. *What in the world?* And now he was stalking toward them like a man on a mission.

THIRTY-FOUR

"Where have you been?"

Wil didn't even wait for her to step out of Blake's truck before firing off questions. "You two have been gone for hours." He waited for her to clear the door before slamming it shut.

"Oh, I'm sorry, Wil. I didn't realize Cassidy was on a time schedule," Blake said as he got out on his side of the truck.

Cassidy watched Wil shoot Blake a warning look to back off. It irritated her that he thought it was any of his business. "I'm a big girl, Wil. You don't need to watch my every move. I can take care of myself."

He locked eyes with her, then took a step back. "I'm sorry. I didn't mean to be rude. I was just getting worried."

"Nothing to worry about." Blake sauntered around the back of the truck and stopped next to her. "Cassidy and I rode out to the Gentry place, and I guess we just lost track of time. She has some great ideas for the project. In fact, she's coming over to my place tonight to go over some of the finer details."

Cassidy turned to Blake to correct him. "But I said—"

"I don't think that's such a great idea, Cassidy," Wil cut her off with a patronizing tone and stare.

Embarrassed by his interference, she fired back, "Frankly, Wil, I don't see how this is any of your business."

"Well, I'm making it my business!" Wil rebutted loudly, drawing the attention and the frowns of a few passersby on the sidewalk. He grasped her arm, pulled her aside, and lowered his voice. "Cassidy, what do you think you're doing?" he scolded. "This guy isn't interested in your ideas. He's interested in you. Period. Can't you see that?"

Cassidy yanked her arm free, deeply insulted Wil assumed her talent wasn't good enough to garner someone's attention.

"Maybe Blake *is* interested in me. But what's it to you? I'm not your responsibility. I am an adult capable of making my own decisions."

"Not very good ones," Wil muttered.

Cassidy wanted to scream. Even though she wasn't interested in going to Blake's place, she would go now just to defy Wil. She turned from him and walked over to where Blake was resting against the side of his truck. "So, what time should I be there?"

Blake smiled, then looked at his watch. "I'm almost done for the day. So . . . let's say . . . seven o'clock." He wrote his address on the back of his business card and handed it to her. With a very pleased smile and one last glance at Wil, he got into his truck and pulled away.

Cassidy marched to her truck as Wil stood on the sidewalk, hands on his hips, head hung between his shoulders. "You're making a mistake, Cassidy. You're only going to get hurt."

"It's okay, Wil. I'm used to it." Cassidy slammed the door to the old truck and pulled away.

Roaring home with enough pent-up energy to run a marathon, she screeched to a stop, marched up the front steps, and slammed the living room door behind her.

"Whoa, whoa, whoa . . . what's this all about?" Joseph said from his place on the couch.

"Nothing. I'm going out tonight, and I need to get cleaned up."

Cassidy slammed her bedroom door, wanting to scream at the top of her lungs, but thought better of it. She hurried to the bathroom, turned the shower on as hot as she could stand it, then stood under its scalding flow. *Wil has no right treating me like this. Insulting and rude. Obviously, he doesn't think I'm as talented as he led me to believe. Maybe he just said those things to make me feel good.*

It hurt more than she would ever let him know.

Cassidy dried herself off and stood in front of her closet. Fingering through her clothes, it struck her what she was doing and cringed. *I'm going to Blake's for all the wrong reasons. I'm only going to annoy Wil. Now I have to hope Blake doesn't get the wrong impression.* Even though she knew he probably already had.

Finally settling on jeans and a black cashmere turtleneck, she held them against herself and looked in the mirror. *Elegant but not provocative. Good. I need to keep this professional.*

After blow drying her hair, she pulled on her stiletto boots and grabbed her purse and black leather jacket. Marching downstairs, she looked at the clock over the fireplace, and realized she still had an hour before she needed to leave. When her father glanced at her from where he sat on the couch, she waited for him to say something.

"What?" Cassidy asked, defensively.

"For someone who's going out, you don't look too happy about it," he said.

"It's Wil." Cassidy started pacing in front of the fireplace. "Sometimes he can be so exasperating."

"So why are you going out with him?"

She stopped. "I'm not going out with him."

"Oh?"

Cassidy looked at her dad knowing he was waiting for more information.

"I'm going out with Blake Simpson. He's the contractor working on Wil's building. He saw some of the plans I drew up for Wil's place, and we struck up a conversation. He asked for my opinion on another job he is working on, and we just kind of hit it off."

Her dad didn't have to say a word for her to know he didn't like the idea, but he told her so any way. "Do you really think that's what you should be doing right now?"

"Why not?" she argued.

"Well . . . I just don't think it looks right. You are still married. People could get the wrong idea."

"What people? I'll be at his house. No one will see us. Besides, I don't care what people think."

He sighed heavily. His sanctimonious 'I know better than you' sigh. Cassidy was ready to fire off at him, when she noticed the tired look creasing his face. "Are you okay, Dad? You look tired."

"I guess I'm just not as young as I use to be." He massaged his worried brows then kneaded the back of his neck. "So, what do you know about this Blake fella?"

"Not much," she said with a cavalier chuckle. "But I'm sure I'll find out more at dinner."

"Cassidy Ann!" Joseph used his disciplinarian tone. "You're going out with someone you know nothing about? It's just reckless."

"Fine!" Cassidy planted her hands on her hips. "If you must

know, he's very good looking, probably ten years older than me, divorced, and he thinks I'm a talented designer."

"He's divorced?"

"Yes, Dad, he's divorced. His wife cheated on him, then asked for a divorce. Sound familiar?"

"So that's it?"

"That's what?" Cassidy raised her voice but caught herself before she said anything more. "Nothing."

Cassidy couldn't tell if her father was conceding because he was tired, or if he was just giving up on her all together.

"You don't get it, Dad, do you? I know what you want. You want me to settle down with someone like Wil. Stay home. Have babies. Well, that's not going to happen. Wil isn't interested in me, and I'm not exactly what men would consider the cream of the crop. Blake's different. He understands what I'm going through and doesn't give me that judgmental look you and Wil keep throwing my way. He's been through the same thing. He understands how I feel."

"But Cassidy, going from one relationship to another is not going to help you. You're trying to fill a void in your life only God can fill. Sure, this Blake character knows how you're feeling, but if you think he's going to nurse your wounds without looking for a little nursing himself, you're only kidding yourself."

"Well, you know what, Dad, maybe I'm ready to give out a little nursing. I know this will come as a shock to you, but I'm a woman, not a little girl. Maybe Blake Simpson is exactly what I need to get over Mark. God knows I would never be suitable enough for your precious Wil."

"Don't talk like that, Cassidy. You're making a mistake. And as long as you live in my house, I think I have some say about the matter."

Her dad was seriously upset, the color of his complexion belying his frustration. But she didn't care. She would not be treated like a child.

"Fine . . . I'll find a place of my own tomorrow." She glared at him, then headed to the door. With a backward glance, she added, "Don't wait up. I don't expect to be home anytime soon."

THIRTY-FIVE

Cassidy was shaking as she drove to Blake's house. In fact, she drove past his street and continued on for another twenty minutes before turning back around. She was so angry at her father and his self-righteous attitude, she wanted to scream. He didn't understand her. He didn't understand anything. He lived in such an unrealistic world; he couldn't even comprehend the struggles she was feeling.

Mark had hurt her deeply and crushed her feelings of self-worth. Wil constantly reprimanded her and made her feel like a child in need of discipline. On the other hand, Blake understood the emptiness she was feeling. He'd been betrayed just like her. He knew what it was like to have what others thought was a perfect world, crumble around you. Not only that, he recognized her talent and was encouraging her to do things she had never done before. How could that be wrong? How could positive reinforcement be bad for a change? Cassidy pondered the question as she pulled into Blake's driveway.

His house was impressive. Large and expansive. The log cabin style fit his masculine demeanor, and his attention to detail reinforced his talent as a builder.

Blake was waiting for her at the door wearing a crisp pair of jeans and a casual, navy, crewneck sweater. Leaning on the doorframe with his arms crossed against his chest, Cassidy watched as his eyes slowly traveled the length of her body. When his eyes met hers, he smiled. Feeling reckless, she questioned what she was doing. There was no denying the sexual tension between them, and by accepting Blake's invitation to join him as his place, she was pretty much waving a green flag. But was this what she wanted? Was she really attracted to Blake or was she just trying to punish her father and Wil for their disapproving attitudes toward her?

I'm a big girl. I can do what I want with whom I want.

When she reached the front door, Blake placed a light kiss on her cheek and slipped his arm around her waist.

"You have a lovely home, Blake." Cassidy tried to act as if his familiar behavior didn't bother her, even though she felt unsettled by his forwardness.

"I have good taste," he said as he looked into her eyes and leaned in once again for another kiss, this time placing one on her lips.

Cassidy's heart thundered inside her chest while her conscience condemned her. *I'm not ready for this. This is wrong.* The only reason she wasn't discouraging Blake's attention was out of spite. To get even with Mark. To anger her father. To put Wil in his place. But she knew she wasn't ready for this.

Encouragement, yes.

Intimacy, no.

Cassidy slipped away from Blake's hold. "So, why don't you give me the grand tour?"

He nodded, then smiled with a—*I get the point*—smile. "Let me help you off with your jacket, before I show you the place."

Cassidy hung her purse on the rack next to her jacket, then followed Blake through the house. Not a house, a mansion. Complete with media room, wine cellar, office space, and game room. It was amazing. Five bedrooms. Six bathrooms. Each one impeccably decorated and unique in design. Finally, they walked to the end of the upstairs hall, and with a grand sweep of his arms, Blake pushed open the double doors to his master suite.

"And this is my sanctuary."

It was like déjà vu. The night Mark took her home for the first time. Introduced her to his world.

Am I ready to do this again?

"Cassidy, are you okay?" Blake gave her hand a squeeze.

"Yes, I'm fine." She pulled her hand away and slowly crossed the room. Glancing to her left, she noticed the massive leather headboard, to her right, a two-sided rock fireplace, with an en suite bath on the other side. It was masculine—all of it. From the club chairs in the sitting area to the rich colors tying it all together. Standing in front of the floor to ceiling windows, she took a deep breath. *I can stop this anytime I want to. I'm not a naïve college student. I'm a woman. And I will not be controlled by any man.* "The view is breathtaking."

"Yes, it is." Blake walked up behind her. "Breathtaking, but lonely."

Cassidy shuddered at his closeness. *I need to tell him this isn't—*

"So . . . are you hungry?" He backed away and walked toward the double doors.

Thank you. She sighed, then turned around. "Ah . . . yes, I mean, no. I mean I'm thirsty. I could use a drink."

"Sure thing." Blake said as she crossed the room to join him. "What will you have?"

"How about a diet Coke?"

"Are you sure you don't want something a little stronger? Unlike some people, I don't see a problem with the occasional drink."

"No. Coke is fine."

"Okay, but I need something with a little more bite to it."

Blake led Cassidy to the gourmet kitchen where he mixed himself a drink that was heavy on the liquor and light on the orange juice. He iced a glass for her soda and handed it to her with a clink. "Cheers." He downed more than half his drink in one swig and quickly poured a refill.

Stepping onto the large tiered deck off the kitchen, Cassidy watched Blake as he lifted the lid on the built-in barbecue. The night air was crisp, so she quickly wrapped her arms across her chest.

"I know it's cold, but I thought grilled steaks sounded good." Blake comment as he pulled a plate of meat from the outdoor refrigerator.

"It sounds wonderful. I'll just go get my jacket." Cassidy slipped back into the house and retrieved her jacket from the entryway coat rack. When she turned to walk away, she heard the muffled ring of her phone. Pulling it out of her purse, she saw Wil's name on the screen.

Really? Are you really that immature?

He knew she was at Blake's. What did he hope to accomplish by calling her here? She silenced the ringer then dropped her phone back inside her purse. She was going to enjoy the rest of her evening, not caring if Wil approved or not.

Dinner was delicious and so was the tasty fondue Blake had made for dessert. Cassidy was completely relaxed and wondered why she had been nervous to begin with. Blake was a great host. They talked at length about some of the projects he'd worked on, but he always swayed the conversation back to interior design and the ideas she had conjured up for the Gentry place. There were a few times when he'd gotten a little friendly with his hands, but it was nothing Cassidy couldn't handle. So far, the evening had gone great.

After Blake cleared the coffee table of the fondue pot and assorted fruit tray, he sat down next to her, handing her a freshly poured drink. She took a couple of sips before Blake nestled closer and kissed her on the neck. She closed her eyes and tried not to overreact. *It's just a kiss.* He continued though, nuzzling her ear, biting her lobe. *It's no big deal. You're an adult.*

"Why don't we go upstairs where we can get more comfortable?" he murmured between kisses.

She cringed. *I should have stopped him sooner.* Taking a deep breath, she whispered, "I'm not ready for that, Blake."

"We can take it slow. Nothing says we have to do anything tonight." Blake persisted as his kisses moved closer to her lips.

"I don't think so, Blake." Cassidy scooted to the edge of the couch and was about to stand when Blake tossed his head back against the couch cushions and groaned.

"Come on, Cassidy, you're not really the 'wet blanket' Ella says you are, are you? Or as 'fragile and unhinged' as *choirboy* seems to think?"

Cassidy was stunned! Absolutely stunned!

She didn't care what Ella said about her. The woman was a tramp, trying to eliminate the competition. But was that what Wil really thought about her? *Fragile? Unhinged?*

Cassidy sat on the edge of the couch, anger boiling inside her.

Blake scooted closer, pushed her hair aside, exposing her neck. "Let's forget them." He kissed behind her ear. "Wil has no idea what an amazing, desirable woman you are." He kissed her again. "You don't need anyone's approval or permission to move on with your life." And again. "You're an adult. A sexy, free-spirit, who should live life to the fullest." And again. "No boundaries. No rules."

Cassidy turned to capture Blake's lips. She kissed him, deep and full. She was her own person. She didn't need anyone's opinions or criticisms. Never again would she allow a man to control her the way Mark had.

She kissed Blake with passion.

She was in control, not Blake.

Not her father.

Not Wil.

Blake pulled back, his eyes brimming with desire. "Come on, Cassidy, let's go upstairs."

His breathless words pierced her anger, and somewhere in the recesses of her mind, she heard herself screaming to stop. But why? So she could prove Wil and Ella right? So she could allow someone else's ideals or outdated philosophies to control her?

No. The thought of Wil wagging his finger in her face only fueled her rebellion.

She stood and followed Blake upstairs.

He led her to the edge of his bed and sat down in front of her. Removing his sweater, Blake exposed his sculpted abs and rounded biceps. Then, he reached up and framed her face with his large hands, and gently pulled her closer until their lips met. Slowing, she descended to the bed with him. Grasping her hands, Blake extended them over her head, and in one quick move, flipped her onto her back, the weight of his body pressing her into the mattress.

Cassidy no longer felt in control and started to panic.

This wasn't what she wanted. Regardless what Wil or Ella thought, she wasn't *fragile* or a *wet blanket,* but she wasn't ready for this either. When Cassidy felt the warmth of Blake's hand push her sweater up, she quickly whispered, "Blake, stop."

"Come on, Cassidy. Just relax."

She struggled, trying to get out from under him, but he had her pinned down. "No, I need to go. This is wrong."

"It's not wrong." He continued kissing her. "Admit it, Cassidy, this is what you wanted, or you wouldn't have come up here to begin with. You're just too worried what Wil and your father will think. Be an adult, Cassidy. Make up your own mind. Don't let others do it for you."

With a burst of rage, Cassidy broke free from Blake's hold. Hurrying to her feet, she pulled her sweater down where it belonged. Blake lay with the backs of his hands across his forehead, his eyes pinned on the ceiling.

"You know what, Blake? You're right. I can make up my own mind, and I've decided to call it a night."

"Come on, Cassidy," he sat up. "Don't be like that. Nothing needs to happen, but you don't have to go either. Let's go back downstairs and talk. Like we were earlier."

Suddenly, there was banging at the front door, followed by repetitive ringing of the doorbell, then more banging.

———— • ————

"What in the . . ." Blake bounded from the bed and went to the front door. He was ready to cuss out whoever was standing there, but when he saw who it was, he decided to change his tactics. He ruffled his fingers through his hair, undid the top button on his jeans, then opened the door.

"Sorry, Wil. I guess we couldn't hear you from upstairs. We were a little . . . preoccupied." Blake made a point of buttoning his jeans as he stood before Wil bare-chested and breathing hard.

"Where's Cassidy?" Wil said, completely ignoring Blake's state of undress.

"She's a little indisposed at the moment, but I'll be sure to tell her you dropped by." Blake tried to shut the door, but Wil pushed hard, forcing his way in.

"Cassidy!" Wil yelled as he took the stairs two at a time.

———— • ————

"Cassidy!" Wil rushed into the master suite where Cassidy stood, looking a little disheveled.

"What are you doing here, Wil? Get out! You have no business barging in here. I am not—"

Wil lunged at her, grabbed her arms, and gave her a shake. "Shut up and listen!"

She broke free, then pushed him away. "What do you think you're doing?"

"Cassidy . . . it's your dad." He waited. Locked eyes with her. Made sure she was listening. "He's had a heart attack."

She looked at him like he was speaking a foreign language. She just stood there, saying nothing. He reached for her but was gentler this time. "Did you hear me, Cassidy? Your dad . . . he's is in critical condition."

THIRTY-SIX

It took a moment for it to sink in.

Her dad was at the hospital.

In critical condition.

When her brain finally engaged the rest of her body, Cassidy rushed downstairs, past Blake, grabbed her purse and jacket, then ran out the front door and jumped into Wil's pickup.

She didn't remember Wil getting into the vehicle or when they hit the highway, but suddenly, she realized road markers were whizzing by the passenger window.

"When did it happen?"

"Near as I can tell, two, maybe three hours ago. I went to the house and—"

"Three hours ago?!" Cassidy hollered. "Why didn't you call me sooner? Why did you wait so long? You should have called me right away. I should be with him right now."

"Check your phone, Cassidy!" Wil yelled back. "I've been calling you all night. I finally had to call Ella to get Blake's address."

Oh no! Cassidy rummaged around in her purse and pulled out her phone. Seven missed calls. All from Wil. She swallowed back the bile rising in her throat as tears slipped down her cheeks.

"How bad is it?" she asked, then braced for the answer.

It took a moment for Wil to reply. "Bad," he whispered, his voice tight with emotion.

"But he's not . . ."

"No. He's hanging on."

Cassidy closed her eyes and pictured her father sitting on the couch. *I should have known something was wrong. He looked so tired.* He'd been resting on the couch when she came home. Something completely out of character for him. *Why didn't I pay*

closer attention? Why did I argue with him?
Because she cared only about herself.
About proving everyone else wrong.
About making Wil jealous.

She closed her eyes, her head spinning with childhood memories. Her first pony ride. Her first ringer in horseshoes. Her first tumble from the saddle. Her dad had been there for every one of them. She had not thought of those memories for years. Why now?

Please, God, don't take him from me.

Cassidy pleaded with the invisible God, who had already claimed her mother. She stifled a morbid chuckle, finding it ironic that she would ask such a huge favor from the God she had chosen to ignore for years.

When Wil pulled into the hospital's emergency entrance, Cassidy looked up, shocked. The hospital hadn't changed at all. It was still small. Old. The same place her mother died twelve years ago. Her first plan of action would be to get her father moved to a better medical facility.

Rushing through the automatic glass doors, Cassidy stood in the middle of a large, sterile hallway. Looking from right to left, she tried to focus on the signs, the arrows on the floor, but none of it made sense.

"This way, Cassidy." Wil led her by a gently placed hand on the small of her back. They rode the elevator to the third floor and then rushed down a white corridor to the nurses' station. Wil quietly spoke to one of the nurses. "This is Cassidy Grayson, Joseph Martin's daughter."

The nurse stood and came around the front of the white partition.

"Mrs. Grayson, if you'll follow me." The nurse walked casually down the hallway like they had all the time in the world. Cassidy wanted to hurry her along but fell into step behind her. The nurse stopped and turned abruptly. Cassidy almost ran into her.

"Mrs. Grayson, your father has had a massive heart attack. His condition is critical, but stable. You can see him, but just for a few moments. Only speak words of encouragement, nothing that will agitate him."

Cassidy didn't appreciate the nurse's instructions. What did she think she would do? Go into his room ranting and raving?

Moving past the woman, Cassidy took a breath, wiped her face, then slowly pushed open the large white door. Stepping into the dimly lit room, she brought her hand up to her mouth to silence the gasp rising inside her. Her dad lay completely still and looked as pale as the room surrounding him. As she stepped closer to his bed, she heard the humming and beeping from the machines he was hooked up to. Feeling like she was going to collapse, Cassidy clutched the bed rail with all the strength she could muster.

Just then, she noticed a flutter. It took a moment, but her father finally opened his eyes. They looked like glass. Gone was the vibrant blue that had always been his most attractive feature.

He moved his frail hand closer to the rail, and she instantly reached for it and gave him a gentle squeeze. "I'm here, Dad. Everything is going to be okay."

He mouthed the words more than he spoke them, but she could still make out what he said.

"I love you too, Dad." Cassidy let the tears run down her face over lips that forced a smile. "Now you need to get your rest and do everything the nurses and doctors tell you, okay?"

He smiled a weak smile then closed his eyes. His breathing labored, but at least it was still there.

Cassidy stepped into the hallway and braced herself against the wall. She felt her legs buckle, but Wil immediately pulled her into his arms and held her up as she sobbed against his chest.

"It's going to be okay, Cassidy."

She heard Wil's words of assurance and felt as he stroked her hair and hushed her cries. But she couldn't respond. Her mind was spinning.

With his arm around her shoulders, Wil led her to the waiting room at the end of the hall. He lowered her into a chair, then swung one around to face her. He sat down and held her hands. Caressing her fingers with his thumbs, he asked, "Are you okay?"

Cassidy sniffled and shook her head. "It's my fault. I had an argument with him before I left the house. I told him I was going to move out. This is all my fault, Wil. I did this."

With her face in her hands, she bawled, not caring who heard her. Wil moved to sit next to her, pulling her close as she cried.

They sat in silence for what felt like an eternity. Cassidy rested her head on Wil's shoulder, neither of them saying a word. The only noise was the occasional shudder from her crying jag. For the hundredth time, she looked at the clock on the wall, doing and redoing the math. Two hours. Almost three. But still, nobody had come to talk to them. She stood to leave, when a man in a white coat, holding an iPad walked in.

"Mrs. Grayson?" he asked as he looked up from the tablet.

"Yes, I'm Mrs. Grayson. How is my father? Is he going to be okay?"

"Let's sit down a moment, Mrs. Grayson, Mr. Grayson." The doctor nodded at Wil assuming he was the Mr. who went with her Mrs. Cassidy didn't bother to correct him. Pulling a chair around so he could sit in from of them, the doctor looked at Cassidy sternly. "Mrs. Grayson, I'm not going to mince words. Your father has had a very serious heart attack."

"But he's going to make it, right?" Cassidy asked, then held her breath waiting for the doctor to assure her everything was going to be okay.

He took too long.

She gasped. "He has to be okay, doctor. He's all I've got." Her eyes swelled once again with tears, before spilling over. "I'll do anything. Work the ranch, sell the ranch, anything to help him get better. I'll—"

The doctor raised his hand. "Mrs. Grayson . . . Mrs. Grayson, please, let me finish."

Cassidy calmed herself and tried to listen.

"Barring any complications, I see no reason why your father won't be able to recover."

"Thank you!" Cassidy clasped her hands together. "Thank you. Thank you. Thank you."

"But, Mrs. Grayson, it will not be a *full* recovery."

"What?"

"Your father's heart attack has damaged a portion of his heart. Unfortunately, there is nothing we can do to repair it."

"Okay." That was a little sobering. Her father has a damaged heart, and it was her fault. *But he's going to be okay. That's what matters.* "When can he come home?" she asked.

"We will be keeping him several days for observation and monitoring. It's a day-to-day prognosis. If he has no setbacks during that time, he should be able to go home in a week, maybe sooner."

"Do you expect there to be setbacks?" Cassidy asked, not sure she was ready for the answer.

"We will just have to wait and see."

"Can I see him again?"

"Yes, but don't tire him out. Right now, even the simplest thing like talking or trying to follow a conversation takes a great deal of energy. He needs to stay as quiet as possible for the next forty-eight hours." "I understand." Cassidy stood, and Wil stood with her. The doctor extended his hand to Cassidy, then to Wil. "I suggest you go home and get some sleep, Mrs. Grayson. We can take care of your father here, but when he goes home it will be up to you to take care of him. You're going to need all the energy you can get." With that, the doctor walked away and disappeared down the fluorescent lit corridor.

Cassidy turned to Wil. "I want to see him again, even if it is just for a moment."

Wil nodded. "I'll wait here."

Cassidy walked to the nurses' station and explained that the doctor said she could see her father again, then quietly pushed open his door, and tiptoed inside. Sitting in the chair alongside her father's bed, she laid her hand over his, noticing the contrast. Her hand was tanned and healthy, his translucent and frail.

She rested her head on the rail and closed her eyes, concentrating on the feel of his hand. As long as she was touching him, she felt the life that ran through him. She wanted to stay all night. To hear him breathe and hold his hand.

She felt herself drifting, exhaustion taking over, when her father muttered something. She lifted her head and strained to make out what he was saying. Finally, she understood. It was his favorite Scripture passage. Psalm Twenty-Three. He was reciting it in his sleep.

Cassidy remembered the many times she had repeated the Psalm with him over the years. The words were crystal clear in her heart and her mind. She started whispering along with him.

"He leadeth me beside the still waters, He restoreth my soul; He leadeth me in the path of righteousness for His name's sake. Yea, though I walk through the valley of the shadow of death I will fear no evil." Cassidy stopped. Was her fathering thinking about death? Could he really face it without fear? It was more than she could fathom. She listened as her father drifted in and out.

She felt a gentle hand on her shoulder and turned to see Wil standing alongside of her. "Cassidy, it's time to go."

"But I can't leave him, Wil. I need to be here. What if

something happens, and I'm not here for him?"

"Cassidy . . . you need to get some rest. I'll bring you back first thing in the morning. The nurses' station has our cell numbers and the house numbers. They'll be able to get a hold of us if they need to. Come on . . . let's go home."

Cassidy looked from her father to Wil and back to her father again. She couldn't bring herself to let go of his hand.

Finally, a nurse came in the room and told Cassidy she needed to go. She stood slowly, but it took her a few seconds before she could leave her father's bedside.

Wil held her close as they rode the elevator and crossed the parking lot. She climbed into his vehicle, leaned back against the headrest and started to cry. Thankfully, Wil didn't try to talk or pull her into needless conversation; he just drove.

———— • ————

Wil glanced at Cassidy. He had so much to say, but he knew she needed time to process all that had happened. Instead, he prayed— for Cassidy more than Joseph. He knew Joseph wasn't afraid to die. He was a godly man with peace within his soul. And even though Wil would miss Joseph terribly if he went home to be with the Lord, it was Cassidy he was worried about. She had completely turned her back on God when her mother passed away. What would she do if she lost her father too?

Wil stole a few glances at her as she stared out the window. She was in a faraway place, deep in thought. *Please, God, don't let her go off the deep end.*

Pulling up in front of the house, Wil stepped from the truck and walked around to Cassidy's door. Holding it open, he waited for her to get out, but she just sat there, looking at the house.

"Cassidy, what's wrong?"

"I can't go inside. Not now. I was so angry with him when I left tonight. It's my fault. If he hadn't gotten upset with me none of this would have happened."

"Cassidy." Wil leaned on the side of the door. "That's not true. The doctors said it was inevitable. The blockage he had was extensive. It was only a matter of time."

"But I should have known something wasn't right. When I got home, he was sitting on the couch, looking so tired. But I didn't say anything. I was so upset with you, and your condescending attitude,

I didn't even pay attention to him. When I told him, I was going out with Blake, he got agitated, and I got defensive and . . . it was such a mess." She looked up at him. "I can't go in there, Wil. Not right now."

"It's okay, Cassidy, you don't have to." He closed her door, got in, and drove to his place.

When she got out of the truck, she trudged up the front stairs, looking completely exhausted.

"I'll make some coffee," Wil said, then disappeared inside the kitchen.

When he walked back into the living room a few minutes later, Cassidy was curled up in a fetal position on the couch, her eyes closed, tears running down her cheek.

"Cassidy . . ."

She looked up at him, then closed her eyes again. "I just keep seeing him, his skin pale, his eyes glassy."

He watched as she curled up tighter, her arms shaking.

He pulled the blanket from the back of the couch and draped it over her. "You can't blame yourself, Cassidy." He tucked the blanket under her toes, then sat next to her feet.

"But if I had been home, I could have gotten him to the hospital faster. Maybe they would have been able to do something. What if he had died? What if I had come home and he . . . I mean . . . I would have found . . ."

"But you didn't, Cassidy." He gently stroked her calf. "He's going to be okay. The ambulance got here in record time, and he never lost consciousness."

"But, Wil, he must have been so scared."

"Actually, he was more worried about you. He was afraid to leave you all alone in the world."

"What? He told you that?" Cassidy sat up, urgent to know exactly what her father had said.

Wil nodded. "Yes. I think that's what made him hold on. He's ready to die, Cassidy, he's just not ready to leave you."

THIRTY-SEVEN

Wil opened his eyes, feeling beat up. His neck was stiff, his arm was asleep, and his head was pounding. But seeing Cassidy asleep, in the crook of his arm, was worth the pain. She needed her rest, and he didn't want to disturb her.

Carefully propping his feet up on the coffee table, he stretched his good arm out in front of him and squinted at his watch. Four in the morning. He laid his head back against the couch cushion and closed his eyes, but sleep eluded him. He kept replaying the same scene in his head.

Cassidy at Blake's house.

No, not just at his house, in his bedroom.

He wasn't sure who he was angrier with. Blake for being such a scumbag opportunist? Cassidy for her self-destructive behavior? Or himself? Just knowing his behavior was the catalyst that sent Cassidy to Blake's, made him want to puke.

"What are you thinking?" Cassidy asked, sounding half asleep.

That I want to stay here, just like this, and protect you from the 'Blakes' in the world. "Nothing. But how did you know I was awake?"

"I felt your heart beating faster." Cassidy craned her neck and looked up at him. "What time is it anyway?"

"After four."

Cassidy pushed herself up to a sitting position and dropped her feet off the side of the couch. Rubbing her face, she laid her head back against the couch and stared at the ceiling.

"What is it with you and this ceiling? You stare at it whenever you're here."

She looked at him, then back up at the ceiling, her eyes turning red.

"Cassidy, what's wrong?"

A tear trickled down her cheek, and she sighed. "After my

mother died, I came here with every intention of killing myself."

"What?" Wil sat up straighter, shocked by her admission.

"Yep. Just me, a rope, and that beam. I was going to . . . you know." She brushed away a tear. "But I couldn't do it. I didn't have the guts to."

He laid his hand on her leg, gave it a squeeze, and whispered, "I'm glad you didn't."

She looked at him and shrugged. "On days like this, I wonder if I made the right decision. I could've saved myself a lot of pain."

"But your father would've been heartbroken."

"I think he is anyway."

"That's not true, Cassidy."

"Well, I certainly haven't given him much joy over the years."

When Cassidy closed her eyes, Wil hoped she would fall back to sleep. He looked up at the solid beam above them, his mind reeling from her revelation.

The thought of Cassidy contemplating suicide was almost more than he could comprehend. He knew how he felt when his parents died; he was devastated. But even then, he never thought about taking his own life.

Please, God, be her source of strength. Don't allow her to get that overwhelmed again.

Rolling her head toward him, Cassidy nudged his shoulder. "What time do you think we can go back to the hospital?"

"Visiting hours don't start until eight. Just try to get a little more sleep."

"I can't. Sleeping is worse than being awake. I keep picturing Dad looking so lifeless in that sterile hospital bed." She leaned forward and laid her head on her knees. "I think I'll head back to the hospital and wait there. Maybe they'll take pity on me and let me in early."

"Cassidy, they have rules. There's no reason to go if they aren't going to let you see him."

"But being this far away is driving me crazy. What if something happens? What if he takes a turn for the worse?" She swiped a tear from her cheek. "I might not be able to make it in time."

Wil got up, stretched his stiff back and tight shoulders, then walked to the entry table and picked up his keys. "I'll take you home so you can shower and change, then I'll swing by in an hour or so to take you back to the hospital."

"That's okay," Cassidy said as she stretched, then slipped on her boots. "I can drive myself."

"No you can't."

———— • ————

His argumentative attitude immediately ignited her short fuse. "Look, Wil, I appreciate what you've done, but quit telling me what I can and cannot do!"

"Your truck is still at Blake's house, Cassidy. Were you going to call him for a ride? I'm sure he'd enjoy that."

She didn't miss the innuendo in his words, or the coldness in his tone. He would not even look at her.

"I guess I don't have a choice, do I?"

"Of course you have a choice!" he snapped. "I said I would drive you to the hospital."

"But I need to get my truck sooner or later. So, I might as well take care of it now."

"So, you want to hit Blake up for a favor? Are you sure that's a good idea? He might expect something in return."

"Knock it off, Wil. Nothing happened. Well . . . nothing I didn't want to happen." *Chew on that.* She marched out the door, down the steps, and to his vehicle.

Wil followed behind, mumbling under his breath.

"Did you have something to say?" Cassidy asked, when he slid behind the wheel.

But he ignored her. He just yanked on the gearshift and drove.

"Are you going to tell me what you said?"

He kept his steely eyes glued on the windshield.

"The silent treatment? Real mature," she turned away, wanting to scream.

Wil pulled parallel to the front porch. "I'll be back to get you in an hour."

"Don't bother."

Pounding up the front steps, she pushed through the weathered front door, then stopped. There, on the living room floor, plastic bags and sterile wrappers were strewn about. And the furniture was haphazardly pushed out of the way. The evidence of EMTs doing everything they could to save her father's life.

Her feet felt like lead as she moved across the living room. She tossed her purse on the couch and bent down to pick up the wrappers. Pushing the furniture back in place, she saw her father's Bible on the floor. Fighting back tears, she picked it up and saw a note pad lying next to it. Through blurry eyes, she read her name at the top of the page.

It was a letter.

She sunk to the couch.

He was writing me when he had his heart attack? Was it because of their fight? Or the way she'd been acting? Or her unwillingness to listen to him when he tried to help? Her blurry eyes kept her from reading the letter, or maybe she was just too scared it would prove she had caused her father's heart attack.

Leaving the letter on the coffee table, she ran upstairs, pulled off her clothes, stood in the shower and cried.

Why? Why did I come back home?

She sunk to the tile floor, the water pouring over her, but it would never wash away her guilt. She was the cause of her father's health problems. Not only had she screwed up her life, but now her choices were causing him to suffer emotionally and physically.

When the hot water eventually ran cold, she stepped out of the shower convinced of what she must do. Once her father was home from the hospital and feeling stronger, she would leave.

Coming home was just another big mistake.

She had already caused her father years of heartache, when he deserved so much better. His home should be his sanctuary. His place of rest. But as long as she was there, they'd have tension. Arguments. Differences in opinion. She would never be good enough. She'd be a burden to him, a pain-in-the-neck to Wil, and an embarrassment to herself.

Just thinking about her behavior with Blake made her cringe. It was inexcusable. She had no business being at his place. She'd only done it to get a rise out of Wil.

But why?

Because, if she wanted to admit it or not, she liked Wil.

A lot.

She was attracted to him. Not only for his good looks, but because he was everything Mark was not. Good. Kind. Caring. He thought of others before himself. He had taken care of her father when he needed someone around. He knew how to treat people with respect.

But that was just it. She didn't deserve his respect. She would never be the devout, Christian woman Wil was looking for. So, she hid her true feelings behind behavior he found unacceptable. Sabotaging any chance they had at a relationship was easier than developing feelings for Wil, only to have him reject her later when he realized she wasn't good enough.

I can't have just one more person reject me. I just can't.

Wrapped in a towel, Cassidy walked into her bedroom. The first thing she needed to do was get her truck. Which meant she needed to call Blake. When she turned to her desk to get her phone, it wasn't there. *My purse? Where is my purse?* She closed her eyes, mentally retracing her steps. Downstairs. On the couch. Pulling the towel tighter, she walked to the upstairs landing and looked down into the living room. She saw her purse on the couch.

And the letter on the coffee table.

She closed her eyes in defeat.

I can't. I can't read it right now.

With singular focus, she crossed the living room to the couch. When she reached for her purse, the front door swung open, the cool air sending a shiver down her spine.

"What are you doing here?" Cassidy asked as she clutched the towel tighter to her chest.

Wil looked her up and down, obviously stunned by what she was *not* wearing. "I said I would pick you up in an hour."

"And I said I would call Blake."

"Oh, I'm sorry," Wil said, clearly irritated. "I didn't mean to interrupt your plans." He looked her up and down again. "And after you got all dressed up for him."

Fine! You want to act like a jerk . . . I'll play along. "Actually, I thought Blake and I could pick up where we left off. I rushed out of there so fast last night, I didn't get a chance to thank him properly for such a . . . wonderful evening."

"Knock it off, Cassidy."

"Whatever do you mean?" she teased as she moved closer.

"I mean . . . you're playing a dangerous game."

"So what? It's my choice what I do with my life." She turned to walk away, but Wil grabbed her arm and spun her around.

"Then why not play with me?"

"What?"

Wil stroked her bare arm, but she pulled away, unsettled by his behavior.

"What's wrong, Cassidy?" He reached out for her again, held onto her elbows and pulled her close. "Isn't this the kind of attention you want? You don't need Blake. I'll give it to you." She glared at him, her wet hair dripping on her shoulder, but refused to give him the reaction he was looking for. "I need to get dressed." She tried pulling away, but Wil looped his hand around her waist and held her even tighter.

"What's the hurry? We have all morning."

Wil bent to kiss her, but she quickly turned away. "Stop it!" Cassidy struggled, shocked at his behavior.

"Just think of this as an apology." Wil stroked her face with the back of his hand. "I was giving you your space, but now I see that's not what you wanted after all. So, why should I exclude myself from something you're so willing to give someone else?"

Again, Cassidy tried to pull away, but he just tightened his grip.

He was scaring her. Just like Mark had every time he came home in a crazed mood. How many times had he grabbed her, caressed her, just to turn around and hit her? How many times had he told her to shut up and enjoy it?

"Please, Wil," she looked at him, holding back tears. "Please. Stop."

Wil immediately released his hold on her but didn't back away. "I knew you were bluffing, Cassidy. But would Blake?"

"Would Blake what?" She took a step back.

"Would Blake know it was just a game? Would he have stopped when you asked him to, or would he have called your bluff?"

"What do you care?" She turned around, ran upstairs, and sat on the edge of her bed, crying. She thought about what Wil had said, and the way she had struggled to break free from Blake's hold.

What if Wil had not come when he did?

Would Blake have given up or been more insistent?

Cassidy was still shaking when she pulled on her jeans and a bulky sweater. She glanced at herself in the mirror, pressed on her swollen eyelids and massaged her blotchy cheeks. Sighing, she brushed her hair, then pulled it back in a ponytail.

When she went downstairs, Wil was waiting for her. She grabbed her purse from the couch, then looked around the living room. It seemed cold, as if the life of the house depended on her father. Wil stood holding the door open for her. She walked out the door, too embarrassed to even look at him.

Once Wil pulled onto the road, Cassidy cleared her throat and spoke. "Could you drive me to the hospital instead of Blake's? I don't think I feel up to driving myself." She looked at her hands. Even though she had them clasped together, she couldn't get them to stop shaking.

"Cassidy, I'm sorry." Wil glanced at her hands, then at her eyes. "I didn't mean to scare you."

"Yes, you did," she said matter-of-fact.

"Cassidy, I—"

"But you were right," she interrupted. "I asked for it. I was toying with Blake. If you hadn't shown up when you did, I'm not sure what would have happened. Even so, it would have been my fault. It was stupid of me, Wil. I realize that now."

————— ● —————

He was dumbfounded. There was no trace of attitude or arrogance in Cassidy's tone, only defeat and exhaustion. He felt horrible. He didn't mean to crush her. He only wanted her to realize that what she was doing was dangerous. A man's sexuality was not something to fool with.

Wil turned to Cassidy to apologize, but saw her eyes were closed. He gazed at her for a moment, feeling a vice tightening around his heart.

He loved her.

He knew he did.

No matter how many times he'd told himself differently, he knew the truth. He was in love with Cassidy.

But what could he do about it?

She was angry and rebellious and had no use for God.

Wil turned the question over and over in his head as he drove to the hospital.

But he had no answers.

THIRTY-EIGHT

Cassidy walked toward the nurses' station, feeling like she was going to puke. When she let out a deep breath to calm herself, Wil draped his arm around her shoulders and gave her a squeeze.

"He's going to be okay, Cassidy. Joseph is too stubborn to go out without a fight."

She forced a smile, then leaned against the high white counter top. "Good morning, I'm here for Joseph Martin."

The nurse smiled up at her. "You must be Cassidy."

"Yes, I'm his daughter."

"He's been asking about you."

"That's good, right? He's awake and talking."

She smiled. "Mr. Martin did well through the night, and his vitals have stabilized. However, he gets agitated when he asks to see you, and we tell him he needs to rest."

"When can I see him?"

The nurse smiled. "You can see him now, if you promise to keep it short."

Cassidy glanced at the clock on the wall. "But it's too early?"

"I know. Technically, visiting hours don't start until eight, but maybe he'll get some rest once he sees you're okay."

Cassidy looked at Wil, puzzled, then back to the nurse. "I don't understand. Why is he worried about me?"

"For whatever reason, he keeps insisting you shouldn't be alone. Maybe if you tell him you're not," the nurse glanced at Wil, "he'll get some rest."

Cassidy walked past the nurses' station and tiptoed into her father's room. Sure enough, he was awake. "Hey, Dad," she walked over to his bedside. "How are you feeling?" She took a seat beside him. When he moved his hand closer to the rail, she reached for it and gave it a squeeze.

217

"Like I got caught in the middle of a stampede." He smiled, then closed his eyes.

"Well, don't talk. You need to rest." Cassidy stroked his hand trying to warm the chill she felt in his fingers.

"I was afraid I wasn't going to get a chance to say goodbye, Sunshine."

"Don't say that, Dad. No one is saying goodbye. You're going to be just fine. Before you know it, you'll be home, and things will be back to normal."

He squeezed her hand, "I worry about you, Sunshine. I knew you'd be afraid, and I didn't want to leave you alone."

"You're not going anywhere, Dad, and I'm not alone. Wil's with me. In fact, he's right outside."

A sweet smile filled her father's face. "So . . . Wil finally told you how he feels."

"What?" She was confused.

"He's a man . . . a good man. And he'll wait. It's your decision, and he'll wait. But it has to be your decision."

He wasn't making any sense. Though Cassidy could make out what he was saying, it just didn't add up.

Oh well. It doesn't matter.

"Just get some rest, Dad, we can talk more later." She sat, stroking his hand, watching his chest rise and fall, thankful when it finally slowed into an easy rhythm.

When the nurse walked in, she smiled. "Good. He's finally resting." She checked the monitors, pushed some buttons, then updated the computer on the rolling cart. "Just seeing you made all the difference. And now that he's comfortable . . ."

"I understand." She squeezed her dad's hand and kissed his forehead. "I'll be back a little later, Dad. You rest."

Cassidy walked out of the room and down the corridor, still trying to piece together what her father had said. Wil was sitting in the waiting room, but when he saw her coming, he sprang to his feet.

"How's he doing?"

What did he mean by 'he'll wait?'

"Cassidy, what's wrong?"

She realized she hadn't answered Wil. "Nothing. I mean, he's doing good. As well as can be expected, I guess."

Wil's shoulders slumped, obviously relieved. "You scared me there for a moment. You looked so bewildered; I was afraid something had gone wrong."

She looked at Wil, exhaustion weighing him down. Her heart ached for him. It wasn't fair that only immediate family could see critical patients. Wil was like a son to her father, and yet he had to wait to find out secondhand how he was doing.

"But you're sure he's okay?" Wil asked again.

"Yes. I mean, he seems a little confused, but he looks better than he did last night."

"That's good."

"Excuse me." A nurse came up behind Cassidy and Wil. "I assume you'll be waiting to visit your father again?" Cassidy nodded. "Then let me show you to one of our private waiting rooms."

Cassidy and Wil followed the nurse to a room at the end of the hall. "This is one of our long-term waiting rooms. It gives you a little more privacy."

Cassidy looked around, surprised at its homey atmosphere. A couch on one wall and a large chair on another. A small refrigerator and microwave in a kitchen-type nook, and a flat screen on the wall.

"You can relax better here, and the nurses' station will call you directly when you can visit next." She pointed to the cordless phone on one of the side tables. "The snacks in the refrigerator and cupboards are complimentary, so feel free to eat something when you're hungry. There's a direct line on that phone you can give out to other family members and friends who might need to get in touch with you. I hope this makes your time here a little more comfortable." The nurse excused herself from the room as Wil and Cassidy took it all in.

"The luxuries of a privately funded hospital." Wil said as he checked out the refrigerator.

Cassidy felt embarrassed. Her initial reaction to the small hospital was that it would be substandard. She was wrong. The care her father was receiving, and the attention given to family members was top-notch.

Wil walked toward the chair.

"No, Wil." Cassidy stopped him with a tug on his arm. "You take the couch. You look exhausted, and I know you couldn't have slept well last night. I'll take the chair."

Wil didn't argue. He just walked over to the couch while she curled up in the oversized chair. She sighed and closed her eyes.

But even though she was tired and wanted to rest, she kept thinking about what her father had said. What had Wil told him? And why was her father glad when he thought Wil had finally spoken to her? Cassidy stole a glance at Wil resting on the couch.

What was it he said . . . something about giving me space?

Cassidy struggled to stay awake, but it was a losing battle. She fell asleep, while the conversation with her dad played over and over in her mind.

———— • ————

Cassidy woke to a buzzing sound but didn't want to open her eyes. When she heard a muffled voice, she opened one eye and saw Wil on the phone. Then her mental checklist kicked in.

Hospital.

Waiting room.

Phone.

Nurses.

Dad.

She quickly sat up. "Is something wrong? Has something happened?"

Wil hung up the phone. "No, it was the nurses' station saying you can go visit now." Wil rubbed his eyes and stretched his arms over his shoulders.

"Why don't you go, Wil? I know you'll feel a lot better if you can see dad for yourself."

"I'm not allowed; immediate family only."

"That's ridiculous." Cassidy picked up the phone and pushed the button for the nurses' station. "Yes, this is Cassidy Grayson, Joseph Martin's daughter. I was wondering what the limitations are for visitors? Wil has waited all night, and I know he would feel much better if he could see my dad for himself."

"Oh, that's no problem, Mrs. Grayson. In-laws are always considered immediate family. Your husband can visit your father. We just ask that you go in one at a time."

"Thank you so much. I'll let him know." She hung up the phone. "The nurse said as long as we go in one at a time there's no problem." Cassidy conveniently withheld the fact that the nurse thought Wil was her husband.

Instantly, relief swept over Wil's face as he stood, straightened his shirt, and ran his hand through his hair. Then he looked at her. "Are you sure, Cassidy? I can wait until the next hour. You should go."

"No, I think it will be good for both of you. Tell dad I'll see him next."

Cassidy sat alone with her thoughts. Even though she wanted to ask her father what he had meant earlier, it was important for Wil to see he was doing better. Wil had found him near death, and had only seen him briefly last night when he was still asleep. He needed to replace those images with something more encouraging.

———— • ————

Wil made his way down the hall and slowly pushed open the large hospital room door. Joseph's eyes were open and fixed on the doorway. "Hey Joseph."

"Wil." Joseph sighed and smiled.

Walking to his bedside, Wil felt such a sense of relief. Joseph looked so much better than he had the night before.

"Wil, how is Cassidy doing?"

"She's okay."

"She told me you were taking care of her. I'm so glad you finally told her how you feel."

Wil took a breath. "I didn't get the chance to tell her how I feel."

"But I thought . . ."

"You thought what?" Wil couldn't exactly read Joseph's expression. "What gave you the idea I had talked to her?"

Joseph's brows knitted together. "Maybe it was the way she said you were taking care of her. She sounded . . . different." Joseph closed his eyes, clearly tired from their brief exchange of words.

Wil stood by, silently praying while Joseph rested. When he opened his eyes again, he looked slightly flustered.

"Joseph, I'm going to go now, so you can rest. But you don't need to worry about Cassidy. I assure you, I'm watching out for her."

Joseph didn't respond verbally he just nodded with a smile, then asked Wil to bring him a few things from home, before closing his eyes again. That was Wil's cue to leave.

Cassidy was curled up on the couch when Wil returned to the waiting room. He stared at her, picturing her as a teenager with a rope in her hand, hopelessness in her heart.

God, please don't ever let her feel that low again.
He quietly looked through the cupboards for a snack and grabbed a soda from the refrigerator. Stretching out in the chair, he pulled back on the soda can tab, the pop sound making Cassidy jump.
"Sorry, I didn't mean to wake you."
"That's okay." Cassidy yawned and curled up into a tighter ball, wrapping her arms around her. Wil reached into the cupboard and pulled out a folded blanket and laid it across her shoulders.
"Thanks."
"No problem," he said, then sat down in the oversized chair.
"How's Dad?"
"He looks good. A lot better than when I saw him last."
"What happened, Wil? You never told me what made you go to the house."
Wil thought about the reason he'd gone to the house: to tell Cassidy how he felt, and to stop her from going out with Blake. But he was too late. Cassidy was gone, and what Wil found struck terror inside him. Joseph. On the floor. The phone in his hand. His Bible and a scribbled note to Cassidy by his side.
"I was just stopping by. He was on the floor, struggling to use the phone. So I called 911, gave him an aspirin, and waited for the ambulance." Wil watched as silent tears ran done Cassidy's face, and waited to see if she would say anything. He finally just asked, "Did you read the letter?"
Cassidy shook her head. "I couldn't. It's my fault he had a heart attack. Knowing he was writing me . . . thinking he was dying . . ." Cassidy's words drifted off.
"It wasn't your fault, Cassidy."
She looked at him, her eyes filled with guilt, then looked away.
They sat in silence, each deep in thought. But after a few minutes, Wil stood. "Your dad asked me to bring him a few things from the house. Is there anything you want me to get for you?"
"Actually, do you think you could wait until I visit dad one more time, then I could go with you?"
"Sure." Wil sat back down and slouched in the chair to get comfortable, with his arms crossed against his chest. He waited until Cassidy closed her eyes, then closed his own, feeling a little more at peace now that he had seen Joseph for himself.
"Wil?" Cassidy whispered.
"Yeah," he answered with his eyes closed.
"My dad said something that has me kind of confused."

222

Wil knew what was coming but was glad. He would finally be honest with Cassidy about his feelings. Joseph's heart attack had been an eye-opener, reminding him life was all too fleeting. He cared too much for Cassidy to not just come right out and say it. Sure, they would have obstacles . . . that is, if she even had feelings for him at all. But regardless of how she felt, he needed to be honest with her.

"He gave me the impression you wanted to talk to me about something."

Wil sat up straighter as he tried to gather his thoughts. He could just blurt out 'I love you' and go from there, but he wanted to be a little more eloquent than that.

"I wanted to talk to you but wasn't sure how to go about it. I was afraid I would overwhelm you, since you were already dealing with so much. And then I decided it was better left unsaid. But now," he stood, unable to sit still, "now I know what I need to say, I'm just not sure—"

The door flung open, interrupting Wil. He turned and saw Ella burst through the door, throwing herself into his arms. "Oh, Wil, I'm so sorry I couldn't be here for you sooner. I know how much Joseph means to you."

He gently pulled Ella's arms from around his neck and took a step back. "I'm fine."

He saw the hurt in her eyes, but she smiled and stroked his cheek anyway. "You look so tired. Have you gotten any sleep at all?"

"Yes, I—"

The phone rang, interrupting him again. Wil watched Cassidy sit up straight, answer the phone, then stand. She crossed the room, then turned when she reached the door. "I'm going to see my father." She quickly glanced at Ella, then Wil. "You can leave without me."

THIRTY-NINE

Needing a moment to gather her thoughts, Cassidy leaned her forehead against the wall next to her father's room and sighed. *Why did Ella have to show up? Of all times!*

Cassidy had a gut feeling what Wil was going to say to her, only to have Ella interrupt him.

Or, maybe I'm seeing something that just isn't there.

Standing up straight, she pushed her hair back from her eyes. *Dad is my priority right now. I'll just have to figure out the Wil thing later.*

Pushing the door open, she plastered on a smile and walked inside.

Fifteen minutes later, Cassidy left her father's room, feeling grateful. He looked so much better than he had earlier. Caught up in her joy, she didn't even notice Blake standing in the hallway until she turned and bumped right into him. "Blake?"

He reached out to steady her. "Can I assume from the smile on your face, your father is doing better?" he asked, grinning.

Cassidy was surprised he was there. When she had left his house, he was not too happy with her. And even though he had acted like a total jerk, it was her fault for leading him on. She owed him an apology.

"Blake, I—"

He leaned forward to kiss her, but Cassidy turned her head, so his lips barely grazed her cheek. When she turned back, she saw a nurse watching them, a look of disapproval on her face. Of course, that's because the nurses thought Wil was her husband, and now she looked like an unfaithful wife. She grabbed Blake's elbow and walked him around the corner to the empty waiting room.

"Blake, I owe you an apology."

"What?"

"I had no business going to your place last night. I was confused and mistook your flattery for attraction." She bit her lip. "No, that's not true either. I knew exactly what I was doing when I went to your house. I was mad at Wil and my father, so I . . . it was wrong, and I'm sorry."

Blake reached for Cassidy's arms with a smile. "But you were right, Cassidy. I am attracted to you."

"But I'm not attracted to you." It was blunt, but at least she'd said it.

Blake let his arms drop at his sides and took a step back.

"I'm sorry, Blake. I didn't mean for that to sound so harsh. You're a very attractive man, and you have a lot to offer a woman. It's just that . . . I mean I was . . . I wasn't attracted to you for you." She looked him straight in the eye. "I was using you, Blake, and I'm sorry. I see now it was a horrible mistake. And mean."

Blake grinned. "I knew that, Cassidy, but I was willing to take my chances."

"What do you mean, 'take your chances?' "

Blake took a deep breath then let it out slowly. "Ella wanted me to work on Wil's project for more than just business reasons. She wanted me to run interference with you."

"Interference with me? I don't understand."

"She has the hots for Wil and was afraid you were going to get your claws into him. Her words not mine."

"So, inviting me to your house was just a ploy? What were you supposed to do, seduce me, get me into bed, then make sure Wil found out about it?"

"Heck no! Well . . . yeah . . . that was the plan, at first, but once I laid eyes on you, I was in it for myself. I thought you were hot. I figured I could make you forget about Wil, and we could have some fun. I was playing the angles too, Cassidy. I knew what I was getting into."

Cassidy couldn't believe they were having this conversation. She felt humiliated and ashamed. She had almost gone to bed with Blake to make Wil jealous, and Blake had tried seducing her not with hopes of having a relationship, but only 'to have some fun.' She wanted to be mad at Blake, but couldn't. His motives were no worse than her own.

Blake reached out for her hand, turned it over, and dropped her keys in her hand. "I brought your truck. I figured you'd be needing it."

"Thanks," she whispered, unable to look him in the face.

"How's your dad?"

"Recovering. The doctors say he's going to be fine."

"That's good."

She nodded.

"Cassidy . . . look at me."

She looked up, feeling so embarrassed.

"I was hoping we could put last night behind us. I was an idiot for letting Ella rope me into this, and my behavior was inexcusable. I acted like a grade-A jerk."

"I wasn't much better," Cassidy mumbled.

"Okay, so we both admit it wasn't our finest moments, but Cassidy, I still want to work on Wil's project, and set up a meeting with you and Mrs. Gentry. You're a talented designer, and I would like the opportunity to collaborate with you in the future."

Cassidy thought about it, wondering if Wil would still be interested in working with Blake after last night? She wasn't sure, but she knew she still wanted a chance to work on the Gentry project. But would she even have the time? When her father came home, he would be her focus. "I don't know what kind of time I can devote to your project, Blake. My dad is going to need a lot of attention when he gets home."

"I completely understand, and I'll work around any timetable you give me. I'll go ahead and talk to Mrs. Gentry about some of the ideas we've already discussed. I know you would present them better, but I'll see what she says. If she's interested in hearing more, I'll explain you've had a family emergency and see if I can set a time that would work for both of you. What do you say?"

She smiled, even though she still felt embarrassed. "It sounds good to me, but only if we agree to forget last night ever happened."

"And what about Wil? I know I acted like a real jerk. Do you think he'll give me a chance to redeem myself?"

Cassidy had to give Blake credit. He didn't back down from things he wanted, and he owned up to his mistakes. "I'll put in a good word for you."

Before she knew it, Blake had her in a bear hug. She knew it was just a 'thank you' hug, but the nurse who had seen Blake kiss her earlier happened to walk by at the same time. She made eye contact with Cassidy and gave her an icy stare. *Great!*

Cassidy walked back to the private waiting room to see if Wil wanted to drive home with her, but when she heard Ella's voice through the door, she couldn't bear to see her with Wil. Even though she knew the truth and wanted to burst in and tell Wil exactly what kind of person Ella was, she did not have the energy for a confrontation.

Turning around, she headed back to the nurse's station to let them know she was leaving. Leaning on the little white counter, she cleared her throat. "Excuse me?"

The nurse who was sitting at the station looked up, her cheery smile quickly transforming into a deadly glare.

"I'm going to go home and take care of a few things."

"Uh-hum," the older nurse said as she stood.

"I just wanted to let you know in case you need to reach me."

"Don't worry, Mrs. Martin," the woman glared. "Go ahead and take care of your . . . business."

Cassidy watched as the woman walked away, then started after her so she could set her straight. But the nurse went into a patient's room before Cassidy could catch up with her. *Just one more person's disapproval.* Walking to the elevator she felt tired and defeated. It shouldn't matter to her what the nurse thought about her.

But it did.

Driving straight home, Cassidy wanting nothing more than a nice hot shower. She crossed the living room without making eye contact with the couch and living area. She knew she was being ridiculous. Her father was doing fine and would be home soon, but she just kept remembering the anger and disappointment she read on her father's face before she stormed out of the house.

The pulsating shower had been exactly what she needed. Having stood under its massaging stream for almost twenty minutes, it did wonders for her tense and knotted muscles.

Sliding a few hangers, she decided on a navy, velour, jogging suit, figuring it would be more comfortable to curl up in at the hospital. She folded a couple of shirts and took a few personal items and tossed them in her overnight bag. She would have no reason to leave the hospital for a few days if need be.

She headed downstairs and then remembered Wil was going to get some things for her dad. She called Wil's phone and quickly received his voicemail. She called the hospital and asked to be connected to the private waiting room in the ICU area but got the runaround from the hospital operator. Finally, she slammed the phone down in frustration and decided to improvise.

She wandered into her father's room, a room she had scarcely be in since her mother's death. Her eyes traveled around the familiar furniture and knick-knacks that filled the room. She walked over to her mother's vanity to find after all these years, her dad still had her mother's sterling mirror and hairbrush set right where she had always left them. Cassidy picked up the brush, remembering the way she loved it when her mother would brush her hair. She would do a hundred strokes each night before Cassidy would go to bed. Closing her eyes, she allowed the brush to glide through her hair. She smiled at the memory.

Looking around the rest of the room, she sighed, then began gathering some of the personal things her father would probably need. Toothbrush, toothpaste, T-shirts and boxers, bathrobe and slippers. A change of clothes. Not knowing where he kept his luggage—or if he even had any—she used one of the pieces she brought from New York.

She was almost to the door, when she remembered his Bible. Leaving the luggage by the front door, she walked to the coffee table. There was his Bible, along with the note he'd been writing to her. She slowly lowered herself to the couch and set both the Bible and the note on her lap. Her eyes were already glassy, but she knew she had to read what was so important to her father that he would use his last ounce of strength to write to her. Silently, she read his familiar but frail writing.

Cassidy,

Since the day you were born, you have been my sunshine. You are my most prized possession and the one thing I fear parting with the most. I look forward to being with your mother, oh how I have missed her, but my heart cannot leave this body until I know you have put your trust in Jesus. You need to realize there are tragedies in this world—like the one that took your

Mother—but God loves you and wants to make you His own. I know as a little girl you called Jesus your friend, but you've been running from Him for so long, I fear your commitment to Him as a child was not one of deep conviction, just make believe like children play. Please, Cassidy, rely on God for your strength. Turn to Him before it's too late. I wish I could be with you always, but life is not that way.

I love you, Cassidy, even though at times I know you didn't feel that love. I did the best I could as a single parent, but I wish I had taken more time to show you how special you are to me. I should have visited you in New York. Supported your art career. Met your husband. It's too late for that, but not for you. I love you more than I can say, but Your Father in heaven loves you even more. Turn to Him, Cassidy. Turn to Him before it's too late. Your mother and I will be waiting for you. And if angels really do sing when a single soul turns to Jesus, know that we will be waiting for the angel choir to announce your new birth.

With all my love, Daddy

Cassidy cried uncontrollably after reading her father's letter. Anguish tore at her soul. She realized now, he knew he was dying. He didn't write the letter because he was too angry to speak with her. He wrote the letter because he was afraid he would never be able to speak to her again. With shaking hands, she folded the letter and put it in her purse, then picked up her father's Bible and pressed it to her chest.

He took what he thought was his last ounce of strength to plead with me about the condition of my heart.

Cassidy's lip quivered as she spoke out loud to an empty room. "Lord, if you're real, then show me. Show me You haven't given up on me. Spare my father, so I will have someone to help me find my way back to You. I want to learn to trust You, Jesus. I want to know I won't be left alone someday."

Cassidy had to compose herself before she could think of driving. Just getting up from the couch seemed an impossible task.

Finally calm, Cassidy smiled, knowing how happy her father would be when he found out she was ready to open her heart to Jesus. Picking up her purse, she felt her phone vibrating inside.

"Hello?"

"Cassidy, are you okay?" Wil asked, sounding worried. "I came to look for you, and the nurse said you left with some man. I was going to head home, but I didn't want to leave until I found you."

"I'm okay, Wil, and I didn't leave with 'some man.' Blake brought my truck to the hospital, and I went home to get some things. I was going to tell you, but you were still talking with Ella, and I didn't want to interrupt. I got a few of my father's things together, and I'm on my way back to the hospital, now. Can you think of anything my father wanted right away?"

"His Bible. He really wanted his Bible."

Cassidy smiled as she held it to her chest. "I already have it. I was thinking maybe I could read it to him when he's feeling up to it. I have a few things I need him to explain to me, so I thought now is as good a time as any."

FORTY

When Cassidy arrived at the hospital, she went to the private waiting room to check in with Wil, but he wasn't there.

Hum . . . he must be in with Dad.

Setting down her overnight bag on one of the chairs, and the suitcase she'd packed for her dad on the floor, she headed to her father's room. Even if Wil was in with him, she figured she could slip by the nurses unnoticed, and give her dad his Bible. She knew it would mean so much to him to have it at his side.

She casually walked the hall while watching the nurses' station, then, when no one was looking, she quickly backed into her dad's room. Pleased with herself, she smiled, but when she turned around, her smile turned to horror. The bed her father had occupied just hours before was empty. The machines sat silent, and the bed linens were neatly made without a patient to occupy them.

Cassidy felt like she was going to pass out. Her legs were numb, and her heart raced out of control. With her eyes fixed on the empty bed, she stood there, unable to move.

No. This isn't happening. It can't be.

She reached for the door handle behind her, but it was too heavy for her trembling hand to pull open. She felt locked in a nightmare.

He can't be gone, God. I have too much to ask Him. I need him. He can't be gone . . . he can't be gone . . .

Cassidy was still mumbling when she yanked the door open and freed herself from the cold, lifeless room. She stood in front of the door, staring at it, her mind a tangled mess of unanswered questions. He'd been doing better.

He looked better. He was talking and smiling. What happened? What changed? What am I going to do without him?

Cassidy stood with her eyes transfixed on the door, barely

remembering to breathe.

"Cassidy . . . Cassidy . . ."

She heard Wil but didn't have the strength to turn toward him.

"Cassidy, I was hoping I would get to you before you went in." She felt Wil's hand on the small of her back but didn't move. "I was going to call and tell you but knew you were headed back."

"Where is he?" Cassidy whispered, not even sure how she was able to form the words.

"I'll take you to him." Wil's arm lapped around her shoulder as he led her further down the hall. Cassidy walked with Wil, still clutching her father's Bible against her chest. She swallowed several times, trying to get the knot in her throat to move so she could talk. "When did this happen? I mean, why wasn't I called immediately?"

"I was going to, but things happened so suddenly. About an hour ago, his conditioned changed so dramatically the doctors themselves were shocked."

Wil's words were so casual it grated on her. Cassidy understood he and her father held the keys to heaven upon their death, but to show no remorse was almost more than she could handle. She walked with Wil; her feet heavy like clay. She did not want to see her father lying in a state of peace. She wanted to be able to talk to him; to tell him about her decision. Tell him she was no longer going to run from God. She was going to try to understand His ways better.

Suddenly, Cassidy realized what was happening. She had said she would trust God. *He's testing me. He's seeing if my decision to trust Him was a decision based on making my father happy or a decision I made for real.*

Cassidy asked herself the same question and was surprised at the answer that echoed inside her. She *would* trust God. Even though He had taken her mother and now her father, she would still cling to the promise God would not leave her or forsake her. She'd been running far too long and no longer wanted to be alone.

Wil stopped in front of a door. Though she felt like she'd been walking for hours, they were only a corridor away from where her father had been before. She was surprised they would allow a deceased patient to occupy a room but was glad. This would be better than saying goodbye in the coldness of the morgue.

Cassidy took a quick breath and held it. She pushed the door open and stepped inside with her eyes squeezed shut. She felt her steps falter, and Wil's quick arm helped her regain her balance. She prepared herself to say goodbye, but before she could open her tightly closed eyes, she heard her father's voice.

"Good . . . you brought my Bible."

Cassidy's eyes flew open, and she whimpered where she stood.

"Cassidy, what is it? What's wrong?" Wil asked, holding her tighter.

She rushed to her father's side, throwing herself on his chest. He winced slightly, then began to stroke her hair as she sobbed uncontrollably.

"Sunshine . . . what is it? You're shaking like a leaf."

Wil pulled Cassidy from her father and held her steady. He looked at her like she was a crazy person. "Cassidy, what's wrong?"

"His bed was empty. Clean. He was gone." Cassidy's words tumble out of her mouth too fast to make any sense.

Wil squeezed her arms. "Cassidy . . . slow down." She looked up at him and saw the concern in his eyes. "What's wrong?"

She inhaled deep and slowly let it out. "When I went to Dad's room he was gone. I thought he had . . ."

Understanding registered on Wil's face. "But Cassidy, I told you I would take you to him."

"Yes, but I didn't know he was alive. You said his condition changed so quickly, even the doctors were shocked."

"For the better, Cassidy, for the better."

"You didn't say that."

Cassidy completely lost it. If it weren't for Wil's arms around her, holding her up, she would have slid to the floor in a heap. Her shoulders shook and her voice quivered. Wil whispered words of assurance as he rocked her. Gradually, she felt the flutter of her heart begin to slow. When she turned her head, she saw her father looking at her, smiling. He reached his hand out to her, and she grasped it, releasing another sob. She looked around, noticing most of the machines were gone. And a hint of pink colored his cheeks.

"Dad, you look so good. What happened?"

"I think you know, Cassidy."

She looked at her father, puzzled. "What do you mean?"

"Just a little while ago I was lying in bed when a sense of deep peace and comfort filled my heart. I felt a burden lift; a burden I have carried for so many years. When I closed my eyes,

I saw you, Sunshine, and I knew where that peace had come from. The Lord was letting me know you were going to be okay."

Cassidy thought about her prayer, asking God to make Himself real to her, that she wanted to trust Him again. She glanced at her watch and wondered . . . then turned to her dad and smiled. "I guess you could say God and I have a new understanding."

"And thank the Lord I get to be around to witness it."

Joseph closed his eyes, overwhelmed by what God had revealed to him. Cassidy had finally unearthed the faith she'd had as a child, brushed it off, and put it to the test. And God, in His amazing grace, accepted her challenge and proved Himself to her when she needed it most.

Joseph knew it wasn't a done deal. Cassidy would falter, have questions, even let her anger get the better of her. But what had happened today between her and God was a start, and he was so thankful he had been allowed to witness it.

Thank You, God. Thank You for showing Yourself to Cassidy when she needed You most. Thank You for giving me peace regarding my little girl. I know now, when it's my time to leave, You will keep her safe in Your care.

Joseph looked at Wil at the foot of his bed. Their eyes met, and he could see Wil was equally shocked by Cassidy's transformation. Wil shook his head, dumbfounded, tears glistening in his eyes. Joseph nodded and smiled, then looked at Cassidy. Her eyes were warmer, no longer void of life. Fear was replaced with peace. Anger replaced with understanding. Hurt replaced with love.

Thank you, God, for leading my baby home.

FORTY-ONE

As Cassidy walked out of the hospital, she felt like she was walking on air. She knew it had to do with her father's miraculous recovery, but it was more than that. The heaviness she'd carried for so many years was finally lifted. Wil signaled to her from across the parking lot that he would follow her home. She waved back, got into her father's old truck, and smiled. Her dad had insisted they both go home and get a good night's rest. Even when she explained about the private waiting room, he didn't budge. "I can't rest if I know you two are all twisted up on hospital furniture. Go home and get some sleep so I can do the same." She shook her head as she recounted his words. He was so stubborn. Even-tempered and soft-spoken. But oh so stubborn.

And I'm so thankful you are, Dad.

When she pulled up alongside the front porch, Wil pulled up right behind her. As he followed her up the front steps, she inwardly cringed, afraid he was going to unleash the lecture he'd probably been suppressing for the last two days.

"Look, Wil, I'm really tired."

"I know, that's why I thought I'd help out with the feeding. You're going to have some mighty ornery animals on your hands."

"Oh no!" Cassidy covered her eyes and rubbed at her brow. "I completely forgot about the animals."

"That's okay, between the two of us, we'll have it done in no time."

They both headed to the barn, and the second they stepped inside, they were met with whinnies and bleating galore.

"For cryin' out loud, they only missed one feeding. You'd think they'd gone without food for an entire week with all the ruckus they're making."

235

Wil just laughed as he headed to the feed. While he took care of the horses, Cassidy attended to the goats and the smaller animals in the outside coops and pens.

After everyone was fed and calm, Wil followed Cassidy inside the house. "I'm going to get a fire going in the fireplace. It's kind of chilly in here." He grabbed a few logs from the woodpile, then knelt in front of the hearth.

"Thanks." She wasn't looking forward to the lecture she was sure to get but was glad he had stuck around. She was not ready to be alone yet. "Then I'll fix us some dinner." Cassidy walked into the kitchen, not sure what to make. They had both been surviving on vending food for the last few days and needed something substantial.

Breakfast sounds good.

With her mind made up, she started pulling things from the refrigerator. After laying several slices of bacon in a skillet, she cracked some eggs into a mixing bowl. Grating cheese into the mixture, she swirled the eggs around in the pan while the bacon popped and sizzled.

When Wil walked in, he didn't say anything, he just started working alongside of her. He plopped four slices of bread in the toaster then turned the bacon in the skillet. She watched as he took a pitcher of orange juice from the refrigerator and noticed the serious expression on his face. She wanted to tell him to just blurt it out, whatever he had to say to her, just say it, but working side by side with him felt so good. So comfortable. She wanted to hold onto that feeling as long as possible.

"That's it, Cassidy, I can't take it any longer."

Oh boy, here we go.

Wil spun her around and pulled her into his arms. Before she could say anything, he pressed his lips to hers and kissed her so passionately, she thought she was going to melt. Though she was beyond shocked, she didn't pull away or protest, or even ask for an explanation. This is exactly where she wanted to be, and she didn't want anything to break the spell.

Wil finally stepped back but kept her wrapped in his arms. Looking into her eyes, he smiled. "I've wanted to do that from the moment you came back to Liberty."

"Me too," she whispered.

He looked at her with a raised brow of doubt.

"Remember, I threw myself at you."

She could see the wheels turning in Wil's head as he recalled their first encounter.

"You also slapped me."

Remembering how she had behaved, Cassidy cringed, her cheeks warmed with embarrassment. "Okay, so maybe my tactics were a little . . . aggressive," she chuckled.

"But what about Blake?" he asked, his tone serious, nervous even.

"I wasn't interested in Blake. Well, maybe slightly." When Cassidy saw Wil's look of concern, she quickly explained. "But only because he showed an interest in my designs, something Mark never did. It was flattering to have a man look at me as not only attractive but talented too."

"But I liked you designs, and I told you so."

"You also had Ella hanging on you at every turn. I just figured I had disgusted you with my behavior when I tried to seduc—" She couldn't even say it, she felt so embarrassed. "Anyway, we were always at each other's throats, and I knew you were looking for certain qualities in a woman. Qualities I obviously didn't have." She shrugged. "I just figured Ella was more to your liking."

"Nothing ever happened between Ella and me. I think she just kind of hung around to see if I would change my mind."

"She also set you up."

"She what?"

Bacon crackled and butter popped. Cassidy quickly turned back to the meal on the stove and gave it her attention for the moment, but Wil wasn't done with their conversation.

"What do you mean, Ella set me up?"

Cassidy hesitated slightly. She knew Wil would be furious once he knew the truth about Ella, and she didn't want to spoil the mood.

"Come on, Cassidy. What did you mean by that?"

Pushing the eggs around in the pan, she spoke softly. "Blake told me she brought him in on your project to try and 'distract' me."

"What?"

"Ella was jealous. She thought we might have something going on. So . . . she told Blake to run interference, so she could make her move. Ella thought if she kept us apart long enough, you would change your mind about her. She figured you wouldn't want me if Blake and I . . . you know . . ."

Wil was livid. He threw a dish towel across the kitchen and reached for his cell phone.

"No Wil, don't." Cassidy reached for his phone and took it away.

"Give me my phone, Cassidy," he said, clearly irritated as he put out his hand, but Cassidy held onto it. "I need to set Ella straight. I knew she was interested in me but hiring Blake to seduce you is going way to far."

"Then you should be mad at me . . . because it almost worked."

Cassidy turned off the flame on both pans and just stood there, waiting for Wil to say something. But he was silent.

"I'm sorry, Wil. I know my behavior has been less than endearing." She cleared her throat, choking back the tears. "I have a tendency to go into self-destruct mode when I'm afraid of getting hurt. So, I push others away and sabotage relationships. It's a protection mechanism. I'd rather hurt myself than allow others to hurt me. Unfortunately, I hurt you and dad instead, and I'm sorry."

Cassidy didn't turn to look at him, but she could hear him breathing deep and pacing back and forth. She closed her eyes and prayed. *It's my fault, God, and I won't blame You if Wil can't forgive me.*

Feeling his hand on her arm, she looked up into his warm brown eyes. He turned her around and stroked her face with the back of his hand. "I think we need a fresh start."

"Right," Cassidy said, even though she wasn't sure what he meant. "How?"

"Why don't we just go from here."

"Where's here?" Cassidy asked.

"Here." Wil framed Cassidy's face in his, strong, calloused, hands and kissed her again.

Kissed her anew.

Kissed her the way she wanted him to for months.

———— • ————

Cassidy and Wil ate their dinner in front of the fireplace where it was warm.

"So, what happened with my dad after I left this morning?"

Wil munched on a strip of bacon as he answered. "It was incredible, Cassidy. He was just resting, when all of a sudden, he took a large breath and sighed. I would have thought something was wrong except for the smile on his face. His grin grew larger, and I thought he was experiencing some kind of daydream then he said, 'Cassidy's going to be okay.' It was like this incredible sense of peace filled him. He relaxed in bed and in a matter of minutes, the nurse came in to see if something was wrong with the machines. The improvement in his readings made her think they were malfunctioning.

"Anyway, the doctor came in to look at him and soon another doctor joined him. I was getting anxious, but not worried. I knew what I saw, so I knew whatever they were discussing was good news. The doctors came out of his room shaking their heads. Dr. Craig finally approached me and explained."

"What did he say?" Cassidy was hanging on Wil's every word. She put her plate down no longer feeling the need to eat.

"He explained to me the importance of emotion during a time of healing. Only one other time in his career had he witnessed such a profound effect on a patient because of his emotions. Except then, he witnessed a patient die of what he felt was a broken heart, literally. He felt your father's recovery was the exact opposite. After talking to Joseph about what he had experienced, Dr. Craig feels your father truly felt the lifting of a burden that had been weighing him down for years. Even though Dr. Craig isn't a Christian, he believes your father actually heard God speak to him."

"What . . . God spoke to my father?" Cassidy was shocked. "Were you there? Did you see anything or hear anything?"

"I was there and yes, I saw the expressions on your father's face, but I didn't realize it was because God was talking to him."

"Are the doctor's sure? I mean, dad could have been hallucinating or dreaming."

Wil shook his head with a chuckle and leaned forward to stack his plate on Cassidy's. "I don't know, Cassidy. But I do know your father had a sense of relief that was visible, and he told me 'Cassidy's going to be okay.' When you saw him today, he said you knew what he was talking about. Do you?"

"I don't know, Wil. I mean . . . this all seems so surreal."

"What happened when you went home this afternoon?"

"I was packing up Dad's things, and was ready to leave, when I remembered his Bible. It was sitting here, on the coffee table."

"Along with the note," Wil added.

She nodded.

"Did you read it?"

"I did."

"And?"

After a long hesitation, Cassidy explained. "I prayed, Wil. I asked God to spare my father and prove He hadn't given up on me. I asked Him to show me He was real."

Wil leaned back on the couch, astonished. "You think Joseph actually felt that in his heart? Could God have really comforted him with the thought that you had turned to Him?"

"I don't know, but it hurts to think my father's burden for me was so great, it actually caused him physical pain. I knew he cared, but I guess I never really knew how much."

Wil reached up and cupped Cassidy's cheek as he spoke. "And how do you feel now?"

"Different. I feel different. When I got to the hospital, and I thought my father was dead, I thought God was testing me."

"Testing you?"

"Yes. Like He expected me to take it all back when I found out my father was gone."

"Did you feel like that?"

"No. That's the weird part. I didn't. I was horrified God would go to such lengths to test my commitment, but I didn't want to take it back. I actually felt comforted knowing even if my dad was no longer with me, I wouldn't be alone."

Wil pulled Cassidy against his chest and stroked her arm. Resting in the crook of his arm, she closed her eyes. "This is how it feels, isn't it? That even though your world is turned upside down, and you're not sure where you're going to go from here, you still have a sense of comfort, a sense that you'll make it."

"Yep. Peace is an amazing thing."

FORTY-TWO

Her father had only been home for a week but was already proving to be a very difficult patient. Because of the restrictions his doctor had given him, he was not allowed to do many of the daily tasks he'd been doing since he was a boy. Instead, he sat in the living room, fidgeting, unable to hide his boredom.

Cassidy did her best to keep him entertained and used her time with him to get reacquainted with the Bible. She sat and talked with him for hours on faith, prayer, and forgiveness. She listened as he told her, with tears in his eyes, how God had helped him through the ordeal of losing her mom. It helped Cassidy better understand why her dad had looked so strong, when she had felt her whole world had shattered into a million pieces.

Cassidy hardly saw Wil that first week. Between making house calls to his patients, and taking over the workload of the ranch, it left them very little time to explore their new relationship. Or for Wil to work on his office space. He had fired Blake immediately from the project but hadn't found time to look for a new contractor. He'd also had a very uncomfortable conversation with Ella.

The day after her dad came home from the hospital, Wil called Ella to set her straight. He insisted Cassidy be there when he made the call and put it on speakerphone. When he confronted Ella with the details of her little scheme, she tried denying it, insisting it was a misunderstanding, throwing Blake under the bus in the process. But when Ella turned the tables on Wil, and accused him of leading her on, he nearly came unglued. Though he maintained his composure, Wil told Ella exactly what he thought of her, and clarified that regardless of what she thought, their relationship had never been anything more than business, and now that their business was concluded, there was no reason for them to cross paths in the future. Neither Wil nor Cassidy had spoken of Ella or Blake since.

But that was about to change.

After lunch, while her dad rested in the living room, Cassidy motioned for Wil to follow her. "I want to talk to you about something," she whispered, as she led him out onto the back porch. Once the door was closed behind them, Wil wasted no time pulling her into his arms and giving her a long, lingering kiss.

"What was that for?" she asked, feeling a crimson blush warm her face.

"Because I felt like it."

His smile made her knees weak, her insides flutter, and caused her to lose her train of thought. She just stood there staring into his comforting eyes.

He chuckled, "You wanted to talk to be about something?"

She did. But now she wasn't so sure it was the right time to bring it up.

"What is it, Cassidy?"

"Never mind, we can talk about it after dinner."

She moved to go back inside the house, but he stopped her, looking serious. "Now you have me worried."

"It's nothing, really," she smiled, reassuringly. "We can talk later."

"Or . . . we can talk now." He walked over to the porch swing and pulled her down beside him. "What's up?"

She wrapped her arms around her, trying to ward off the cold. "I wanted to talk to you about . . . Blake."

Wil stood, clearly angered. "What's there to talk about? He's not coming anywhere near my project. Or you, for that matter."

"But Wil, he was as much a pawn in Ella's scheme as we were."

"So now you're defending him? After what he did?"

Cassidy could tell Wil was hurt but wanted to try to make him understand. "I'm not defending Blake. I just think you're hurting yourself by not letting him work on your project. You're so busy with your patients and the ranch, you haven't had time to look for a new contractor. Blake knows what you want. He'll do a great job."

Wil crossed his arms and clenched his jaw. "And what about that project of his? Do you still want to work on it?"

She did. But not enough to hurt Wil's feelings. "I don't care about the Gentry project." She stood and moved closer to him. "I care about you, and your future. You need to get your office built."

"Correction." He tipped her chin up, looked into her eyes. "Our future."

FORTY-THREE

When Wil pulled up outside his building the following day, Blake was already waiting for him at the curb. Clenching the steering wheel tighter, Wil had to work hard to push down the anger simmering inside him. It took a lot to call Blake last night and set up this meeting. He didn't do it because of his project, because he knew it would eventually get done. He did it because he knew how much it meant to Cassidy.

Suppressing his desire to pin Blake up against the side of the building and threaten him within an inch of his life, he chose instead to walk directly to his building, unlock it, and wait inside.

Blake followed him in, looking over confident, glib even. "Hey, Wil, I just want to—"

"Shut up!" Wil snapped, pointing a calloused finger directly in Blake's face. "The only reason I'm here is because Cassidy begged me to speak with you. And the only reason I agreed was so I could set you straight." Wil crossed his arms against his chest, feeling the need to restrain himself.

"What you did to Cassidy was completely reprehensible. She was already struggling from the insecurities of a failed marriage, and you, like a vulture, swooped in on easy prey. You flattered and complimented and flirted until she was completely confused. Give me one good reason why I should keep you on this project?"

"Because I can renovate your building exactly the way you want and still maintain the architectural integrity."

Wil just stared at him, not wanting to listen to anything he said.

"Look, Wil," Blake hung his head. "I'm sorry I went along with Ella's stupid scheme, but I'm not sorry I met Cassidy." He stood straighter. "She's extremely talented, and I don't think you should stand in the way of her doing something she's so good at."

"We're talking about my project, not yours."

"But Cassidy should be allowed to—"

"You're kidding, right?" He laughed, not believing Blake could be so bold. "You actually think I trust you enough to let her work on your project?"

"You don't need to trust me. You trust her."

Wil's jaw tightened.

"Look, if I thought I had half a chance with Cassidy, I certainly wouldn't be here talking to you about a job. My focus would be on her. But I know it's not going to happen. I told Ella her plan wasn't going to work, but she didn't listen. I knew from the moment I saw the two of you in the same room, Cassidy had feelings for you."

"Yet you still tried bedding her. What's to say if I let her work on this project of yours, you're not going to try and do it again?"

"Because she's no longer confused or frustrated. She was dealing with emotions that had gone unanswered or unacknowledged."

Blake's insinuation was like a punch to the gut.

"She now knows who she is and where she belongs. She loves you. She doesn't need to look to me to bolster her self-esteem."

Wil turned away. He wanted to believe Blake but wasn't sure he could.

"I'm sorry, Wil. I don't know what else I can say. I acted like a complete jackass, and I'm sorry."

When Wil turned around Blake's hand was extended to him. Wil looked at it, then up at Blake. It took every ounce of strength he had to shake Blake's extended hand of apology.

"Just let me get one thing straight. You're right. I trust Cassidy, and I don't want to come between her and something she loves. She's spent the last five years with a man who ignored her gifts and stifled her talent. I don't want to be 'that' guy. But if I feel, for even one second, your behavior is anything less than professional, I'll drop you where you stand. Got it?" Wil's grip tightened on Blake's hand to add emphasis to his statement.

Blake held Wil's stare. "Got it."

———— • ————

Cassidy looked at the clock for the hundredth time, wondering how Wil and Blake's meeting had gone. Though she busied herself decorating the house for Christmas, all she could think about was Wil.

Maybe I was wrong to suggest they meet? What if Blake goads Wil or says something stupid about the night at his place. I should have left well enough alone. Please, God, don't let things get out of hand.

When Wil finally called, it was to let her know he would not be home for some time. Besides the patients he had to check on, he'd gotten an emergency call from a rancher in the next county. When she asked about his meeting with Blake, he assured her it went fine, but didn't elaborate. Only that he would be home late, and they could talk about it then. Thankful Wil didn't sound riled or upset, Cassidy decided to let it go, immersing herself in Christmas decorating.

———— • ————

A couple hours later, Cassidy looked around the house at all the decorations and smiled at the finished product. Wreaths were suspended in every window with red velvet ribbon, and garland was laced around the banister leading upstairs. She carefully placed her mother's favorite decorations—a set of golden angels—on the mantel and nested them on angel hair just like her mother had always done.

She reminisced about Christmas' past: wearing matching pajamas with her mom, drinking hot chocolate by the fireplace, turning off all the lights except for the tree, Dad reading the Christmas story. And how he always acted surprised when he opened his gifts, even though she gave him the same thing every year. New leather gloves and a bottle of his favorite aftershave.

Everything looked festive, except for the corner where the tree should go. Even though it was only a week until Christmas, she still wanted to get a tree. She was hoping to get one tonight after Wil got home.

Walking over to the window seat where the boxes of ornaments were stacked, she sat down next to them. The boxes were brown and tattered, some of them older than her. She lifted the lids on each set, remembering the story that went with them. When she got to the box labeled 'Cassidy' in her mother's perfect cursive, emotion welled inside of her.

Removing the lid, she looked at the delicate handmade ornaments her mother had made just for her. Every year her mom crafted something unique and different. She had fifteen in all. Fingering the intricate shapes, Cassidy remembered how much fun she had each year finding the newest ornament hanging on the tree. She sat back, tears in her eyes as she reflected on memories she had suppressed for so long.

When she heard her father coming down the stairs, she quickly brushed the tears from her cheeks and put the lid back on the box. Even though they were happy memories, she didn't want her melancholy mood to make him sad.

Instead, she met him at the bottom of the stairs and planted a delicate kiss on his cheek.

"What was that for?" he asked, a sweet expression filling his face.

"Just because." She smiled, then headed toward the kitchen. "Lunch will be ready in just a few minutes."

After they ate a nice, low cholesterol lunch, Cassidy and her dad took a slow stroll down the driveway and back. He'd been encouraged to walk for exercise, as long as he didn't overdo it. So, Cassidy accompanied him every day after lunch.

Once they were back inside, and her dad had his nose firmly planted in a book, she decided to do some painting. Wil wanted her to do the artwork for his waiting room, and even though that was months away, her technique was rusty, and she needed to practice with her oils. It had been years since using them, the last time being when she was still in art school. Normally, she used chalks or pencils when she was in a creative mood because they were easier to manage and store. But today, she wanted to work with her easel and oil paints. She felt motivated, inspired, and wanted to capture it on a canvas.

"Dad, I'm going to let the horses run in the east holding area. I need some inspiration. Call me on the walkie-talkie if you need me." Cassidy had purchased walkie-talkies before her father left the hospital. It gave her peace of mind to know he could reach her, even if she was outside. He nodded, acknowledging he'd heard her before she slipped out the door.

Cassidy set up her easel and watched the horses for quite some time before squeezing tubes of color onto her palette. She looked around at the beauty and serenity surrounding her and again wondered why she had ever left. She had wasted so much time dwelling on her mother's death, instead of her life. She had left the ranch with hatred, vowing never to return, but it was the hate within her that had followed her throughout her life. Now, with new eyes and a new heart, she could see why her mother and father loved the outdoors so much. The beauty of wide-open spaces. Nature surrounding them on all sides.

It was a gift.

A love affair.

A rebirth.

Quickly, a painting of rich browns, amber golds, and mossy greens filled her canvas. When she stepped back to examine it, she was surprised to see depth and feeling, something that had always been lacking in her paintings of Central Park or the Hudson River. Now she knew why. Those pictures were make-believe. She had been trying to capture something she couldn't feel. But the picture standing on the easel in front of her came from her soul.

This is where she lived.

What she loved.

Where she belonged.

Cassidy spent time watching the horses' mannerisms. Rooster was stoic, regal, prideful. Whiskers was playful and curious, and Sassy was mischievous as always. Watching them, Cassidy memorized their movements, then returned to her canvas and transferred her observations to her brush. Each stroke added life to the painting. The beauty of the day was being translated to canvas. The tranquility of the moment would forever be held in oils and brush strokes for all to see.

Cassidy was so immersed in what she was doing, time stood still. Or so she thought. When she finally made the connection between the pink-tinted sky and the time, she realized she needed to call it a day. Stepping back again, she looked at her canvas and felt a sense of pride. She still had some finish work to do, but she immediately recognized it to be her best work to date. She wasn't rusty or out of practice, she just needed the right muse. She couldn't wait to show Wil.

No. I'll surprise him with it for Christmas.

Carrying the wet oil painting home, she crept into the house. When she saw her dad was asleep, she rushed upstairs and carefully leaned it against the wall. Tiptoeing down the stairs, she hurried toward the front door, but not fast enough.

"Whoa, whoa, whoa," her dad said, swiveling his chair around to face her. "What's all the running around for?"

"I'll be right back, Dad. I have to get my supplies and bring in the horses."

Jogging to the field, she gathered her easel and supplies and took them to the barn. Seeing Rooster's harness on the hook by his stall, gave her an idea. Grabbing it, she went back to the field where the horses were grazing. It took a little coaxing to get Rooster harnessed, but once she did, she hopped on his back and headed for home, the other horses following behind them.

——— • ———

Wil watched from the front porch, leaning against the handrail, hat pushed back from his brow. Cassidy was a natural. Even though she had been out of the saddle for years, her natural abilities made her and the horse look like one. He watched as she led Whiskers and Sassy into the corral, then walked over to the stables.

"Need a hand?"

Cassidy slid from Roosters back, then turned around. "Wil, how long have you been home?"

"Just a few minutes." He opened Sassy and Whisker's stalls and helped lead them in. When Gent nickered for attention, Wil gave him a handful of oats and a little TLC.

With all the horses back in their stalls, Wil walked over to Cassidy, slid his index fingers through the belt loops on her jeans, and tugged her closer. He didn't say anything he just smiled.

"What?" Cassidy smiled in return.

"Nothing."

"Then why are you staring at me like that?"

"I'm just admiring the view." Wil leaned down and gave her a kiss, then walked arm and arm with her to the house.

"So, how is our patient doing?"

"Okay. I know he's trying to behave, but it's driving him stir crazy to sit still."

"And what did you do today?"

Cassidy smiled, pushed open the front door, and with arms spread wide, said, "Ta-dah!"

"Wow!" He stepped into the living room and took it all in. "Everything looks so beautiful."

"Doesn't it look great?" Joseph added from where he sat near the fireplace. "All we need to finish it off is a tree."

Cassidy turned to Wil. "I was thinking we could go get one tonight . . . if you feel like it. I realize it will only be up for a couple weeks, but it wouldn't be Christmas without one."

"Sure. Let's go after dinner."

"Which I will go make right now." She started backing up toward the kitchen when she added, "You know . . . it would go faster if I had a little help."

He smiled. "I'll be there in a minute; I just want to talk with your dad about something." He waited for Cassidy to disappear into the kitchen, then took a seat on the sofa opposite Joseph.

"I think Cassidy was angling for some help in the kitchen."

Wil chuckled. "She doesn't need my help, she just wants to know how my conversation with Blake went."

"And . . ."

"I wanted to deck him, Joseph. Just seeing him, knowing how he treated Cassidy . . ." Wil hadn't gone into detail with Joseph, but enough to let him know Blake and Ella had teamed up to try and keep Cassidy and him apart.

"But you didn't."

Wil shook his head. "No. And I might have made an even bigger mistake by agreeing to let him work on my building."

"So why did you?"

He looked at Joseph. "Because I don't want Cassidy to think I don't trust her."

"Trust her with Blake?" Joseph shook his head, amused. "She doesn't have feelings for Blake. She only has feelings for you."

Wil's gut tightened. "And how do you feel about that?"

"Are you asking if I approve?"

He nodded.

"How could you think I wouldn't approve? You're like a son to me."

"But Cassidy's divorce isn't even final. People might think we're being . . ."

"Wil, you know I've never been in favor of divorce. God is very clear on the subject. But this last week, Cassidy and I have had a lot of time to talk. She told me a little about Mark . . . her marriage . . . if that's what you could call it." Joseph paused, and Wil could see the emotion in his eyes. "She didn't come right out and say it, but he abused her, Wil," Joseph whispered. "Emotionally and physically. I don't know to what extent, but she's been living in fear of her own husband."

Clutching his hands together, Wil felt like he was going to puke. "Then why didn't she come home sooner? Why did she put up with it for so long?"

Joseph hung his head. "Because she didn't think she *could* come home. She felt God was punishing her for being rebellious. She thought her behavior was so unforgivable, I wouldn't want her to come home. So, she stayed—stayed with a man who terrorized her."

"Until she found out he was having an affair."

Joseph nodded. "She said he couldn't hurt her any more than he already had, so she left."

"But if he didn't care, why did he come all this way to serve her with papers?"

"I thought the same thing. But when he talked about Cassidy, it was like he was talking about a failed business transaction. To listen to the man, who took my daughter away, who hurt her . . . speak about her with such little feeling . . ." Joseph cleared his throat and continued. "Her divorce will be final soon enough. As long as you and Cassidy take it slow, you'll be all right. Now, tell me," Joseph gave him a slap on the knee, "how are things going at your building?"

"Wil, could you give me a hand?"

He turned to see Cassidy poke her head out of the kitchen.

"Yeah, I'll be right there." Wil quickly brought Joseph up to speed. He was switching gears. Since he no longer felt the need to move out of the cottage, he wanted work to start on the office space before the apartment. And when construction did happen upstairs, it would be Cassidy overseeing the details.

———— • ————

Cassidy pushed the beef strips around in the marinade as it sizzled on the stovetop. The rice was already done, and since Wil was still talking to her dad, she started working on the salad.

As she ripped the lettuce leaves, and sliced the tomatoes, she felt her irritation building. Wil had talked to Blake but not told her how it went. He didn't seem angry or upset, so it must have gone okay.

At least I hope it did.

But in case it didn't, she decided to wait until they went to get the Christmas tree to ask. Since her dad still didn't know what went on between her and Blake, there was no sense stressing him out about it now.

"Dinner's ready," she called from the kitchen doorway.

Wil looked at his watch, then at her. He jumped up from where he was sitting and quickly moved to the kitchen doorway. "I'm sorry, Cassidy. I didn't realize I had been talking for so long." He glanced at the dining room table and saw that everything was already done.

Cassidy raised her eyebrow as she glanced at him. "Uh huh."

"Really, Cassidy, I needed to discuss a few things with your dad and then when we got on the subject of the building, I guess I . . ."

"Smells good, Sunshine." Joseph inhaled deeply.

"Da-d," she protested.

"Okay, so what is with 'Sunshine?' " Wil looked between her and her dad. "Every time your father uses it, it makes you cringe. Why?"

Cassidy groaned. "It's a nickname my father gave me when I was little. It was fine when I was child, but I think I've outgrown it."

"You'll never outgrow it, Cassidy. You'll always be my Sunshine."

The way her father looked at her tugged at her heart. During her rebellious years, she refused to even acknowledge him if he called her by his pet name. She knew it hurt his feelings, but she didn't care. She was dealing with her own hurt after her mother's death, she didn't care about anyone but herself.

"Well, I think it's cute, and it describes you perfectly . . . when you're in a good mood." Wil smiled, then gave her a quick kiss.

"Ask her how she got it."

"Da-d. Come on, that was so long ago I don't even remember."

"Well, I remember like it was yesterday." Her dad took a seat then turned to Wil. "Her favorite song, when she was a little girl, was 'You are My Sunshine.' She used to sing it all the time. When she did her chores, when we went riding, all the time. I told her she was my sunshine and started calling her Sunshine from then on."

Cassidy saw love in her dad's expression as he recounted the story to Wil. She'd actually forgotten how she got the nickname, along with so many other childhood memories she'd pushed to the recesses of her mind.

Wil started humming the tune, then her dad chimed in with the words. Cassidy tried to ignore them as she grabbed two Cokes from the refrigerator and her dad's iced tea, but they got louder and louder. Soon, Wil was singing the words along with her dad. Cassidy shook her head in disbelief and crossed her arms in objection but couldn't hold back her smile. "Okay, okay, you win," she laughed as she took her seat. "Now . . . can we eat our dinner in peace and quiet?"

Her dad smiled as he reached for her hand. "Sure thing, Sunshine, just let me say grace." He bowed his head. "Our gracious and heavenly Father, I come before You with thanksgiving. For bringing Cassidy back to me and drawing her back to Yourself, and gratitude for this man who cares for her so much." Cassidy felt Wil reach for her other hand and give it a squeeze while her father continued. "Your plan is sometimes hard for us to understand, Lord, but we know it's always best. As the season is near for the world to celebrate Your birth, may they not forget to celebrate Your life. Thank you for this food before us and may it nourish our bodies for another day in Your service. Amen."

FORTY-FOUR

It was just starting to snow when they climbed into her dad's truck and headed to the Christmas tree lot. Wil whistled along with a Christmas tune on the radio while Cassidy waited patiently for him to say something about his conversation with Blake. But when his whistling turned to humming, then to all out singing, Cassidy couldn't wait any longer. She reached for the radio dial and turned it off.

"Okay, enough with the Christmas carols, are you going to tell me about your conversation with Blake, or not?"

Wil was silent.

"Okay, the "or not", is not an option. What did you say to him?"

"I told him I didn't trust him."

Cassidy nodded, then turned toward the passenger window to hide her disappointment. Even though she had told herself she would understand if Wil wanted to break all ties with Blake, she was discouraged just the same.

"What, no rebuttal?" Wil asked, clearly expecting one. "No argument? No debate?"

"No. I told myself I would be okay with whatever you decided." She looked at Wil and smiled, trying to look convincing.

"Okay, then let me finish. I told him I didn't trust him . . . but, Cassidy . . . I do trust you." He reached over and gave her knee a squeezed. "And I know how important this is to you."

She looked at him. "You mean . . . I can still work with him on the Gentry house?"

"That's what you want, right?"

"Well . . . yes . . . but not if it's going to make you feel uncomfortable."

Wil gave her a sideways glance. "Well, I'm not going to lie. It does make me feel uncomfortable, but I'll get over it."

He stared out the windshield, his brows knit with concern. "But there is something else that's been gnawing at me since we got into the truck."

Cassidy thought for a moment what it might be but came up empty. "What?"

With his eyes on the road and a smile raising the corners of his lips he asked, "Why are you sitting way over there?" He offered her a quick glance. "The best part about these old trucks is the bench seat."

Cassidy smiled as she scooted closer. Lacing her arm through his, she rested her head against his shoulder. The butterflies in her stomach took flight again, just like they always did when she was this close to Wil. The feelings she had when she was around him were so different than the emotions she'd felt with Mark.

Mark had brought out her insecurities. She always had to strive for his approval. Her mannerisms and behaviors were skills she had learned by watching the other women who traveled in Mark's circle. Seduction. That's what she had mastered in her time with Mark.

But when she was with Wil, she felt like herself again. She didn't need to be alluring or provocative. He knew who she was, had even seen her at her worst. But he wasn't discouraged. It was refreshing to be real. She no longer was running from who she was or where she came from. If anything, she was trying to find the girl she buried along with her mother years ago. She wanted to be the daughter her father deserved to have. She wanted to be plain old Cassidy Martin again.

"You're awfully quiet. I expected nonstop chatter about the Gentry house, and the ideas you want to pitch to her."

"It's not that important. I'm just enjoying the company."

"Me too."

They sat in silence for a while, then Cassidy remembered the pow-wow Wil had with her father earlier. "Hey . . . what were you talking to Dad about when you got home? You two seemed so serious."

"I was just making sure he was okay with . . . us."

"Us?" She chuckled. "Dad thinks the world of you. Why would you think he'd have a problem with 'us?' " She air-quoted.

"Cassidy, I know it might not seem like it, but you still are married. I just wanted to make sure your dad was comfortable with us spending time together, that he didn't think it was inappropriate."

"So, you think our relationship is inappropriate? That's great." She scooted to the far side of the truck and turned away.

"Come on, Cassidy, you know that's not true, but other people could get the wrong impression. I was just being respectful of your dad."

Cassidy wanted to be mad, but Wil was right. Legally she was still married to Mark, even thought that part of her life seemed like an eternity ago. She sat quietly, her head down in thought.

"I didn't mean to upset you. I was just looking out for you . . . for us."

"No . . . you're right. I mean I don't think people in Liberty have a very high opinion of me anyway, but I would hate for anyone to think badly of you or my dad." Cassidy scooted closer. "So, what did he say?"

Wil lifted his arm over her head and around her shoulder, pulling her closer still. "He encouraged us to take it slow, but other than that, he's glad we're together."

Wil pulled into the Christmas tree lot, killed the engine, then opened his door. As he was getting out, Cassidy asked, "And what about you, Wil, how do you feel about us?"

As she scooted across the seat of the truck, she thought about his reputation, his values, and the conservative lifestyle he lived.

The people of Liberty will think I seduced him.

Would it damage his reputation or his business? She hadn't thought about it. She hated the idea of Wil being subjected to the judgment she deserved. People could be cruel and slow to forgive.

How long will it take people to see I'm not the same person who returned to Liberty filled with anger and resentment? And what will they think of Wil in the meantime?

Getting out of the truck, she quickly pulled the hood of her jacket up over her head. Wil closed the door behind her, but still had not answered her question.

So, he does have doubts.

"You know, Wil, if it takes that long to figure out how you feel about us, maybe this isn't a good idea."

Cassidy tried to step around him, but he stepped closer to her, pressing her back against the truck. She didn't look at him—she couldn't. Not without crying.

"Cassidy . . . look at me."

She looked off in the distance.

"Cassidy . . ."

"Then tell me, Wil." She looked up, tears spilling from her eyes. "Tell me how you feel."

"No."

Cassidy wanted to run, but before she could, Wil brought his hands up to frame her face. "But I will show you." He softly touched his lips to hers, then kissed her. Slowly at first, then he wrapped his arms around her and held her tight. He looked into her eyes, his thumbs gently caressing her cheek. "I love you, Cassidy."

She smiled through her tears, "I love you too, Wil. But why was it so hard for you to say so?"

"It wasn't hard at all," he smiled. "But I could see in your eyes you were wrestling with your own thoughts. I just wanted to make sure you heard me."

Cassidy stood in front of Wil, her hands hooked in her back pockets, her boot lightly brushing over the smattering of snow on the ground. "I'm just afraid what people are going to say about you. They'll think I've lured you to the dark side. That I'm a wicked city woman who put a hex on you," she giggled, trying to make light of it. Then looked into his eyes. "But I don't want people to look down on you, Wil. I don't want to ruin your reputation or your business."

"That's not going to happen, Cassidy, and even if it did, it wouldn't matter to me. I know the real Cassidy . . . and she's the one I love."

FORTY-FIVE

"Dad we're home," Cassidy shouted as she and Wil dragged an eight-foot tree into the living room, complete with a dusting of snow.

Joseph emerged from the kitchen with a cup of coffee in hand. "My word, Wil, did you have to get the biggest one you could find?"

Wil laughed. "That was Cassidy's idea. I believe her exact words were, 'The bigger the better.' "

He helped her pull a side chair and a small end table away from the front window, then carefully lifted the tree into place. When they took a step back, the tree swayed slightly, snow glittering to the ground.

"I'm going to go get some more wood to reinforce the stand, I'll be right back." Wil gave Cassidy a peck on the cheek then headed out the door.

"So . . . you and Wil?" Her dad asked as he took a seat on the couch.

Cassidy smiled while watching the tree continue to sway, then chanced a glance at her dad. "You're okay with that, right?"

He didn't answer.

"Dad . . . Wil said you were okay with this."

Her father remained quiet.

She stepped back from the tree, watching the branches sway, but thinking it would hold. "Dad, what is it?" She moved to the chair nearest her father and perched on the arm.

Her dad looked at her, his kind eyes saying more than words. Immediately, she felt like a little girl again, caught doing something wrong. "Dad . . . Wil said he talked to you."

"He did, but I didn't talk to you." He sipped his coffee slowly, then asked, "Sunshine, are you ready for this? A relationship so soon after . . ."

So, he doesn't approve. She felt her heart tumble to her knees. *Please, God, don't make me choose between Wil and Dad.*

"Cassidy, what is it you see in Wil?"

"You're kidding, right?" But Cassidy could tell he was far from kidding.

"Wil's a wonderful guy, Sunshine. I know that. But what is it *you* see in him?"

Dumbfounded with where her father was going with this, she sat back, sighed, and thought about how best to describe how she felt about Wil. "He makes me feel safe. Wil knows the worst about me, has seen the worst in me, but says he loves me anyway. It's like he was waiting for me all along, and now that I'm back here and we're together, I can't image life without him."

Cassidy thought her words would encourage her dad, prove to him her feelings were real, but he looked even more somber. She placed a gentle hand on his knee. "Dad, what's with the worried face? I thought you'd be happy for me . . . for us."

He looked intently at her. Subdued. Worried. "Cassidy . . . if Wil makes you feel all those things, will you still have room in your life for God?"

He dad's words pierced her heart. She slid into the chair unable to answer.

"Cassidy, you ran away from here years ago looking to fill a void in your life. You were able to for a little while before the emptiness drove you home, brought you to a point where you acknowledged your need for God in your life. But what will happen now? Now that things are turning around for you? Will you still see a need for God if Wil provides you with security, love, and comfort?"

Cassidy couldn't say anything because she wasn't sure she knew the answer. Just then, Wil walked in with the supplies for the tree stand unaware of the shifting mood in the room.

"Sorry it took me so long," he said with a smile. "I figured if I was going to reinforce the stand, I might as well do it right." Wil dropped a couple two-by-fours at the foot of the tree and a handful of nails. When he looked between her and her dad, his smile faded. "Did I do something—"

"Wil," she got up from where she was sitting, rubbing her forehead. "I know we planned on decorating the tree tonight, but I'm kind of tired. How about we do it tomorrow?"

"But Cassidy . . ."

"I'll see you in the morning, Wil," she smiled, then quickly climbed the stairs.

"Okay . . . I'll be by to pick you and Joseph up for church at ten o'clock."

She nodded, then went to her room.

After showering, she sat brushing her hair while pondering her father's words. Was he right? Would she come to rely on Wil instead of God? She gazed out her window and saw the dim lights of Wil's place. He had looked so dejected and confused when she excused herself earlier. She felt horrible for leaving without an explanation, but how could she assure him of something she wasn't sure of herself. Maybe her father was right. Maybe she and Wil needed to slow down. They'd become too comfortable with each other over the last few weeks. He was already feeling like a natural extension of herself.

Confused, she curled up on her bed and closed her eyes, fearful she was going to lose everything all over again.

———— • ————

Wil saw the light from Cassidy's window. He sat in his kitchen, a cup of coffee in his hand and a chill in his bones. He wasn't sure what had happened between Cassidy and her dad to cause the evening to take such a drastic turn, but he knew who did.

He slowly climbed the stairs, fell across his bed, and stared at the ceiling. "I'm confused, Lord. I know this hasn't taken you by surprise, but it sure has me. Help Cassidy and Joseph with whatever is causing the difficulty between them and allow me to be patient and understanding in the process."

Wil rolled off his bed, headed to the shower, and continued his conversation with God.

———— • ————

Cassidy could not sleep.

Every time she closed her eyes, she debated with her soul. Pros and cons. Do's and don'ts. Wil vs God.

I spend the first hour of every day in the Word, talking with God. I do ask for His direction. I am seeking His guidance.

Or am I?

She thought about how she spent the majority of her days. With her dad. Her art. The horses. Wil.

Just thinking about Wil made her smile. He was amazing and kind and patient. Being with him made her want to be a better person. She craved his touch and the warmth she felt whenever he was close to her. He was the first thing she thought about in the morning and the last thing she smiled about before going to sleep at night.

Oh, no. She choked back a sob. *Dad is right.*

She wasn't relying on God. Even though she had restored her relationship with Him and was communicating with Him like she had when she was a child, her comfort . . . her *true* comfort came from Wil.

Closing her eyes, she tried processing what she was thinking, what she was feeling.

I need time. Even if it is just a few days. I need time to sort things out.

She needed to make sure her relationship with God was real, not just a good feeling because things were going right. He needed to be first in her life.

Regardless of circumstances.

It was the right thing to do.

Then why does it hurt so much? she questioned before crying herself to sleep.

FORTY-SIX

Cassidy woke up early the next morning, her decision of the previous night weighing heavy on her. She would talk to Wil after church. She wasn't sure what she would say, but it's what she had to do.

"Okay, Lord. I'm relying on you," she whispered, sitting on her bed, her head against her drawn up knees. "I don't want to do this, and I'm not sure I have the strength to go through with it, but I know I need to. I have to know for myself, if Wil was no longer a part of my life, would You be enough?"

———— • ————

Wil was up and ready for church before dawn.

He was anxious to see Cassidy, needing assurance that whatever had transpired the previous night had nothing to do with him. Trying to distract himself from his overactive imagination, he rolled out the blueprints to his office space and visualized what it would look like when the penciled lines became real walls. Blake would be on site first thing tomorrow morning and had assured Wil, he and his crew would be able to make up the time they had lost due to their *misunderstanding*. Wil wasn't worried about it. He was more worried about Blake spending time with Cassidy. He knew it was just his insecurities messing with his mind.

Cassidy loved him.

She said so.

But then something changed.

———— • ————

Wil knocked on Cassidy's front door a little before ten, then pushed it open. "Church bus is here," he joked. When he glanced at the bare Christmas tree in the corner, he remembered the tension from the previous night.

Joseph emerged from the kitchen as Cassidy slowly descended the stairs. Wearing wool slacks in a houndstooth pattern and a black wool blazer, she looked stunning, sophisticated. But the fact that she wasn't making eye contact with him, tightened his gut.

That can't be good.

"Good morning, Cassidy." Wil said, sounding more chipper than he felt.

"Good morning, Wil." Cassidy's voice was barely above a whisper and again, there was no eye contact. She breezed past him, grabbed her purse off the coat rack, and headed for the truck.

Wil followed her out and reached for her arm. She stopped but didn't turn around. "What is it, Cassidy, what's wrong?"

"Not now, Wil. We need to get to church."

"Then at least tell me it isn't me. If you're angry because you had disagreement with your dad last night, I get it. But I have to know it isn't me."

Cassidy stepped off the porch and got into the truck without a word.

———— • ————

The drive to church was grueling. After a few failed attempts at conversation, Wil focused on driving, while she did all she could to not burst into tears.

Her dad squeezed her hand, silently letting her know he was there for her, but the tortured expression on Wil's face was almost more than she could bear. To try and explain herself in the few minutes they had before church would only make matters worse, so she needed to wait until they got home.

When she scooted out the passenger side, her dad gave her hand a tug. She looked at him, but quickly turned away.

"Cassidy, this is my fault. The tension between you two. I shouldn't have said what I did last night."

She shook her head. "No, Dad," she whispered, "you had every right to say what you did. The problem is, I'm not sure of my answer."

"But shutting Wil out isn't right either. You need to talk to him."

"I will. Just not right now."

"Cassidy, please don't leave again. I need you here."

"Dad," she looked at him, her heart nearly breaking. "I'm not going anywhere."

"But what if you do?" His eyes welled with tears. "I'm afraid you're going to disappear inside yourself again. I lost you for nine years. I can't lose you again."

"You're not going to lose me, Dad. I promise."

———— • ————

Church was awkward, to say the least.

Politeness dictated Cassidy and Wil exchange pleasantries with members of the congregation. Questions about Wil's practice were easy enough to answer, but the well-meaning older women were harder to ignore.

"Hold on to him, Cassidy. He's a treasure," Mrs. Beals whispered in her ear, while Wil assured Mr. Beals, he would still make house calls on the stock animals after his office opened.

Then Mrs. Boothby gave her a hug, reminding Cassidy she was the wedding coordinator for the church. "Just in case you ever need my services, sweetie."

Of course, there were the dissenters too. Those who felt Cassidy was city trash, and Wil was a fly caught in her web. Those women stared at Cassidy while their husbands spoke with Wil. He got the smiles; she got the glares. The women never came right out and said how they felt. Cassidy was sure it was only out of respect for her dad, but they made it clear what they thought and how they felt. And on a day like today, with her decision weighing heavy on her heart, she all but agreed with them.

Wil deserved so much more.

When the organ started to play, everyone took their seats; her dad on her left, Wil on her right. After a few songs from the choir, the announcements, and the offering, the pastor stepped up to the pulpit and addressed the congregation. "Today's message is a simple one, but there are times when we need to be refreshed on the simplicity of our faith. Today's message is on Dependency. Dependency on God."

When Cassidy looked up, she was sure the preacher was looking directly at her.

Am I that transparent?

Cassidy braced herself and listened. Because surely God had arranged this message just for her.

FORTY-SEVEN

The drive home was just as quiet and torturous as the drive to church.

After service, Wil ushered Cassidy straight to the truck, not visiting with anyone like he normally did. He wanted to ask her right then and there what was wrong, and why she had cried silent tears during the pastor's message. But Joseph followed them to the truck, obviously sensing Wil's urgency to get home.

When he pulled up to the front porch, Joseph excused himself to the house. Cassidy moved to slide across the seat, but Wil stopped her. "Cassidy, I'm dying here. You need to tell me what's going on. Why are you so upset?"

"I'm not upset, Wil, but we do need to talk." Cassidy got out of the truck and walked over to the fence line, not caring that it was cold.

Wil sat for a moment, his mind rewinding for the hundredth time back to the night before. He racked his brain for anything he might have said or done to hurt Cassidy, but just like every time before, he drew a blank.

When he joined Cassidy along the fence line, she was staring out over the property like she was seeing it for the first time. Finally, she turned to him.

"Wil, I need some time to myself, just for a little while, to sort some things out."

He reached for her forearms and pulled her close. "What is it, Cassidy? What's wrong? If I said or did something to upset you, just tell me."

Cassidy didn't say anything, she simply leaned against his chest and cried.

Wil's heart sank. He held her close and tried to formulate his next question, but the knot in his throat made it near impossible to speak.

"Cassidy, I didn't mean to pressure you last night. You asked me how I felt so I told you. If you don't feel the same way, that's okay. I didn't mean to rush you. If you don't—"

"Wil . . . I do love you . . . I do, but I'm afraid."

"Afraid? Afraid of what?" Wil held Cassidy's head to his chest and rocked her back and forth. "I don't understand."

"Neither do I or at least I won't until I have some time to think. I don't want to mess up again, Wil. It's too painful. I allowed one person to crush my world because that person *became* my world. I don't want that to happen again."

"But Cassidy, I would never hurt you the way Mark did." He tipped her chin up and looked into her eyes, wanting her to see the truth in his. "You've got to know that."

"I know, Wil. This isn't about you . . . it's me. I'm confused right now. I just need a little time to think, to pray, to listen with something other than my selfish heart."

He was more confused than ever. "I'm sorry, Cassidy. I'm not trying to make this harder on you, really I'm not, but you're not making any sense. If you say you love me, and you trust me, then why? Why don't you want to be with me?"

Cassidy stepped back from him and took a deep breath. "I'm afraid . . . I'm afraid I'm allowing you to fill areas in my life that are meant for God."

He was stunned. "Why would you say that?"

"Because my father challenged me last night, and as much as I wanted to be angry with him and tell him he was wrong, I couldn't. I wasn't sure."

"Wasn't sure about what?"

"Wil, I need to trust God for my peace and my strength. For comfort and unconditional love. But right now, I'm trusting you for all that. When I'm with you, I feel strong again. Loved again. But what would happen if you were gone? I need to know . . . if God was to remove you from my life . . . I wouldn't make the same mistakes again. I need to know I would be okay . . . that I could survive."

He hugged her close, sighing with relief, knowing the transformation he'd seen in Cassidy was real. "Of course you would."

She shook her head and pulled away. "No, I don't know that, Wil." She started to pace. "When God took my mom, something inside me died. I can't even begin to describe the emptiness and sense of betrayal I felt. The anger and the resentment. I walked away from everything I thought I knew, because I refused to believe in a God who could be so cruel."

"Cassidy," Wil stopped her pacing and allowed his fingers to brush the tears from her cheeks. "You're no longer that angry little girl. When you thought you lost your dad, you were devastated, but you knew your strength would come from the Lord. I saw that in you."

She hung her head, looking defeated.

"But . . . if you need time to prove it to yourself, I'll wait." He tipped her chin up and waited for her to look at him. "I love you, Cassidy, and I can't stand the thought of being apart from you . . . but I understand—at least I'm trying to." Wil forced a reassuring smile to his lips. "So, what are we talking here? No contact of any kind? No phone calls? No passing notes in school?"

Cassidy smiled.

He sighed with relief. *If she can still smile, it can't be too bad; I hope.*

"I'm not sure. I mean, Dad still needs your help around here, and if you or Blake have questions about the project designs, I don't want you to fall behind because you're afraid to call me. I just think I need to have some time to myself to figure out who I am in the Lord, not who I am when I'm with you."

"But next week is Christmas. I really don't want to spend it apart."

"Me either." She pressed her hands to his chest. "Even if I don't have things figured out by then, we'll still spend Christmas together. Starting with presents at eight o'clock in the morning." She smiled, but he could tell it was forced.

"Okay," Wil agreed, even though his heart constricted. "I'll keep up with the chores, but I'll give you some space. I won't come looking for you in the evenings or stay for meals. I'll let you call me when you're ready."

They walked back to the house hand-in-hand. Wil squeezed Cassidy's hand, just as she let go of his. Standing on the front porch, she took a deep breath. "This is for the best, Wil. I know it is. Otherwise, it wouldn't be so difficult." She raised up on her tiptoes and kissed him softly on the cheek before going into the house.

Staring at the closed door, Wil prayed. "Please, God, don't let that be a goodbye."

Cassidy went straight to her room. She needed to cry and get it over with. Kicking off her shoes, she took off her blazer, and curled up on the bed. Pressing her pillow against her aching heart, she prayed, "Okay, God, it's just You and me now. Please show me Your ways and grant me Your peace."

And please . . . please don't take Wil away from me.

FORTY-EIGHT

Wil drove downtown wishing he was seeing anyone else but
Blake. He was supposed to meet with him first thing this morning,
but an emergency with one of his patients called him away before
dawn, and his day went downhill from there.

He pulled up in front of the building, and when he walked inside,
he saw Blake's crew hard at work.

"Hey, Wil," Blake walked across the room and shook his hand.
"I took the liberty of using Ella's key. I figured she didn't need it
anymore, and I wanted to get an early start."

Wil looked around and saw Blake's men had already made a lot
of progress. "I appreciate you getting started even though I was
delayed."

"That's the beauty of working with a blank canvas. We've nearly
got the framework done and should be ready to pull the electrical
tomorrow."

Wil walked in and out of doorways that would make up the exam
rooms, reception area, and office. His dream was taking shape. He
felt a sense of excitement, but it lasted for only a moment. It would
be better if he was sharing it with Cassidy.

He and Blake discussed the plumbing and the electrical in detail.
Blake explained—even though Wil was committed to being on
property any chance he got—he needed as much information as
possible, so work didn't stall when Wil wasn't around. Blake pulled
out the more detailed plans for one of the exam rooms, and was
talking about something, but Wil wasn't listening. Instead, he was
remembering the night Cassidy and he went over her sketches for
the downstairs.

"Wil . . . are you with me?"

He quickly turned to Blake. "What? Sorry, I wasn't listening."

"I wanted to get a feel for it. The details."

"Excuse me, what?"

"I said, I checked out a vet's office in Clearlake to see how the exam rooms were set up." Blake stared at him, clearly waiting for him to say something. "Okay, Wil, you're a million miles away. What's wrong?"

"Sorry. I'm just a little distracted." He turned his attention back to Blake. "How was the office?"

"Nice. Top notch. That's why I went there."

"You must have gone to Abernathy's."

"How'd you know?"

"He's known for his money as well as his veterinary skills."

"Well he spared no expense. Everything was top-of-the-line."

"Was it helpful seeing it first hand?"

"It really was. Abernathy explained why some of the drawers and cupboards had such unique dimensions and what they housed. I took down all the dimensions, just to be on the safe side. I know your notes were specific, but I didn't see the harm in double-checking. You know the old adage, 'measure twice, cut once.' "

Wil and Blake went over every aspect of the design. Every measurement, every door, every hinge. Wil was impressed with Blake's attention to even the smallest details.

"Thanks, Blake. I can see you've put a lot of your own time into this."

"Hey, contrary to popular belief, I don't spend all my free time with women."

Wil gave him a drop-dead stare.

"Sorry," he chuckled nervously, "I should have let that one go. Anyway," he turned back to the counter, "I brought wood chips and countertop samples, if you want to go ahead and choose a color scheme."

Wil would've liked Cassidy's opinion, but went ahead and chose a nice oak, and a dark countertop to complement it. "I really like wood with character, so if you could find some oak with a lot of veining, I'd appreciate it."

"No problem." Blake jotted down a few notes. "Now let's talk about the sinks and fixtures."

They hammered out every decision pertaining to the exam rooms, knowing the office space and reception areas could wait. Wil appreciated the way Blake took notes every time Wil made a specific request. He also noticed for the third time, Blake looking at his watch.

"Okay . . . well, I need to get going. I have another appointment." Blake gathered up the plans and his notes. "I'll only proceed with information you've confirmed. Any other questions will wait for your walk-throughs or if need be, I'll give you a call."

"Don't worry, I plan on being around a lot, especially when it comes to the finish work."

Wil stayed after Blake left and soon found himself helping the crew with the framework. Physical labor had always been a good distraction for him. And that's what he needed right now, that and a lot of prayer. Otherwise, he was going to drive himself crazy thinking about Cassidy.

———— • ————

Cassidy got dressed for her appointment with Blake. He was introducing her to Mrs. Gentry today and she, in return, would be presenting some of her ideas.

Scrutinizing her appearance in the full-length mirror, Cassidy made sure she looked professional but not too stuffy. She chose a chocolate-colored linen suit with a creamy silk blouse. The tailored ensemble gave her the classic look she was hoping for. Grabbing her camel colored Peacoat from the closet, she headed downstairs.

She drove to Blake's house, but his truck wasn't in the driveway. Just as she was about to text him, he pulled in behind her, got out of his truck, and walked up to her window. "Are you ready?"

"As I'll ever be." She scooted out of the truck and followed behind Blake. When he turned around, his eyes instantly swallowed her up from head-to-toe, followed by a whistle and a groan, "Man, oh man, to think I gave up all that without a fight. I must be getting old."

Immediately, Cassidy turned on her heels and headed back to her own truck. Blake caught up to her and reached for her arm, but she quickly shook him off. "I can't handle this right now, Blake. Please give my apologies to Mrs. Gentry."

"Hey, hey, hey, I was only teasing," he chuckled, his hands raised in surrender. "Gees, you and Wil need to get yourselves a sense of humor or this old world is going to chew you up and spit you out." Blake put his hands on Cassidy's shoulders and marched her back to the passenger side of his pickup. "Now, let's go see Mrs. Gentry so you can woo her with all your fancy ideas."

Once they were on their way, Blake was all about business. He explained to Cassidy what he had already discussed with Helen Gentry, and gave her a rundown on the woman's eccentricities. She listened intently, feeling like she was going to be sick.

"Cassidy, are you all right?"

"Sure . . . I'll be fine." She closed her eyes and prayed. *Lord, please help calm my nerves. I feel so unsure of myself. If this isn't a career I should pursue, please let me know today. I don't want to get my hopes up just to fail.*

"Cassidy, relax. You're going to do fine."

They pulled into the dirt lot and parked behind a Mercedes-Benz. Blake helped Cassidy out of the truck and walked beside her to what would soon be the grand entry.

"There you are." A larger-than-life woman approached them.

"Helen Gentry, this is Cassidy Grayson. Cassidy, Mrs. Helen Gentry."

"Nice to meet you, Mrs. Gentry." Cassidy stared at the woman in bedazzled jeans, teal-colored cowboy boots, and a rhinestone jacket to match. She was a large woman, not heavy, just large; and she oozed self-confidence and sass. She extended a heavily jeweled hand to Cassidy and smiled.

"You too, dearie. Blake can't say enough nice things about you, and now I can see why." She turned her attention to Blake. "No wonder you want her on this project. She's a lot prettier than the last designer you recommended. What was her name again? Isme . . . Hisme . . ."

"Esme."

Mrs. Gentry swung her arm like she was batting at a fly. "Whatever. She was an idiot. Only had two colors in her decorator palette. Black and white. Anyway," Mrs. Gentry turned back to Cassidy and grinned. "You got yourself a real hottie here," she pointed a thumb at Blake. "I told Mr. Gentry, if I was twenty years younger, Blake might give him a run for his money. But don't worry, sweetie, I'm not gonna give you any competition." She laughed and gave Cassidy a wink.

Cassidy looked at Blake, wondering what he had told her.

"Helen," Blake cleared his throat. "Cassidy and I aren't an item. She's already spoken for."

"Oh really? Anyone I know?"

"She's seeing—"

"Actually, Mrs. Gentry," Cassidy cut Blake off. "I'm not sure what my personal life has to do with this job, but I'd love to

273

show you some of the ideas I've come up with."

"Cassidy," Blake whispered sharply.

She looked at Blake, saw fire in his eyes, then turned back to Mrs. Gentry. The older woman's fuchsia lips were pressed together tightly, and her hands were propped on her ample hips, clearly taken aback by Cassidy's directness. Realizing she might have come off a little to blunt, Cassidy braced herself for a verbal assault. Then, the woman's demeanor changed completely, and she burst out laughing. "You're quite the spitfire, missy. No one has talked to me like that for years. I like it. Reminds me of me."

Blake sighed, then smiled.

"And you can wipe the stupid grin off your face, Blake Simpson. If you think you'll get away with talking to me like that, you're sadly mistaken."

Helen Gentry took Cassidy by the arm and walked alongside her as they entered the shell of her dream home. She explained to Cassidy the look she was going for, the materials she wanted to use.

"Like a villa," Cassidy suggested.

"Yes! A villa set in the vineyards of Italy."

"I thought you said French Country," Blake cut in.

"No. I said I wasn't sure what I wanted. You're the one who said French Country, but Cassidy is right. I want a villa. You know . . . rough hone walls, tile floors, openness. I want my guests to feel like they're dining outside, even when they're not. I want it to feel spacious even though I'll need seating for many people. I want the furniture to be exquisite, but I also want it to disappear into its surroundings. When people leave my house, I want their feeling to be, Wow! But I don't want any one piece to stand out or detract from the others. Do you know what I mean?"

Cassidy didn't answer; she just moved around the room remembering what she had seen while vacationing in Rome with Mark. Well, she had been on vacation; Mark had turned it into a business trip. While she wandered the streets of Trastevere, Mark met with potential clients.

Opening her eyes, she started rattling off ideas and suggestions. Her arms expressed open arches. Her fingers spoke of natural mortar and suede furnishings. Mrs. Gentry got more and more animated with each detail Cassidy explained. Golds, browns, and olive greens were the colors that would bring Mrs. Gentry's vision to life.

When Cassidy was done with her walk-through of the main

floor, Mrs. Gentry could barely contain her excitement. "Okay, Blake, hear me, and hear me good. I give Cassidy full reign from here on out."

"What?" Both Cassidy and Blake exclaimed at the same time.

"You heard me." She pointed to Cassidy. "You, my dear, have just taken me to the vineyards of Sicily and back. You must have been there yourself and loved the country as much as I do."

"It was several years ago, but I did fall in love with the architecture and the old-world charm."

"That's exactly it! Old-world charm. That's what I want." She headed toward the imaginary doorway with Cassidy and Blake following behind. "Okay, Blake, it's all yours. You don't need me hanging around anymore, giving you grief. I will be leaving for New York at the end of the week, and then I'm off to Switzerland. I will be back in three months. I know you won't be finished by then, but you should be well on your way. I'll be in touch."

Without warning, Mrs. Gentry pulled Cassidy into a bear hug. "You, sweetie, are a treasure. It's as if you climbed into my thoughts and pictured every detail. If you have any questions, Blake has my number." She stepped away from them both and headed to her Mercedes. "Oh, Cassidy, if you think we need to look for any authentic pieces of furniture or accessories, just let me know. I would love the excuse to shop in Italy. You could come with me and show me where you stayed." With a wave of her hand, she looped around on the dirt lot and roared away in a cloud of dust.

Blake looked at Cassidy and laughed. "So, what do you think of the demure Mrs. Gentry?"

"I think I've never met anyone quite like her." Cassidy let out a breath, then smiled. "And I met some pretty over-the-top women when I was in New York."

"Well . . . you did it! You sealed the deal!" Blake scooped her up and spun her around, then set her down gently. "You're incredible!" When he leaned forward, Cassidy quickly backed away, and walked to the passenger side of his truck. When Blake got in, he rested his forearms and head on the steering wheel. "I'm sorry, Cassidy."

"Don't be sorry, Blake. Just don't let it happen again. I won't be able to work with you if this is the way it's going to be."

"I said I was sorry. I was just happy. Believe me, I have no intentions of moving in on Wil's territory."

"Hey! Don't say that. I am no one's territory. Got it?"

"Got it." Blake was quiet, but only for a second. "Are you telling me, you and Wil split up already?"

"No. I'm not saying that either. I'm just . . . taking some time for myself. I'm dealing with a lot right now, and I'll do better without personal distractions."

"But you still want to work on this project, right? You're not going to go scooters on me in the middle of it? Helen just gave you carte blanche. I'll never get that back if you walk away."

"Creating is not a distraction. It's therapy."

"Whatever you say."

The ride back to Blake's was quiet. When he pulled up alongside her truck, she reached for the door handle, but before she got out, she couldn't help but ask, "How are things going at Wil's?"

"Good. He picked out a lot of the materials today. In fact, I'm headed back there right now."

She nodded. "That's great." Then got out of his truck and stepped to hers.

"Cassidy," Blake called after her.

When she turned around, he was leaning over, looking at her through the passenger window. "For what it's worth, I'm sorry about you and Wil . . . and I promise to give you your space."

"Thanks, Blake."

FORTY-NINE

Blake noticed Wil's pickup was still parked out front when he pulled up. He entered the building to the sound of hammers and saws. Waving to get his foreman's attention, Steve acknowledged him and stepped away from the sawhorse.

"Looking good, Steve."

"Well, having an extra set of hands helps." Steve glanced to where Wil was working with Tim.

"Has he been here all day?" Blake asked.

"Left for about an hour, but that's all. He really knows what he's doing. If he ever wants to give up the vet thing, he'd make a great carpenter."

Blake walked over to where Tim and Wil had just finished framing out the fourth exam room. "I hear you're showing up my guys."

Wil brushed the sawdust from his jeans and wiped his brow with the back of his arm. "I forgot how much I loved this kind of work. It's like therapy."

"You too, huh?"

"What?"

"Cassidy. She said the same thing about the Gentry project."

"Really? I didn't realize her meeting was today. So, how did she do?"

"Great! Mrs. Gentry is going to Switzerland and leaving her in charge."

"You're kidding!"

"I'm not. Cassidy was fantastic."

Wil cast his eyes downward.

"Hey . . . Wil, for what it's worth, I'm sorry about you and Cassidy. I mean, go figure women. One minute they're hot, another minute they're cold."

"She told you?" Wil snapped.

277

Blake didn't mean to tick him off, but from Wil's tone, and the clench of his jaw, it was pretty clear he had. "Not exactly. I just kind of put it together."

"And how exactly did you do that?"

Choose your words carefully, or you're going to be picking yourself up of the ground.

"She said something like . . . she didn't want any personal distractions, and that she needed her space. Something like that. I just put two and two together and figured she had jumped ship. Some women just have a thing about commitment."

"And you're an expert?" Wil tossed down the hammer he was holding and snatched his jacket from the sawhorse behind him.

Blake took a step back. "Hey, man, I didn't mean to tick you off, or put myself in the middle of whatever is going on between the two of you. Maybe it would be better for you to talk to Cassidy about this stuff in the future."

———— • ————

Wil chirped his tires as he pulled away from the curb and sped down Main Street. He knew he shouldn't be mad. He'd opened the door by asking the question. Blake just answered. Well, he did more than answer, he tried psychoanalyzing Cassidy. Acting like he knew her. That's what put him over the edge.

When he saw Joseph's truck in the driveway, Wil stopped, then looked at the front door.

I said I wouldn't go looking for her; I would give her some space. He killed the engine. *But that doesn't mean I can't check in on Joseph.*

Wil poked his head in the house. It hurt seeing the decorated Christmas tree, knowing Cassidy had done it without him.

"Hey, Wil." Joseph spoke low.

"How you doing, Joseph?"

"Oh, you know, the good comes with the bad."

Wil quickly looked around the living room, then glanced upstairs.

"She's in the barn."

"Is it that obvious?"

"Yes, but I don't blame you. In fact, this is all my fault. When I asked Cassidy about your relationship, I had no idea she would go to this extreme."

Wil chuckled slightly. "If you haven't figured her out after all these years, what hope is there for me?"

"There's hope, Wil. You've got to know that."

"Just pray for me, Joseph. I know Cassidy said it would only be for a little while, but what if it's not? What if she decides there isn't an 'us?' I love her, Joseph. I am madly in love with your daughter. For me, there is no going back."

"Believe me, Wil, prayer and the Word of God are about my only companions these days. You're being well represented before the Lord."

Wil felt a sense of peace, knowing prayer would be the only thing keeping him sane in the days ahead. "I heard she was a real hit with Mrs. Gentry."

"Yep. She's been sketching like crazy. Says she's been left in charge of the whole project."

"Then I guess she'll be putting in long hours with Blake." Wil wanted to kick himself the minute her verbalized his fear.

"Now, Wil . . . don't go borrowing trouble for yourself."

"I know, I know," he sighed. "Well, I'd better go. I'll try to check in on you tomorrow."

Wil could see light flickering from inside the barn.

She said she expected we would still have some contact. Especially, if we're both doing chores.

So, he decided congratulating her on her business venture would be as good excuse as any.

Slipping through the heavy barn doors, he saw her across the way, mucking out a stall. He heard her humming as he moved closer but couldn't make out the tune. "Congratulations, Cassidy."

She gasped and jumped back, the pitchfork dropping from her hand. "Wil, you scared me half to death."

"I'm sorry. I didn't mean to."

She picked up the pitchfork and continued mucking. "What are you doing here?"

"I came to congratulate you on your new job."

"Dad told you?"

"No. Blake did."

She stopped for a moment, glanced at him, then wheeled over a barrow of fresh hay.

"He said you did a great job presenting your ideas. I guess you'll be spending a lot of time with him, I mean on the job site."

Cassidy stopped and leaned against the pitchfork. "Wil, please don't make more of it than it is."

"I'm not." He tried to keep his voice controlled. "Blake assured me he wouldn't take advantage of your availability." For the second time in less than five minutes, he spoke before he thought.

"Don't act like that, Wil!" Cassidy marched from the stall and tossed the fork against the wall.

"I'm sorry. I shouldn't have said that, but why are you sharing personal information with Blake Simpson?"

"I didn't mean to . . . it just kind of came out." Cassidy led Rooster back into his newly lined stall, gave him a handful of oats, then flipped the switch, leaving her and Wil in shadows.

"Good night, Wil."

Walking to his truck, he watched as Cassidy climbed the front stairs and disappeared inside the house. Looking at the Christmas lights twinkling through the living room window, he prayed Christmas would be a time of celebration. Not just of the Savior's birth, but for Cassidy and him, as well.

FIFTY

A week had passed.

A long tortuous week away from Wil.

It has been difficult, but productive.

Cassidy's coping mechanism . . . stay busy.

Moving from one project to another, left her little time for self-loathing and doubt. Even though she used her extra time to have some amazing conversations with God—filled with affection and affirmation—the busy thing really helped.

She was up at five o'clock every morning in order to beat her dad to the barn and get the labor-intensive chores out of the way. He was a reluctant patient and refused to wither away by doing nothing. So, Cassidy did the heavy lifting while he took care of the easier tasks. Once she was done there, she spent time in God's Word and in prayer. Daily, she asked the Lord for guidance and strength, and carried on conversations with Him as she moved about the property. God had become her companion again, and she felt the peace that came with the rekindled relationship.

Once everything was taken care of on the home front, she drove out to the Gentry project to see how things were progressing. The first two days she'd shown up at the site, Blake was glad to see her. He flirted with her harmlessly, but that wore off quick enough; because, whenever she showed up, she pointed out areas that needed slight changes. Nothing major. Not really. But Blake moaned and groaned over even the smallest modifications. Nevertheless, all Cassidy had to do is remind him she had Mrs. Gentry on speed dial. She would pull out her phone, scroll to Mrs. Gentry's contact information, then hold it out to him.

Today was one of those mornings.

"You realize every time you make one of your *slight*

modifications, it pushes the timeline back?"

"It will be worth it, Blake, believe me. When it's all said and done, Mrs. Gentry won't even care about the delays. She'll have the house of her dreams, and she'll have you to thank for it." Cassidy looked at Blake, not batting an eye.

Finally, he caved. "Fine. I'll take care of it. But show me again what you want."

She walked with Blake over to the solid wall. "This needs to be arched, and this area will be cut out. A fountain with tile will sit here."

"That means I need to plumb for water."

"But it's doable, right?"

"It's doable but . . ."

"I know, I know. It's time consuming."

"Maybe I'd better think twice about having you on any of my other projects. When you get an idea in your head, you just don't let it go."

"But it will be worth it; you'll see." Cassidy looked at the view the Gentry's would have, then turned to walk to her truck. "So . . . how's Wil's place coming?" She tried to sound nonchalant.

"It's coming along pretty fast. He's a bigger asset than I thought he would be. He's busy during the day with patients, but he comes over after hours and does work on his own. I bet he's putting in another four or five hours every night after my crew has gone home. We've got framing, electrical, and some plumbing already done. We're set to drywall next week."

Cassidy knew Wil was coming home late. She heard him drive past the house each night, after she was in bed.

"Well, Merry Christmas, Blake." Cassidy reached into her truck and pulled out a large decorated plate of homemade cookies and candies all wrapped in colorful cellophane.

"When did you have time to do this?"

"I have plenty of time in the evenings, and I like to stay busy."

"You know, Cassidy, there's no reason for you to be alone in the evenings."

Cassidy cringed inside, afraid Blake was going to ask her out or something. "Blake . . ."

"Cassidy, I see Wil almost every day, and it's obvious he's dying inside. What are you searching for?"

Cassidy didn't answer.

"If you're going to break it off for good—do it already. I don't think the guy can take much more."

Cassidy knew what Blake meant. Time away from Wil was grueling, but she'd also found out a lot about herself. "Blake, I know you're just trying to help, but I have to do things my way." "I know, I know." Blake passed a small package through her open window and smiled. "Merry Christmas, Cassidy."

"Blake, you didn't need to do that."

"Oh, believe me, I did. Go ahead, open it. You'll understand what I mean."

Cassidy pulled the paper from around the small object in her hand. She laughed when she saw it was a pink tape measure. Blake always teased her about her measurements. She measured the old-fashion way. From her nose to the tip of her finger. From her elbow to her hand. Her arms spread wide. Blake was constantly having to remeasure everything for her to make sure things were accurate. "Thank you, Blake. It's exactly what I needed."

"And there's no mistaking it with anyone else's on the crew."

They laughed together as she started the engine. "Merry Christmas, Blake."

"Merry Christmas, Cassidy."

———— • ————

"Dad, dinner's ready."

He walked into the kitchen and joined her at the table. They had prayer and then Cassidy spoke up. "Dad, I think I can answer your question now."

"What question?" he asked as he cut into his pork chop.

"You asked me if I felt a need for God in my life."

He looked up.

"Yes, I still feel the need for God in my life."

Realization flooded his face. "So, this week has been good for you?"

"It really has. I've missed Wil like crazy, but it gave me a lot of time to think and pray. I've made so many mistakes, thinking I knew better. But I don't want to repeat those mistakes. I don't want to put anything or anyone ahead of my relationship with God."

She reached for her dad's hand, tears in her eyes.

"If I hadn't stormed off to New York like I did, I never would have met Mark, or been seduced by his wealth and power. I was so taken by everything he did and everything he said. It was completely opposite to how you brought me up, yet he was hugely successful and beyond wealthy. He laughed when I told him how I was raised. He said, 'If that's the best God can do; I wanted nothing to do with Him.' I agreed. I though it proved you and mom were wrong. That serving God got you nowhere in life. You worked so hard, Dad. Everyday. But we weren't rich. People didn't look at you and say, 'There goes a successful man.' Or so I thought. But now I know the difference between having wealth and being rich. And it has nothing to do with the size of your bank account."

Her dad pushed tears aside and gave her hand a squeeze. "Welcome home, Sunshine. Welcome home."

FIFTY-ONE

It was colder than she expected, so Cassidy pulled up the collar of her jacket to cover her ears and stuffed her hands into her pockets. Wanting to surprise Wil, she'd decided to walk to his place instead of driving. Now she wasn't sure it was the brightest idea.

Oh well. I'll be warm soon enough. She smiled just thinking about being wrapped up in Wil's arms.

As she approached his front porch, she tiptoed up the first two steps, then stopped, thinking she heard laughing. She waited a few seconds before climbing the last two steps, then leaned close to the door. She heard it again. Wil laughing. And he was talking to someone too. She could not make out what he was saying, and she didn't hear anyone answer him.

He must be on the phone. Reaching up to knock, she gasped, then quickly pulled her hand away. *But what if he is with someone?*

She immediately thought back to the night she saw Ella leaving his place. Her first reaction was to turn around, but she quickly scoffed at herself.

No! You're not going to freak out. If Wil has someone at his house, there is a perfectly good reason for it. Besides, who says it's a woman.

Pushing down her suspicion, she knocked on the door.

"Just a second," Wil yelled, "I'll . . . I'll be right there."

Cassidy could hear commotion through the door. The scuffing of feet on hardwood floors, and the slamming of doors.

What is he doing?

Again, her suspicions spiked.

When the door jerked open, Wil stood there, out of breath, wearing a pair of sweatpants, no shirt, and his hair was a wet and rumpled mess.

"Cassidy!" He looked shocked to see her.

"If I'm interrupting something, I can come back." Cassidy turned to leave.

"No, no. Come on in," he reached for her arm and pulled her in, closing the door behind her. "I just got out of the shower."

He walked to the living room, perched on the arm of the couch, and ran his fingers through his messy hair. He was still breathing hard, and with every breath, his muscular chest monopolized her attention. She knew she was blushing but couldn't help it. Wil had never looked so good.

"Cassidy, is something wrong? Is it Joseph?" He jumped to his feet, alarm on his face.

"No," she smiled, "Dad is fine." She took a step closer. "I just came by to give you your Christmas present."

He dropped back down on the edge of the couch looking totally dejected. "But I thought we would be exchanging gifts tomorrow. Does this mean we won't be spending Christmas together?"

The heartbreak on his face was almost more than she could bear. But he would have his answer soon enough.

"You need to close your eyes."

"But you didn't answer my question."

"Come on, Wil, don't make this harder than it is."

He looked on the verge of tears, making her feel a twinge of guilt for stringing him along.

"Come on, Cassidy, if I close my eyes, I might find out this was only a dream, and when I open them, you'll be gone."

She groaned. "Don't be so dramatic, I'm not going anywhere. I just didn't have time to wrap your gift and I want it to be a surprise."

Wil put his head down, closed his eyes, then extended his upturned palms, clearly expecting her to put something in his hands.

She giggled. "Okay . . . open your eyes."

Wil opened his eyes, then looked up.

"Merry Christmas, Wil." She smiled while holding a sprig of mistletoe over her head.

Surprise didn't begin to describe the look on his face. He didn't say anything, he just reacted. Pulling her close, he kissed her. Kissed her like he was never going to let her go. She felt his desire and his passion. And when he finally came up for air, she saw the question in his eyes.

"I love you, Wil." She stood before him, stroking his bare arms.

"Are you sure?" he whispered. "I don't want to rush you or confuse you. If you need more time—"

She lunged in for another kiss, anything to silence his doubts. Then, with her hand pressed to his beating heart, she smiled. "That was never in question, Wil. I was just afraid I had become dependent on your strength and your comfort. Afraid I wasn't allowing God His rightful place in my life." Framing his face in her hands, she looked deep into his eyes. "You are an amazing, wonderful gift from God. I just wanted to make sure I wasn't overlooking the Giver."

"So, what now?" he asked.

She grinned mischievously, "Another kiss would be nice."

Wil stood, his large frame towering over her. He cupped her face in his hands and slowly bent to kiss her. Cassidy waiting with anticipation, when suddenly there was a noise from the kitchen. Startled, Cassidy took a step back. "What was that?"

"I didn't hear anything." Wil pulled her close and leaned now to claim her lips.

She heard it again. A scraping sound, like an animal scratching at the back door. Cassidy leaned back from him. "Wil, don't tell me you didn't hear that? Something is trying to get in the back door."

"It's probably just a mouse."

Wil leaned in again, but Cassidy dodged his advances and headed to the kitchen. "That is not a mouse."

Wil followed her to the kitchen and leaned on the doorframe, arms crossed against his chest, making his biceps look even larger than they were. He watched as she listened, waiting for the noise again.

When she heard it, she spun around. "It's coming from the pantry. And it definitely sounds larger than a mouse."

"Yep." Wil didn't even move.

" 'Yep!' That's all you have to say? Aren't you the least bit bothered that a varmint is living in your pantry?"

"Nope."

"Wil! Come on. We can't just leave it in there. We need to try to catch it."

"Okay. You go ahead, and if it gets past you, I'll catch it."

Cassidy could not believe Wil's cavalier attitude. Here she was expecting a somewhat intimate reunion, but instead, she was readying herself to catch who knows what, and Wil was being absolutely no help.

She heard it again. Except this time, the scratching was followed by a whimper. She quickly turned to Wil, then back to the cupboard. When she pulled the door open, the most adorable, yellow Labrador puppy scampered across the kitchen floor. Her legs were gawky and went in four different directions. She slid to a stop at Wil's bare feet then started to bite on his toes.

When Wil started laughing, Cassidy realized it was the same laughing she had heard when she was standing on the front porch. She looked at him in stunned silence.

Wil scooped up the squirming puppy and cradled her in his arms. He walked to Cassidy and held the ball of fur between them. The puppy instantly began to chew on Cassidy's hair.

"Merry Christmas, Cassidy."

Cassidy pulled the puppy into her arms and was immediately assaulted with licking. She laughed as she tried to talk to Wil. "I thought . . . you said . . . we weren't exchanging gifts."

"No. I said, 'I didn't know we were exchanging gifts.' I never said I didn't get you one." He laughed as the puppy continued to assault her. "I was just trying to keep her a surprise until tomorrow."

"Oh my gosh, she's adorable! How long have you had her?"

"I just picked her up today. I was playing with her when you knocked on the door."

"Now it makes sense."

"What makes sense?" Wil asked, taking the puppy to the living room and letting her down so she could run around.

When Cassidy got down on her knees, the puppy quickly jumped on her and tumbled over her legs. She laughed and played, hoping Wil would forget his question.

"What makes sense?"

No such luck.

Wil sat next to her and pulled her chin toward him. "Cassidy, what did you mean?"

She stalled for a moment, dangling her hair over the puppy, watching as she tried to bite it. "For a split-second, I thought you might have a guest."

"A guest? Like who?"

She ducked her head and continued to play with the puppy.

"Cassidy," Wil chuckled, "what would make you think that?"

"Well, don't make it sound completely out of the realm of possibility. I have seen Ella leave your place before. I even saw you kiss her."

"What!? When?" Then he cringed. "Wait, I know what you're talking about. She came over, *uninvited*, to congratulate me on the deal."

"That's what she said."

"And did you believe her?" He arched his brow in challenge.

"Sure. Even the part about you thinking of me more like a little sister."

He laughed. "That's funny, she told me you thought of me like a big brother." He leaned forward and wrapped his hand around her neck. Pulling her closer, he whispered, while his eyes studied her lips. "I dare say I have assured you of my true feelings?"

When he looked into her eyes, a tremor raced through her body. The love she saw . . . the desire she felt, made it hard for her to breathe. She simply nodded her agreement, then felt his lips press into hers.

A whimper, followed by a pint-size bark, interrupted their special moment.

"Oh, I see how it is," Wil said, stroking the pup's ear. "You're not happy unless you're the center of attention."

She yelped in agreement, and both Wil and Cassidy laughed.

Wil ruffled her head and tossed her about, rough housing her but in a gentle way. "So, what are you going to name her?"

Cassidy picked up the pup and held her to her face. The puppy cocked her ears and turned her head as if wondering for herself. Finally, Cassidy knew the perfect name. "Grace. I'm going to call her Grace," she said with absolute confidence.

"Grace?" Wil chuckled. "That seems a bit tame. You realize how much trouble she's going to get into, right?"

"Yes. That's exactly my reason. I've been extended so much grace in my lifetime, without even knowing it. Her name will remind me to be more lenient on her when she screws up."

Wil leaned into Cassidy causing her to lose her balance. She, Grace and Wil tumbled backwards onto the living room floor. She laughed while Grace scampered away. But Wil propped himself up on one elbow and stared at her.

"What?" She smiled as she drank in the smolder in his eyes.

"I love you, Cassidy."

He looked ready to cry, causing tears to sting in her eyes. "I love you too, Wil."

Leaning over, Wil kissed her forehead, then her cheek, her lips, her neck. Cassidy's heart raced so fast, she actually felt light-headed. Just then, the phone rang. Wil sighed heavily and rested his forehead on hers. It rang again, but Wil didn't move to answer it.

"Aren't you going to get that?"

"The machine can get it." Wil whispered in the ear he was kissing.

"Will."

He rolled to one side and stared at the ceiling. "This better be divine intervention or else I'm going to be very upset."

Wil's outgoing message was already playing so he waited.

"Screening your calls," she laughed.

He shushed her and listened. "It's just me."

It was her dad.

Wil scrambled to his feet and hurried across the room, but Grace got so excited, she raced after him.

"I was just wondering what was taking Cassidy so long," her dad continued, while Wil stumbled and teetered trying not to step on Grace's paws.

The phone clicked before Wil got to it, and Cassidy couldn't help but laugh at Wil's dance across the floor. "Come her, Grace!" Cassidy clapped her hands and bent down. The puppy immediately ran to her, sliding the last few inches, right into Cassidy's arms.

"Well, let's get you and Grace home before I break my neck."

Wil ran upstairs and grabbed a shirt while Cassidy and Grace cuddled. After putting the puppy supplies in the bed of his pickup, they all piled in and headed to Cassidy's house.

"What made you think of a puppy for a gift?" she asked as Grace squirmed on her lap.

"I wanted to make sure when you came home at night you knew I was thinking about you." Wil reached for Cassidy's hand and gave it a squeeze. "Besides, I was going to demand visiting rights."

Grace wiggled and yipped all the way home. So much so, Cassidy didn't even notice the strange car in the driveway until they pulled up next to it.

"Were you expecting company?" Wil asked as he killed the engine.

"No. Maybe someone from church came to visit Dad."

"On Christmas Eve?" Wil grabbed Grace's bed, food, toys, and bowl from the back of the truck while Cassidy snuggled Grace. She hurried up the stairs, excited to show her off.

"Dad, look what Wil . . ." Cassidy stopped. Astonished. "Hello, Cassie." Mark stood up and smiled.

FIFTY-TWO

Cassidy couldn't believe her eyes.

Mark was standing in her living room, his hair askew, tie loose, overcoat rumpled, looking as contrite as she'd ever seen him.

Wil walked in with his hands full, bumping into her. "Coming through," he laughed.

Cassidy moved slightly as Wil set everything against the wall. When he turned around, she watched his complexion fade to gray. Their eyes met for an instant before she turned back to Mark. "What are you doing here?"

"I want to talk to you, Cass."

"Then you should have called," she snapped while holding onto a wiggling Grace.

"I tried calling, numerous times, but you never picked up or returned my messages. You gave me no choice."

She'd blocked Mark's number weeks ago. "Fine. You want to talk, talk."

"Do you think we can talk privately?" He glanced at Wil, then focused on her.

She looked at Wil, unsure what she should do. She turned to her father and saw his concern. "Mark, I don't think we really have anything left to talk about."

"Please, Cassie. I came all this way. Frank was pretty ticked when I called him to ready the jet. And landing at that rinky-dink airport, made him none too happy," he joked, and for the first time in her life she saw Mark Grayson look awkward. Out of his element. "Please, Cass . . ."

Cassidy still didn't know what to do, but she knew she wanted Mark gone. If talking with him was the only way to get him to leave, she would do it. She turned to Wil. "Would you mind if I . . ."

Wil glanced at Mark, then at Cassidy. "Are you sure you want to?" he whispered.

292

"Yes. The faster we talk, the faster he leaves," she spoke quietly.

"But I'd feel better if I was here."

She would too. But in case Mark decided to drudge up dirty laundry, she preferred Wil not be there to hear it. "I'll be fine, really. Why don't you take Grace home for a little while, so she can run around? I'll call you when he's gone."

Wil glanced once more at Mark, at Joseph, then back to Cassidy. He gave her a reassuring smile and whispered in her ear. "I'll be praying. Call me when he's gone." He scooped Grace from her arms and left her standing in the entryway.

"Dad, could you give us a couple of minutes?" she asked as she walked toward the chair he was sitting in. He stood and gave her a hug. "Are you sure?" he whispered in her ear.

She hugged him back. "It's all right. It won't take long."

He cleared his throat as he let her go. "I've got some reading to do in my room." He nodded politely to Mark, but his eyes were fierce with protectiveness. "I'll be upstairs."

Cassidy turned toward Mark, then sat in the chair her father had occupied.

He can't hurt me anymore. I'm home. Where I belong. God is with me. No matter what.

Then why do I feel so afraid?

"You look good, Cassie."

She felt self-conscious under his lingering stare, but the lilt in his voice, her nickname spoken again, it took her back to happier days spent with him. However, that feeling lasted only a split second before the darker more *painful* memories flooded her mind.

And the way Amanda looked in his arms.

"Did you get the boxes I sent you?" he asked.

"Yes."

"Good. I know how important your art is to you."

She rolled her eyes at the small talk. "What do you want, Mark?"

"I've been thinking about you, Cassie." He scooted to the edge of the couch, his knees nearly touching hers. When he reached for her hand, she pulled away. He sighed in resignation. "I've missed you."

She crossed her arms against her chest and leaned back into the safe confines of the wing chair.

"I've changed, Cassie."

"So have I." She kept her answers short, wanting their conversation to be over as quick as possible.

"And is that guy part of your change?" he asked calmly, but Cassidy saw him clench his fists.

"Yes."

"So that's it! Our divorce isn't even final, yet you've found yourself someone new?"

Though Cassidy could tell Mark was trying to control his temper, his sharp words revealed his anger simmering just beneath the surface.

"I didn't think you would mind since our marriage didn't interfere with *your* personal relationships." Cassidy's lip quivered with fear. She'd never spoken to Mark that way before.

But it felt good.

"I was wrong, Cassie. I still love you, and I came here to give us a second chance. I have it all set up. We'll fly to Morocco tonight. Start over."

Cassidy couldn't believe what he was saying—what he was suggesting. She stood abruptly, cutting him off. "No . . . no, there's no way. I'm different now, Mark. I'm not the same scared little girl who ran to New York nine years ago. I was wrong to run. I was wrong to turn my back on my Dad and on God."

"So that's it!" Mark got to his feet and moved closer. "Your father has brainwashed you with his religious crap."

She slapped Mark before she could control the reflex. Her hand stung, and his eyes ignited. He was clearly shocked. He didn't expect her to stand up for herself.

She never had before.

Cassidy saw a glint in his eyes. Anger and something more. He grabbed her by the forearms and squeezed them tight. "That's the thanks I get for all I've done for you?"

She jerked away from him. "For what you've done for me? What would that be? The unfaithfulness, the intimidation, the abuse . . . the pain?"

"I provided a good living for you, Cassie, and you know it. The expense account, the big parties, the BMW in your parking space. I made you."

"And I paid dearly for those things," she gritted between clenched teeth, not wanting to raise her voice and worry her dad. "I became a non-person when I was with you. I wasn't Cassidy. I was

Mrs. Mark Grayson. I was who you made me to be, and even that wasn't good enough for you." Cassidy stepped away from him, the fireplace warm on her back. Straightening her shoulders, she took a deep breath. "You need to leave. We have nothing left to talk about. Our divorce should be final any day now, and when it is, I see no reason for further communication between us. So don't contact me again."

Mark dropped his head and his shoulders. He actually looked pitiful. "You're right, Cassie, and I feel terrible." He stepped forward. "I never meant to change you." He gently squeezed her shoulders. She flinched, but he held them just the same. "You just seemed so frail and without direction. I never meant to overpower you. I was trying to make you the person I knew you could be. I know some of my tactics were harsh, but I only wanted the best for you." He bent and placed a tender kiss against her neck.

"Mark, don't," she flinched again.

"You can't tell me, you don't feel something for me, Cassie." He kissed her again.

Please, God, don't let this be a test. I know how you feel about divorce, but do you really want this? Is this my punishment? Did you send Mark to stop me from going through with it? But what about Wil? I love him, God. Have I sinned? I've fallen in love with one man while married to another. Which sin is worse? What should I do, Lord? There's no room in Mark's life for You, and I can't live without You again. I need Your help now more than ever."

Mark held her close, and she didn't know what to do. She couldn't believe this is what God wanted for her.

Ask him about Amanda?

Cassidy wasn't sure where the thought came from, but she acted on it. "What about Amanda?"

Mark stiffened slightly. "What about her?" His voice was laced with hatred.

"Does she still work for you? Are you still seeing her?"

"I don't want to talk about Amanda." He brushed off the question. "I love you, Cassie; that's all that matters."

"You didn't answer the question." Cassidy looked at him, her resolve strengthening, Mark's calmness diminishing. She knew if she pushed him far enough, he would show his true colors. As much as he tried, he was never able to control his rage whenever she challenged him.

"You haven't changed at all. You're still seeing her, aren't you?" He didn't say anything, so she drew her answer from his silence. "That's what I thought. So why are you here, Mark? What . . . did people find out I left you instead of you dumping me?"

He glared at her, his fists tight at his side.

"That's it, isn't it? The guys at the club found out you're not perfect; you're not a demigod to be revered. I guess your pedestal wasn't as strong as you thought it was. Goodbye, Mark. You can see your way out."

Cassidy turned away, but Mark swung her around to face him. "Don't walk away from me, Cassie."

"I already did." She looked at him, feeling nothing. "Face it, Mark, I'm just one of your deals that ended up in the loss column."

He grabbed a handful of her hair and yanked her to within inches of his face, his controlled demeanor collapsing in a fit of rage. "It's not over until I say it is." He pushed her to the couch with such force she nearly bounced onto the floor.

"Stop it, Mark. You can't hurt me anymore. I'm no longer your property."

Mark lunged at her, a gun appearing out of nowhere. With one hand pressed against her neck, the other pressed the barrel of the gun to her temple.

"Mark, what are you doing?" Cassidy clawed at his hand, trying to speak, to breath. "Have you lost your mind?" She'd never seen Mark with a gun before. Ever.

"That's just it, Cassie, I've never lost anything in my entire life, and I'm not about to start with you."

Cassidy struggled to break free. When she thought she had the upper hand, his fist came across her face so quick, she couldn't react. She tasted blood, her tongue sliding across the cut on her lip. When she looked at Mark, she could tell there was something different fueling his behavior. Not control. Not dominance. But fear. Irrational, terrifying fear.

"Mark, what's wrong? What's happened?"

"None of your business. All you need to know is I'm not giving you up without a fight. Someday you'll come to appreciate me and see I was right."

Cassidy tried to move out from under him, but he pressed himself to her and whispered in her ear. "You're not really interested in that hayseed, are you?" Mark smiled, his words seductive. "I mean, what can he give you that I can't? Don't you remember all the good times we had?" Mark's hand began to travel down her body. "I do."

"Stop it!"

She tried again to push him away, but he only became more forceful, kissing her with lips void of passion, filled instead with desperation. She tried to scream . . . yell . . . anything to get her father's attention, but Mark was too strong. He pressed down on her mouth with his hand, pinning her head to the couch. He straddled her and looked at her with eyes no longer belonging to a human being. Something had snapped inside him.

"What are you doing!? What's going on!?"

Cassidy looked up and saw her dad on the upstairs landing, then watched as Mark swung around and pointed the gun at him. "No!!" she screamed, just as a shot rang out. She saw a look of shock register on her dad's face, just as a spot bloomed red on his shirt, then he fell back from sight.

She lunged for the gun, knocking it from Mark's hand, hearing it clank against the brick fireplace. "What have you done?" she hollered, pushing him off balance and onto the coffee table. With her legs free, she jumped over the back of the couch and ran toward the stairs, but Mark tackled her to the floor. She fought with everything she had in her, but when Mark flipped her around and slammed his fist into her cheek, she lost focus.

Don't let me blackout, God. Please . . . I need to help Dad. He needs to be okay.

With blurred vision, she watched as Mark crawled to the fireplace where the gun had landed near a log, flames licking dangerously close. He got to his feet, grabbed the poker, and tried flipping the gun from the fire, but a log tumbled out along with the gun. Embers burst gold and bright before descending onto the rug.

Mark tossed the log back into the fire, yelping and cursing as it burned his hand, then stomped on the rug where the embers began to smolder.

While Mark was distracted trying to snuff out the fire, Cassidy grabbed a small horse sculpture from the end table and raised if over her head. With all her weight and momentum, she closed her eyes and brought it down on Mark, missing his head, hitting his shoulder instead. They both crumpled to the floor, Mark moaning in pain, momentarily dazed. When Cassidy saw the gun by the hearth, she rolled to one side and on hands and knees, scrambled toward it. Wrapping her fingers around the heated barrel, she tried pushing to her feet, but not fast enough. Mark yanked on her ankle and pulled her back toward him, wrestling the gun from her hand.

Smoked filled the air while Mark straddled her chest, pinning her arms above her head. "Dad!" she screamed. "The house is on fire! You need to get out!" but he didn't answer.

Cassidy struggled to break free, but Mark just laughed at her as if they were playing a game. "I'm stronger than you, Cassie," he howled, sounding more animal than man. "I will always be stronger than you." Then he yanked her to her feet and pulled her back against his chest; his forearm pressed against her neck. "Now . . . you're going to come with me and we're going to leave this place."

Cassidy struggled, gripping his arm, trying to breath. "Please, Mark, my father is hurt. Just let me help him."

"He's got his god. He doesn't need your help."

As Mark dragged her toward the door, she saw flames begin to slither across the carpet toward the Christmas tree. "Mark, please. We have to help my dad."

He ignored her as he moved slowly toward the door.

Please, Lord. Help me. Help Dad.

"Let her go."

A shout came from upstairs. Cassidy looked up to see her father standing with a shotgun aimed at Mark, the shoulder of his shirt bloodied.

Mark tightened the strangle hold he had on her and aimed the gun behind her ear. "Give it up old man, or I'll kill her."

The fire had reached the Christmas tree and instantly there was an eruption of flames. It quickly engulfed the tree and moved to the curtains. Mark dragged Cassidy backwards toward the door, but she knew he kept his eye on her dad.

"What kind of . . . coward uses a . . . woman as . . . a shield?" Her dad taunted, even as he struggled for every word. "What kind of man . . . forces a woman . . . to love him?" The shotgun shook in his hands.

"I don't need to force a woman to love me. I've had many lovers through the years. Your daughter just happens to be the most satisfying. Maybe it's because she's so eager to please."

"Let her go, Mark . . . and I'll let you walk out of here. Otherwise . . . you better be prepared to die, because if it is . . . the last thing . . . I do, I will make sure . . . you pay for what you've done."

Flames crossed the ceiling. Windows exploded. Again, Mark laughed, sounding deranged and psychotic. He bent close, his lips brushing against her ear. "Say goodbye to your daddy, Cassidy." In a burst of motion, Mark flung her to the ground, took aim at her dad, and pulled the trigger.

FIFTY-THREE

Amen.

Wil got up from where he had been kneeling in prayer. He asked God for direction, intervention, and strength. Grace had whimpered the whole time as if she was keenly aware something was wrong. "I know," he patted her head. "But everything is going to be all right." He stood, turned around, and saw something through the living room window. "What the . . ."

He hurried to the window and saw flames dancing in the distance. "Cassidy, no!" He grabbed his cell phone and dialed as he ran to his truck.

The first floor of the house was completely engulfed by the time Wil screeched to a halt. "Cassidy! Cassidy!" Wil cried out in horror.

In a flash, he was transported back to the day his parents died. Flames claimed his family, his home, his childhood memories. Numbness overtook his body and terror gripped at his heart.

Please, God, not again.

He would not lose the people he loved again. Not like this.

Running to the barn, Wil dunked his jacket in the water barrel. Covering his head and his hands, he raced through the cold air and up the front steps. Reaching for the doorknob, he threw it open, only to be blown back by the flames and the suffocating heat.

A body lay by the door, but he couldn't make out who it was through all the smoke. He grappled for limbs and started to pull. He could tell from the weight, it wasn't Cassidy. On the porch, he got a look at Mark, but his mind couldn't comprehend what he was seeing. His shirt was covered in blood. He looked like he'd been shot.

"Cassidy!"

Wil plunged back into the house and quickly dropped to his hands and knees. Crawling forward, he yelled for Cassidy, and prayed for guidance.

Where God? Where is she?

Coughing uncontrollably, Wil was having a hard time covering his mouth and crawling at the same time. When his ears began to ring, he prayed it was sirens, that help was on its way. Unable to see, he swept his hands from side to side in front of him, then called out for Cassidy but the smoke swallowed his words. When his hand hit something soft, he immediately felt his way around. It was Cassidy, in a fetal position, under the end table.

But she wasn't moving.

Wasn't talking.

Had she been shot too?

Flinging the end table aside, Wil pulled on Cassidy's arms. When she cried out in anguish, it was music to his ears. Crying meant she was alive, hurt but alive. He carefully cradled her in his arms and draped the now scorched jacket over her, but when he started toward the front door, a burning beam fell in front of him, cutting off his exit. Even though a wall of flames stood between him and the door, he ducked his head, jumped through the flames and stumbled out the front door, just as the first fire engine roared up the driveway.

Almost dropping Cassidy, he regained his balance and hurried down the stairs, trying to get as far from the house as possible. He laid her limp body in the snow, in front of the barn, the amber light casting shadows across her face. He knelt down next to her and patted her cheek.

"Cassidy," he choked and coughed, his throat raw. "Talk to me, honey!" He coughed again, having a hard time catching his breath. "You have to be okay." He looked at the gash on her head, saw it was deep, and bleeding a lot. Leaning close, he waited for it, then felt the warmth of her breath on his ear. She was breathing. "Say something, baby," he choked, and had to turn his head to puke. Wiping his sleeve across his lips, he clutched her hand and begged, "Come on, Sunshine, let me know you're still with me."

He felt it.

It was small. Weak. But he felt her squeeze his hand.

Another window exploded, drawing his attention back to the fire. Fireman rushed from the truck, yelled instructions, while others pulled hoses and manned pumps. So many sounds, so many noises, but all he wanted to hear was Cassidy's voice.

"Is there anyone else in the house?"

Wil turned and looked at a man swathed in protective gear.

"Is there anyone else in the house?" he repeated.

Wil had to think, had to process what the man was saying. Then when he tried to speak, he started coughing uncontrollably. When the fireman turned to walk away, Wil clutched onto his arm. "Joseph," he choked. "You've got to get to him."

The fireman jumped into action, yelling instructions to two other men. *Joseph.* Wil hung his head. He'd pulled Mark out, but not Joseph.

Looking at the inferno, Wil wanted to help, needed to help, but he couldn't leave Cassidy. She needed him too.

"Wil, what happened?"

He turned and saw Blake, along with the rest of the volunteer fire department descend onto the scene.

"Blake, give me your coat."

Immediately, Blake stripped off his heavy turnout jacket.

Wil tucked it around Cassidy, then stood. "Stay with her. I need to help them find Joseph."

Wil stepped forward, but Blake jerked him back. "You can't go in there. The place is ready to go."

"No . . . I won't stand by again. I can't."

Wil ran towards the house but was wrestled back by two firemen. "You've got to stay back. It's too dangerous. There's nothing you can do."

The words echoed in Wil's head, just like they had when he lost his parents, but he could not let it happen again. Cassidy would never forgive him. He was struggling to break free from their hold, when he saw another fireman plunge through the flames with a body draped over his shoulders. Wil followed the fireman across the yard and watched as he gently laid Joseph near Cassidy, a medic already working on her. The fireman dipped his head to Joseph's chest, felt for his pulse, then shouted, "We need some more help over here."

Two men rushed toward them, taking position on either side of Joseph. Immediately, they got to work, the three paramedics volleying information back and forth, their hands moving quickly, talking on radios, communicating with the hospital.

Wil knelt next to Cassidy's feet, wanting to be close—needing to be close. He watched the blur of commotion. And tried to follow the comments.

Lost a lot of blood. Not responding. Pulse thready. GSW to the shoulder.

A man walked over and mumbled about there being another body with a gunshot wound. Finally, one of the medics turned to Wil and asked, "What went on in there?"

"I don't know." Wil looked up at the raging inferno while firemen worked the perimeter. The first floor was a total loss, but they seemed to be getting the upper hand. They bathed the house in water, making sure embers or debris didn't spread to the other structures.

Wil turned back to Cassidy while an ambulance attendant rolled a gurney toward them.

"Wil, I'm going to have to ask you some questions."

He looked up at Sheriff Turner. *When did he show up?*

"Okay, but can it wait?"

"I'm afraid not, Wil. We've got two gunshot victims—one fatal. This is a crime scene, and I need to investigate it."

Fatal? Mark is dead? Wil hung his head, looking at Cassidy. *What happened? Why didn't I insist on staying?*

"Wil . . . do you know who the other man is?"

"Yes. His name is Mark Grayson. He's Cassidy's . . . *I can't believe I'm saying this* . . . he's Cassidy's husband."

The sheriff's eyes lifted from the note pad he was writing on and stared directly at Wil. "I'm not going to find out this is some kind of sordid love triangle, am I?"

"No, it wasn't like that." Wil defended.

"But you *were* seeing Cassidy, right?"

Wil didn't know what to say.

"Come on, Wil, I don't buy into gossip, but nevertheless, I do hear the town scuttle."

Wil cleared his throat, feeling the burn. "Mark came to see Cassidy. I don't know why. I left so they could talk. I went home for a while, was praying, and when I looked up, I saw the house was on fire. I found Mark by the front door, dragged him out, then went back in for Cassidy. When the fire department arrived, they went in for Joseph. That's all I know."

The Sheriff wrote a few things down, "So you weren't here when the fire started?"

"No."

"And you don't know what transpired between Joseph and Mr. Grayson?"

"No. Like I said, I left so he and Cassidy could talk."

The sheriff scribbled a few more things, then closed his notebook and put it in his pocket. "Okay, Wil, that's it for now. I can see you're pretty shaken up and in need of some medical attentions yourself." The sheriff glanced at his blistered arm, and for the first time, Wil realized he was injured. "But Wil, I'm going to need you to stick around in case I have more questions."

Wil looked at Cassidy's frail body as the attendants lifted her onto the stretcher and tucked a blanket around her. Her eyes were still closed, and one of the technicians was still working on her. "You'll find me at the hospital. I'm not going anywhere until I know Cassidy and Joseph are going to be okay."

"Sir, let me take a look at your arm."

One of the other EMTs turned his attention to Wil, but Wil shook him off. "I'm fine." He could feel the burn, saw his blistered skin, but he didn't care. "Can I ride with her?" Wil asked as he walked alongside the stretcher.

"I'm afraid not. It's going to be tight enough with both patients in the ambulance, and we're still trying to get them stabilized. Can you call someone to drive you?"

"I'll drive him." Wil turned around and saw Blake standing behind him. "Come on. We'll take your truck. I can get mine later."

Blake followed behind the ambulance, staying right on their tail. Wil kept his eyes on the rear door, watching the technicians work, wondering what they were doing. He closed his eyes to pray . . . no, to plead with God. And as he did, he felt the throbbing in his arm. The pain was finally registering.

"Wil, what happened tonight?" Blake asked.

He opened his eyes, stared in front of him. "I don't know. I can't even imagine. One minute Cassidy and I are laughing and kissing, celebrating Christmas; the next thing I know, her house is in flames, Mark's dead, she's unconscious, and her father's been shot." Wil leaned his head against the passenger window.

"But what was her husband doing there? Did she know he was coming? I had no idea Cassidy was even in contact with him."

"No. She was just as surprised as I was."

"So, you don't know what he wanted?"

Wil stared at the flashing lights in front of him. He knew what Mark wanted. He could see it in the way he looked at Cassidy.

Why did I leave? I knew I should have stayed. Please, God, I can't lose her.

Not now. Not this way.

FIFTY-FOUR

Wil wasn't sure how long he'd been at the hospital. He sat on an examination table while the nurse cleaned the soot from his arm and applied salve to the burns. He was having trouble keeping his thoughts in the present. He was caught somewhere between the fire that had claimed his parents years ago, and the fire this evening. He kept asking the nurses and attendants who walked by the draped examine room, if there was any word about Cassidy or Joseph, but they would just give him a sympathetic smile and move on.

Dr. Craig pulled back the privacy drape, the metal rings squealing on the rail. He was wearing a jogging suit under his lab coat. Obviously, he'd been off duty.

"Doctor, have you seen Cassidy or Joseph?"

"Just a minute, Wil."

Dr. Craig stepped forward and examined his arm.

"I'm okay, Doctor, how's Cass—" he choked, the cough painful.

"These are second degree, possibly third-degree burns, Wil. This in nothing to take lightly. And your chart shows you may have acute inhalation burns."

"I understand that, Dr. Craig, but how are Cassidy and Joseph? Have they regained consciousness?"

"I don't know, Wil, but I think we need to go ahead and admit you. You're going to need medical supervision."

Dr. Craig was ignoring him. And on top of that, he was talking about admitting him to the hospital.

"What are you talking about? I'm fine. I just need to see Cassidy—I need to know she's okay."

Just then, Sheriff Turner stepped into view. "So, doc, are you done here?"

"I'm afraid not, Sheriff. Wil is not going anywhere. I'm

305

admitting him for observation. These burns are pretty severe, and we're going to have to keep a close watch on his breathing." Wil wanted to object but Dr. Craig's stare seemed to be relaying a message. "You'll have to do your interrogation here."

Is Dr. Craig running inference for me?

Sheriff Turner looked from Wil to the doctor and back at Wil again. "Okay. Let me know when he's in a room." The sheriff left, not the least bit satisfied with the situation.

Wil made sure the sheriff was out of earshot before he asked the doctor, "What was that all about?"

"I need to ask you something, and you need to be straight with me." Gone was Dr. Craig's bedside manner. ". . . and so help me, if I put my butt on the line for you and I find out you lied to me, there will be consequences."

"What are you talking about? Why would I lie to you?"

Dr Craig continued, "Sheriff Turner wanted to take you downtown for questioning, but I knew you'd want to be here with Cassidy and Joseph. So . . . I might have made your injuries sound a little more serious than they really are."

Wil felt like he was in an episode of the Twilight Zone. "I don't get it. I told him everything I know. What more does he want from me?"

Dr. Craig started working on Wil's bandages. "Put yourself in his place. A fire. Two gunshot victims. A husband *and* a boyfriend. It's the stuff soap operas are made of."

"But I didn't do it. I wasn't even in the house." Wil felt the need to defend himself once again, but Dr. Craig stopped him with a raised hand.

"I trust you, Wil. That's why I'm admitting you."

Wil winced at the slight pressure the weight of the bandages applied to his arm. "How's Cassidy?"

Dr. Craig looked up solemnly. "She's still unconscious."

"And Joseph?"

"He should be fine. He was shot in the shoulder, but he was lucky. The bullet barely grazed him. It's the smoke inhalation and the excitement putting a strain on his heart I'm worried about. But if I didn't know better, I'd say the man has nine lives."

Wil was glad Joseph was going to be okay, but he was desperate to see Cassidy. "Can I see her?"

"First, I have to admit you and get you into a room. Otherwise, Turner's going to be suspicious."

Wil wanted to argue, but knew the doctor was doing him a favor. He just needed to be patient.

As Dr. Craig worked on his arm, the pain seemed to amplify. Wil had to close his eyes and concentrate to combat a wave of nausea.

"The pain getting to you?" Dr. Craig asked.

Wil looked up. "Yeah. A little."

"I'd say it's more than a little. You've gone from pale to green." The doctor walked away, then came back with two paper cups; one with pills, the other with water. "Take this, it will help with the pain."

"But I don't want to take anything until I find out about Cassidy."

"And sitting here in extreme pain is not going to do her any good."

Wil wanted to argue but didn't. The pain was excruciating. Like a hot branding iron searing into his flesh, and his stomach was not handling it well. He took the pills, washed them down with water, then closed his eyes again, to steady himself.

"Okay, I think we're done for now."

A nurse magically appeared at the doctor's side. He rattled off instructions while she typed on the tablet.

"Hey, doc, if I'm going to be here overnight, I have some things I need taken care of. Can you see if the guy who drove me here is still around?"

"I'll take a look," the nurse said. "What's your friend's name?"

Friend? Not exactly how he would categorize Blake, but that didn't matter right now. "Blake Simpson."

When she left, the doctor continued. "Someone will be by to get you situated in a room. I'll make sure they know you want updates on Cassidy and Joseph."

"Thanks, Doc."

"I'll be by to check on you later."

As the doctor walked away, Wil dropped his head forward. The pain and nausea were vying for attention, while his head was spinning with questions. Questions he knew he'd be asked again, and still he'd have no answers.

"Hey, man, are you all right?" Blake whispered as he walked into Wil's not-so-private cubicle.

"Yeah," Wil kept his head down, "but the doctor is keeping

me overnight."

"That serious?" Blake questioned.

"I don't think so—other than the pain—but Dr. Craig is running interference for me with the sheriff, so I can stay close to Cassidy." Wil sighed, feeling the effects of the pain medication beginning to sink in. "I need to ask you a favor, Blake."

"Sure, whatever you need."

"I bought Cassidy a puppy for Christmas. She's at my place and is probably going nuts." Wil looked up at Blake. "Do you think you could keep an eye on her for me? I know it's a lot to ask. Especially since we haven't been on the best of terms, but I haven't had the chance to call anyone." Again, Wil closed his eyes, knowing a drug-induced sleep was quickly approaching.

"No problem, man. I'll take her to my house for a few days until you're up on your feet."

"Her name is Grace."

Wil fought sleep as he was rolled into a private room. It took every ounce of strength to change into the hospital issued gown, then crawl back into bed. He still hadn't been told any information regarding Cassidy's condition, other than she was stable but unconscious. His last thoughts were of Cassidy, cradled in his arms. It was the last picture in his mind before he drifted off to sleep.

FIFTY-FIVE

Cassidy felt herself disconnect from her body. She walked down a garden path, lined with roses, to where she did not know. Then, as if by magic, her mother appeared. Cassidy reached out a timid hand to touch her, but she was just out of reach.

"Not yet, Sunshine," her mother whispered with a smile.

"But I've missed you." Cassidy wanted to step closer, hug her, but something kept her from moving forward.

"I know, but your dad still needs you."

"Then why, Mom? Why am I here?"

"Because I want you to know everything is going to be okay."

Cassidy closed her eyes, allowed her mother's words to wash over her. "But I want to be with you, Mom. I don't want to live in fear anymore."

"It will all be over soon, Cassidy. You're safe now. No one is ever going to hurt you again. I'm so thankful you found your way back home."

"But what about Dad, is he going to be okay?"

"Yes, dear, he's waiting for you."

A cool breeze swirled around her mother. She was drifting—drifting from her. "Don't go, Mom." Cassidy reached out, only to feel a brush of the wind.

"It's okay, Cassidy. I'll be waiting here for you."

She opened her eyes, tried to focus, tried to orientate herself, but the lights were low, and her eyes were having a hard time adjusting. When she saw a shadow hovering over her, she reached out. "Mom?"

"No honey. My name is Catherine. I'll be taking care of you."

Hospital. I'm in the hospital.

Swallowing back tears, Cassidy whispered, "My mother's name was Catherine."

"What a coincidence."

But Cassidy knew it wasn't.

Closing her eyes, she tried to make sense of what just happened. *Was I hallucinating? But it felt so real.*

She had talked to her mother. Carried on a conversation. Asked her questions. And her mother answered her back. *Or was it just a dream?*

Opening her eyes again, Cassidy watched as Catherine pushed buttons on the machine alongside the bed and changed her IV bag. "Where is my father?"

"He's waiting for you."

Exactly what Mom told me.

*She **was** here. She **was** speaking to me. She **was** with me when I needed her most.*

Cassidy took a deep breath, a sense of peace washing over her. "Can I see him?"

"In a little while. There are a few other people who want to talk to you too, but they'll have to wait until after the doctor sees you." Catherine smiled. "I'll tell the doctor you're awake."

When Cassidy reached to touch her forehead, her hand sprung back from the bandage, her touch amplifying the pain. She tried to remember what happened, how she got here, make sense of the snapshots flashing through her head, but her brain felt like mush and offered little help.

Dad . . . we had just had dinner.

Wil . . . I went to his house. Mistletoe.

She smiled at the memory.

A puppy! Wil got me a puppy for Christmas.

We took her to show Dad.

"Mark!" she gasped.

Mark was at the house. But why?

A tall, slender doctor strolled into her room, iPad in hand. He swiped through information, then turned his attention to Cassidy. With an extended hand, he introduced himself. "Hi, I'm Dr. Peterson."

She shook his hand. "I'm Cassidy."

He chuckled. "Yes, you are, and you have quite a nasty cut on your head. Catherine, can you turn up the lights a little?" He pulled his pen light from his coat pocket and examined her eyes. "How are you feeling?"

"My head is killing me, and it hurts to swallow."

"It will feel like that for a few days. You have inhalation burns from the fire."

Fire! Now she remembered. There was a fire.

"Anything else?" the doctor inquired as he continued his exam.

"This eye feels blurry." She brought her hand up to point to her right eye, felt pain in her arm, and saw it was wrapped in gauze.

Did I get burned?

She closed her eyes, saw her Mom again, and remembered what they had talked about.

I asked if Dad was okay. He must be hurt too.

She opened her eyes and looked up at the doctor. "Is my dad okay?"

"He's having difficulty breathing, but he's going to be fine."

"Difficulty breathing? Is it his heart? What happened?" Cassidy felt like she was juggling a hundred puzzle pieces, but none of them connected together.

"You don't remember?" Dr. Peterson looked at her more intently.

"It's all fuzzy. You said there was a fire." Cassidy furrowed her exposed eyebrow trying to think. "I remember that, but I don't remember much else."

"It will come back to you, just give it some time."

"Can't you just tell me?"

"I don't have all the details. Besides, Sheriff Turner will be here soon to get your statement. It's best if you save the questions for him." Dr. Peterson closed the iPad. "But the good news is, you're going to be fine." He walked toward the exit. "And after the Sheriff gives the all clear, we'll make arrangements for you to visit your dad. Until then, try to rest."

The doctor left, Catherine following behind him, dimming the lights as she went.

What sheriff? Why would the sheriff be involved with a house fire?

———— • ————

Sheriff Turner waited outside Cassidy's room. He'd heard she was finally awake and talking, and he needed to question her while everything was fresh in her mind, or before she could fabricate a lie.

When he saw the doctor and nurse exit her room, he approached them. "So how is she? Can I go in and see her?"

Dr. Peterson handed the nurse the iPad he was holding, then turned to him.

"I don't know if now would be the best time."

"But doctor, I need to talk to her as soon as possible, while the details are fresh in her mind."

"But she doesn't remember much. She didn't even remember there was a fire until I explained why her throat hurt."

"You told her what happened?!" he barked, furious the doctor gave her information.

Dr. Peterson took a step closer and glared at him. "Do not raise your voice to me. I did not tell her what happened. I explained her injuries. I am not trying to interfere with your investigation, Sheriff. I am only looking out for the well-being of my patient. Having said that, I think it would be best to wait a few hours, give her body a chance to recover from the shock before you barrage her with questions. It's Christmas," he smiled. "Go home. Spend time with your family. Come back after dinner."

"Fine." He crossed his arms and took a stance. "But she can't have any visitors until I've had the chance to question her."

"That is not your call to make. She's my patient, her father is the only family she has, and she needs to see for herself that he's okay."

"Sorry, no visitors unless I'm present. I can't take the chance of them syncing their stories. Look, doc, I'm not trying to be a jerk, but I need some answers. I have a body in the morgue with a gunshot wound and three possible suspects. You can't allow them to talk to each other until I've had a chance to get their individual statements."

The doctor stroked his chin and pulled on the back of his neck. "Fine. Go ahead and talk to her . . . but make it brief. No badgering. She's still my patient and regardless if you get the answers you're looking for, she *will* see her dad today. It's paramount to her own recovery."

"What about Marsh? Are you going to let him see her too? He's not family."

"But he's her—"

"Boyfriend?" he snapped sarcastically. "Sorry. Not immediate family."

"Come on, Sheriff!" The doctor threw up his hands.

"Put yourself in my place, Doc. I've got a father, a wife, a husband, *and* a boyfriend."

"I'm very aware of the situation, Sheriff. Dr. Craig filled me in. Her husband was divorcing her. It's not as illicit as you make it sound."

"You don't know that. If Mark Grayson was divorcing his wife, what was he doing on her ranch? And how did he end up dead?"

Dr. Peterson shoved his hands in the pockets of his lab coat, clearly frustrated. "Look, I can't have her worrying about everyone else's condition, jeopardizing her own. I've got to relieve as much mental strain on her as possible. I understand you have a job to do, Sheriff, but so do I."

"And I can't let you interfere with a murder investigation. If Marsh is going to be allowed to see her, I need to be present."

"Fine. Just don't upset her." Dr. Peterson turned to the nurse who had stood by the whole time they were talking. "Mrs. Grayson can have visitors, but please make sure she doesn't get agitated."

Turner knew the caveat was for his benefit.

"Yes, Doctor. I'll confer with Dr. Craig regarding her father."

Dr. Peterson started down the hall, then turned back around. "Sheriff, her mental state is very delicate. Don't send her over the edge."

"I understand, Dr. Peterson, really I do. I have no intentions of hindering her recovery. I just need some answers."

FIFTY-SIX

Cassidy's eyes were closed when she felt the tiniest breeze. Looking toward the door, she was hoping to see her dad or Wil. But as the shadow moved forward, she saw a man in a sheriff's uniform with a stoic face and a stern disposition. He was older, graying at the temples, and when he removed his hat, he exposed his shiny bald scalp. He approached her bed, held out his hand, and offered a friendly smile. Unfortunately, his uniform assured her this was anything but a social visit.

"Cassidy, this is Sheriff Turner," Catherine made the introduction.

She awkwardly extended her left hand to shake his because it was too painful to lift her right.

"I need to ask you a few questions about what happened last night."

Last night?

Is it morning already? With the curtains closed and the lights down low, she thought it was still night.

"I'll try, sheriff, but it's all still pretty fuzzy."

"Just tell me what you remember."

Cassidy closed her eyes, trying to fit the puzzle pieces together she'd been juggling since she woke up. "Mark was at the house. He was sitting on the couch. We were talking."

"Was it just the two of you?"

Cassidy opened her eyes and thought for a moment. "Yes. Dad went upstairs and Wil . . . left."

"Left?"

"Yes. He left so I could talk with Mark alone."

"And then what happened?" the sheriff asked as he jotted on his notepad.

"Mark said he still loved me and wanted a second chance." Cassidy remembered his words, but a flash of Mark's face startled her. Her entire body shuddered.

"What is it, Mrs. Grayson?"

"Mark . . . he was angry. He said my dad was brainwashing me." Her mind played like a video on fast-forward. She remembered him hitting her . . . the taste of blood . . . she gasped, "He had a gun."

"Who had a gun?"

"Mark." Tears rolled down her face and her breathing intensified. "He held it to my head." Cassidy's breathing turned to panting. She knotted the bed covers in her left hand as she blurted out pieces of information.

"Sheriff, I think that's enough," Catherine interrupted. "She's getting too upset."

"He shot him . . . there were flames . . ." Cassidy continued, as the images funneled through her mind. "I hit my head on something, then everything went black."

"Who shot who, Mrs. Grayson?"

"Mark . . . Mark shot my father."

"Then who shot Mark?"

"Dad." Cassidy said, astonished. "I thought Mark killed him, but he didn't. Mark was dragging me away when I heard my father shout at him."

"Where was Wil when all this was happening?"

"I don't know." Cassidy sobbed. "Everything was happening so fast."

"Are you sure he wasn't in the house? Maybe he came back to check on you?"

Cassidy shook her head, crying in pain, not knowing anything for sure.

"Sheriff, that's enough," Catherine said, firmly. "You got what you wanted. She told you what happened. And now you're causing her physical pain. You need to leave."

"But I'm not finished. I need to—"

"Yes, you are," Catherine insisted. "Dr. Peterson told you not to upset Mrs. Grayson, which she clearly is. It's time for you to go."

Cassidy was thankful for Catherine's interference. When the sheriff left, mumbling something to himself, Catherine turned to her. "I'm sorry. I should have made him leave right away."

"It's not your fault. I know he has a job to do. It's just so messed up in my head. None of it makes any sense."

———— • ————

"Can I help you, Sheriff?"

He turned around to see Dr. Craig approaching.

"I need to ask Mr. Martin a few questions, if that's all right with you."

"Have you spoken with his daughter, yet?"

"Yes. I just came from her room. She doesn't remember much, but she seems to be doing okay."

"Great, Joseph will be relieved to hear that. Now, Sheriff, I don't need to warn you about your questioning, do I? Joseph's condition is fragile, and I don't want him to become agitated."

"I understand, doctor. I just need to get his account of what happened. His daughter said it was him who shot Mark Grayson."

"What?" Dr. Craig said, shocked. "Are you sure?"

"That's what she said."

"Then it must have been self-defense or in defense of his daughter. Need I remind you, Joseph was shot too?"

"No doctor, you don't need to remind me what happened at *my* crime scene. But I do need to find out from Mr. Martin what exactly happened."

"But you're not here to arrest him, correct? I mean, you have to know whatever he did—he did for good reason."

"I'm not going to comment on information that hasn't been substantiated yet."

"Well, I don't think he's strong enough if your plan is to go in there and accuse him of murder."

"I'm not accusing him of anything. I'm taking his statement."

The two professionals eyed each other, knowing they each had a job to do.

"So, can I go in?" the sheriff persisted.

"Yes, but if you don't mind I would like to be present."

He shrugged his shoulder. "Have it your way."

FIFTY-SEVEN

Wil's sleep was interrupted by a hospital staff member placing breakfast on his tray. When he opened his eyes, a young kid smiled at him.

"Merry Christmas, Mr. Marsh. Would you like me to open the curtains?"

"Sure," Wil looked at his badge, "Dave. I'd appreciate it."

Wil had not slept well. Between the nurses checking on him every few hours, the pain in his arm, and the time spent thinking about Cassidy and Joseph, it all made for a very long night. Whenever he asked a nurse or hospital staff member how Cassidy was doing, he was told 'about the same.' The problem was, he didn't know what that meant, and whenever he tried to explain that, they just smiled, told him to rest, and that the doctor would be in to see him in the morning.

"Hey, the doctor said I would be able to see Cassidy this morning. Can you tell me what room she's in?" Wil asked casually, like it was no big deal.

"No sir. I'm not allowed to give out that information."

"I'm not asking you to tell me her condition, just what room she's in." Wil could tell he wasn't being very convincing, so he decided to exaggerate his story a little. "She's dead, isn't she?" he said abruptly, flinging his head back against his pillow. "I know she is! No one will talk to me! No one will give me a straight answer! I can't take it anymore! Just tell me!" He began to sob . . . sort of.

"Don't freak out on me, man. She's not dead!"

Wil snapped his head back up and looked at Dave. "Then what room is she in?" he asked calmly.

"Aw, man, you duped me."

"I'm sorry, okay? I won't tell anyone. But I've been going crazy all night. You're sure you know who I'm talking about?"

"Sure I do. You guys are the talk of the hospital. It's not everyday someone is murdered in Liberty."

The word struck like a sucker punch.

Murder?

Will Cassidy or Joseph be charged with murder?

No way. There's just no way.

"But you're sure she's okay?"

"Dude. I just took her breakfast. When I asked if she wanted the curtains pulled, she told me she'd rather they stay closed."

It was all Wil could do not to jump out of bed.

She's conscious and talking. Thank you, God. Thank you! Thank you! Thank you!

After Dave left, Wil managed to get himself dressed. Pulling his shirt over his arm took grit and determination, but he did it. He had to. He needed to see Cassidy for himself and make sure she was really okay.

Dave said he had just given Cassidy her breakfast.

So, Wil peaked outside his room to see which direction Dave was headed . . . then turned the other way.

The first room he came to had a group of visitors in it; no one he recognized. The next room, the door was closed.

Okay, I didn't think this through. I still don't know what room Cassidy is in.

Wil was one room away from the nurse's station and would have to choose either right or left.

Come on, God, give me a clue, a hint.

"I have a delivery for Cassidy Martin."

Wil quickly slipped into a small alcove with a water fountain.

Wow, that was fast. Thanks, God.

He chanced a look at the nurse's station and saw a delivery boy holding a vase of flowers.

"We don't have a Cassidy Martin," the nurse said from behind the counter. "We have a Cassidy Gray . . . oh wait a minute." The nurse turned to her computer and typed something. "That's her maiden name. Go ahead and leave the flowers here. I'll have someone take them to her room."

Wil stayed where he was and watched for someone to take the flowers.

". . . well it sounds pretty suspicious to me. A husband *and* a boyfriend?"

Wil pretended to use the water fountain as two nurses walked by having a heated discussion.

"Well, I don't believe it, Kim. I was working the cardiac care unit last month when her father was admitted. There's no way that sweet girl arranged all this."

"Who are we talking about?" Another nurse joined them as they approached the nurse's station.

"Some guy was murdered last night, and the girl in five-twenty might be the one who did it."

Wil hurried down the hall just as the nurse behind the counter started chastising the others for gossiping. He wanted to join in. Read them the riot act. Tell them their behavior was atrocious and unacceptable and that he planned on reporting them to the medical board, but he wasn't going to stick around. He had the information he needed.

Pushing the door open on room five-twenty, Wil craned his neck around the corner. When he saw Cassidy lying in the bed, he thought he was going to fall apart. Her eyes were closed, but when the door moaned shut behind him, she opened her eyes.

"Wil!" Cassidy bolted upright, then winced. "Where have you been?" Her eyes darted to his arm, then back to his eyes. "What happened to your arm? What's wrong?"

He walked to her bed, leaned over the rail, and kissed her hungrily. When he felt her respond, his heart hammered in double-time. She was okay. They were going to be okay. Pulling back slowly, he looked into her eyes. "Merry Christmas, Cassidy."

She gasped, her eyes glistening. "I completely forgot it was Christmas."

"I know. Our kiss under the mistletoe seems like a lifetime ago." Wil said as he allowed his finger to trace her profile. "I was so worried about you."

"Your arm, Wil, what happened?"

"Just a little burn, nothing serious."

"You were there? In the fire? What happened, Wil? I can only remember pieces . . . and even those don't seem to fit together."

"I don't know, Cassidy. By the time I got to the house, it was completely engulfed. When I went inside, I found Mark near the door and you under the end table. I never saw Joseph. One of the firemen pulled him out." Wil paused for a moment. "Cassidy . . . Mark's dead."

319

Cassidy looked at him in stunned disbelief. "That's what she meant when she said no one would ever hurt me again."

"Who, Cassidy? Who told you that?"

"My mom."

FIFTY-EIGHT

"Joseph, this is Sheriff Turner. He needs to ask you a few questions about what happened last night."

Joseph turned to the sheriff. "It's my fault. It's all my fault. I had—"

"Wait a minute, Joseph," Dr. Craig stopped him. "You must not be thinking clearly. You don't mean you killed that man?"

"Yes, I do."

Joseph watched as the sheriff pulled out his note pad, poised and ready. "Would you like to explain yourself, Mr. Martin?"

He closed his eyes so he could organize his thoughts. "Mark came to visit Cassidy. I knew she wasn't expecting him, but he insisted on seeing her. She was at Wil's house, so I—"

"To clarify, you're referring to Wilbur Marsh. A resident on your property?"

"Yes," Joseph confirmed. "I called to see how much longer she would be, but no one answered." He took a breath. "But they were at the house soon enough."

Joseph stopped, remembering how Mark looked when he saw Cassidy walk in with Wil. "Mark was clearly upset to see Cassidy with Wil. He didn't say anything, but I could tell by his expression and the way his body tensed. Wil wasn't too happy either when Cassidy asked him to leave."

"Why did she ask Marsh to leave?"

"Mark asked to talk to her privately. I think Cassidy was being agreeable, so he wouldn't cause a scene. Once Wil was gone, she asked me to give them some privacy, so I went upstairs." He shook his head. "I had no idea the rage Mark was holding in. If I had, I never would have left Cassidy alone with him."

"What happened next?"

Joseph took a deep breath. "I heard arguing, then crying.

When I walked to the landing, I saw Mark holding a gun to Cassidy's head, strangling her with the other. When I yelled at him to stop, he turned the gun on me and shot."

"And hit you in the shoulder?"

"Yes." Joseph nodded. "I must have blacked out, because when I came to, I was on the floor. I heard Mark yelling and Cassidy pleading. And there was smoke in the house. So, I crawled to my room, got my shotgun, then went back to the landing. That's when I realized the house was on fire, and Mark was dragging Cassidy toward the front door. I knew I had to stop him. He was going to kill her; I was sure of it."

Joseph reached for the cup of water on his tray, his hand shaking. Dr. Craig stepped closer and assisted him with the cup. "Joseph, you really shouldn't overdo it. You're still very weak."

"I'm okay, I just need to catch my breath." He took a couple of deep breaths, then continued. "I yelled at Mark to let her go, but he pointed the gun at Cassidy's head and told me he was going to kill her, then me. I was shaking too much to shoot him while he was holding Cassidy, so I taunted him."

"What do you mean, 'taunted him?'" The sheriff interrupted.

"I told him he was a coward because he was using a woman as a shield. I mocked him. I said whatever I needed to so he would direct his anger at me, not Cassidy. I was trying to buy time."

"And what did Mark do?"

"He finally got angry enough and flung Cassidy to the ground, then pointed the gun at me. So, I took my shot." Joseph turned and looked at the sheriff. "I shot him, because I had to."

The sheriff wrote without speaking, then looked up at him. "Is there anything else?"

"The house was an inferno. The fire . . . the smoke . . . I remember stumbling, losing my balance. The next thing I know, I'm being carried through the flames." He cleared his throat. "That's what happened, Sheriff. I never would have thought I could do something so . . . so heinous. But, seeing the fear on Cassidy's face and the hate in Mark's eyes, I knew I had to do something." He laid his head back on his pillow, exhausted from the memory, emotion trailing down his cheek.

"Do you have what you need?" Dr. Craig looked at Sheriff Turner. "Because Joseph is done for now."

"I still have some questions for him."

"I'll answer all the questions you have, *after* I see my daughter,"

Joseph interrupted. "Once I know she's okay. Once I *see* with my own eyes that she's going to be okay; you can do what you want with me."

———— • ————

Sheriff Turner stepped from Joseph's room, Dr Craig quick on his heels. "You have your confession. Now what?"

He flipped his notepad closed and with a sigh, slipped it into his shirt pocket. "I'll talk with the D.A."

"He was defending his daughter for crying out loud. You can't charge him for that!"

"If everything happened like Mr. Martin said, the D.A. will declare it justifiable homicide, and he won't be charged."

"How can you be sure?"

He looked squarely at the doctor. "Because I believe Joseph. He was defending his daughter and himself. Grayson shot first. His behavior was psychotic. Unpredictable. If Joseph had allowed him to leave with Cassidy, there's no telling what he would have done to her. And . . . nothing Joseph said contradicted his daughter's statement. As long as we don't find evidence that proves otherwise, it will be an open-and-shut case."

Dr. Craig hung his head. "I'm sorry. I didn't mean to come at you like that. It's just . . ."

"I get it. You were protecting your patient; that's your job. My job is to get to the truth of this very unfortunate event. Believe it or not, we're on the same side."

———— • ————

Turner knocked before entering Cassidy's room, and was shocked to say the least. There she lay, Wil Marsh stretched out beside her, Cassidy's head resting on his chest, sound asleep.

Wil heard him as he walked in because he opened his eyes, and immediately extended his index finger to his lips to hush him.

Feeling his blood pressure rising, he walked across the room as Wil slowly slipped out of bed. Cassidy stirred, but Marsh said something to her, and she went right back to sleep.

"What are you doing here?" He kept his voice low but did nothing to hide his anger. "You were *not* to see her before I got her testimony."

"Cassidy said she already spoke to you," Wil whispered, moving further away from her bed.

"I wasn't finished questioning her. She was too upset so I had to stop. Now you've compromised my entire investigation," he barked, pacing a few steps then back again. "How do I know you didn't coach her, tell her what to say?"

"Wil?" Cassidy stirred.

He glared at the sheriff. "Thanks a lot. You could've waited another hour or so, but no. You'd rather question her when she's fragile enough you can badger her and twist her words."

"That is not my intention."

"Sheriff Turner . . ."

They both turned to Cassidy and watched as she pushed herself up to a sitting position.

"Have you seen my dad yet?"

"Yes, Mrs. Grayson, I have."

"Then can I see him?"

He shot a look in Marsh's direction. "Sure. I'll get the nurse." He turned and walked out.

FIFTY-NINE

The reunion with her father was emotional, but not very private. Dr. Craig was there, making sure her dad didn't overdo it, and the sheriff was present to remind them, they weren't allowed to discuss what happened the night before. With her wheelchair alongside her dad's bed, Cassidy listened as the doctor explained his injuries.

"But you're sure he's going to be okay?" she asked, while clutching her father's hand.

"He's weak, and is having a little difficulty breathing, but your dad is going to be fine," the doctor assured her. "I want to keep him a few more days as a precaution, give his lungs a chance to clear, make sure he doesn't overdo it. But other than that, I see no reason why he can't go home by the end of the week."

After a lot of handholding and tears, Dr. Craig encouraged them both to get some rest. When her dad started to drift off to sleep, Sheriff Turner volunteered to push her back to her room. As they rolled down the corridor, Cassidy felt like everyone was looking at her. Judging her. She could only imagine what they were thinking.

"Here we are," Sheriff Turner said as he backed her into the hospital room.

When he swung her around, she scanned the room. It was empty. No Wil. She sighed in disappointment.

"I told Mr. Marsh I would get him when we were through talking."

"Am I that transparent?" she asked, looking over her shoulder.

He shrugged, with a hint of a smile. "Lucky guess." Parking the wheelchair alongside her bed, he put on the brake. "Let me give you some privacy while you get situated."

When the sheriff stepped outside, Cassidy slowly pulled herself up onto the bed, and laid the stiff white sheet over her legs. She closed her eyes, feeling pain all over her body. Touching the bandage on her forehead, she winced.

"Still pretty painful?" The sheriff asked when he walked back into the room.

"Yeah." She sunk against the stack pillows.

"I need to ask you a few more questions, Cassidy."

She sighed. It was like he was asking her to remember things from a hundred years ago. The puzzle in her head still was not fitting together, and he was trying to force the pieces into place.

"I'm pretty sure I told you everything I remember."

"I understand but let's see if you can fill in some of the blank spots."

"I'll try but I don't know if it will do any good."

"Your father said he heard you and Mark arguing, is that right?"

"Yes. At first, Mark tried to sweet talk me. Said he loved me and wanted me back. He even arranged for us to fly to Morocco that night. Told me to pack my bags. But I knew something was wrong. He said he wanted me back, but he was agitated too. So, I started asking questions. That's when he got mad."

"What kind of questions?"

"I asked him about Amanda."

"Who's Amanda?"

"She's his assistant . . . and his mistress." Cassidy clenched her jaw. "That's why I left Mark. I found out he was having an affair."

"So, it was you who asked for the divorce?"

"No. Mark did. That's the part I don't understand." Cassidy shifted, trying to get comfortable. "He drew up the papers and brought them to Liberty weeks ago. He also left a note basically telling me he wasn't cut out for the monogamous life."

"So why do you think he changed his mind?"

"I have no idea. He said he missed me, and things would be different. But when I pressed him with questions and accusations, he snapped. I've seen Mark angry before—plenty of times. But never like that. It's like he became a different person. Someone I didn't know anymore."

"So, he'd been violent before?" the sheriff questioned.

Cassidy squeezed her hands, kneading them like stubborn dough. "Yes, but he was always careful not to hit me where the bruises would show. When he hit me across the face, I was shocked. That's when I knew something was wrong."

"Can you remember what happened next?"

Cassidy could taste the blood on her lips, feel his hand against her neck. "He held a gun to my head." She relived the moment. Mark stroking her. The things he said. "He had me pinned underneath him on the couch. My father must have heard me scream because he yelled at Mark from the upstairs landing and told him to leave me alone. Then Mark turned the gun on him. I knocked the gun out of his hand, but not before he shot my dad. We both went for the gun, wrestled for it. Somehow it ended up in the fireplace. Mark used the poker to get it away from the fire, but a log rolled out with it." Cassidy caught her breath. "That's how the fire started. The log on the carpet. It smoldered. Then there were flames. They spread to the Christmas tree, and then it seemed as if everything was on fire."

Cassidy laid back and closed her eyes. She remembered the smell of smoke. The taste of it in her mouth.

"Okay, Cassidy, you said you and Mark wrestled for the gun, and it ended up in the fireplace." She nodded in agreement. "That Mark fished it out, starting the fire." She nodded again. "Then how did the gun end up by the front door, and you on the other side of the couch?"

Cassidy thought for a moment, stroking her neck, remembering the stranglehold Mark had on her. "He had the gun in his hand and was dragging me toward the front door. He was going to force me to leave with him." She remembered the windows breaking. The roar of the fire. The suffocating feeling from Mark's hold and the smoke.

"Cassidy, what happened next?" The sheriff prompted her.

"My father yelled at him from upstairs, but this time he was pointing a shotgun at him." She relived the moment. "I was so grateful my dad was alive, but I was afraid Mark would shoot him again. Instead, my father taunted Mark, goaded him. Called him a coward." She swallowed a breath and her body shuttered. "That's when Mark shoved me to the ground, and I heard what sounded like an explosion. I remember reaching for my head and knowing I was hurt, but then everything went black."

Cassidy blinked, and for the first time looked at Sheriff Turner. "The next thing I remember is . . ." Cassidy recalled her conversation with her mother, when she thought she was dying, and her mother had come to meet her. But she didn't want to share those thoughts with the sheriff. They were too precious to end up in a police report.

And he would probably just think I was crazy.

"The next thing I remember is waking up here."

She watched as the sheriff finished jotting down notes in his little black book. He asked a few follow-up questions, rephrased them, and asked for more details. But once he seemed satisfied—had all he needed—he thanked her and left.

Wil paced his room. Even though his arm was killing him, he couldn't sit still. When the sheriff walked in, he took a deep breath. "How'd Cassidy do? Did she remember anything else?"

"She did. She corroborated what her father said."

Wil ran his hand through his hair, a wave of relief settling his heart.

"Did she give you any reasons why Mark might have snapped? I mean, I knew he was a major jerk, and a cheat by what she'd already told me. But to be so violent . . . it seems so over the top."

"She commented on his previous behavior, and she too was shocked by the excessive lengths he'd taken. She agrees it was out of the ordinary."

Wil could read between the lines. Cassidy had told the sheriff about Mark's abusive behavior. That this wasn't the first time he'd hit her.

It chilled him to think what would have happened it Joseph hadn't been there to stop him.

"I just came to tell you I'm done for now, and Cassidy is expecting you. I'll be in touch. Hopefully you can enjoy what is left of Christmas."

Wil's stomach churned, thinking of all Cassidy had endured over the years.

God, thank you for bringing her home.

Bringing her to me.

SIXTY

"I was thinking you ditched me." Cassidy yawned as Wil walked into her room. She scooted over to make room for him on the bed.

"You look pretty sleepy. Maybe I should just let you rest." He reached out and gently touched the bruise on her cheek.

She took his hand in hers, knowing what he was thinking, but not wanting to talk about it. Not yet. "But I'll sleep better if you're here."

It didn't take much to change his mind.

Wil stretched his legs up onto the bed and extended his left arm around her shoulders. She snuggled into the crook of his arm and sighed. "How's your arm?"

He shrugged. "It hurts, but I'm okay."

They laid side-by-side, silent. Comfort coming from just being together.

"Who are the flowers from?"

"Blake."

"I didn't even think to send you flowers. What a lousy boyfriend."

She couldn't help but giggle at the teenage-sounding term. "I think you were a little more preoccupied than Blake. I'll give you a pass—this time."

He huffed, sounding annoyed. Annoyed and exhausted. When his breathing deepened, she wondered if he'd fallen asleep. She wouldn't blame him, with all he'd been through.

"Wil?" she whispered, to see if he was still awake.

"Huh?"

"I'm so sorry you had to go through this."

"Me? What about you?"

"But it had to feel like your worst nightmare repeating itself."

She felt a strand of her hair slip through his fingers over and over

329

again.

"It was horrible," he finally said, his words thick with emotion. "I thought I was losing everyone I loved all over again."

Cassidy felt a droplet on her forehead and looked up to see Wil in tears. "Don't cry, Wil. Everything is going to be okay." Cassidy reached up to brush the tears from his jaw. His eyes looked so deep, so full of hurt. "What is it, Wil? What's wrong?"

Tears continued to redden his eyes, but it took a moment before he could gather his composure.

"What is it?" she whispered again. "You can tell me."

"How many times had he hurt you before?"

Cassidy stiffened, letting her hand fall away from Wil's face.

"That's why you didn't want to see him when he came the first time. You weren't angry at him; you were afraid."

Cassidy laid her head on his chest. "It doesn't matter. It's all over now. No one is ever going to hurt me again."

Just like Mom said.

———— • ————

When Wil was sure Cassidy was asleep, he slipped out of her room. He asked at the nurse's station what room Joseph was in, and if he was allowed visitors. They scolded him for not being in his own room but allowed him to check in on Joseph.

"Merry Christmas, Joseph."

"Wil." Relief filled Joseph's face. "I was afraid something worse had happened to you, but nobody wanted to tell me."

"Nope." He lifted his arm. "Just some minor burns. I really didn't need to be admitted, but Dr. Craig ran interference for me. Otherwise, I think I would have ended up down at the police station."

They took stocked of each other's injuries in between moments of silence. Then in his quiet manner, Joseph shared his grief. "I killed a man, Wil."

"No you didn't, Joseph. You saved Cassidy's life. There's a difference."

"Watching him hurt her. Strangling her. A gun to her head. I had to stop him. No matter what."

"You did what you had to do, Joseph. You can't blame yourself. Mark's responsible for his own actions, and his own death."

Speaking Mark's name was enough to make him retch. The man

was dead, and Wil did not feel the least little bit of regret. When he thought about all the years Cassidy lived in fear, Mark terrorizing her, abusing her, it was hard to stomach.

If he wasn't already dead . . .

Dr. Craig walked in all smiles, causing Wil to shove down his anger.

"It's Christmas, gentlemen. You should be celebrating."

"So should you, Dr. Craig. Why aren't you home with your family?"

"All my family is in New York. I'll call them around dinner."

"You're not married?" Wil glanced at the gold band on the man's finger.

"No. The ring is a deterrent." The good looking, middle-aged man smiled. "I know that sounds arrogant, but I'm not up to the forwardness of women these days."

Wil gave him a nod of understanding.

"Look," Dr. Craig turned his attention back to Joseph, "I thought it would be nice if the three of you could have Christmas dinner together."

Joseph's eyes brightened. "That would be great."

"Well, don't get your hopes up too high," he chuckled. "We're still talking hospital food, balanced with your health in mind." He grinned. "But family needs to be together. Since Cassidy's room is larger, we will set everything up in there. I'll have one of the nurses come and get you when the time comes. It should only be another hour or so."

Wil looked at the clock on the wall. Christmas Day had flown by already. It certainly was not the Christmas anyone would have expected.

But they still had plenty to celebrate.

As Wil headed down the hall, his attending nurse caught up with him, scolding him for not staying put in his own room.

"Come on, Sally, can you blame me?" She was a gruff woman and sturdy enough that she could probably take him down if she wanted to, but he appealed to her compassionate side. "The love of my life is in a hospital room just down the hall, the man who is like a father to me is not far from her, and its Christmas. Can you blame me?"

"You have your own injuries to worry about, Mr. Marsh," she said as she followed him into his room.

He carefully removed his shirt and sat on the edge of the bed as she directed. "I know you could have hunted me down sooner if you wanted to, Sally. Admit it, you're a romantic at heart."

The corner of her lip pulled ever so slightly as she removed the bandages from his arm. She glanced at him, then back to his arm. "Is it true? Did the woman's father really kill her husband?"

Wil was shocked to hear it put so bluntly. "Well . . . yes, but there are extenuating circumstances."

"Some of the nurses are saying it was your fault. You were in a lover's triangle, and her husband went berserk."

"I can assure you, her husband went berserk long before last night." His words were sharp. "I'm not going to discuss Cassidy's personal life with you, but believe me, she had every reason to leave him. He would have killed her if her father had not intervened."

"I'm sorry, Mr. Marsh. I shouldn't have said anything. It's none of my business."

"Please, Sally. I think we can be on a first name basis."

She smiled and blushed. "Okay, Wil. Now sit still so I can finish what I'm doing." She examined his arm, turning it over carefully and back again. "Dr. Craig explained that your injuries weren't exactly serious enough for hospitalization, but he felt you would be safer here than in a police station or left to your own devices."

Wil laughed. "He's very astute."

Sally applied a salve before re-bandaging Wil's arm, then covered it with a plastic sleeve so he could take a shower. "That should do it," she said while disposing of the discarded wrappers. "I'll be back to check on you later."

"Hey, Sally," Wil stopped her before she could leave.

"Yes?"

"Please let the other nurses, and whoever else is gossiping about us, know the truth."

"I'll do that, Mr. Marsh."

After Sally left, Wil undressed and stood in a hot shower. The pulsing water felt good on his aching muscles, but he could not get his mind to rest. He kept picturing Cassidy with Mark; wondering what sort of abuse she had endured. How often? How much?

Stop it. This isn't helping anyone.

Clearing his head, he stepped out of the shower and reached for the smoke-filled clothes he'd been admitted with. In place of them, was a stack of neatly folded clothes.

He looked at the jeans. *Right size.*

He looked at the shirt. *Nice color.*

He wondered who would've taken the time to get these things for him. He didn't know, but he was grateful.

It took a little longer to comb his hair and shave with only one good arm, but it was worth putting in the extra effort. After all, it was Christmas.

Slipping on the flimsy hospital slippers, he headed down the hall, feeling *almost* brand new.

When he walked into Cassidy's room, she was standing by the window wearing a beautiful, velour robe in a deep shade of red, looking absolutely stunning.

"Wow! Where did you get that?"

She smiled. "I imagine the same place you got that shirt."

He played the part of a model, did the slow turn. "Pretty nice, huh?" He looked down at the forest green button-down while she smiled appreciatively.

Closing the distance between them, he did so slowly, not wanting to rush the view. "You look beautiful, Cassidy." He pushed her golden hair away from her face and over her shoulders. But she quickly dipped her head and pulled the hair back close to her face, hiding the bruising discoloring her chin and cheek.

"I don't look or feel very beautiful," she said with her head down.

Wil gently cupped her chin and tipped up her head, so she had to look at him. "You're beautiful to me." With his good arm, he reached for her and pulled her closer, then slowly bent and placed a soft kiss to her lips. He pulled back just far enough to whisper to her. "I love you, Cassidy."

She stepped back from his embrace and leaned again on the window sill, her form rigid. Wil thought about the way they had curled up in her hospital bed. She felt safe with him, she loved him, he knew she did.

Then why is she acting so cold . . . so distant?

"I heard the nurses talking, Wil. They think I'm some sort of tramp, that I got what I deserve. Maybe I did. Maybe I was just kidding myself into thinking I could have something better. I was married to Mark and carrying on with you. It was wrong to get involved with you. It was wrong to think I could walk away from my past and not have to pay for my actions. Maybe if I had not become involved with you, things would have turned out differently last night."

Wil was livid. He wasn't sure who he was more upset with, Cassidy for thinking what they had was a mistake, or the nurses for gossiping about her and planting doubt in her head. "How can you say that, Cassidy? What happened last night was Mark's fault. His behavior was criminal, both last night and when you were married. The way I see it, his punishment fits his crimes."

Cassidy spun on her heals and stumbled, reaching for the end of the bed to balance herself. "So, what about me, Wil? Shouldn't I be punished for my behavior? For my mistakes?"

"You have!" he shouted. "How many times did Mark hurt you, Cassidy? How many times? How many times did he terrorize you and make you feel worthless? You almost paid with your life. Isn't that enough?" Seeing her tears, he stepped forward and gently brushed them away. "You can't spend the rest of your life punishing yourself, Cassidy. Remember, you are saved by grace?"

She fell into his arms and sobbed.

Wincing slightly, Wil held her tight. The pain he felt was measureless compared to hers. His wounds would heal in time. He could only pray hers would do the same. "You should be lying down," he whispered as he stroked her back.

"No. I'm tired of lying down." She padded over to the chair alongside the window, and slowly lowered herself into it.

"Are you comfortable?" He squatted down in front of her. She nodded, but not very convincingly. "Okay, I'll be right back."

"Where are you going?"

"I have some business to attend to." His strides were long and determined.

"What kind of business?" she yelled after him.

But he didn't answer. He had a more important matter to discuss with an insensitive team of nurses.

He walked to their station, slammed his good hand down on the countertop and lunged forward. "I thought your profession dealt in facts?" The two women standing with tablets in their hands stared at him, clearly shocked.

"Mr. Marsh, please keep your voice down." Catherine took hold of his arm and pulled him into a waiting area. "What is the matter?"

"I want to know the nurses who are assigned to Cassidy, and I want to speak to them right now!"

"Well, we're just getting ready for a shift change. They're going over patient information. Can I help you?"

"Well, you'd better speak to them." Wil paced, then jabbed his finger at her. "Because of their gossiping about something they know nothing about, Cassidy is in her room, beside herself with guilt. She said she heard them talking about her. They called her a tramp and said that she got what she deserved."

Catherine looked horrified. It was obvious this was news to her.

"Wil, I'm so sorry. I can assure you I knew nothing about this. But I will take care of it immediately."

He watched as Catherine marched into the breakroom, then saw Dr. Craig about to enter Cassidy's room. "Dr. Craig." Wil got his attention. "I never got a chance to thank you for sticking your neck out for me." Wil extended his hand.

"No problem, Wil. My instincts sort of took over on this one." He shook Wil's hand, then put his arm around his shoulder. "I like to think I'm a good judge of character. The way the two of you rallied around Joseph when he was in here before, I just couldn't imagine you being involved with anything criminal."

"Well, I appreciate it."

"Hey, the shirt looks nice."

"It was you who sent it?"

"I wanted your Christmas dinner to be as festive as possible." He patted Wil's shoulder as they walked into Cassidy's room together.

Joseph was sitting alongside Cassidy in a wheelchair. He too, was wearing a new robe. Blue velour.

"Look who's here." Wil pointed to Dr. Craig. "Santa Claus."

Cassidy looked puzzled but when Wil tugged at his shirt, she realized what he meant.

"Dr. Craig . . . you picked out all these things?"

"No. Actually, Catherine picked them out. I just paid for them."

Wil cringed, thinking about the way he had just spoken to her. "If you'll excuse me, I have some groveling to do." He turned to leave when Catherine came bursting into the room.

"Turn on the TV!"

SIXTY-ONE

Everyone looked confused as Catherine reached for the controls on the side of the bed rail and pressed buttons until she found the station she was looking for. She then turned up the volume just as a reporter, standing in front of the famous Wall Street Bull, repeated his story.

"Again, the grisly discovery of the bodies of financier, Nathan Davis, and a woman identified as Amanda Banes has rocked the New York financial community."

Wil looked at Cassidy. She rose from where she was sitting and moved closer to the television.

"New evidence has been found linking financier, Mark Grayson to both victims. Amanda Banes was the personal assistant to Mr. Grayson, and he and Mr. Davis were known to have had their differences in the past. Though the police are not saying if Grayson is a suspect, they do want to question him in regard to his relationship with both victims. Currently, the whereabouts of Mark Grayson remain unknown."

"Steve, you said there was evidence linking Mark Grayson to the victims. Do we know what that is?" The studio anchorman asked.

"It is speculation at this time, but it has been rumored Ms. Banes was actually working for Nathan Davis while she was employed by Mark Grayson. Embezzlement seems to be the buzz word on Wall Street. But police will not confirm or deny it. Back to you, Scott."

All eyes were on Cassidy. Wil braced her shaky limbs and led her back to the chair. He held her hand and looked into her vacant eyes.

"Cassidy, are you going to be all right?" Dr. Craig bent close, clearly trying to read her condition.

"She knew." Cassidy whispered to herself. "Mom knew it would all be over soon."

Joseph looked at Wil, then back to Cassidy. "What are you

talking about, Sunshine?"

"I saw her, Dad. I saw mom . . . after I was pulled from the fire. I wanted to go to her, but she wouldn't let me. She said I was safe now. She told me it would all be over soon."

Wil watched as Joseph was overwhelmed with emotion.

"She said she'd be waiting for us, Dad."

Cassidy knelt at her father's feet, laid her head in his lap, and cried. Joseph sniffed away the knot in his throat. "She's right, Cassidy. You're safe now." He stroked her hair. "Everything is going to be all right."

When Wil, Dr. Craig, and Catherine stepped out of the room to allow Cassidy and Joseph some time together, Sheriff Turner was working his way down the hall.

"So, did you hear?" he said, looking like he was ready to burst.

"We heard," Wil answered. "Have you contacted the authorities in New York?"

"Yep, told them they could stop searching for Grayson."

"Did they tell you anymore about what happened there?"

"Seems Grayson found out his assistant was embezzling from him. She was working for one of his rivals and was secretly handling money transfers. When Grayson found out, he followed her to the man's high rise, confronted them, then killed 'em both."

"They're sure it was Mark?" Wil asked.

He nodded. "They even have a witness. They withheld that information because they were hoping Grayson would come forward on his own, just for questioning."

"So, why do you think he came here? Do you think his intentions were to kill Cassidy too?" Wil asked.

"No. I think he was running. Cassidy said something about Mark wanting them to go to Morocco."

"What!?" Wil shook his head. "Why?"

"My guess, the U.S. doesn't have an extradition treaty with Morocco. I think he was spiraling. Grasping at straws. He filed a false flight plan to throw the cops off his track, then came here to claim what he thought was his before he lost everything. I mean, I'm no psychologist, but that's what I think."

The sheriff looked at him. "Sorry I was so hard on you, Wil, but I couldn't be too careful, you know?"

"I understand."

"Well, I have a body to release. Merry Christmas, Wil. And Dr. Craig . . . next time you admit a patient and willfully obstruct justice, I'm going to call you on it." He tipped his hat with a smirk and left.

A rolling cart was coming toward them as they stood in the hall. "I think your dinner is here," Dr. Craig said. "I guess it's not going to be as joyous as I had hoped."

"Yes, it is. It's tragic what happened tonight, but we still have plenty to be thankful for." He shook the doctor's hand. "Thank you, Dr. Craig, for everything."

Wil took the cart from the attendant and rolled it into the room. Cassidy was in the bathroom washing her face, and Joseph was staring out the window from his wheelchair. Wil set everyone's dishes on the small table in the corner and waited for Cassidy to sit down.

"You okay?"

She nodded, smiling as best she could. Wil turned over his hand and Cassidy gently place hers in his. Wil reached for Joseph's hand and Cassidy finished the circle. They all bowed as Wil began to pray.

"Our gracious Heavenly Father, as we celebrate Your birth tonight, we celebrate life. We thank You for the safety You provided for all of us over the last year and especially last night. We thank You for bringing Cassidy back home where she belongs, and that she has found You again. We thank You for Joseph's improving health even in the face of setbacks. And I thank You for allowing me to find the love of my life." He squeezed Cassidy's hand. "Through laughter and tears, highs and lows, may we always know what it is we have in You. May we never take for granted the love and the grace You bestow on us daily. Amen."

"Praise God, from Whom all blessings flow . . ." In his strong, tenor voice, Joseph started to sing the doxology. ". . . praise Him, all creatures here below."

Wil struggled with emotion but joined in. "Praise Him above, ye heavenly host." Cassidy's whisper completed the chorus. "Praise Father, Son, and Holy Ghost. A-men."

SIXTY-TWO

Wil helped Cassidy into his pickup, then handed her the flowers she would have to juggle on her lap.

"I don't know why you don't just leave those with your dad." Cassidy was sad her dad wasn't coming home with her, but so thankful he was going to make a complete recovery. "Because I want to stop somewhere on our way home."

Wil looked at her and smile. "I think I know where." He then pulled out from the hospital driveway.

They drove in silence, and soon enough Wil edged to the side of the road. He steadied her as she got out of the truck. "Do you want me to go with you?" he asked.

"No. I need to do this alone."

Cassidy made a path through the snow to the memorial cross her father had erected so many years before. She leaned down, placed the flowers in front of it, then stood. "Mom . . ." her voice broke slightly. "I was mad when you left. You never even said goodbye. I was so afraid. I didn't think I could go on without you. I felt abandoned, like you didn't even care. But now I know I was wrong."

Her voice quivered. "You were there all along. Watching me, protecting me, keeping me safe until I could find my way back home. I didn't know. I didn't understand why God took you away from me and Dad. I didn't think it was fair. I turned my back on God, thinking I was punishing Him. But now I know I was only punishing myself. I know it was your voice I heard the day I left Mark. You told me to run. It was you who helped me find my way back to home." Cassidy's tears fell unrestrained. "Thank you, Mom. Thank you for always being there for me even when I didn't know it. Thank you for bringing me back to Daddy. I should have never left him. I've lost so much time that can never be replaced. I pray we still have many years together to make up for it."

Cassidy knelt down and stroked the outline of the cross. "You'd like Wil," she whispered. "He's wonderful and strong. He loves the Lord, and he loves me. And I love him, but then you probably already know that." Cassidy chuckled, then swallowed back more tears. "I wish I could be with you, Mom, but I'll just have to be content to know I'll see you again."

Cassidy leaned forward and placed a kiss to the weathered metal. She stood slowly feeling the ache in her chest, but knowing it was there because her heart was full. She turned around. Wil was leaning against the side of his truck, hands in his pockets, patiently waiting for her. He held out his arms as she approached and wrapped her in his strong protective care.

"You okay?"

"Yeah."

"Then let's go home."

They slowly drove home.

Or what was left of it.

Cassidy's eyes were closed as they approached the house because she wasn't sure she was going to be able to handle what she saw. Wil shifted into park, then reached for her hand. "Are you sure you're ready for this?"

"No. I'm not sure, but I don't think it will get any easier."

The smell of smoke assaulted her nostrils. Cassidy opened her eyes and slowly turned toward the house. She pushed through the initial shocked and stepped from the truck. Wil held her close, almost blocking her view. "We can do this another time, Cassidy." With her head resting on his chest, she took a deep breath.

"No, I can do this."

She held his hand tight as they stared at the blackened frame. She had been told the house was a total loss, so she expected to see nothing but a pile of rubble, but instead the house was still standing.

"I thought they said it was a total loss?" She looked up, amazed.

"It is. The lower structure has been compromised. The top floor will have to come down."

"But did the fire spread to the second floor?"

"In some areas."

Hope sparked inside her. "What about my room?"

"I'm not sure. Until right now, the only thing I cared about was you and Joseph."

Cassidy turned to him and like a shot she was up the front steps.

"Cassidy, stop!"

Wil grabbed her before she could go through the doorway. They both stood on the threshold surveying the destroyed living room. "Can you call someone? See if we can go in and look for things?"

"Sure . . . I guess." He pulled out his cell phone and dialed. "Blake, it's Wil. Hey, we're at the house . . . yeah, she got out this morning. Look, could you call someone and see if it's okay to go into the house. Cassidy wants to look for some things, but I'm not sure it's safe. Okay, call me back. Sure, that would be great."

Wil hung up the phone and tugged at Cassidy. "Come on. We're not going any further without permission. I'm not about to lose you now."

How could she argue? She stepped away from the house with Wil, hoping beyond hope not everything in the house was ruined.

When they got to Wil's place, she sighed once she was inside. A resemblance of normalcy. It felt better than she could even imagine.

"Why don't I fix us something for lunch?" he suggested.

"Can it wait a little while? I just want to sit for a moment and relax."

Wil smiled and sat down next to her. She rested her head on his chest, listening to the rhythm of his heart. He circled his arm around her and pressed her to his side. Cassidy melted in the security she felt in his arms. They sat in silence. She knew Wil had questions about Mark, about their relationship. She'd seen it in his eyes.

She didn't want any secrets between them. It was just so painful and demoralizing to admit she had allowed Mark to control her for so long. After a few minutes of quiet, she took a deep breath and began to explain. "At first Mark only intimidated me. He yelled or lectured. Used scare tactics. Then it became physical."

"Cassidy, you don't have to . . ."

"Yes, I do. I don't want you to wonder forever or to imagine things. I want you to know the truth. I want to be able to put it behind me, or at least try."

Wil kissed the top of her head and held her close as she explained the worst years of her life.

SIXTY-THREE

Wil watched Cassidy sleep. It had been an emotional time for them both. Cassidy because she lived it, Wil because he was unable to do anything about it.

He listened as she described how Mark controlled her, how he made her believe she was nothing without him. He instilled weakness and ineptness in her. And after he succeeded at that, he became more demanding and demeaning.

Wil couldn't get out of his head the things she told him. How Mark body shamed her to near starvation. How he purposely bought her dresses two sizes too small, insisting she wear them to whatever lavish function they were expected to attend. Then he would parade her around in front of his business associates like she was the main course. Mark intimidated her into submission, but his psychological abuse and deviant behaviors were just as toxic.

She was bruised, battered, flung against walls, pushed to the ground, forced to do things she didn't want to do. All because Mark could get away with it. Thinking she had no place to go, Cassidy endured it. She was too afraid to leave. Too terrified to defy him.

Cassidy explained how things had gotten better the last several months, how she thought their marriage had turned a corner. The fighting, the arguments, the abuse had all stopped. When Mark came home, he was pleasant, loving, not demanding. But it wasn't until she found out about Amanda, she realized why the change. Amanda was his stress relief. She gave him what he wanted. She was the reason Mark no longer put demands on her.

When Wil asked Cassidy how she finally found the nerve to leave, she told him it was her mom who told her to leave.

She went on to explain to him the voice she'd heard, telling her to run the day she left Mark. The same voice she heard right before Mark went crazy. And how she carried on a full conversation with her mother while she was unconscious. Cassidy was convinced it was God and her mom who saved her from Mark's continual abuse.

Wil looked down at Cassidy asleep in his lap. Stroking her hair, caressing her face, he thanked God for protecting her, and that Mark could never hurt her again. She would have scars, but hopefully, someday, she would be able to put her past behind her.

Wil had just closed his eyes, when there was a knock at the door. He slowly scooted from underneath Cassidy's head, causing her to stir. "Go ahead and rest. I'll get it." He slipped a pillow under her head, and she hugged it tight and closed her eyes.

"Hey, Blake." Wil spoke in a hushed tone.

"How's Cassidy doing?" Blake whispered, Grace squirming in his arms.

"She'd doing okay." Wil took Grace and held her to his cheek.

"I talked to the fire chief. He said he would be out later to escort you through the house."

"Thanks, Blake . . . for everything."

"No problem and just so you know, take whatever time you need with Cassidy. I've got things handled at the site. The inspector is scheduled to sign-off the electrical and plumbing on Monday, and then we're going to knock it out of the park."

Wil smiled, even though he was disappointed.

"What's wrong, Wil? I thought you'd be thrilled."

"I just wish I had stuck to the original plan and started on the apartment. Joseph and Cassidy can stay here, that's not the problem. I'll just have to move my stuff into the work zone." Wil spoke out loud the issues he was shifting around in his head, but Grace's squirming and face licking distracted him, making him laugh.

"Thanks again, Blake. I'll touch base with you when I can."

Wil watched Grace scamper across the wooden floors, slipping and sliding, curiosity leading the way. When she saw Cassidy on the couch, she headed straight for her. Stretching her pudgy little body, Grace bathed Cassidy's cheek with puppy dog kisses.

The smile on Cassidy's face lit up the room. She swung her feet off the couch and pulled Grace up into her lap, but soon she was sitting on the floor, puppy teeth nipping at her toes.

Wil laughed. "Why don't you keep her company while I fix lunch? But watch out, she can be a real handful."

"She won't give me any problems." Cassidy chuckled as Grace pulled on her hair.

"I was talking to Grace."

———— • ————

Lunch was over, and Grace had finally worn herself out. She was snuggled in a blanket Wil had laid in the corner of the kitchen; the oven door cracked open to warm the space.

"Cassidy, I can finish these. Why don't you go lay down?"

She dried the dish she was holding and lifted it to the cupboard shelf. "Because I'm tired of watching people flit around me while I lay like a bump on a log. I had enough of that in the hospital."

Wil continued with the dishes, while he watched Cassidy out of the corner of his eye. She glanced at him between dishes, but whenever Wil turned to her, she quickly looked away. Finally, without warning, he grabbed her around the waist and clenched her to his chest. "You think you're so sly. I see you watching me."

She blushed, giggling. "I have no idea what you're talking about."

He looked at her longingly, then pressed a slow, satisfying kiss to her lips. Cassidy stretched to her tiptoes, wrapped her arms around his shoulders, and kissed him with surprising intensity. Then he realized why. She was free to love him. She was no longer married, and they no longer had a reason to wait for what it was they both wanted.

Wil allowed his fingers to stroke her back, to feel her muscles flex under his touch. His hands slid down the curves outlining her body, enjoying the feel of her pressed against him.

But he was enjoying it too much.

Way too much.

Pulling away, his hands slid to her waist and his forehead pressed to hers. "We'd better stop," he whispered.

She lowered herself from her tiptoes, then rested her hands on his forearms. Looking at him with those gorgeous blue eyes, she had no idea the power she held over him.

"But we'll be careful. We won't let it go too far." She pressed her lips to his neck and kissed him some more.

He stepped back, putting even more space between them. "I

don't trust myself to have that kind of self-control, Cassidy."

Her shoulders stiffened, and her eyes grew moist. Then she just walked away.

Wil hung his head and took a deep breath. "That went great," he mumbled under his breath, but Grace perked up and gave him one of those doggie head tilts. "What? I was being honest."

And now I am carrying on a conversation with a dog. Real smooth.

Taking a second to regain his footing, he walked into the living room and saw Cassidy sitting on the couch, knees pulled up against her chest, looking very closed off.

He sat down next to her, reached for her hand, and laced his fingers with hers. "I'm sorry. I didn't mean to hurt your feelings." He brought her hand up to his lips and kissed her.

She shook her head, avoiding eye contact. "You have nothing to be sorry about. I don't know what I was thinking . . . or maybe I do. But it was wrong and for that I'm sorry. Not very flattering, to say the least."

"Cassidy, don't be so hard on yourself." He bent low to whisper in her ear. "I would like nothing better than to take you upstairs right now and make love to you." Cassidy looked at him with furrowed brows. "Why does that surprise you?"

"Because it would be wrong."

"Yes, it would be wrong, but that doesn't mean I don't desire you. I just know we need to wait until the time is right. The time God has appointed for us."

"When do you think that will be?"

"Soon . . . very soon."

SIXTY-FOUR

When Cassidy and Wil pulled up to the house, the fire chief was already there, leaning against his vehicle, looking quite inconvenienced.

"Paul, thanks for meeting us here." Wil extended his hand.

"Sure thing, Wil, but you have to follow my lead. If I say it's unsafe, it's unsafe. If I say no, it's a no. I don't want anyone getting hurt."

Wil nodded in agreement.

"Cassidy, understand?" The chief looked at her. "Your father has been through enough these past few weeks. I don't want to have to explain to him how you got hurt rummaging around in the debris."

"I understand."

Slowly, the three of them walked through the house, stepping over charred beams and around destroyed furniture. Cassidy looked around, numb. Everything from her childhood was gone.

Wil reached for her hand, giving it a squeeze. "You okay?"

"Yes," she said, forcing back tears. "I just want to see if there's anything upstairs."

She followed the fire chief upstairs, stepping where he stepped, looking at everything charred and ruined. Stopping in front of her father's bedroom door, the chief gave a cursory looked then stepped out of the way.

"I can go in?"

"Yes. Just be careful."

She picked up the silver brush set from on top of the dresser. It was black with soot and the bristles were partially melted, but it could be salvaged.

Thank you, God.

If nothing else was saved, she was glad to have at least this one keepsake from her mother. Then she saw the cedar chest at the foot of her father's bed. Knowing it was where her mother kept important papers and mementos, she knelt before it and said a prayer before lifting the heavy lid, then smiled. Everything looked as if it had been spared. She turned to the chief. "Do you think we could get this downstairs?"

"How about we just remove the contents?"

"But it was my mom's cedar chest. It'll mean a lot to Dad if we're able to salvage it."

He didn't exactly eye-roll, put she could tell he wasn't thrilled.

"Yeah," he sighed. "I'll have Wil give me a hand with it." He looked around. "Is there anything else you want?"

"Not in here, but I have some things in my room, if they're not ruined."

He rubbed his jaw. "I'm sorry to say that section of the house suffered quite a bit more damage. Don't expect much."

She nodded. "Just a quick look. I promise."

"Okay," he said looking as if he was losing his patience. He stepped into the room, glanced around, moved some things out of the way. "Stay away from the east wall, and do not move any of the furniture."

Cassidy stepped carefully over some debris and peered into her room. It was a mess. The canopy that had hung over her bed since she was a little girl looked like a black cloud. Her walls were completely black and there was broken glass all over the floor. She quickly glanced at her closet. Nothing of importance. Clothes were replaceable. What she really wanted was covered in cloth, leaning behind her door.

She pulled the door forward and sighed at what she saw. The cloth draped over Wil's painting was completely black with soot. She stepped around the door and squatted down, hesitating before pulling the cloth from the painting, then turned it around. Wil's present stared back at her, completely undamaged. She choked back a sob.

"Are you okay?"

She looked over her shoulder at the fire chief, happy tears moistening her face. "Look . . . it's perfect . . . I can't believe it." Cassidy lifted the large frame from the floor.

"It's beautiful. A collector's piece?" he asked as he studied the picture.

Cassidy beamed with pride. "No. A gift."

Carrying the painting down the steps, she saw Wil walk out

of the kitchen, wiping soot from his hands. Well . . . what used to be the kitchen.

"Nothing can be saved from the living room, but there are some things in the kitchen I think can be cleaned up." He nodded at the picture. "What's that?"

"A miracle." Cassidy said as she maneuvered the picture around so he could see it. "Merry Christmas, Wil."

He stood mesmerized for a second before stepping forward. Taking hold of the frame, he held it, examining it from corner to corner. "Cassidy, it's wonderful. I mean the detail . . . the colors. When did you do this?"

"The day you went to talk with Blake. I had so much nervous energy, I had to do something. It still might not be completely dry. I've added some details to it here and there, so some of it could still be wet." Cassidy smiled. "So, you really like it?"

"I love it." He turned his gaze from the canvas to her. "I love you." He leaned over the frame and gave her a kiss.

The fire chief cleared his throat as if to remind them he was still there. "So, is there anything else?"

"No. This and the chest from my father's room are the only things that mattered."

"Okay then, Wil, why don't you let Cassidy hang on to the picture, so you can give me a hand with the cedar chest upstairs."

She watched as Wil and the chief carried the chest down the stairs with its creaks and moans, then looked around the room again. Emotion flooded her heart with the many memories of time spent in this house with her dad and her mom. It was ironic. She had tried for nine years to erase the memories, to put behind her the sadness that hung in the house. But now . . . now she realized the sadness had only come because of her rebellion. The memories of love and laughter were still there. The days spent with her mother in the kitchen or her father reading by the fireplace were still very much alive deep within her. Yes, the house would be gone, but the love that was born and nurtured there would never be lost.

Once the cedar chest was put in the barn and the painting safely in the truck, Wil thanked Paul for his time and extended his hand. The chief accepted it with a smile, then turned to Cassidy.

"That painting of yours was something else. I was wondering, do you do any commissioned projects?"

Cassidy looked to Wil and then back to the chief. "Like what?"

"Well, my brother has a stud ranch in Texas. He's been looking for someone to paint his three top breeders. He wants them for his office. He has photographs now, but it's not the quality he's looking for."

Cassidy was so excited, she didn't know what to say. It took Wil nudging her elbow to get her to speak up. "Well, I'm flattered you think my work is that good. I have a few other projects I need to take care of first. But if you think he would be interested, I would love the opportunity."

"Okay then. I'll give him a call." The chief shook her hand, got in his vehicle, and drove away.

Cassidy squealed with delight, then threw her hands around Wil's neck and planted a kiss on his lips. "Can you believe it? He actually thinks I'm good enough to recommend to somebody else. I can't believe it."

"I can. I always thought your stuff was good enough."

"Yes, but you're bias."

"No, I've always admired your talent . . . and a few other things." The look in Wil's eyes . . . the way he blushed, then turned away with a smile.

Cassidy stepped back from him and grinned. "You had a crush on me in high school, didn't you?"

"What guy didn't?"

Cassidy thought back, embarrassed. Her last few years of school were filled with rebellion and anger. She did a lot of flirting, seductive behavior, but it was all a façade. She thought about letting her virginity go as a punishment to her dad, but she never did. She didn't want anything that would tie her to Liberty. Maybe her mother had been protecting her even back then.

"Hey, I didn't mean to kill the mood." Wil said as he stepped closer, wrapped her in his arms and gave her a kiss, then another.

"What was that for?"

He shrugged. "Because I can, something I will never take lightly."

Cassidy turned back to the house and took a deep breath. "What now?"

"I've already talked to Blake about doing the demolition. Of course, that will have to wait until the insurance is settled." Wil walked her to the pickup, helped her in, then resumed their conversation as he drove home.

"But where are we going to live? We need to stay on the property to be able to keep up with the herd and the other animals. Should I get a trailer and hook it up next to the barn?"

"Joseph can stay at my place and I can move to the office building."

"But it's not even close to being finished. You'll be living in sawdust and fiberglass. No, there's got to be a better solution. Besides, I need a place to stay too."

Cassidy's head was spinning, trying to come up with a plan. It was her turn to step up to the plate, to care for her father, to be the responsible one. Wil was saying something, offering some sort of suggestion, but she wasn't really listening. Not until she caught a word that got her attention.

"What did you just say?"

He smirked. "I said, 'Joseph can stay at my place, and Blake can finish up the apartment while we're on our honeymoon.'"

Wil parked and got out of the truck as casually as if he had just asked her out for coffee. He grabbed the painting from behind his seat while Cassidy sat in stunned silence. Finally, she jumped from the pickup and caught up with Wil on the porch. "What did you say?"

Wil smiled, then leaned the painting against the house. "Maybe this will help." He got down on one knee. "Cassidy, I know your life has been difficult and there are still some major hurdles you have to deal with." She quickly thought about Mark's death and the complications that went with it. "I want to be with you. I want to hold you at night, all night. I don't want to leave you alone. I love you, Cassidy and I want you to be my wife. Cassidy Ann Martin, will you marry me?"

Cassidy's knees felt weak, and she was shaking. There was nothing she wanted more than to be with Wil for the rest of her life. But the baggage she was bringing into their relationship was complicated and messy, especially with the death of Mark.

"Are you sure, Wil? Maybe we should just take things slow. Get past Mark, and the fire, and—"

Wil quickly got to his feet, pulled her close, and kissed her deeply. Cassidy knew Wil's love was true and right, but she would always struggle with the thought he deserved so much more—someone better than her.

Wil framed her face with his calloused fingers and looked into her eyes. "Don't doubt us, Cassidy. I love you, and I know you love me. And with God as our center, there's nothing we can't handle. Nothing."

She shrugged nervously. "So now you can read my mind?"

He smiled. "It's one of my super powers."

She rested her head against his sturdy chest and heard the beat of his heart race in tandem with hers. She felt peace. Love. God's hand.

She felt whole.

"Cassidy," Wil pressed a kiss to the top of her head, "you still haven't answered my question."

Cassidy looked up into his eyes of love, peace washing over her like rain.

Thank you, God. Thank you for giving me everything I don't deserve.

"I would love nothing better than to be Mrs. Wilbur Marsh. I will love you, honor you, protect you, and respect you because you make me feel loved, honored, protected, and respected. This is my commitment to you and God."

Wil's kiss spoke of promise, love, and so much more.

Cassidy realized, maybe for the first time, the grace of God was more powerful than anything she had ever experienced before. She thought about the closing line to her mother's favorite hymn.

". . . 'twas grace hath brought us safe thus far, and grace will lead us home."

Epilogue
Four Years Later

"I think I'm going to have to pass, Blake. I've got too much going on as it is." Cassidy rested the phone against her chin as she put the finishing touches on dinner. "I know, I know." Cassidy sighed. *Someday I have to learn how to say 'no.'* "Okay, Blake. I'll do one consultation, one preliminary, and the final draft, but that's it. I'm not going to try to wheel and deal. If she likes my proposal, fine. If not, she'll have to find another designer." Cassidy heard the front door open and knew Wil was home. "Blake, I've got to go. Yeah, I'll call you back to set up a time." Cassidy hung up the phone just as Wil walked into the kitchen.

His arms slipped around her waist as he nuzzled his chin against her neck. "Something smells good."

"Lasagna." Cassidy said as she ripped lettuce leaves and put them into the bowl.

"No . . . no, I think its Obsession," he said as he dotted her neck with kisses.

She scrunched up her shoulders. "Don't start something you can't finish, Mr. Marsh." Smiling, she moved to the oven, pulled out the casserole dish, and set it on the butcher block.

He followed her, pulling her to his chest. "Who says I can't finish?"

"Me. Dad is coming over for dinner, and he'll be walking through the door any minute." Cassidy gave Wil a peck on the cheek and then turned her attention to the vegetables steaming on the stovetop.

"Where's Grace?" Wil asked, winking.

Cassidy saw movement out of the corner of her eye "I don't know," she answered with dramatic exaggeration. "She was here just a minute ago. Where do you think she could have gone?"

352

"Here I am, Daddy." Out jumped the toddler from behind the backdoor, giggling and laughing at her game of hide-and-seek. Wil bent and scooped her up, hugging her tight. "Has Daddy's little girl been helping Mommy?" She shook her head, blond curls bobbing over her shoulders.

It was a scene Cassidy never tired of. "Why don't you help Grace wash up while I get everything on the table."

Grace and Wil entered the little washroom off the kitchen, the sound of giggles bringing a smile to Cassidy's face. Her life was so full, so different than it had been just a few short years ago.

After Mark's death, there had been a few unforeseen hurdles they needed to navigate before she and Wil could move on. Though the police eventually confirmed Mark's self-destructive behavior had been fueled by Amanda and Davis' embezzlement scheme, Cassidy and Wil were shocked to find out she was under investigation by the FBI.

With assistance from a forensic accountant, the FBI uncovered numerous shell companies Mark had set up in Cassidy's name. Since the accounts were legal, and Cassidy stood to gain millions, the FBI had to make sure Mark's death, and the subsequent house fire were not elaborate schemes orchestrated by Cassidy to exact her revenge and cut Mark out of the money. The investigation eventually cleared Cassidy of all wrongdoing, labeled Mark's death justifiable homicide, and answered the question—why did Mark come after her that Christmas Eve?

Because he panicked.

The FBI believed the deaths of Amanda and Davis were accidents, that Mark had only intended on confronting them to get his money back. But driven by jealousy and anger, his confrontation turned to murder. Realizing his empire was crumbling, Mark needed Cassidy to access the hidden accounts. And since Morocco has no extradition treaty with the U.S., he planned on starting a new life there with Cassidy and his money.

Even though Cassidy and her dad were cleared, the first few months after the investigation were rough. Cassidy struggled with guilt over Mark's death, and the tabloids sensationalized and insinuated that Cassidy had more to do with Mark's death than the FBI had uncovered. Overnight, Cassidy was labeled a millionaire, and had just as many eyes watching her to see what she would do with the money.

Under the guidance of a financial advisor, Cassidy made several large donations to missionary organizations around the world and established The Sunshine Foundation for the Arts, a scholarship program for underprivileged teens with artistic talents. But the highlight of the year had been when she and Wil were married in a quiet ceremony in the living room of Wil's cottage—now her father's home.

Unbeknownst to them, her dad transferred the main house to her and Wil. Upon completion of the rebuild, he presented them with the deed as a wedding gift, with only one stipulation. He wanted grandchildren while he was young enough to enjoy them.

Now, four years later, Cassidy, Wil, and their precious daughter, Catherine Grace lived in her childhood home. Though some of the things that had made it special when she was a child were gone, the memories were strong as ever. And now the three of them were making new memories of their own.

Wil's downtown property turned out beautifully, exactly as he and Cassidy had designed. Wil used the upstairs apartment whenever he had to stay overnight with patients, and sometimes he and Cassidy would escape to it when they needed a little quiet time to themselves.

Cassidy's career as an artist had bloomed into more than she ever dreamed. After everything involving Mark was over, and she had finished the paintings for Wil's office, she flew to Texas to meet with Harold Smith, the fire chief's brother. He loved Cassidy's work so much, he commissioned several paintings, not just for his office, but for his home as well. Now, work came to her from all over the south. Harold Turner's office worked as Cassidy's private little gallery. Anyone who had business dealings with him was immediately drawn to the paintings that brought such life and realism to its subjects. She became so busy, she actually had to turn business away. And on top of all that, she still worked with Blake from time to time on some of his more extravagant projects.

But two years after Wil and she were married, Cassidy's career took a backseat to an even bigger project. The birth of their first child. Catherine Grace came into the world on a breezy fall day in October. Her dad was speechless when Cassidy told him her daughter would be named after her mother. And when he held Catherine Grace for the first time, he wept tears of joy as he prayed over her. Cassidy had thanked God a thousand times for blessing her with a child before the years caught up with her dad. Catherine's arrival had breathed new life into him.

But soon, Catherine was going by the name Grace, and had the ability to turn her daddy into a giant marshmallow. Wil held her for hours when she first came home from the hospital and studied her like she was a priceless jewel. He got up for night feedings more times than not, never complaining, afraid if he didn't, he would miss out on something special.

The Labrador pup Wil had surprised Cassidy with for Christmas was now full-grown and could be found following Joseph around on the ranch. She attached herself to him when he watched her after the birth of Catherine Grace. Cassidy noticed the bond they shared and realized it was good for her dad to have someone to keep him company. So, the four-legged Grace became his constant companion.

Grace's giggles brought Cassidy back to the present. She watched as her daughter welcomed the canine Grace with a squeeze around the neck while the patient dog licked her face. The Labrador had always been careful and tolerant of the tail tugging and tight hugs at the hands of the precocious toddler. They were quite the pair to watch, though at times, having two Graces in the house got confusing.

Wil and Cassidy thought long and hard about calling their daughter Grace. They didn't want her to grow up with the stigma of being named after the dog. But they knew that wasn't the reason they felt led to call her Grace. The name was a declaration of what God had done in their lives. Catherine Grace was the perfect name and God had given them an *almost* perfect little girl.

Everyone took their place at the table, even Grace curled up at Joseph's feet knowing she would get the best table scraps a dog could ask for. Everyone bowed their heads and waited for Wil to say the blessing.

"Thank you, Father, once again for giving us a day full of hard work, good company, and Your grace. Bless this food to our bodies. Give us strength for a new day tomorrow and may the four of us always be able to gather around the table and sing Your praises together. We give You honor, and glory, and praise. Amen."

Everyone shared about their day as they ate dinner. Little Grace excitedly told Grandpop how she had drawn her own picture while her mommy worked on hers.

"Can I see it?" Her grandpa asked as if she had just painted a Monet.

"Uh huh." Grace nodded, her mouth full of food.

They excused themselves from the table. Grace taking Grandpop's hand and leading him into Cassidy's studio that branched off the kitchen.

Wil showed some attention to the four-legged Grace before she waddled off to keep an eye on the other two. "I heard you talking to Blake when I came home. A new project?" Wil asked as he cleared the table.

"Yes. He wants me to help him on the Lander's house. Well, the Lander's master suite to be exact." Cassidy answered as she stretched her back and rolled her neck.

"You look tired, honey." Wil said, sounding concerned. "Has my Energizer Bunny met her match?"

Cassidy shrugged off Wil's teasing, even though it was true. Keeping up with Grace, the house, her art, the foundation, projects with Blake, and the riding lessons she'd started giving Grace, her days were definitely filled to capacity.

But that was not why she was tired.

"What do you say to calling it an early night?" Wil said as he gently massaged her shoulders.

"I don't know if I have the energy to call it 'an early night.'"

"Cassidy Marsh," he turned her around. "I'm offended you think I would take advantage of you when you're not feeling well." He looked at her with his wounded puppy dog eyes, but Cassidy saw right through it.

Hugging him close, she asked, "What's the use of calling it 'an early night' if you're not going to take advantage of me?" Her sexy smile let him know she wasn't *that* tired.

Wil bent down to kiss her pouty lips, but just as he touched them, Joseph, Catherine Grace, and Grace came in from the studio. Her Dad cleared his throat to signal Wil, they were no longer alone.

"I think we have a little artist here who might be ready for bed."

As if on cue, Grace stretched, then covered a huge yawned.

"Come on, sweetheart. Daddy will get you ready for bed and then Mommy can come up and say prayers with us." Wil picked up his bundle of joy with little effort. Grace laid her tired head on Wil's shoulder, her eyelids already heavy. "Good night, Joseph. See you tomorrow," Wil said as he left the room.

Her dad waved good night to Wil as he left with Grace, then

turned to Cassidy and sighed.

"What is it, Dad? Are you okay?" Cassidy was immediately concerned.

He stood a moment longer, his eyes beginning to glass over. "You've made me so proud, Cassidy. I could never have imagined I could be this happy without your mother."

Cassidy moved forward to hug her dad. "That's just it, Dad. We're not without Mom. She's still here with us. I feel her every day."

They embraced for a moment before Grace whimpered at Joseph's heels. Cassidy squatted down to stroke the faithful dog. "Still have to be the center of attention, don't you, Grace?" Cassidy stroked her ears and gave her a hug. "Go on you two. You need to get home."

Her dad kissed her on the cheek and headed for the front door. Grace bounded after him, knowing she would have him all to herself for the rest of the evening.

Cassidy finished up in the kitchen and turned off lights as she made her way upstairs. Wil was reading to Grace, on her bed, when Cassidy peeked in on them.

"Ready for prayers?"

"Yes, Mommy." Grace said as she stretched with another yawn. Grace laid in her big girl's bed, with daddy next to her and mommy kneeling on the floor. Grace prayed for everyone and everything. From the animals to the butterflies and all the people she knew. When she was done, Wil closed their time of prayer. When Cassidy opened her eyes, she saw Grace was already asleep and Wil was staring at her.

"Do you know how happy you've made me, Mrs. Marsh?"

"I think I have an idea." Cassidy stood and stretched as Wil slowly moved from the bed.

"Why don't you go take a nice hot bath?" Wil suggested as they walked to their bedroom.

"I think I will." Cassidy pulled some lingerie from her dresser drawer and headed for the bathroom.

"Did you want a little company? I could work on some of those sore muscles?"

"Ah, so you did plan on taking advantage of me," she teased.

"Patience, Mr. Marsh. I won't be long."

Cassidy finally emerged from the bathroom, her satiny nightie clinging to her still moist body. She watched Wil watching her, his look of wanting igniting her senses. She stood alongside the bed and allowed the thin straps of her gown to slip from her shoulders. Wil pulled the covers back from his body allowing her to nuzzle in close to him.

"I can't believe my life is this amazing," Wil said. "I've got it all. A beautiful daughter, a great business, a wonderful father-in-law, God's love, and a wife who can still send chills down my spine and make me blush at my own thoughts. I couldn't image it getting any better than this."

Cassidy was glad Wil couldn't see the huge smile on her face. It would have surely given her away. Snuggling closer she sighed, trying to sound casual even though she was bursting with joy.

"Not bad for a mother of two."

ABOUT THE AUTHOR

Tamara Tilley writes from her home at Hume Lake Christian Camps, located in the beautiful Sequoia National Forest. She and her husband, Walter, have been on full-time staff at Hume for more than twenty-five years. Tamara is a retail manager who loves to read, spend time with her grandkids, and craft greeting cards. Visit her website at www.tamaratilley.com to read excerpts from her other books.

Made in the USA
Columbia, SC
13 April 2020